The
Marriage
Lie

BOOKS BY ALI MERCER

Lost Daughter
His Secret Family
My Mother's Choice

The Marriage Lie

Ali Mercer

Bookouture

Published by Bookouture in 2021

An imprint of Storyfire Ltd.
Carmelite House
50 Victoria Embankment
London EC4Y 0DZ

www.bookouture.com

ISBN: 978-1-83888-694-3
eBook ISBN: 978-1-83888-693-6

For Katie and Gary

Chapter One

Rob had reserved a table for us, though he needn't have bothered. There was plenty of space, not surprisingly given that it was a weekday lunchtime. But it was my birthday, and he wouldn't have wanted to leave anything to chance.

Most of the other customers had gravitated to the beer garden, overlooking the river, but Rob wasn't a fan of eating outside – too many insects, too much weather, too much risk of other people's kids running round or being noisy. Inside it was calm and quiet and there were just a few other diners, who were either elderly or looked as if they were out on business and eating on expenses. There would be no interruptions to fray Rob's nerves, and nobody would be close enough to eavesdrop on us. We'd be able to have a proper conversation without anybody else listening in.

The oak-panelled walls had been painted a dark shade of grey that soaked up the sunshine coming in through the tall sash windows, and the silver cutlery and crystal glasses on the tables gleamed in the muted light like jewellery in an old painting. Our table was set slightly apart from the others in its own little alcove, which was as shadowy and private as if it was dusk in winter rather than midday in June. As I took my seat I felt as if I had entered a dark cave, lit up by rectangles of brightness from a distant outside world.

Just for a moment, it was like one of those dreams where you start to panic and try to ask the people around you for help. But they're too far away and too preoccupied to hear you, and anyway, you've lost the ability to speak.

I reminded myself to breathe. Here I was in the newly renovated dining room of one of the top-rated gastropubs in Oxfordshire, out for lunch with my husband sitting opposite me. My good-looking, successful, generous husband, who had brought me here as a treat to celebrate my fortieth birthday. I was safe. Our daughter was safe. Nothing bad was going to happen.

Live in the present. That was what they said. I had to let myself enjoy the here and now, because why not? What else was there?

Rob reached across the table to tap the menu resting in front of me.

'Maybe you could start thinking about what you'd like to have,' he said. 'I'm pretty hungry.'

It was a reproof, but a gentle one. After all, it *was* my birthday. 'Sure,' I said.

I opened my menu and looked through it, and Rob did the same with his. The silence that fell between us was more or less companionable, though there was something about it that was just a touch off-key – an almost inaudible note that set my teeth on edge.

Nothing unusual there, though. My whole life was off-key. I just had to try to get by without anyone else noticing. Though Rob noticed. He saw and knew everything.

Sometimes all it took to make me feel small was to look at him when he was looking back at me.

But still… we had a beautiful daughter. A beautiful home. And here we were, just the two of us, about to eat a meal that would cost as much as it took to feed us and Georgie for a week, if I was careful.

The past was the past. These days, we had a good life, didn't we? A fortunate life?

Or at least, that was what other people thought.

I decided to do as Rob had told me and focus on deciding what to eat.

Cost wasn't the problem. It was the calories I had to look out for. Being a Greek god with a gym habit, Rob could eat potato dauphinoise till the cows came home without any obvious consequences. Not so for me. Especially not now I'd turned forty. And if I couldn't get into the lingerie Rob had bought for me... he'd definitely notice.

I read through the list of starters yet again, but didn't take it in. I couldn't help thinking about Georgie. Four days, three nights. That was all. She was not far off fifteen now and I really ought to be able to let her go, at least for that long. Which wasn't really very long at all.

But this whole thing of not being able to get in touch with her... so unnecessary. Even on my birthday! All I really wanted was one little text message from her saying she was OK. Then I'd be fine. I'd be able to relax. I might even be able to begin to enjoy myself.

It wasn't really being overprotective. It was only natural for a mother to worry about her daughter being out there in the back of beyond, wandering around with nothing but a couple of other kids and a paper map to help her orientate herself. OK, so there were supervisors, but they were few and far between and they couldn't watch the kids all the time.

Also, I knew all too well how easy it was for any school trip to come close to catastrophe. That heart-stopping moment when you counted heads for the coach back and realised someone was missing... And then they turned up, or were found, and the world righted itself. But you always knew that there could be a time when that didn't happen, when the lost stayed lost and there was no miraculous restoration of normality, and no relief. There was so much that could go wrong.

There were so many ways for kids to vanish. What if Georgie got separated from the others in her group? What if someone else was watching... the wrong kind of someone? She was so trusting. She'd never yet had cause to learn that not all grown-ups could, or should, be trusted.

There was no way we could tell her she couldn't trust *us*. It was much, much too late for that.

'You all right?' Rob said.

I gave myself a little shake and managed to smile at him.

'Of course I am. Couldn't be better. This is wonderful. Thank you.'

The only way to stay sane – as I often reminded myself – was to be grateful for what you had. I had been lucky. I had got what I wanted. It was just that, one way or another, there was a price to be paid. But then, you couldn't expect to gain your heart's desire for free…

The champagne arrived and the waitress poured it and withdrew, and Rob and I raised our glasses to each other.

The crystal glittered and chinked and the booze fizzed, but I didn't see it. Instead I glimpsed a different scene: a long straight road through woodland on another summer's day, and something half seen in the shadows at the verge.

I blinked and my vision cleared. I was back in the restaurant and my handsome husband was toasting me. Rob said, 'Happy birthday,' and we clinked glasses again and drank.

Then he said something strange. 'Make the most of it, because there'll never be another one. Not like this.'

What on earth did he mean? Had I misheard him?

I set down my glass. Best not overdo it. I'd skipped breakfast this morning to avoid bloating. A jumpsuit wasn't the most forgiving garment if you had a less than perfectly flat stomach. He liked me in it, though, which is why I'd picked it out.

The first time I'd worn it, he tore it at the front and I had to get it mended. *It makes you look like a sexy mama. Which is what you are.*

Would tonight be one of those nights? Did I want it to be? Would I want it to be, when it came to it?

The room swam – the tables, the people eating, the dark panelling on the walls that seemed to absorb the sunlight – then righted itself. Rob was smiling. He seemed to be waiting for me to get the joke.

I said, 'What do you mean, "there'll never be another one"?'

His smile widened but didn't reach his eyes.

'Just that you always used to say you were going to stop having birthdays after you turned forty.'

'I never said that.' I attempted a smile in return. After all, he was only joking. 'I said I was going to stop counting. I didn't mean I was going to stop celebrating. Or having presents, so don't get any ideas about that.'

I was still waiting for my birthday present from him, which was going to be a surprise, as usual. He never let slip what he was planning in advance. *A gift has to be unexpected,* was what he always said. *Otherwise it's not a proper present. It's just part of an exchange.* All he'd been willing to tell me was that I'd have to wait until after lunch to find out.

It would be jewellery, probably – something in a box that he would hand over when we got home, or leave on the bed for me to find. Diamonds? Gold? Or it could be an experience – a trip to a spa, or a family holiday.

Rob said, 'Do you like the table they've given us? I thought you'd like to be seen but not heard.'

He had let me have the seat with the best view of the restaurant, while he had his back to everyone else. *It's absolutely fine by me,* he'd said. *You're the only person I'm interested in right now.*

In the far corner to my right a silver-haired couple were holding hands across the table and talking in low voices. The picture of what we could be, one day? Two elderly people, content to be together as only those who have kept each other's secrets for decades can be? To the left there was a man in a suit and a woman in a formal shift dress. Their conversation had flagged. The woman was picking over what was left of her salad, and the man looked as if he had the beginnings of indigestion.

'It's a great spot,' I said, and sipped some more champagne.

Maybe I should just knock it back. Insist on having more. After all, it *was* my birthday.

But no… you just couldn't do that kind of thing when you were married and a mother. And a teacher at a local school. When you had a certain reputation to uphold, even if it was a quiet one. You certainly couldn't get smashed at lunchtime, in public.

Anyway, Georgie wasn't going to be away *that* long.

If I could just focus on that – the moment when the coach would arrive back at school on Saturday evening, and I'd spot her waving from the window – I'd be able to keep it together between now and then.

Knowing her, she'd be desperate to get back. She liked her home comforts.

'I'm glad you approve of the restaurant,' Rob said. 'I must say, I like the way they've done the place up.'

'It's *perfect*,' I said, and gave him my best, most winning smile, the one I usually saved for photos.

I was conscious of the woman to my left, the one who was on a business lunch, watching us. I didn't want her thinking I was miserable. After all, it should be easy to come across as happy if you and your date are safely out of earshot.

She was still picking at her salad, and still struggling to make small talk to the man she was with. Maybe she even envied me. Drinking champagne, being toasted. Celebrating my special day.

Then she caught my eye. I felt my smile turn rigid and falter and both of us looked away.

Rob paid for lunch, as he always did. He had always picked up the tab when we went out, right from the start. Back then I'd just thought it was nice to be treated. It hadn't occurred to me that I was letting him set a pattern that it might be hard to break.

After lunch, again as always, he was the one who drove us home.

Which was fine by me. If it wasn't for Georgie, I could quite happily have never driven again. It still terrified me. But Georgie needed ferrying around and Rob worked long hours and was often away. There wasn't much choice but to get on with it and do my best not to let anyone see how I felt.

And that was nothing, really, in the scheme of things. Nothing compared to what I would have been prepared to do for her.

When it came down to it, it was *all* because of her, all for her.

I had always wanted her to have the things I hadn't had. A storybook childhood: the house in the country, roses round the door, fresh-baked cake on the table. Stability. Security. A good education. Routine, even if that was a little boring for her sometimes – but that meant no nasty surprises. A dad who adored her and told her she could be anything she wanted and the world was hers for the taking. A mum who was there for her no matter what, who was willing to put her first…

The choices that had been made, the sacrifices – it had worked. She was the living proof of that, and I was so proud of her she made my heart want to burst.

OK, there had been had a few slammed doors, a few pensive moods. But she'd never really been difficult. She still talked to me. Confided in me. Let me hug her. She had bought me a new purse for my birthday, maroon leather from the gift shop in Kettlebridge, which she'd chosen herself and paid for out of her pocket money. She'd even baked me a cake, all off her own bat, without asking for a recipe or ingredients or anything.

As she was due to go off on her school trip the day before my birthday, she'd made the cake in advance, at the weekend. As soon as her Saturday morning maths lesson was finished and the tutor had gone, she'd set to work. At teatime she'd brought the cake ceremoniously out to the dining room, where I was sitting at the table marking homework, and set it down in front of me. The candles were already lit, and there was a piped message on top of the just-set water icing: HAPPY BIRTHDAY MUM.

Rob had been just behind her, having come in from his garden office, and as I admired the cake he'd watched me with just a hint of challenge.

'Aren't you the lucky one,' he'd said, with a coolly questioning look.

'I certainly am,' I'd told him.

And I was. She was such a loving daughter. The ideal daughter. So kind-hearted, so good-natured. So sheltered. Rob had always insisted on sending her to private schools, and I'd had my doubts, not just because of the expense. I had worried that she might learn to be a snob, that we were cutting her off from other kids in the neighbourhood and the community we had chosen to live in, and that one day she might even learn to look down on us. Then I'd ended up teaching part-time at her secondary school. She had taken that in her stride. If she had ever found it embarrassing or awkward, she had never admitted it.

She worried about other people – people who were less happy and less lucky than we were – and wished she could do more to help them. For her, cruelty and injustice were far away and outside the home, in the news. Still, they troubled her.

Once she had asked me – hesitantly, because she was smart enough to know that it was a sensitive topic – 'Did you and Dad ever think of having any more children?'

And I had told her, 'No, Georgie. You were enough for us. You were all we ever wanted.'

Then, as an afterthought, in answer to the question she hadn't asked – *why* hadn't we had more children? – 'To be honest, it was hard enough having you.'

I had been so lost in thoughts of Georgie that I hadn't taken any notice of where Rob and I were going. But then I saw that the scenery around us was completely unfamiliar. We were in the middle of nowhere when we should have been well on the way home.

'Rob, where are we?'

Rob tapped the satnav to remind me the answer was right there, if I could only be bothered to look for it. The satnav was new, and

I'd never used it. I didn't have one in my car. Rob had said that if I did, I'd probably end up following it down a one-way street.

'Heading towards Fox Hill,' he said.

'But Rob... that's completely the wrong direction.'

He didn't reply. The road ahead of us was completely deserted and led straight between fields of wheat to vanish into woodland on the horizon. I told myself there was no reason to feel uneasy. Maybe this was all part of my birthday surprise.

I said, 'Is this the scenic route or something?'

'Patience is a virtue, virtue is a grace. Isn't that how the old rhyme goes? Patience, Stella. Hang on in there, and it will all begin to make sense. Now hush up and enjoy the ride.'

By and by we came to the woodland on Fox Hill. Between the trees I glimpsed scattered houses set back from the road. Some of them were half-timbered and thatched, while others were Victorian Gothic places with steeply angled roofs and there were one or two new builds, square concrete houses with solar panels and huge windows gleaming in the sun.

Right at the end of the lane, Rob pulled up in front of a white-painted, stucco-fronted cottage set behind a substantial gate with a security keypad. I guessed it had maybe been built sometime before the Second World War and modernised since, though it was hard to tell. It had the slightly dead-eyed look of a house that hasn't been lived in for a while and has just been done up.

Maybe this was one of his property development projects. But why had he brought *me* here? He didn't usually care for my opinion on these things.

He hopped out of the car and punched a code into the keypad. The gate opened. He got back into the car and drove us through and the gate shut smoothly behind us.

Would you be able to get out and drive away if you didn't know the code? Maybe not. You'd have to walk. Or run. There was a pedestrian gate to the side and that was secured with a keypad too. You'd have to start by climbing…

But that was a paranoid thought, anyway. Rob was always telling me I had an overactive imagination. He knew better than anyone how often I slept badly, and how little it took for me to start obsessing about possible disasters. There had been a time when he'd been able to sympathise, but these days my habitual anxiety just wore him down.

He killed the engine and turned to face me.

'Well,' he said, 'what do you think?'

'It's very… quiet, isn't it?'

'It's up-and-coming,' he said. 'On the other side of the hill, with views of Oxford, places like this cost a fortune. The centre of the village is only ten minutes' walk away. OK, there isn't that much there – convenience store, church, pub, primary school – but day-to-day, it's all you need. It's a fifteen-minute drive to Kettlebridge, twenty in rush hour, and then you've got the supermarkets and so on. Same distance to Oxford – though if you time it wrong, you'll be sitting in traffic till you've lost the will to live.' He opened his car door. 'Let's go in. If there's anything you don't like about the décor, do let me know.'

'Really?'

'Really.'

And then he smiled at me with a warmth I hadn't seen for ages.

'Don't worry, I won't take offence,' he said. 'Not today. After all, it is your birthday.'

'OK, then take me on the tour. You know I love nosing round other people's houses.'

'Everybody does,' he said.

I thought he might be about to lean across and kiss me, but instead he got out of the car and strode purposefully towards the front door. I was wearing a new pair of high heels, spindly things designed more to show off a pedicure than for actual walking, and nearly twisted an ankle as I hurried to keep up.

Inside, my first impression was of whiteness, brightness and emptiness. It was like walking into a lightbox.

I knew that was the look Rob favoured – pale walls, a lack of clutter, a little bit of natural wood and a few splashes of accent colour for contrast. Over the years, I'd quietly resisted it back home in Kettlebridge, with limited success. We'd ended up with a compromise between my hankering for cosiness and his more austere tastes: minimalism plus mementoes and a few carefully maintained pot plants. But the inside of this house was pure unadulterated Rob, and as immaculate as if the decorators had just moved out – which perhaps they had.

The entrance hall was unusually wide, almost square, with a chequerboard tiled floor. There were closed doors to the left and at the end of the hallway, and a wooden floating staircase rising to the first floor. Behind me, the front porch had a rack for shoes – in Rob's view, shoes needed somewhere to go, and should always be lined up. There was also a short row of rubberised coat hooks in a quirky shade of orange, which was the kind of design flourish Rob liked.

There was less storage space for outdoor things than we had back home at Fairfield Road: any family living here would have to be disciplined about how many coats they kept to hand. And there wouldn't be much extra space if they had visitors, or a party. But I decided not to say anything about that. It was unusual for Rob to ask me for my opinion, and I had a hunch that criticism wouldn't be what he wanted to hear.

Rob was smiling at me like the magician at the beginning of a trick, patient and knowing, willing to indulge his audience in the build-up to the big reveal.

He said, 'Ready?'

'Sure.'

'We'll start with the kitchen-diner. It's really the heart of the house.'

The reply that came to mind was, *Come on, you can spare me the sales patter.* I bit my tongue.

You couldn't say that kind of thing to your husband, not after he'd just taken you out for a nice lunch on your birthday. You shouldn't say that kind of thing to your husband *ever*. You shouldn't even *think* that kind of thing, because it was just evidence of how critical and ungrateful you'd become. Anyway, Rob couldn't help it. He'd spent years doing this kind of thing. He'd been working in the world of property so long, he'd absorbed its language and used it as if it was his own.

He held open the door at the end of the hallway and waved me through. The gesture was ironic, as if letting me go first was some kind of private joke. Mocking, even. As if he was treating me like a lady when both of us knew I didn't deserve that kind of courtesy.

As I went into the kitchen I caught sight of something out of the corner of my eye – something moving, a white shadow against white. But it must just have been a trick of the light. There was no breeze coming in and no curtains to stir. In fact, the room was stifling.

'Very nice. Plenty of space,' I said.

It was L-shaped, and ran the full length of the house as well as behind the width of the hall. The kitchen units were at the back, so you could stand at the sink and look out into the garden. It was all done out in white. With windows at either end, on a sunny day like today it was almost dazzling. The echo of my heels on the shiny tiled floor was like a ricochet.

There was a small round wooden table in the middle of the room, with a chair on either side. Rob must be planning to let the place part-furnished. It seemed an odd size of table to choose, whether he was looking for a family to rent it out to or a group of young professional housemates. Surely they'd want something bigger? And it wasn't the kind of starter place a couple would look for.

'Come and check out the living room,' Rob said. He seemed to be enjoying himself, as if this little tour was all part of some kind of grand unveiling and he'd been looking forward to it for longer than he dared say.

The living room was part-furnished too. A flat screen TV stood on an otherwise empty matte white unit in one corner, near a small grey sofa that seemed to float in the space like a piece of furniture bobbing on top of an expanse of water after a flood. The wooden floor was spotless and unmarked, as if nobody had ever walked on it. Perhaps nobody had, apart from the workmen and Rob and now me.

I was drawn to the garden at the back of the house. Drawn to it and vaguely appalled by it, though I didn't let on. It was framed by French windows that gave onto a small paved patio and a modest square of lawn with gravelled borders, surrounded by a high wooden fence that had been freshly painted with oak-brown creosote. There were no trees, no flowers, no bushes or shrubs. If anything had been growing there, Rob had torn it out.

'The turf looks like you've just laid it,' I said.

'It's artificial, actually. It's very convincing, isn't it? A lot of people like it, nowadays. It's very hardwearing, and saves all the trouble with weeds and mowing.'

Barren. The word echoed in my head so loudly I almost thought I'd said it out loud. A harsh, bleak word. It conjured up a landscape of dust. A weeping woman with red-rimmed eyes. An empty cradle and blood on the sheets with nothing to show for it.

The house was silent. I pressed my hand to my heart: I could feel it beating through the black crepe of my jumpsuit. I was beginning to sweat.

'You've thought of everything,' I said.

'I try,' Rob told me. 'Are you ready to go upstairs? I want to show you the bedrooms.'

'Sure. Ready when you are,' I said. We went back into the hall, and he waved me on to make my way up the slippery wooden stairs before him.

*

There were three bedrooms and an immaculate white-and-grey bathroom. Two of the bedrooms were empty, but one, the largest, which overlooked the front of the house, had a single bed in it. Decent quality, by the look of it, with a good plump mattress. Rob hadn't skimped. But then, he never did. That was another of his maxims, that it was worth a little bit of extra outlay to create the effect you wanted.

The bed smelt brand new, as if it had only just been delivered and stripped of its packaging. It was odd that Rob hadn't ordered a double – there was easily space for one, and if he let the place to a family, this would probably be the parents' room. Or, if it was a house-share, a young professional couple might take it. Or a singleton with a love life, who might sometimes have a boyfriend or girlfriend staying over.

Why were the other bedrooms still unfurnished? Maybe there was a delivery on the way.

They were obvious questions. Reasonable questions, you might think. Maybe they had reasonable answers. But I still didn't say anything. I knew from experience that there was a difference between Rob asking for an opinion and being pleased to hear one.

He led the way back downstairs and I followed him, slow and careful on the stairs in my awkwardly high heels. My heart was still racing. Maybe because I half expected him to be irritated with me for not keeping up. Or maybe for some other reason that I couldn't quite put my finger on yet.

We ended up back where we'd started, in the hallway with the chequerboard floor. I touched my forehead and felt beads of sweat. Rob would be repulsed; he disliked any sign of perspiration on me unless it was just after exercise. But he didn't seem to have noticed. He wasn't sweating at all. He was smiling still, and waiting for my verdict.

'Well?'

The whole place seemed unreal. Or perhaps just as if it was waiting to be put to use. A blank canvas. A set for a certain kind of drama, the sort where lonely people had affairs and tried to kill each other, and maybe succeeded. Or sought revenge. Or were haunted.

My throat was dry and it was an effort to speak.

'It's lovely. Very classy,' I said.

I sounded nervous. And defensive, as if the house itself was some kind of threat.

But that was ridiculous. Taking paranoia to whole new heights. It really was time to get a grip.

'No criticisms? Don't hold back,' Rob said. 'I can take it.'

It was as if he *wanted* me to find fault. Was he looking to pick a fight? I was going to have to come up with something to say.

'Well… it's quite isolated. Tucked away at the end of the lane with the woods all around. That might not suit everybody. In the middle of winter, in bad weather… if there was heavy snowfall… it could end up being cut off. The only way to get out would be on foot, and you wouldn't be able to get much further than the village. If you could manage even that.'

I hesitated. Rob pulled a little face as if to say, *Fair point.* I tried to take heart. Perhaps I was on safer ground commenting on the location than I would be if I questioned the way he'd done the place up, or the furniture he'd chosen.

'It could be spooky if you were here on your own at night,' I went on. 'Also, you'd pretty much have to get in the car to go anywhere. I mean, I guess there is a bus service, but it's probably about once a day. But for a certain kind of family I guess it could work… or if you can find tenants who want to live in the country and don't mind a bit of a commute…'

I ground to a halt. It was on the tip of my tongue to ask him whether he was planning to sell the place or let it out. But something stopped me.

Rob frowned. 'So do you think you could be happy here?'

For once, I decided to risk being blunt.

'This might be somebody's dream house,' I said. 'But it would never be mine.'

'I'm sure you'll adapt,' he said.

Then he reached into his pocket and held out a set of keys.

I didn't take them. Instead I glanced round the hallway as if half expecting someone to spring forward out of hiding to explain it all. But nothing stirred – not even dust.

I said, 'What is this? Is this some kind of practical joke?'

'No, it's not a joke. It's a surprise. Your birthday surprise.' He shook his outstretched hand so the keys rattled. 'Go on, take them. Congratulations! The place is as good as yours – just a few formalities to complete first, but we can sort all of that out in good time. I think I'm right in saying this will be the first house you've ever owned outright.'

It was as if I had been hypnotised. I cupped my hand and held it out without wanting to or meaning to, just because it was what he expected, and he dropped the keys into it.

They were cool and heavy. Substantial keys for substantial locks. He must have thought carefully about security when he was doing the place up. That was a good thing, wasn't it? He didn't want anything bad to happen to me here.

To *me*? But why would I even be here? I had a house. *Our* house. And who did he think I might need protecting from?

'It's a very generous present,' I said.

'I'm glad you think so. As I said, it's up-and-coming, so it's as good as a nest egg. I think you'll like it here.'

'But Rob, I don't understand. What do you mean? We have a house. I don't mean to sound ungrateful, but... why would you give me this one? And why would we move here? What would Georgie say? We haven't even consulted her.'

He looked at me very directly and coldly. It was the gaze of someone peering down the barrel of a gun with prey at the other end of it. This was it: it was time for the big reveal, the killer blow.

'Stella, *we* aren't going to be living here. *You* are.'

I was still holding the keys. I didn't know what else to do with them. Maybe this was some kind of hoax. A practical joke. There must have been something I'd missed. This was like the times when he repeated a punchline and all I could do was look blank or fake a response. It wasn't always easy to get the point of the pay-off if you hadn't been listening to the set-up.

Somewhere along the line I must have lost focus. I'd got careless. I hadn't been giving Rob the kind of attention he needed.

I said, 'Is this your way of telling me you want a divorce?'

His eyes were still icy, but now he was smiling again too, as if he was pleased with the way the surprise was going down so far.

'It's not just that I want one. It's what's going to happen,' he said. 'You're quite right, though. We do need to sit down and talk to Georgie. The sooner the better. This weekend, ideally. If you could pop over sometime on Sunday, maybe we could do it then.'

'Pop over...? What is this? You seriously think you can give me the keys to a house and just expect me to take them and say thank you and quietly move in?'

Rob sighed and folded his arms. 'Stella, I don't think you understand this yet. But you'll get there. Look, I think what I'm proposing is pretty generous. I'll carry on paying Georgie's school fees, of course. I'm sure we both want what's best for her, and that means keeping the disruption to her life and her education to a minimum. I'm prepared to give you this house outright, and I'm not going to stop you from seeing Georgie. I want you to have a good relationship with each other. As good as possible. But she'll be better off living with me.'

'With you? No way. I'm her mum. She belongs with me.'

His eyebrows went up. *This* was it. This was the real killer blow. And there was nothing I could do to fend it off.

'Think about what you're saying, Stella. Think what you're really saying. Think what it means. And think what matters to you most. There's an awful lot, isn't there, that would be much better kept under wraps? For your sake. Georgie's sake. And my sake, too.'

'Are you threatening me? That's blackmail.'

He shrugged. 'Call it what you want. It's always possible to find ugly names for things. I'm actually trying to spare your feelings here. I know how much in denial you are. But I can remind you of the facts if you'd like. I suspect you might find those ugly too.'

'You can't do this. I won't let you.' I held up the keys. 'Do what you like with these. I don't want them.'

I threw them at him. And missed. He stepped back and the keys landed on the floor.

The jangle of metal hitting tile was as explosive as gunshot. Then the house was silent again.

Chapter Two

Rob shook his head as if I'd just made a rookie mistake.

'You should take a step back, Stella,' he said. 'Try a few deep breaths. What would Georgie think if she could see you now? Look at you. You're shaking.'

I glanced down at my hands and he was right – they were trembling. I could feel the rhythm of fear in my fingertips and toes, as if my blood was coming to the boil.

'I understand that this is hard for you,' Rob went on. He was still smiling – the particular smile of a man who wants to make it clear that he is above being touched by any female display of emotion, however raw or alarming. 'I get it, Stella, honestly I do. There are certain unpalatable facts that you just don't want to have to revisit. And it hasn't got any better with time, has it? Here we are in the new millennium. We still haven't come clean about something we did back in the last century. And we aren't going to, are we? Oh, I know you used to say you would one day. But let's face it, you're never going to do it if you can help it. You're incapable of it. I know how much it frightens you. You can't even bear to think about it, can you? Let alone talk about it.

'But look, we don't have to dwell on all that right now, do we? Let's think about some other facts that might be a little easier for you to get your head around. Your finances, for example. Your income is, how shall I put it? Modest. You're barely in a position to support yourself, let alone to take care of Georgie. And as for the school fees – forget it. So what about your assets? Let's face it, Stella, you don't have any. Your name isn't on the deeds of the house on

Fairfield Road. It never was. That's *my* house. I found it and bought it and paid for it. *You* barely contributed to it.'

'That's a lie.' My voice sounded strained and throaty, as if I'd been screaming. 'I looked after Georgie and I helped do up one place after another and I worked in the evenings, and once I got my degree and was qualified I got a job and started bringing money in. I know I don't earn as much as you. But I always paid for as much as I could.'

'Oh, come on. These days Georgie pretty much looks after herself. All you have to do is drive her round occasionally and make sure there's food in the cupboards. OK, so you used to do the odd bit of freelancing, and now you're teaching. Three days a week at a nice private school with nice, easy pupils. A pretty cushy number, really, isn't it? And before that there were years of studying, and then training, and I supported you through all of that. You're a part-time history teacher. How far do you think your salary would go on accommodation anywhere round here?' He mentioned my job with pure contempt, as if he was talking about work that no capable or competent person would ever even consider – as if it was either just a pointless sop to my vanity or demeaning, or both. 'Let me break it down for you, Stella. If I wasn't willing to let you have this place, if you were completely on your own, you might just about be able to rent a room in a shared house. Or maybe a very small studio flat, if you cast the net a little wider. But you'd struggle to buy your own home, even as part of a shared ownership scheme, and you'd certainly struggle to own the kind of place that you might actually want Georgie to live in.'

'This is crazy. Have you lost your mind? You thought it was great when I got the job at Georgie's school. It meant we got a discount on the fees. Don't you remember? I can't believe you're saying this. We agreed that I should work part-time. You said at the time you thought it would be the best thing for Georgie, given that you're away such a lot.'

'Yes, but that was a couple of years back. She was younger then. And now she isn't quite so young any more.'

He was smiling as he said this. He was batting my objections away absolutely confidently, as if he was an expert tennis player dealing with a novice. He was enjoying himself.

'One of these days, she's going to head off to live her own life,' he went on. 'And then what? What will you and I have left? It won't be enough, Stella. Maybe it would be enough for you, but I know it won't be enough for me. Anyway, look, we've been married for a long time. It's reasonable to assume that you're entitled to *something*, and I don't want to see you destitute. That wouldn't be in anybody's interests. Once you've adjusted to living here, I think you'll find it's perfectly pleasant. I'm sure Georgie will be more than happy to come and visit.'

He paused and held up his hand as if I was about to rush him and he was stopping me in my tracks, or as if this was a debate and I was being unruly, and he was reminding me that it was his turn to speak.

'I know you've been through some difficult times,' he said. 'What with one thing and another. How could I forget? I'm very mindful of all of that. That's part of why I'm willing to be so generous. And I know you love our daughter, and she loves you, and I love her. But Stella, I don't love you, not any more. I don't need you. I can have Georgie in my life without you. And you know what, if certain facts from the past ever did come to light, I think you would be the one she would find impossible to forgive.'

A weird sound came out of me, part scream and part howl. Almost not a human sound. My hands formed into fists and I moved towards him and he raised his hand further still to warn me to back down.

'Don't even think about it,' he said. 'You know perfectly well that if you try to hit me, you'll only regret it. I don't want to have to show you how easy it is for me to stop you. I'm the one who practises martial arts, remember? Also, the legal consequences might embarrass you. Being arrested for assault and battery would only add to your stress and anxiety at what is clearly going to be a testing time.'

Up close like this, his absurdly handsome, familiar face looked more than ever like a mask. I could see his pores, the golden hairs of his eyebrows, the coordinated tension of the muscles around his mouth, the planes of his cheekbones and the taut lines of his jaw. All of it signalled self-belief. There was no missing his conviction, and no doubt that he meant what he said.

I let my fists drop. It wasn't self-control that held me back, or knowing it would have been wrong to attack him. What stopped me was recognising that he was right. He was stronger than I was.

'Good girl,' he said. 'You don't want to get into all that. You really don't want to make things worse for yourself. If you lash out at me now and end up in court you could lose your job, and I really don't think you can afford for that to happen. And, of course, it could make the divorce more difficult, for you at any rate. Judges tend to take a very dim view of domestic abuse. It might affect contact arrangements. You could end up with supervised visits only. And that would be traumatic for Georgie, too. I don't want her to have to pick sides – that's the last thing I want. But under those circumstances, if she did have to choose, which one of us do you think she would put her trust in? The victim, or the aggressor? I suspect you know the answer as well as I do. And once she's an adult, free to choose her path in life for herself – what then? Do you really want her to be afraid of you?'

I said, 'How could you?'

It came out as a shriek. This was no way to land a blow on him. It wasn't going to begin to touch him. But I couldn't stop myself. For once, I was going to tell him what I thought.

'You timed this deliberately, for maximum effect, so you could hurt me as much as possible. And for when you knew Georgie would be away.'

I could feel tears coming to my eyes, though the last thing I wanted was to break down and cry. My hands were moving loosely, as if I was scrabbling to keep a hold on a cliff edge. At the same time part of me had detached from the situation I was in and was seeing it as if from the outside, like a helpless witness.

'This morning, after I got back from dropping Georgie off... the breakfast, the birthday flowers, the expensive lunch... All the time, you knew you were going to spring this on me. You must have known for weeks. Months, even.' Something else occurred to me. 'When we last made love...' When had it been? A fortnight ago? Not much more. It was bins night, I could remember that much. 'You must have known then.'

He shrugged. 'In any relationship, there's always going to be a first time and a last time. That was it. That was the last time. And this was the only way of presenting you with a clean break. Something I believe you have been known to favour, for other people, anyway. Think of it as being cruel to be kind. Think of it as karma. You got what you wanted once. But not this time. This time it's your turn to give up and let go. That's how karma works, Stella. It's indirect, and it creeps up on you when you least expect it.'

I said, 'I have done nothing to deserve this.'

I didn't sound convinced. Or convincing. I sounded as if I knew I was guilty and just couldn't take what I'd had coming all along.

He raised his eyebrows. 'Really? You really think that you have absolutely nothing to reproach yourself with?'

'Everything I did, you did too,' I said.

'Only because you talked me into it. It was never part of the deal. Not to start with. It was a fluke. It was about your family and a chance you couldn't bring yourself to pass up. I went along with it, but it wasn't my idea and you know it. I don't regret it. But that doesn't mean I'm willing to be trapped with you for the rest of my life.'

'You don't get to bail out on me like that,' I said. 'You're complicit.'

He shook his head, as if I was testing his patience but he was confident of being able to resolve any differences in his favour. 'I really don't want this to get any nastier than it has to,' he said. 'You know what Georgie's like. She's so sensitive and idealistic, and sometimes she has rather unyielding views on justice and fairness. If she were ever to find out about those things that you and I usually prefer not to discuss, she'd have so many questions for both of us. And they would be very difficult questions to answer, for you especially, I think. And then there's your mother to think of. Poor Pam. Such a lot on her plate right now. Last thing she needs is all that coming out into the open. So do those questions really need to be asked? Personally, I don't think so. I really don't see that it would be to anybody's benefit. Why open a can of worms if you have the option to leave it well enough alone? I'm sure you'll agree with me once you've had a little time to reflect and come to the right decision.'

'Don't you drag my mother into this. What kind of man are you, to try and hold what we did over me? Because we both did it. You wanted it too. And you agreed about keeping quiet about it.'

He shrugged. 'Yours was the bigger lie. It was down to you to take the lead. I was really an accessory after the fact. And I suspect Georgie will see it that way, too. But I like a calculated gamble, as you know. I'm willing to bet that you would do almost anything to stop her finding out. Especially now. It's a delicate stage, isn't it, being a teenager? People can really take against their parents. Of course, there are some things there's never going to be a good time to tell.'

'Rob… you're twisting it all. You know I went into this with the best of intentions…'

'Oh, spare me the self-justification. Look, Stella, here's the thing.' He was fond of that phrase. For the first time I realised how much I hated it. 'Times change. People change. You've changed. You're not the girl I fell in love with, and you haven't been her for a long time. Next time you're in front of a mirror, try and see things from my point of view. You're a shadow of who you used to be. You're history, babe.'

Then I saw myself as he might see me, as if I was standing in his shoes, pointing a camera in my direction and looking into the viewfinder to line up the shot. A no-longer-young, almost-hysterical woman in high heels and a black crepe jumpsuit, with long, carefully styled, expensively highlighted hair that was now slightly in disarray. A woman who, in the normal way of things, might have been deemed attractive, apart from the air of suppressed unease and the signs of middle age: lines on the neck, lines on the forehead, lines on the backs of the hands.

Someone who was on the verge of losing control, with trembling hands and beads of sweat around her hairline.

A woman who was guilty. Who had spent years hiding something that she knew full well shouldn't be hidden, and that, unlike other kinds of secret, was more likely, rather than less, to be uncovered as time went by.

I said, 'How could I not have realised how much you hated me?'

He shrugged again. 'We had our moments, once. We had something. *You* had something. I'll grant you that. But for years it's just been about going through the motions. It's a long time since I've been happy.'

'Happy? What's happy got to do with it? Life isn't about being *happy*.'

'There we must agree to disagree,' he said. 'I thought Georgie might like the bedroom at the back, by the way. Overlooking the garden. For when she comes to stay. But anyway, you should probably see what she thinks when you show her round.'

'Show her round? Georgie is never coming to this house. Over my dead body.'

'Oh, you won't die, Stella. After all, how would that help Georgie? Look, you are going to end up saying yes to me, so why pretend otherwise?'

'If you're willing to gamble with Georgie's happiness, you're not fit to take care of her.'

'Don't try reaching for the high ground. You won't make it. Are you really so sure you're someone Georgie can trust? Who *anyone* could trust?'

I had stopped shaking, and I found I was able to stand very still as we stared into each other's eyes. But my sense of where and when I was had begun to give way, as if it was possible for me to be here and simultaneously in some other place and time when I had been someone else. Someone Rob had found it possible to love.

A summer afternoon long ago, when we'd just started going out and had ended up arm wrestling at a table in a pub garden...

I had known he was going to win, and he did and I didn't put up too much of a fight. That had been the point: to charm him by resisting a little, and then giving way. So he would tease me and then say something affectionate and go and buy me another drink.

That was the pattern: I was the one who yielded. I had only broken it once, and I had paid for it. But not enough. Not nearly enough to make up for what I owed...

Rob kicked the keys across the floor towards me.

'I'd like to move forward with the divorce as quickly as we can,' he said. 'It doesn't have to be a particularly tortuous or expensive process, and it doesn't have to take forever. Not if we agree on the finances and the custody arrangements, and focus on planning for the future. You'll find some paperwork in the top drawer by the cooker. I suggest you take some time to read through it, and if we can, I'd like to meet with the mediator tomorrow morning to kick things off.'

'A mediator? Tomorrow morning? Have you spoken to a solicitor about this?'

He raised his eyebrows as if it was both foolish to ask this and foolish to expect an answer. 'Just show up, Stella. Come with an open mind and find out about the process. It won't cost you anything – I'll be paying for the meeting. I hope you'll see that there's no reason why this can't be resolved amicably. The more we agree on, the less solicitors will need to be involved, the less time and money will be wasted and the less Georgie will need to be dragged into it. This is about finding a way forward, not raking over the past.'

How could he seriously imagine that it might be possible to find a way out of our marriage without our history coming into play? But clearly he believed that he could get through this the way he wanted, as long as he had already persuaded me to comply. Presumably all kinds of couples, with all kinds of shared pasts and knowledge of each other's mistakes, managed to separate without their secrets coming out into the open. Celebrities. Politicians. Not to mention gangsters and other criminals...

'Oh, and by the way, the security code for the front gate is the date of your mother's birthday,' he went on. 'I thought you'd find that easy to remember, but you can change it if you want. There's an intercom by the front door and an exit button on the gate, so don't worry, you won't have any problems getting out. The instructions are in the drawer, along with everything else.'

With that he moved towards the front door and opened it. I said, 'Where do you think you're going?'

He turned back and looked at me with the exact same expression he always had if I missed part of the plot of a show and he had to explain it.

'I hope you're not expecting a ride home. This is where you belong now. Check the cupboards. You'll find everything you need. If you want to pop back to Fairfield Road you'll have to call ahead to arrange a time. I'm having the locks changed, so you won't be able to get in unless you ring first. Otherwise, I'll see you tomorrow.'

And then he was out of the house before I could stop him, and had slammed the door in my face.

My breath was coming in big uneven gulps. I felt as if I'd been buried alive and he had sealed me in. I scrabbled at the door handle, struggling to open it, getting nowhere. There had to be a knack. Something I was doing wrong. From outside I heard him starting the car and the wheels turning on the gravel.

When I finally managed to fling the door open he had already gone.

The sound of the car thinned out into the distance as he sped away from me. The sun hit me full in the face; it was baking hot and there was no shade. Ahead of me, the view of the gravelled parking area and the gate gave way to the thickly clustered trees of the wood on the far side of the lane.

The trees were the only other living things in sight. I was so completely alone it was almost as if I was no longer alive myself.

Chapter Three

I couldn't cry. I was too shocked. I retreated back into the house and closed the front door carefully behind me. Then I sank down on the chequerboard floor of the hall and curled up into a ball with my arms round my knees and my head resting on them.

Breathe. Think. Pull yourself together.

There had to be *something* I could do.

When you lose a lifelong partner, I've heard it said that you still find yourself talking to them and hear them talking back to you, as if they're just in the next room. Rob was, as far as I knew, very much still alive, and currently speeding away from me back to our house in Kettlebridge – *his* house, as he seemed to think of it. But I heard his voice in my head as if something fatal had happened to him on the way and his ghost had returned to mock me.

Like I said, Stella, you're going to give me exactly what I want. At least that way you get to keep some of what you *want. Whereas who knows what you'll end up with if I blow the whole thing apart?*

My body ached as if I'd been beaten. Rob never would have done that, though. Not his style. You probably shouldn't feel pleased with yourself for being with a man who isn't going to physically hurt you, but there had been a time when I had seen it as something to be grateful for.

With men, as with so much else in life, it all depends on who you're comparing them to.

I could still picture it: the pale white skin of a young girl's upper arm marked with a bruise as dense and dark as a tattoo. A pattern of ink-dark circles scored with red. A puzzle that resolved itself into the imprint of someone's hand: the bruises were fingerprints and the red marks had been scored by nails.

Molly. My long-lost little sister. That was the first time I'd realised what a thug her boyfriend was. She had been ashamed that I had seen it, and her first response had been to tug down her sleeve and to glare at me as if it was my fault for looking.

I shook my head to clear it and found myself back in the present, in the almost-empty house that my husband wanted me to live in.

The house keys were still where they'd fallen. I shifted forwards and picked them up, and thought of him imagining me doing that, on my hands and knees.

There, you see? You've come to your senses. It didn't even take that long.

'I'm not planning on staying,' I said out loud.

Maybe he would come back for me. This could all just be intended to get the message across and show me that he was in earnest. First the shock, then the making peace. Like the kind of parent who turfs a badly behaved kid out of the car to teach them a lesson, then drives round the block and picks them up again.

He never would have done that to Georgie, but then, I never would have let him. And Georgie had never been badly behaved.

You're just kidding yourself, Stella. I'm not coming back to rescue you. Nobody is. You really are on your own.

I scooped up my handbag from the floor by my feet, put the keys in it and went into the kitchen. It must have clouded over, because the light coming in was muted, and the room was as still and dead as a tomb.

If this was meant to be the heart of the house, then the house lacked a pulse. It was so stark, so… soulless. Had he really thought that being abandoned here would induce me to accept his terms – including the custody arrangements he wanted? Would anyone want to live in a place that felt so lonely and abandoned? Perhaps he had just decided that it would do, that the value of the property was enough to wipe out any misgivings I might have.

Just as if he was standing right next to me, I heard his voice again. *She's my daughter just as much as she is yours.*

But the room was still perfectly empty, apart from the table and chairs he had so thoughtfully installed for me.

He was possessive. Had been with me too, once upon a time. And proud. He believed in ownership, as long as it was him doing the owning and calling the shots when the time came to dispose of something. He tended to think that anything could be sold and everything was for sale, if only the price was right. Or, as he preferred to put it, if you could establish the right combination of push factors and pull factors. That was how he made his money, after all: making deals, doing places up, then making even better deals. He wasn't sentimental about property. Back in the early nineties after the house prices crashed, when Georgie was little, we'd moved from one place to another before we settled in Kettlebridge, living in a constant state of renovation. He'd never found anywhere hard to leave.

'You're not thinking about what's best for Georgie,' I said out loud.

The comment that came back was unanswerable. *Are you?*

As he'd promised, he'd left a leaflet about mediation in the top drawer nearest the oven, along with a business card giving an address in an office block on one of the three main roads in Kettlebridge. On the back of the business card he'd written, *Friday 11.00 a.m.* No question mark.

He really believed I was going to go along with this. Or else he'd decided his best hope of railroading me was to behave as if I would. It was a gamble, the whole thing. But as Rob had said to me more than once, it wasn't gambling if you'd studied the odds and were sure you could win.

The leaflet explained what mediation involved in bullet points, stressing the importance of compromise. *Compromise!* That had never been Rob's strong point. What he had in mind was a sham – the real negotiation was the one that had just taken place, which had ended up with me on the hallway floor.

But I agreed that we could have a child together.

He could say that. It was true. It was fair. I couldn't argue with it. It was a statement of fact.

That was a compromise. And then I learned to love her.

That was true too. Once Georgie had arrived, he had loved her.

I put the leaflet away. The drawer shut smoothly, almost silently, and then the loudest noise in the empty house was my breathing, which was as fast and loud as if I'd just been running.

Attention to detail was important to Rob: he wouldn't have wanted anything to go wrong. I pictured him moving round the house, probably as recently as yesterday, checking everything was in order, putting the finishing touches to his plan. Setting the trap.

And I could still hear him. *I owe you that much, don't I? And Georgie. And myself. In the end you might even forget, some of the time, that there was ever a chance of anything being different.*

Yes, he really did mean it. That was why he'd done it this way. He intended to leave no room for doubt and very little room for manoeuvre. He was using a strategy that I'd sometimes heard him talk about approvingly, as if it was a book or a film he'd particularly enjoyed. Take it or leave it.

He despised me. And if it was a shock it was only because I had never wanted to see it before. It wasn't just the ordinary familiarity-breeds-contempt type of weariness that you might expect to settle into after spending the best part of twenty years together, nearly fifteen of those as parents. What he felt for me was a kind of horror.

If Georgie found out what we'd done – if? when? – he'd be able to claim that he'd just been going along with what I wanted, but in the end it had made it impossible for him to stay with me.

He'd be able to claim a kind of belated innocence. And it would be believable. He *was* believable. He had the gift of making whatever he said sound reasonable, the kind of thing that any sound-minded person would go along with.

Georgie might not know who or what to believe. But he was right about one thing: she would blame me more.

The sunlight was pitching in again, as if somebody had turned a dial. It was even more dazzling than before. I closed my eyes as I leaned back against the kitchen counter and a vivid image came to me of newborn Georgie sleeping in the crook of my arm, a warm little bundle with a perfectly tiny nose and a milky mouth. Her eyes closed so tight they looked like creases in her soft new skin, fringed with almost imperceptible eyelashes.

So quiet, so sweet, so peaceful and so right.

As if I'd been dropped back in time, I was back in that little house in the countryside near Bristol, sitting on the faded yellow sofa we'd had for a while till Rob decided we could afford to get rid of it. Georgie was in my arms and Rob was next to me, gazing down at her too, as enchanted as I was.

Enchanted – and anxious. He wasn't yet confident about holding her. It was as if he didn't trust himself not to drop her or do something terrible to her. I knew how he felt because I felt the same, but I was her mother and it was down to me to overcome the fear and hold her close anyway.

And Mum was sitting opposite us, taking photographs, taking it all in. Delighted to be a grandmother. Even prouder than she'd been when I got married, and already softer with Georgie than I'd ever seen her.

Georgie was easy to love, wasn't she?

That was what Rob would say if he was next to me in the present, and looking back too.

She was easy to love, and that makes your life with her easy to remember. But what about when it's hard to love and hard to forget?

When I opened my eyes there was nothing to see but the bright and almost-empty kitchen. It was as if the years I'd spent with Rob and Georgie had been a fairy tale and now the spell was broken and they had vanished. And here I was in a lonely house in the woods, with a leaflet on mediation in a drawer in the kitchen and a single bed upstairs.

I checked the keys Rob had left for me. One of them was small and silver. I leaned across the draining board to try it in the internal lock of the kitchen window overlooking the garden. It fit. I pushed open the bigger of the two window flaps and breathed deep as a little eddy of cooler air made its way in. Then I rummaged in my bag for my phone.

My heart sank as soon as I unlocked it.

Rob sometimes referred to it as my drug dealer phone, since it was apparently the kind they used and threw out before they could be tracked down. It was an oldish pay-as-you-go Nokia that I needed to get round to replacing. The battery was a little temperamental and it had chosen this particular moment – the worst possible moment, when it was my only connection to the outside world – to lose almost all its charge.

Also, Rob hadn't called.

I made my way back upstairs, taking extra care on the wooden steps. If I fell and broke my neck, it might be quite some time before anyone found me. And if I did myself some lesser injury, my phone would die on me before I could call for help.

In the master bedroom, the chemical smell of the new single bed was even more noticeable than before.

I slid back the door to the fitted wardrobe and saw the clothes hanging inside it.

New clothes. Not mine, but the kind of thing I might wear. Black trousers, a cotton shirt patterned with light green leaves, a long flowery skirt, a pastel-blue T-shirt with three-quarter-length sleeves. In the bottom of the wardrobe there were white cotton waffle slippers and a pair of flat leather sandals.

He'd provided bedding, too. In the shelving compartment on the right was a summer-weight duvet still in its box and a pillow still in its case. There was a plastic-wrapped pillowcase, duvet cover and fitted sheet, all in matching duck-egg blue Egyptian cotton, plus a towelling bathrobe and pyjamas in the same colour, neatly folded. On the top shelf was a wicker basket that turned out to have toiletries inside – soap, shower gel, shampoo, toothpaste, toothbrush.

If I checked the kitchen cupboards I knew I'd find food. Ready-made meals in the freezer, suitably low-fat. Semi-skimmed milk. Coffee. Porridge oats. And there would be a couple of pots and pans and cutlery, and glasses. No doubt the electricity and water were on, and the TV and the cooker would work. There was probably a microwave that I hadn't noticed yet, and a radio in a cupboard waiting for me to find it.

He'd kitted me out as if this was a doll's house and he had all the money and time he needed to play with me.

I slid the door of the fitted wardrobe shut. The minute I took my shoes off and put those slippers on, or went downstairs and helped myself to food, I was doomed. Using anything here was the slippery slope to accepting Rob's terms.

Anyway, I wasn't hungry.

Suddenly I was hit by a wave of dizziness so intense that I had to sit down on the single bed and double over to get my head down to my knees.

It would pass. It was the shock, that was all. Shock and airlessness, and how ruthless Rob was prepared to be.

I already knew that about him, of course. Single-minded. That was Rob. Focused. He liked to get what he wanted, and he usually did.

A loud bang from somewhere in the house startled me into getting to my feet.

A door slamming. That was all. But there wasn't anybody else in the house, or much of a breeze.

I retraced my steps downstairs to close the kitchen window. Once it was locked again the house seemed more than ever like a prison. I got out my phone again and unlocked it and the screen promptly went black.

Nothing. Not even a glimmer of charge. Dead as a dodo.

Was everything conspiring to keep me here?

I marched out of the place and slammed the front door behind me as if I was leaving behind someone I'd had a row with.

The gate! Rob had sounded so pleased with himself when he told me that the entry code was my mother's date of birth. How many husbands would remember their mother-in-law's birthday? But Rob always did. Sent her a bouquet every year. I sometimes told acquaintances about this: *Rob adores my mum and the feeling is entirely mutual. When those two are together I don't get a look-in! And Georgie's the apple of her eye. Being the only grandchild. When we have family get-togethers I end up feeling like a spare part.*

I tried to sound self-deprecatory, but it probably came across as a kind of boasting. Still, you had to come up with *something* to say to people. Even if what you really wanted was to keep them at arm's length because there were other things you had no intention of telling them…

What would Mum say when she knew what Rob had done? She would be heartbroken. It meant everything to her to see us happily settled together, and if we weren't always all that happy, well… she didn't have to know that, did she?

Given how fond Rob had always seemed to be of her, how could he do this to her now? He was right – from her point of view, it was a terrible time. She was under so much strain already. If he couldn't bring himself to wait for Georgie's sake, at least until she was a little closer to adulthood, couldn't he have held on out of respect for Mum? Had it really been so unbearable for him to carry on as we were that he had felt he had no choice?

I pressed the exit button by the pedestrian gate. There was a click, then a brief, unnerving delay before a motor sprang into action and it opened. After I'd passed through, as the gate slid shut behind me, I allowed myself one final glance back at the house. It was still a dead-eyed place in the middle of nowhere, with the kind of fresh paint job that is applied to distract the unwary from any number of hidden faults.

If anything, it looked even more ominous than when I'd first laid eyes on it. It looked like the kind of place where anything could go on and nobody would ever know. It looked like a good place to hide, and I could see why Rob had thought that would suit me, and why he had assumed he would be able to lead me into the trap and leave me there.

Still, ambitious men who like to gamble have been known to miscalculate from time to time. Especially when they underestimate the opposition. If he seriously expected me to give up just like that, he had another think coming.

Chapter Four

Even though there was no one else around, it was impossible not to feel conspicuous. You just wouldn't expect to see a woman dressed the way I was – in a date outfit and shoes that weren't made for walking – several miles from the nearest bar or restaurant and trudging along a quiet rural lane. If you did, you'd probably conclude that you were witnessing either a walk of shame or the aftermath of a crime.

I was just thinking about the blisters I was going to have by the time I found a bus stop when my ankle gave way under me and I crashed down onto the ground.

The indignity was more of a shock than the hurt. I had instinctively gone down onto my right side, onto the elbow that had never been broken. I'd grazed my forearm and as I examined it blood welled up through the scraped skin. My knees smarted and the jumpsuit fabric had snagged but hadn't torn.

It was going to be even harder than I'd expected to get out of here. The heel of one of my sandals had snapped clean off.

As I got to my feet a man in cycling lycra emerged from the nearest front garden and approached me. The neighbour. My instinct was to recoil from him. Before I could stop myself I had reached up to shield my face. I didn't want anyone seeing the state I was in.

He said, 'Hello there, are you OK? That was quite a tumble.'

I forced myself to act normally. Well, as normally as possible. I could do that, couldn't I? I'd had plenty of practice.

All he would see, all I needed him to see, was a silly woman who'd made a bit of a fool of herself and was mildly embarrassed, no harm done…

I managed an ingratiating, sheepish smile and held up my broken heel, a thin sliver of disco gold that screamed impracticality. Then, not knowing what else to do with it, I slipped it into my handbag.

'Yes! Yes, I'm fine, thank you. Can't say the same for my shoe.'

He glanced down at my feet, then up at my face. He was looking at me as if I was a good person, a decent person – he was giving me the benefit of the doubt, the way you do when you meet someone new.

'Do you have far to go?' He glanced up the lane as if he half expected to see a car there waiting for me.

'Oh, just back to Kettlebridge. Not far at all.' I gave him my best feckless-female smile. With any luck, he'd just conclude I was slightly mad.

He didn't reply straight away, but carried on standing there and studying me as if I was an unexpected puzzle. He was slightly taller than me, about the same height as Rob and possibly a few years older, with sandy-coloured hair streaked with silver and a small, tight-lipped smile. He looked as if he kept in shape, but not as if he would care about being top of the league tables down the gym, and he wasn't self-conscious in his lycra the way Rob might have been. Instead he was focused on me. He looked as if he was on the verge of finding my situation troubling and wasn't sure whether he should let it go.

Was he attractive? Maybe. The lack of self-consciousness was attractive in itself. But maybe that was just because it was a contrast to Rob, and a change was as good as a rest.

It was unwise to compare your husband to other men – every wife knew that. It could never be comparing like with like – the devil you knew, and the devil you didn't…

He said, 'If you don't mind me asking… what brings you here?'

I should have known better than to respond to a stranger's polite curiosity. But I wanted to. I had to make it normal. To turn what had just happened into something it was possible to talk about.

'My husband has been doing up the place next to you,' I told him, and waved a hand towards the house at the end of the lane. 'We were checking it out, and I stayed behind, and I would have called for a cab but then my phone died. And then my shoe died too. I don't suppose you could tell me where the nearest bus stop is, could you?'

'It'll take you a while to walk there, and you'll be waiting forever. Look, why don't I call a cab to take you back to Kettlebridge? I'm sure one would come soon.'

Was this a stroke of luck? Or should I just get out now while the going was good, and walk away?

If you know you're not what you seem, you tend to think the same might be true of everyone else. I couldn't help but suspect him, though I wasn't sure what of. Wouldn't any woman be a little on edge, talking to a strange man in a strange place with no one else around? Especially if she was dressed as I was, with a broken shoe that would make it hard to run…

For all that, he still looked like a nice, normal chap who just wanted to help out a hapless passer-by.

'That's very kind. Thank you. Nice to meet you.'

I moved to hold out my hand for him to shake, hesitated, thought better of it, glanced down at it – no blood. It was only my arm that was scraped and bleeding. My hand was soft, clean and well cared for, with no varnish on the nails because Rob didn't like it, and preferred a more natural look.

An unobjectionable hand. Just a hint of tarmac dust from contact with the pavement, as you would expect, nothing too incriminating.

I felt the same little frisson I sometimes felt when I looked in a mirror and the face staring back at me caught me by surprise. Was that really my hand? The hand other people saw? I wiped it surreptitiously on the leg of my jumpsuit and offered it to him. He took it without hesitation and without looking at me askance, as if, as far as he was concerned, I had as much right to fall over in front of his house as anyone else did.

'I'm Stella Castle.'

His touch was light and dry and he let me go almost instantly. 'Tony Everdene,' he said.

I heard Rob's voice in my head again. *Making friends with the neighbours already, Stella? Way to go! Are you hoping this man will be your ally? Your shoulder to cry on? If so, how much are you going to tell him?*

Rob had always been jealous. Thrillingly so, at first. Later on, his jealousy had been more of a joke, as if he was resigned to the likelihood of me being attracted to other people and willing to take it in his stride. The funny thing was, whenever he accused me of fancying someone, he was always right. Exaggerating, perhaps. But he had an eagle eye for who I might like. Often I would have barely even realised or admitted it to myself.

Had I taken a shine to Tony? I wasn't sure. It was too awkward for it to be easy to tell. As for him… he was just being nice. And he was curious. I certainly had his full attention.

He reached into the back pocket of his cycling jersey, fished out his phone, pressed a couple of buttons and passed it to me.

'Just tell them where you want to go,' he said.

I gave my address. The woman at the other end said, 'Picking up from where?'

'Er…' I looked round and caught sight of a 2 etched on a slate number plate next to the front door of Tony's house. 'Number 2, Fox Hill Lane.'

The woman said the car would arrive in about twenty minutes and the driver would call when he got there, then hung up.

I thanked Tony and passed back the phone, and he put it away and said, 'Come in and wait inside, if you would like?'

I knew I ought to say no. I barely knew him and I didn't want to start behaving as if I was actually going to live here. And I wouldn't have wanted to explain what had just happened to anybody, let alone to a complete stranger.

Still, I hesitated. It was hot and I was sweating again, and it seemed silly to wait outside if I didn't have to. Besides, it was only twenty minutes. Surely I could manage twenty minutes.

'You've been very kind, but it looks like you're on your way out and I wouldn't want to impose,' I said finally.

'You sure? I'm not in a rush, and you'd be doing me a favour. My name will be mud if it comes out that I met you and didn't take the opportunity to grill you.'

I blenched at that. I didn't much like the idea of being grilled.

'Only kidding,' Tony said. 'I'm not a nosy neighbour, I promise you. But at least let give you some antiseptic for that graze.'

'Oh, it doesn't really need it. But I suppose it might be an idea to wash it. Thank you.'

I limped behind him towards the house, past the family estate car parked on the drive. His bike was upright on a kickstand on the lawn. Tony said, 'I'll just put this away. I'm afraid you have to be careful round here, even though it seems as if it should be safe as houses.'

He took a bunch of keys out of another pocket, unlocked the garage door and flipped it open. Inside it was immaculate and mostly empty. There was a well-swept expanse of floor, a tidy array of tools on the walls and a chest freezer, which would probably be packed, come autumn, with Tupperware boxes of stewed apples from the tree in the front garden and blackberries picked from the hedgerows of Fox Hill.

Tony put his bike in the garage and locked it up again. A careful, helpful, security-conscious person. The ideal neighbour.

For someone else. Not me. This was all just a detour, and soon enough I'd be back in Fairfield Road with old Mrs Mott on one side and the boys who were always kicking their ball over the hedge on the other. There was no way Rob could mean what he'd just said. Could he? This was just his way of letting me know how unhappy he was… Surely I'd be able to persuade him to give us another chance… I'd have to get to the bottom of what it was that had

made him so dissatisfied, and then I'd have to fix it. Do better, try
harder… Give him whatever it was he was missing…

If I could.

Tony unlocked the front door and I glimpsed a perfectly normal
entrance hall: carpet, a cupboard for coats, stairs. Framed needlepoint
on the wall: 'Home Sweet Home' picked out in painstaking stitching,
probably the work of an older relative.

Really, what was the worst that could happen to you in a house
with needlepoint on the wall? It wasn't always right to expect the
worst of people. When Tony said, 'Come on in,' I thanked him
and went through.

*

He pointed out the cloakroom, and I went in to wash my arm
and hands. The liquid soap was green and antiseptic, and stung.
Rob would have disapproved. He viewed luxury handwash as an
essential bathroom accessory, especially when trying to impress
potential buyers.

My reflection in the mirror didn't look too bad. Almost normal.
Dim lighting, though. And my expectations of what I might see
were not high.

I lingered in the cloakroom long enough for it to be embarrassing
if I stayed there any longer, then went out to join Tony in the kitchen.

Rob definitely wouldn't have been impressed. Too old-fashioned.
It was done up in antique cream with terracotta floor tiles and
light-green units with brass handles, and there was a big framed
studio photograph of Tony with his wife and children on the wall.
He had two girls, one dark-haired and one blonde, apparently the
same age. The wife was pretty and slim and blonde with a smile
that showed a mouthful of good white teeth.

They all looked happy. Of course they looked happy: the picture
would hardly be hanging right where they could see it every din-
nertime if they didn't.

I'd once suggested getting some studio shots like that of our family, but Rob had declined. We didn't need to flaunt our perfect marriage, he'd said. Let people figure out how much they ought to envy us for themselves. Besides, they'd only get suspicious if we advertised how blessed we were.

Would Mrs Everdene mind me being here? Probably not. She looked pretty secure. The kind of wife who knew her husband loved her and who had no reason to question whether she deserved it. Though those things could change, and the photo looked as if it had been taken some years back. Tony's hair had less silver in it than it did now, and he looked a little fresher-faced and more puppyish in the photo than in the present.

Those girls – late-primary-school-age – might be teenagers now, getting on for being as old as Georgie. I didn't recognise them, thankfully. One of the downsides of being a teacher in a small country town – even if you were only part-time – was that you tended to come across your pupils' parents in all kinds of situations, from the supermarket to the doctor's waiting room, which was, at best, a lovely affirmation of the value of your work but could also be embarrassing and sometimes, as now, had the potential to be downright humiliating.

The last thing I needed was for it to get round that I'd been spotted alone in Fox Hill on my day off, dressed as if I'd just been stood up for a date or – worse still – had fled from one that had gone wrong. Which, since everyone knew I was married, would be taken to mean either that I'd had a row with Rob, or that I was having an affair.

That wouldn't just be humiliating for me – it would be bad for Georgie, too. OK, so she had never complained about having a mum who taught at her school – she said it was fine – but if she thought people were gossiping about her family it would surely become unbearable. Even if she didn't believe a word they said.

I took a seat at the round oak table and Tony gave me a drink of water in a heavy glass tumbler. I almost choked on it: it was as if I'd forgotten how to swallow. That happened sometimes, when I was particularly anxious. It made social occasions less than relaxing. Over the years, I'd left a lot of half-empty glasses and cups of cooling tea and coffee behind me.

I kept hold of the glass. I'd have another go at swallowing in a minute: my mouth was dry. Tony didn't seem to have noticed anything out of the ordinary. He said, 'If you don't mind me asking, are you planning to live at Gamekeeper's yourself, or rent it out? We've all been wondering.'

'Gamekeeper's?'

'Your new place. The house at the end of the lane. That's what it's called, or it always used to be, anyway. Gamekeeper's Cottage. Your husband's done an awful lot of work on it over the last few months. But I guess he didn't mention the name?'

'No, he didn't. To be honest, I don't really keep up to speed with what he's doing. He's done up a lot of different places over the years.' I attempted a smile. 'Maybe I'm wrong about this, but I've always thought that in a marriage, it's best to specialise. He has his work and I have mine. He undoes the lids on jam jars. I put out the spiders. You know the kind of thing.'

It was comforting to talk about Rob as if everything was just fine between us. It almost made it seem as if it was.

Surely, when he'd had a little time to reflect, he would realise he still needed me. Once I'd got to the bottom of whatever it was that was going on, and had promised to make amends.

Tony was looking at me with one eyebrow slightly raised and a small, tight-lipped smile.

'I don't know what's going to be happening with the house. It's all a bit up in the air,' I said.

'Oh. I see.'

There was a small silence that lengthened until it was almost uncomfortable. Perhaps Tony expected me to say more. Maybe he thought that if he left me hanging, I would.

I had actually told him the truth, more or less, but I knew he didn't believe me. He must think I was being deliberately evasive. He would be wondering about what I wasn't telling him. About what I might have to hide.

At least he was too polite to ask outright. I could handle this. I knew what to do. I was used to making out everything was fine – I'd had plenty of practice.

Seize the initiative. Deflect. Even when all you want to do is curl up in a corner and hide, act like you've as much right as anyone to be the one asking the questions.

I said, 'Did you know the people who lived next door before?'

'It was just an old guy who was there on his own. I don't know if he'd ever had a family. I think it was all in quite a state by the time the police went in.'

'The police?'

'Well, yes. After he passed away.'

'Oh. I didn't know he had died there. On his own.'

Tony looked at me sympathetically, as if he was commiserating with me over a personal loss.

'I'm sorry. Perhaps I shouldn't have said. Anyway, the place had pretty much gone to rack and ruin. Like I said, your husband has done a lot to it.'

'Yes, well, he's good at that.'

I had come out in goose pimples. How was it possible to go from baking to freezing so quickly? And how much longer was this taxi going to take?

My husband wanted to wall me up in a house where someone else had died alone…

He must have known.

He couldn't mean it. Not really, not after all we'd been through together.

I decided to change the subject.

'That's a lovely picture of your family,' I said, gazing up at the photo on the wall behind Tony's head.

He turned to glance at it as if he'd almost forgotten it was there. 'Oh. Thank you.'

'Are your girls twins? They look as if they're very close in age.'

'They are. Though people don't often guess, because they're not identical. They tend to assume Livy's the oldest, because she's more confident. She's the dark-haired one. Even with twins, you get this sibling dynamic where they have to work out what their roles are. Or that's how it is with those two, anyway.'

Usually I steered clear of the subject of siblings and sibling relationships, as far as was reasonably practical. I didn't want to have to mention Molly and then explain that I hadn't seen her for years and had no idea where she was. And I didn't want to be quizzed on having an only child, either. I loved talking about Georgie as she was now, and I was more than happy to reminisce about her childhood and the baby years. But as for looking back to her birth, and to the choices we'd made… That was a subject to be avoided at all costs. It was private, anyway. None of anybody else's business…

Tony didn't seem like the type to ask, but you could never tell who would decide to wade in and who would leave well enough alone. Even though it wasn't that unusual to have an only child these days, sometimes people wondered why…

Some of them wanted to know whether it was out of necessity. Had I suffered some kind of medical trauma that meant I couldn't have another child? Had we tried in vain? Or had I just not been up for it? On the face of it, it looked as if we could afford a bigger family. But maybe I had decided I couldn't face the whole business of pregnancy and birth and broken nights all over again? Or was Rob the one who had felt that way? Maybe it was us, me and Rob together. Had we struggled the first time round, and agreed our marriage couldn't take the strain?

I don't know what it was exactly that made me choose to stick with the subject of Tony's twins. Maybe it was because they looked so happy. Maybe it was that old, familiar feeling, the dull pang of yearning that comes from seeing something you have been cut off from and can't quite believe you've lost. I had taken sisterhood for granted. Now it was gone for good.

I said, 'Do they get on? They look as if they do.'

Tony seemed to be pleased by this, though he pulled a self-deprecating face to suggest it wasn't always the case. 'Mostly. They're pretty good friends, on the whole. I think each of them would miss the other one if she wasn't around. But that hardly ever happens, given that they're in the same class at school. They see too much of each other, if anything.'

Another silence. Was this how it was going to be from now on? Would everything people told me about their families remind me of what it was to be lonely?

I cast around for something else to talk about. Work. That would do. Safe ground. Work was all about punctuality and professionalism and public appearance. It wasn't like family life, all that intimacy and resentment, the jockeying for position, loving people and being like them and unlike them and missing them and needing them.

And feeling guilty about them. And fearing them...

Work *could* be like family, at times. In good ways. In bad ways. But there were rules about that. Rules to protect people from what happened when closeness went wrong.

I told Tony I was a part-time teacher; he told me he was on leave today and was a solicitor, specialising in wills and trusts. That figured. I could imagine him leafing through large, dusty-smelling old books, poring over the fine print, mapping the parameters of what was permissible and what was not. Then listening to people talking about money and property and death and gifts, planning for futures they would never see.

What would Rob say if he could see me now?

Inheritance. Now there's a topic for a dinner-party conversation. You might call it dry, or you might call it thought-provoking, depending on the kind of dinner parties you like. But it matters, doesn't it? Everybody knows that. You and I especially. Nobody can undo the brute facts of death and blood and life. And there are records. It's all there in black and white, just waiting for someone to realise it's there to be looked for.

We were interrupted by Tony's phone. He had an unexpected ring tone – a staccato piano riff that I vaguely recognised from a horror film Rob had talked me into watching with him once. Maybe Tony had selected it as a joke. It was certainly distinctive.

'Taxi's here,' Tony said.

He came out with me. As I went down the garden path he locked the front door and opened the garage up again. As my taxi pulled away he was walking his bike towards the road, ready to set off on the ride I'd kept him from. I waved but I wasn't sure he'd noticed.

With any luck, I'd never see him again.

I had to talk to Rob. I had to fix this.

You're history, babe. But I was Rob's history, and he was mine. I had already lost too much. I couldn't lose him too.

If I could keep him – if I could change the story he had decided to write for me, if I could make him want to keep me too – then perhaps I could also keep Georgie safe in the nest of lies we'd built. A nest that was made of all the little evasions and omissions and half-truths I had felt so anxious and guilty about, and had tried, day by day, to forget. I was haunted by irrational fears all the time, but it had never occurred to me that Rob might one day turn on me and threaten to tear down everything we had.

Chapter Five

Within minutes the taxi had left the scattered houses of Fox Hill Lane behind and we were deep in the woods. That was one of the things I'd had to get used to when we moved to the countryside: how quickly you could get away from other people, and find yourself out of sight and in the middle of nowhere. At first having so much empty green space close by made me feel exposed. Then, over time, I realised it was just a different kind of anonymity.

I don't think it was ever much of an issue for Rob. He didn't seem to be affected by his environment in that way, and he wasn't afraid of being isolated. He was always focused on two things: what land was worth, and what he could do with it next. That said, he'd grown up in the countryside and he'd never shown any desire to live in a city, although he'd done some work on properties in the suburbs. If I'd asked him about it he probably would have said that he had gone where he had seen the best opportunities. He wouldn't have admitted to anything as sentimental as wanting to return to the kind of landscape he'd grown up in.

The taxi emerged from the woods onto the crest of the hill overlooking Kettlebridge. Rays of sunlight were breaking through at the edge of a tall mass of white cloud above the hills on the horizon, forming a big dramatic skyscape like a scene from an old painting about justice coming down from above. Kettlebridge came into view, clusters of rooftops reaching across the basin of the valley in a spreading circle, surrounded by hills and fields.

I thought of Georgie and how pleased she would be when the school coach came this way on its return journey. And then I began to picture how her homecoming would play out if I couldn't fix things with Rob – if he meant what he'd said and got what he'd told me he wanted, with me out of the way and cooped up in the house back on Fox Hill...

If I didn't show up to collect her... if Rob went instead... wouldn't she immediately wonder why?

It was never usually him who turned out when she needed picking up. And if I wasn't there when she got back to Fairfield Road, what would she feel then? Had Rob even thought about that? If he had, how could he have gone ahead with what he'd just tried to do?

The road ahead followed the curve of the hill down into the fields. The view flattened out as we descended and started making our way through the outskirts of town.

As the school day had just finished, there were kids everywhere – helmetless kids on bikes riding two or three abreast, younger kids holding their mothers' hands as they waited at the pedestrian crossing, teenagers sauntering along with deliberately bored expressions. Within quarter of an hour they'd all be gone, as if some mysterious Pied Piper had summoned them away.

'It's the next left,' I said, and the taxi turned onto Fairfield Road, which was wide and quiet and planted with tall trees.

Rob had told me I'd like it before he took me to see it, and he had been right. What a magical moment that had been, walking through the big rooms with their worn carpets and furnishings and faded curtains, imagining it as our own. The forever house. The estate agent holding back, keeping her distance and staying quiet, knowing that the house was selling itself.

Mum had approved of it, too: 'Exactly the kind of place where I want to see my little granddaughter grow up.' When Lee took early retirement and they decided to move closer to us she'd hoped to buy something on the same road or just round the corner but nothing suitable had come up, and she'd ended up in a little house in Critchley, the next village, instead.

'Just here,' I said, and the taxi pulled up in front of our driveway.

There it was: home. A big, friendly-looking, double-bay-fronted Edwardian red-brick house with a red front door and pots of lavender and rosemary on the doorstep. Rob's car was there, next to the little runaround we'd bought for me to use couple of years back. All calm, all peaceful.

Before we'd moved in, the house had been owned by an old lady who'd brought up five children here. She specifically wanted it to go to a young family. Or so the estate agent had told Rob, who had gone to work on her with his usual mix of charm and bluster, determined to secure the place for us while also whittling down the price as far as possible.

'Having Georgie was what swung it,' he said to me when our offer was accepted. 'She wanted it to go to us.' And he'd grabbed me and spun me around the dreary kitchen of the house we were living in at the time.

Then Georgie had wandered in. She had been astonished at first, then delighted to see us both so overjoyed. She had come forward to hug us and we had clung together, the three of us, and I had thought how right all this was and how I had everything now, the husband, the child, the home…

That's the problem with happiness. It's addictive. So heady at first, so easy to get used to…

The old lady who had owned the house before us left us a note in the kitchen on moving day, along with a bottle of cava: *I hope the three of you – and maybe more – have many happy years here.* 'She could have gone for champagne, given the size of the mortgage on the place,' Rob had said as he checked out the label.

Would he have made good on his threat to change the locks yet? I paid the taxi driver and was pained by the sight of my brand-new burgundy leather purse, which Georgie had left with Rob, carefully wrapped, to give to me on my birthday.

I had to press on. I had to persuade him to change his mind. Surely, for Georgie's sake, he would reconsider…

As I hobbled towards the house the gravel on the driveway crunched loudly underfoot, as it was supposed to do; we'd been advised to put it down as a security precaution. I thought of the flicker of light that had caught my eye when I first walked into the empty kitchen in the house on Fox Hill, a flash like the headlamps of an approaching driver before they're dipped. Then there had been the door that had slammed so disproportionately loudly in response to the meagre breeze I'd let in, as if to rebuke me. And someone had died there, not so long ago…

But I'd been jumpy and then in shock. Suggestible. In exactly the right state for my mind to start playing tricks on me, conjuring up things that weren't actually there. Anyway, there was always something strange about an empty house. An empty house was between one kind of life and another, waiting for people to turn up and claim it.

It didn't matter. I wouldn't be going back there. *This* was my home.

I had to remind Rob of the good times, and of everything we had that was worth preserving. I couldn't fight him. I couldn't be angry. I couldn't afford to lose control.

This time there could be no sobbing, no accusations, no hysteria. Rob hated all that. I had to remind him who I was. I had to give him a reason to want me again…

The living room window was open, and I made my way over to it. We didn't have net curtains at Fairfield Road. Rob would have been horrified by the very idea. Instead the lower half of each ground-floor window was covered with opaque film to prevent any passing nosy parkers from gawping at us. Still, the window was open wide enough for me to peer inside. Even to climb through, come to that.

When the dust had settled, we might need to have a little chat about security. If you were going to attempt to kick your wife out, you shouldn't make it quite so easy for her to get back in.

From what I could see, he wasn't in the living room. The house seemed quiet. Maybe he was sleeping, though it would be entirely out of character for Rob to take an afternoon nap, especially on a day such as this.

Most likely he had his headphones on and was working out in the bedroom that he'd commandeered as a home gym. The other spare bedroom was reserved for guests, though it was very rare for anyone to sleep there unless it was a friend of Georgie's. It wasn't a deliberate policy: it was just how things had turned out, especially since Mum had moved nearby and hadn't needed to stay overnight.

Rob and I had guests round for dinner… you might even say we had friends… but we didn't let people get *that* close. Not close enough to stay. You could tell things about a house after you'd slept overnight in it that you wouldn't know otherwise, and we hadn't wanted that to happen to us – for a visitor to come to the conclusion that *there was something not quite right*, even if they couldn't put a finger on what it was.

Seen from outside, with Rob somewhere else and the sun on my back, the living room didn't look how I remembered it. I'd been there just that morning… but suddenly it didn't look as if it was mine or had anything to do with me, any more than it would have done if I'd been checking it out in an estate agent's window.

The glossy pot plants, the cheerful patterned rugs, the mid-century furniture with spindly wooden legs and generous upholstery – it struck me as stagey: a pretence put together for people to see and be convinced by.

And then I saw the green cotton cardigan draped over the back of the sofa.

Not mine. Not Georgie's. I didn't recognise it.

Mum's? It could be. But what would she be doing here?

I pulled the window as wide as I could. Then I checked over my shoulder to see if anyone was approaching, and when I was sure the coast was clear I hoisted myself up onto the window ledge and through it, and broke into my own home.

It was quiet. I couldn't hear Rob, or anyone else. I sat down on the sofa and took off my sandals. It was a relief to get out of them.

Next to me, the green cardigan gave off a perfume that reminded me of boiled sweets. Strawberry flavour. Definitely not Mum's. She hated fruity scents.

I left my sandals on the carpet and padded through to the dining room and kitchen. All quiet, and no signs of life. I didn't call out to say that I was home. It really hadn't been that kind of day.

As I went through into the hall I heard voices from upstairs.

Not angry voices. And not grunts and cries of sensual ecstasy, either. What I heard was conversation. Friendly conversation. The voices of people who knew each other well, and liked talking to each other.

One of them was my husband. The other I couldn't place.

I hovered at the bottom of the stairs. Rob said quite distinctly, 'You know, you shouldn't have come. You're very difficult to say no to. But the locksmith's due to show up soon.'

The reply to Rob's comment was inaudible, but I could make out enough to know the person he was with was a woman, one who liked him – maybe even really loved him – and didn't want to leave.

As I crept up the first few steps he laughed. The urge to spy on him was overwhelming – stronger by far than the urge to burst in and start making accusations. Now, while he was blissfully oblivious… this was my best chance to get to the truth of what was going on.

Maybe I didn't need to try too hard to be silent, since they seemed to be completely absorbed in each other. Presumably Rob had decided that whatever he was doing was worth the risk that I might turn up in the middle of it. Maybe he didn't actually care that much if I found out. Or had he just assumed that I would stay in Fox Hill, quivering in a corner, too devastated to do anything other than comply?

Perhaps he was just even keener to have this person in the house than he had been to kick me out of it.

A familiar voice said, 'I'm just worried that you're giving too much up. Making too many sacrifices. And that you'll resent me for it in the end.'

Now I knew who she was.

Oh, Rob... how could he?

And yet he had...

And she was young. Not too young, of course, not illegally young. Respectably young. Young enough to be pretty and fresh and to have that special optimism, that openness and willingness that goes with youth. That bloom. That lovableness. Everybody wants it, all the more when they've lost it, and nobody gets to keep it. It's nothing to do with face lotion or vitamins. It's to do with life and what it takes out of you.

She was in her mid-twenties – I couldn't remember exactly. About ten years older than Georgie, and fifteen years younger than me.

There was a suppressed giggle followed by a sticky silence. I could imagine what they were doing, though I really didn't want to. I'd done that kind of thing with Rob myself when I was her age, and more recently too, though it was fair to say that these days it was a matter of being conscientious. A good wife. A wife who wanted to hang onto her husband, because without a partner in crime where are you? No one wants to be alone with a bad conscience.

I was near the top of the stairs and I wanted to stop but I couldn't. It was the opposite of those nightmares where you're stuck or frozen; I was impelled to keep moving. I had to see for myself and at the same time I knew what I was going to see and I dreaded it. I dreaded having proof. The proof of my own senses, which would be impossible to ignore or deny. Or forget.

He had sounded so tender. I had forgotten he could sound like that.

Love. What I had heard in his voice was love. And it didn't make any difference if I was furious about it or thought it was ridiculous and doomed. Love of any kind was rare and you could never take it for granted, or make any assumption about what people would do or not do for it.

I would have expected it to be the idea of the sex that hurt. Being replaced like that, in a way that obliterated you and turned your body and everything it had been through into nothing. I had never imagined that the real shock would be love.

She'd said she was afraid he was sacrificing too much. But I was the sacrifice he was making, and it didn't matter to him if I was unwilling.

I wanted to weep and vanish at the same time. Because if what Rob felt was real, then all of this was real. The house he wanted me to live in. The distance he wanted me to keep. The daughter he thought would do just fine without me around, at least some of the time. This young woman in our bed.

There was a rustling of sheets. (*My* sheets!) Then she said, 'I'm just really worried that Georgie will never accept me.'

That did it. How dare she talk about my daughter? Without consciously deciding to, I moved up to the top of the stairs and stepped onto the landing.

The bedroom door was ajar. They'd been in a tearing hurry. So rash! So reckless! A trail of clothes led to the bed. Jeans. A T-shirt. The snug-fitting underwear that Rob favoured. Sometimes I walked in on him wearing nothing else and anxiously peering at his reflection in the mirror, as if to check that his body was still the same shape he remembered.

He'd taken good care of himself, stayed fit. Was still lust-worthy, as I often told him, as someone else had obviously decided to discover for herself…

And there they were, stretched out and facing each other, bare-skinned on the tangled sheets, absorbed in each other as if nothing and nobody else mattered.

Chloe – the twentysomething tutor I'd brought into the house to help Georgie with her maths – turned, saw me, squawked and dived for the bedding to cover herself up.

'Hello, Chloe,' I said. 'I wasn't expecting to see you today. Nice of you to pop by.'

Rob sat up but made no attempt to cover himself. He was staring at me with gobsmacked hatred, as if I stood for everything that had ever stopped him from enjoying happiness. Also – and this was gratifying – he looked very slightly afraid.

I wasn't upset. Not this time, not yet. I wasn't about to cry. I was furious, and righteous and cold. The wronged wife. The wronged mother. I just wanted to hurt him back. To scorn him and look down at him the way he had looked down at me.

'I didn't realise you were interested in brushing up your numerical skills,' I said to him. 'You must have needed a *lot* of extra help with your geometry.'

'I told you to stay in the cottage,' he said. 'I had no idea you'd pull a stunt like this. Creeping in like a burglar. I thought you were going to call me if you wanted to come round.'

'Yes, well, you told me you were going to change the locks, and that didn't happen either. I guess things don't always turn out the way you want them to.'

'I told you I would meet you at the mediator's office tomorrow. I'm not going to get into some kind of slanging match now.'

'We need to talk, Rob. Sooner rather than later. I'll be downstairs when you're ready. Chloe, I think it's probably time you left. Oh, and by the way – you're fired.'

My blood was pounding in my ears as if there was enough force in my heart to detonate the whole house. I couldn't stay there looking at them: I was going to lose control completely. For the first time in my life, I could understand how it might be possible to want to kill someone.

I turned and went back downstairs to the kitchen, took the previous night's bottle of white wine out of the fridge and poured myself a glass. It tasted good. It tasted like something I could do with a lot more of. I went back into the living room and perched on the sofa next to Chloe's mumsy green cardigan and forced myself to sip the wine rather than knocking it back the way I would have liked to, and mulled over all the things I was going to say to Rob when he finally got up the courage to come and face me.

The room seemed more vivid than before, as if a spell had been lifted and my vision had suddenly cleared after years of being misted over. A shiver ran through me from head to toe and my heart twisted inside me. It felt as if someone was stretching it and manipulating it into knots, like the balloons turned into animal shapes by the party guy I'd hired for one of Georgie's birthdays long ago.

Did I still want my husband? Could I still want him? Love him? What I was feeling was surely the opposite of love…

She'd have to go. Him, too. I didn't want to have to see him, at least for a while. We'd have to think up something to tell Georgie. But then, maybe… It might be possible to patch things up, give it another shot…

Anyway, I didn't see why *I* should be the one to leave.

But then there was the threat he had made. He had said he would tell Georgie everything. Would he really? Did he mean it?

How could he?

I heard the creak of the stairs and then the two of them moving through the hallway, followed by the sound of the front door opening.

The glass in my hand seemed to drop of its own accord. It didn't break, but the splash of wine I had left immediately darkened a patch of the carpet. It smelt decadent, like the aftermath of an over-the-top party. I sped towards the hallway like someone flying in a dream.

He couldn't. It wasn't possible. He couldn't just walk away with her like this and leave me here alone.

The front door had closed behind them. Immediately it was as if I was back in the house on Fox Hill: the airlessness, the sense of being trapped. I opened the door again and saw him with her in his car.

He was going to drive her home.

'Stop!' I screamed at him. 'Don't you dare!'

Chloe looked petrified. She was a nice girl, really. Naïve. Eager to prove herself. I'd been like that, once. And now? Lies, conspiracy, evasion – I'd done it all. And perhaps I was capable of more.

I picked up one of the aluminium planters from the front door-step and upended it. The rosemary plant tumbled out, scattering earth across the gravel and releasing a sharp medicinal smell. The planter swung in a perfect arc in my hands until it connected with the windscreen in a clean sweep, and then it fell to the ground and I was horrified by what I had just done and covered my face with my hands.

*

Rob was talking to me. A stream of cold, hard words that I could barely stand to hear. He was standing much too close for comfort but had made no move to touch me. He didn't need to when he could beat me just by speaking to me with such relentless contempt.

I stopped crying and took my hands away from my face. I couldn't block him out forever. He looked angrier than I'd ever seen him. Chloe had gone.

Glancing past him, I saw that the windscreen was still intact. I'd only managed to crack it.

Rob said, 'Take your car and go, Stella. I don't care where. If you don't want the house I gave you, find somewhere else. Just stay away from us. You're on notice. If you don't play this by the book – if you so much as step out of line again – I'll file for a restraining order.'

Us. How could he and Chloe possibly be *us*?

The planter was on the ground, the scattered earth, the rosemary. My rosemary. I'd planted it. I'd spent hours in the garden, weeding, pruning, mowing. Absorbed, and thinking of nothing other than what was in front of me. It was the happiest place to be alone. Maybe the only place I was really happy to be alone.

My garden.

My house. My daughter. My family. My marriage.

It took so long for things to grow. So little time to break them.

Rob said, 'Go on then, clear off. You'd better run along before I call the police.'

I said, 'If you were going to do that you'd have done it by now.'

'Don't tempt me.'

'Chloe… is she all right?'

'She's badly shaken up. Unsurprisingly. Be warned, Stella. If any harm comes to her because of you, I will take great pleasure in making you pay for it for the rest of your life.'

'Listen to yourself. You're infatuated. Having some kind of mid-life crisis. That's what it is. It won't last.'

'I'm in love with her. And if you don't understand that, it's because you've forgotten what it's like.' He sighed. 'I've got to say, it's been really nice being happy for a change.'

That hurt. A special kind of pain, mixed up with remorse. Love gone wrong. Even in the middle of everything else, it still wounded me to hear that my husband had been miserable with me, and that being with someone else had been a relief.

But still… I could have hurt her. I could have hurt both of them. I had meant to.

'Will you tell her I'm sorry? I just saw red. You pushed me too far. I couldn't take it any more.'

'Just listen to you, you're a textbook case. Isn't that the kind of thing people who attack their spouses always say?'

'But Rob… how could you? In our house? In our bed?'

'Don't do this, Stella. Next you'll be asking me how long it's been going on. What difference does it make?'

'Have you told her… have you talked to her about us?'

He folded his arms. 'I wondered when you'd get on to that. No, I haven't. Not in the way you mean. I don't particularly want to. I'd much rather never have to talk about it, to be honest. But that's up to you, isn't it? Right now, she has no idea. She would be shocked if she found out. She's a good, sweet, straightforward person, and she assumes other people are straightforward too. You wouldn't believe how relaxing it is being with someone who's got nothing to hide.'

'How can you say she's good and sweet when she's made you do this?'

'She didn't make me. I decided to. What I've got with her is real, and it's what I want. You just have to accept it.'

He looked me up and down, and seemed to soften a little. 'You're a mess. I suggest you get yourself back to Fox Hill, make yourself a nice cup of tea, run a bath and light one of those candles you like. It's all there. All part of your birthday present. You might as well take advantage. I'll expect you to pay for the damage to the car, obviously. We're all very lucky it wasn't worse. Otherwise we would be looking at police involvement, and then all of this would be out of my hands.'

'I haven't got my keys,' I said. 'My bag. I think I dropped it. Or maybe I left it by the sofa. It must be inside the house somewhere.'

'Wait there,' he said.

He went back inside and I forced myself to move. The gravel was rough under my bare feet, a reminder of how he'd left me high and dry in shoes I couldn't walk in.

I'd last used my car the evening before, to bring a few bits and pieces back from the supermarket: the bottle of white wine, ingredients for a quick supper for two and a DVD bought on impulse to watch by myself while Georgie was away. Everything needed for a nice quiet evening.

It *should* have been nice. I'd looked forward to it. But if I was honest, it had given me a strange hollow feeling, too. As if the heart had gone out of me. Driving home, I'd begun to realise what it might be like when she was grown up and free to leave us both behind. The empty nest. It seemed Rob had been thinking about that, too.

He came back with my handbag and gave it to me. He said, 'Drive safely, won't you? You're clearly somewhat overwrought, and Georgie wouldn't want you to come to grief.'

'I'll be careful,' I promised.

Submissive. Complicit. The good little wife. Good to a fault, right up to and including her own demise.

He nodded and I unlocked the car and got in. As he went back into the house he didn't look at all dejected. He actually looked quite jaunty, as if he felt he'd turned a potentially tricky situation to his advantage.

There was always a pair of flat shoes in my car, just in case I needed to change my footwear to drive. Rob didn't approve – he didn't think a car should be a shoe cupboard – but he never used this car anyway. Too small and too cheap. It wasn't a surprise that Rob was willing to let it go.

I slipped on the flats, started the engine, reversed carefully, turned and pulled out onto Fairfield Road.

As I approached the junction with the main road that led out of town I saw the locksmith's van heading towards me. After I'd passed it I spotted it in my mirrors, turning onto our driveway.

If I'd just let Rob and Chloe go, Rob would have missed him and I would have been able to tell him the locksmith he wasn't wanted after all. So much for resisting. So far, all I'd done was make things worse.

But I still wasn't going to go back to Fox Hill.

I didn't even think it through. My body took over. I indicated and turned right and then right again.

She'd always been such a fan of his. It wasn't fair to hit her with the details of what had just happened. She'd be horrified. Devastated. She was so proud of him. The dream son-in-law, she sometimes called him. *Knows just how much tonic to put in my gin.* Playing it down a little so as not to put my stepfather's nose out of joint, but still, always ready to praise him.

She was so proud of *us*. The photogenic couple. The sweet grandchild. And all the trappings: the cars, the holidays, the house.

Still, I couldn't think of where else to turn. I couldn't give up, not yet. Not because of *Chloe*. And Mum was the one person who had almost as much to lose as I did.

Chapter Six

Mum's initial reaction to seeing me, and then realising that I was on my own, was surprise followed by disappointment. No, worse than that. Gloomy resignation, as if I was a chore she hadn't expected to have to do today.

But surely I was overreacting? Maybe she'd been expecting someone else. She'd recently discovered online shopping and had told me several times how much it cheered her up when her purchases arrived. It wasn't exactly flattering that I brightened up her day less than the delivery of a new handbag, but under the circumstances I couldn't hold it against her.

Poor Mum. She had always yearned for glamour and freedom, and yet here she was. Maybe that was one of the functions of marriage: it forced you into roles you never would have imagined taking.

She looked me up and down on the doorstep and took in the scrape on my arm, the snags in my jumpsuit and the scuffed driving shoes that didn't go with the rest of my outfit. She clocked the car I'd arrived in. No Rob. She looked momentarily both lost and vindicated, as if she'd been anticipating disaster for a while but just hadn't known exactly when it was going to strike. Then she gave me her broadest smile and stepped forward to embrace me.

'Stella! Happy birthday! But we weren't expecting you today, were we? I thought you were going out with Rob for a nice lunch. I haven't got anything in.'

'Oh, that doesn't matter. I'm sorry to turn up out of the blue. I won't make a habit of it, I promise. Is now an all right time?'

'Well, dear, as a rule, it *is* helpful if you can let me know when you're planning to pop round.' She dropped her voice the way she always did when she wanted to talk about my stepfather, no matter how far out of earshot he was. 'He can be quite cranky these days. Understandably.' She studied my face and grimaced slightly. 'But anyway, it's lovely to see you. Come on in. We can go out to the garden. Lee's having a nap upstairs, so we'd best be quiet.'

She stepped back and I went in. After we'd gone through to the kitchen she closed the door behind us with exaggerated caution, as if Lee was a sleeping giant who'd come stomping down and eat us both for dinner if we disturbed him.

Their house was the same as ever, with the shades of brown and beige Lee favoured offset by Mum's taste for colour and ornament. Pot plants cluttered the surfaces, along with knick-knacks and various framed photos of them having a good time as a couple, including several of their wedding – they'd finally tied the knot a few years earlier, after twenty years together, before Lee took early retirement and they moved to Critchley.

Mum in particular had thrown herself into her new life here. I knew she'd been looking forward to her sixties, enjoying being a grandmother and spending time with Lee and, of course, going off on plentiful holidays. But it hadn't turned out that way.

There was nothing to indicate what they were going through, not unless you knew where to look. There'd been some talk about adaptations that might be needed later, but Mum had glossed over the details. She'd always been like that – she didn't like to worry about the worst until it happened. As it turned out, putting off thinking about difficult things was quite an effective coping strategy. Especially if there was no other choice.

She made us both tea and we went out to the garden and settled on the swing seat, and I turned to face her and wondered where to start.

When I was younger, I had loved the way Mum presented herself to the world – the make-up, the shiny jewellery. I loved the bright colours she wore when she wasn't in her uniform for work, and I loved the uniform too.

She had always smelt good. Expensive, as if she was about to go out somewhere fancy. She worked on the perfume counter at the big department store in Brickley, and sometimes, when she brought home free samples, I was allowed to try them out. Her dressing table was a treasure trove that I wasn't allowed to touch without permission, but occasionally she let me explore and pick my favourites: the lipsticks with names like Raisin Shimmer and Cherry Dream, the eyeshadow palettes in azure blue.

Then Molly came along, and she was too busy to let me look at anything. And by then I was old enough to wish for a mother who was a little less conspicuous.

When I became a mum myself I had tried not to stand out. I aspired to be unobjectionably pretty, and inoffensively bland. Well-groomed, but not obvious. But that was not Mum's way.

Today she was wearing a maroon tunic over dark-blue slacks, with long glittering gold earrings and dark lipstick that made her look slightly petulant, as if she was pouting, not in a sultry way, but out of general dismay. When she set her cup of tea aside there was a smudge on the rim the colour of old wine. You never had any trouble telling which cup was Mum's.

She was studying me beadily, almost as if she had some inkling of what was coming, and was wondering how I was going to broach it. But that was impossible. Wasn't it?

She was the first to speak. 'How's Georgie getting on?'

'I'm sure she's fine, but I haven't spoken to her since I dropped her off yesterday morning. She's not allowed to call. I can't ring her, either.'

'Oh. Really? Even though it's your birthday?'

'Not even then.'

'But you work at the school. You're an insider. Isn't there some way round it?'

'I can't look for special treatment. It's supposed to be good for them. It's meant to encourage independence.'

'Seems a bit drastic,' Mum sniffed. 'I do wonder about the wisdom of it. Letting a young girl like Georgie roam about the countryside. There are some dodgy people out there, you know. Just because it looks pretty doesn't mean it's safe.'

'She's going to be closely supervised, Mum. All the students are.'

She sniffed. 'Well, they'd better be. I suppose there are boys on this trip.'

'Well, yes, obviously there are. It's a mixed school. But they won't be in the same bedrooms.'

Mum raised her eyebrows. 'I should hope not. And I hope they're going to be supervised at night, too. I know it's a good school – or at least, they're choosy about who they let in. Probably they're nice boys. But they're still boys. She's coming up to the age when things can go pear-shaped. You know that as well as I do.'

I sucked in my breath.

'I really don't think she's interested in all that.'

Mum made a clucking noise with her tongue. 'Well, let's hope nobody gets her interested. I know you've been a vigilant parent. Just don't assume it couldn't happen to *your* daughter. Take it from one who knows.'

'To be honest, I'm more worried about what we're going to tell her when she gets back,' I said.

My hand had started trembling. I remembered what I'd read somewhere about amputees, that they might experience feelings where their limbs used to be; ghost pains, itches they couldn't scratch. The body had its own way of dealing with the aftermath of trauma, and it didn't always involve forgetting. On cold days or in unguarded moments I was still sometimes troubled by odd aches and pains, even in parts of my body that hadn't been injured in the accident; my neck, my feet, my hands.

I moved to put my tea down on the ground and slopped some of it on my knee. Mum was watching me with a mixture of apprehension and something that was more discomforting to see, and more unexpected.

Ruthlessness? Resolve?

She sighed again. 'Go on,' she said.

So I told her. I described the house on Fox Hill and what Rob had said he wanted. I glossed over some of the details – given that Mum had always had a soft spot for Rob, I baulked at disillusioning her completely. I mentioned Tony Everdene and how he'd helped me. Then I explained what had happened when I got back to Fairfield Road, who I'd found Rob with, and, finally – hesitantly, knowing how much she would disapprove – what I had done to his car.

Mum listened to it all with her best poker face, resting her clasped hands on her crossed knees, giving nothing away.

When I finished I didn't cry. I just watched her and waited. I think I already knew what was coming. Some part of me wasn't surprised. But that didn't stop it being a shock when she took his side.

She took her time to speak. Then she cleared her throat and said, 'Fox Hill is really quite desirable these days, you know. And he's prepared to give you a house there, just like that? That's really something.'

I should have known better than to expect sympathy. Why did I never learn? This was Mum. Sympathy wasn't part of the deal.

Besides, on the face of it she was right. The house on Fox Hill wasn't what I wanted. But it was not nothing.

'He wants Georgie,' I said. 'During the week, anyway. He seems to expect me to sign up for just having her at weekends.'

Surely that would focus her on what really mattered. Which was not the house. Mum adored Georgie, who could do absolutely no wrong in her eyes. Georgie went round to her house religiously for tea every Wednesday after school, an event that I knew Mum looked forward to all the more since her life had become more constrained. Surely she wouldn't want anything to jeopardise that.

But even that barely registered.

'I certainly don't think Georgie needs to know about any of this yet,' she said slowly. 'You'll need to find a new maths tutor, of course. Well, that can't be beyond the bounds of possibility. But what you really don't want is Rob suddenly deciding to make good on his threat, and telling Georgie a load of stuff she really doesn't need to know.'

She was looking directly at me now, willing me to agree with her. I said, 'We have to face facts. We should have told her already. I never intended to keep it a secret. And she might find out one day anyway.'

'Yes, eventually. In a few years maybe, when she's older. But that's not right now, is it? It's not just the impact on her. It's the impact on all of us. What if she starts asking questions you don't want to answer? Where's it going to end? Knowledge isn't always power, Stella. Sometimes knowledge is nothing but grief and shame.'

'So you're telling me you think I ought to go along with what Rob wants? So as not to rock the boat?'

'It's a consideration,' Mum said flatly.

'Mum, don't take this the wrong way… but did you know something about all this already?'

She stared at me. 'What exactly are you getting at, Stella? Because I'm tired and I have a lot of problems of my own to deal with. In case you've forgotten. At the moment what I need is support. I don't think that's too much to ask. The last thing I need is you coming round here causing a load of grief.' She shrugged again. 'What can I do about it?'

'What I mean is, did he say anything to you? About her? About what he was planning to do to me?'

'He's your husband. If you don't know what he's up to, how should I know?'

'So he did say something,' I said slowly. 'Didn't he?'

She didn't deny it. He'd got to her somehow, that much was clear. He'd made sure she was on his side.

My own mother. My own husband.

When it turned out that he had betrayed me, at least I had been surprised. I wasn't now. I had no energy left to be surprised with. Rob had dumped me as if dropping me from a great height and Mum had just sidestepped what was left of me. And that was it. I was finished. Beaten. I couldn't imagine how I would ever move from the swing seat and leave her house. The life I had lived with Rob was over, and the person I had been with him was dead. It had all started so brightly and hopefully. And it ended here, facing my mum's fuchsias and geraniums and knowing how easy it had been for him to persuade her to sign up to what he wanted.

'I can see that this has been a shock to you, Stella,' Mum said. 'You need some time.'

Perhaps this was her trying to say the right thing. It got to me in a way that her indifference had failed to do, and stirred up a flicker of something not all that far removed from rage.

I said, 'Is that really all you have to say to me?'

'Marriage is a contract, Stella. It's a deal. If you don't deliver what the other person wants, sooner or later they're going to look elsewhere.'

Her face was still a carefully composed blank, but I glimpsed the glitter of something close to triumph in her eyes. Perhaps not triumph. Satisfaction. The superiority of the wife who is still loved and needed, however difficult the situation she is living through, over one who is not. When she described marriage as a contract that either party was entitled to leave if dissatisfied, she wasn't talking about me. She was talking about Dad, and how right she'd been to leave him.

A sudden noise from the house distracted both of us. It was Lee, my stepfather. He'd woken from his nap and was sliding open the patio doors so he could come out to join us.

He still looked sleepy and puffy-faced, and also a little thinner than when I'd last seen him. In the last few months he'd lost his appetite and the weight had started dropping off him. It was already possible to imagine him becoming gaunt.

'Afternoon, Stella,' he said. 'I didn't know you were coming today.'

That was it. The conversation with Mum was over. It had been as good as over anyway, and there was no way I could even attempt to carry on in front of him.

I got to my feet. 'I hope I didn't wake you up,' I said.

'You look as if you've been asleep yourself.' He rubbed his eyes as if he couldn't quite believe what he was seeing. 'Are those pyjamas you're wearing?'

That was one thing about Lee that hadn't changed: he was as wilfully tactless as ever.

'Lee, leave her alone. You just don't know anything about fashion,' Mum interjected.

'No, I don't. Too late now to learn, I suppose,' Lee said.

He often referred to the finite number of days he had left, sometimes obliquely, sometimes not. Usually Mum or I tried to respond by saying something lighter, as if it wasn't really true that he was sick and facing death. But this time neither of us said anything. Instead I stepped towards Lee and we embraced. A quick, light token hug, the same as always. Then he sat down on the swing seat next to Mum and I remained standing.

Time for me to go. Mum wouldn't want me to stick around, and neither would Lee. He tolerated me visiting but tended to leave me and Mum to it. If he joined us, it was usually a signal he was ready for me to go.

'Seriously,' Lee said, 'what have you been up to? You look like you've been dragged through a hedge backwards.'

'It's Stella's birthday, Lee,' Mum said. 'Aren't you going to wish her many happy returns?'

'Oh, I've stopped celebrating birthdays,' Lee said, folding his arms. 'If I can't look forward to any more of my own, I don't see why I should celebrate other people's. But don't let me put you off having a good time, Stella. Have as good a time as you can manage. Before you know it, it'll all be over, or as good as. Seize the day, that's my advice. Just remember, the future can be a lot shorter than you think.'

'Now Lee, you need to remember about staying positive,' Mum told him.

'Stuff being positive,' Lee said. 'I've got terminal lung cancer and the doctors are all being politely vague about how much longer I've got to live. Is there any chance of something to eat? I'd like to have it out here. Make the most of the sunshine. I might even smoke a cigarette. After all, it doesn't really matter now, does it?'

Mum got to her feet. 'I'll fix you a sandwich.'

'Don't put any of those tomatoes in it,' Lee said. 'Too ripe. Maybe you could bring the paper out while you're at it.'

'I'd better be heading off,' I said. 'It was good to see you, Lee.'

'You never know, it might be the last time. We'll see, won't we? Well, off you go, Pam, you'd better see Stella out, otherwise I'll never get my sandwich. By the time you two have done gassing I'll be on my last legs.'

'We won't be long,' Mum said, and shooed me back inside. She closed the patio doors carefully behind us and came right out to the front of the house with me, and I knew she was going to say something to me that she didn't want Lee to overhear.

'You can see the state he's in,' she said in a low voice. 'And it's only going to get worse. You know I don't really like to leave him, not for long, unless I know someone's around. Even if it's just to get my hair done. Rose next door has been pretty good, but I don't want to wear out her goodwill.'

'You can still call on me whenever you need to, Mum. I won't be far away. Whatever happens.'

She exhaled and fixed her gaze on the horizon, as if looking ahead to a gloomy but inescapable future. 'I'm not going to tell him about your trouble with Rob. I don't think he needs to be bothered with all of that.'

'No. OK. Whatever you think.' I couldn't imagine that Lee would care.

'Maybe you should go to this new house for a bit. Lie low. Think things over.'

'Maybe. Mum…'

She watched me wearily and unblinkingly, as if I was about to ask a favour she didn't have time for. I could almost hear her willing me to give up and go away, so she could get back to Lee and making his sandwich…

Presumably Rob had promised that she'd still be able to see Georgie on a regular basis whatever happened. Maybe he'd even enlisted her help in persuading me to accept what he wanted. I wouldn't have been surprised. He'd always been able to wind her round his little finger.

But anyway, she had plenty of other things on her mind. She had a dying husband to concern herself with, so why should she trouble herself unduly with worrying about mine?

All I wanted to do was ask a question. But I could feel the full force of the past trying to keep me from putting it to her.

'Mum… This may not be a good time to ask. There may never be a good time. But I've been mulling it over, trying to think through all the different ways this could play out.' I drew a deep breath. 'I know this is a taboo subject. It's upsetting for everyone. I'm sorry to bring it up, but I was wondering if you knew where Molly is.'

There. I had said it. The effect of coming out with my sister's name was sudden and extreme. Mum's face seemed to fall inwards, as if her mouth was drawing everything else towards it. It took her a little while to recover herself and compose an answer, but when she spoke it was without hesitation or doubt.

'Stella, no. Why would you even ask that? You need to calm everything down, not stir it up. There is no point going out looking for trouble. Look, here's my advice. Go home. Have a bath. Have a glass of wine. Sleep on it. That's what I always do when the going gets tough. I promise you, you'll feel different in the morning. But for Georgie's sake, and my sake, and everybody's sake... don't even think about getting in touch with Molly. This is about your marriage. It is nothing at all to do with what happened to your sister.'

And then she turned and went back into the house, shutting the door firmly behind her.

I carried on standing there for a little while. Gradually it sank in that by home, she meant Fox Hill. As far as she was concerned, that was now where I belonged.

Chapter Seven

After leaving Mum I called in at the big supermarket on the edge of Kettlebridge to pick up a new pay-as-you-go phone, and by the time I left the rush-hour traffic had begun to build. I sat in one queue after another taking in the still-bright summer sky, the lines of cars and other drivers all purposefully going home, and tried not to think about what lay ahead. And then I found myself back in Fox Hill, heading for the lonely white house at the end of the lane.

Here, there was nobody else around. The Fox Hill commuters probably worked long hours in the City to pay for their mortgages, and were still on their trains back from London Paddington, tapping away at their laptops and ignoring the scenery beyond the windows. Meanwhile, inside those big, quiet houses, set well back from the lane behind pretty gardens, other mothers and the occasional stay-at-home dads were fixing the children's tea, preparing for the witching hour of bathtime and bed. Right up until yesterday, that had been me – the default parent, the one whose responsibility it was to make sure there was something for dinner that night.

Surely Rob wasn't going to take all of that on? How much had he really thought any of this through? Maybe he was planning to switch me for Chloe, and expecting her to do it instead. But if so… did Chloe know?

I got through the gate, parked the car, approached the house and put the key in the front door.

It wouldn't turn. Straight away my heart was in my mouth. The one thing worse than being here would be being here and not being able to get in.

I heard Rob's voice just as clearly as if he was standing at my shoulder: *Really? You really think that's the worst that could happen?*

The key turned suddenly and the door gave way, and I stumbled in. The door seemed to close behind me of its own accord, sealing me into the bright and empty space of the chequerboard-tiled entrance hall.

At Fairfield Road, the smell of the house was usually one of the first things I noticed when I came in – the faint traces of toast or coffee or of whatever we'd eaten the night before, or, in wet weather, the damp coats and drying shoes, or the waxy sweetness of scented candles. But Gamekeeper's Cottage smelt of nothing. The air had the same stale, closed-in quality that a disused warehouse might have towards the end of a hot summer's day.

I went through to the kitchen and dumped my bag on the worktop. Even in my flat shoes, my footsteps on the tiles sounded intrusively loud. But that was because it was still so empty. It just needed more stuff to fill it up and absorb the noise. Then it wouldn't seem so hollow, so much like a white-walled prison…

Was this my future?

The table for two. Of course. He'd imagined me and Georgie eating there, on the weekends when she came to visit, for as long as she would want to.

Could I really live here? Could I give him what he wanted, and go quietly? Was it possible?

I opened the windows at both ends of the room, and the air began to stir as if the place was coming back to life. I fiddled round with my new phone and the old, unreliable one, swapped the SIM card, got the new phone working and texted Georgie: *Just checking this works.* There was no answer, of course. Then the kitchen door slammed shut and I jumped half out of my skin.

It wasn't rational to feel so on edge, as if someone might be about to try and break in at any minute. It wasn't just because the house was relatively isolated – it was because I was alone. A new kind of alone. Had I only felt safe before because Rob was around? Even though he so often wasn't?

Anyway, he wasn't the sort to take risks to defend other people. However he felt about me, I was in no doubt that he really loved Georgie. But would he have attacked an intruder to protect her, or donated a kidney for her, or moved unthinkingly into the path of a speeding car to shove her out of harm's way? I doubted it.

It was something to do with his attitude to his own body, his fear of being violated or maimed and left damaged and in pain. He had to be in control. He could barely bring himself to go to the doctor's, though he rarely needed to. He was almost phobic about the idea of being subjected to any kind of medical treatment, and having to put himself in someone else's hands.

Upstairs in the master bedroom I slid open the door of the fitted wardrobe, stepped out of my shoes and laid out some of the clothes Rob had left for me on the single bed: a pair of not-too-tight jeans and a three-quarter-sleeved T-shirt. Everything was the right size. He'd even left me a selection of nude and black and white underwear, and several pairs of socks.

It wasn't an admission of defeat. It was common sense. I'd feel better after a shower and a change of clothes. I'd rally. I'd be able to figure out what to do next.

OK, so perhaps it *was* an admission of defeat. But wasn't I just exchanging one outfit he had approved of for another?

The jumpsuit had a fixed wrap top, which had confused Rob the first time I'd worn it – he'd pulled at it and it had torn, and he'd apologised and been nonplussed until I had undone the hidden zip under my left arm and wriggled out of the top and let it fall around my waist. The lighting had been dim, the way Rob knew I liked it: a candle on the bedside table that turned us both into a collection of shadows, and made our bodies changeable and obscure.

We really had been tender with each other once, hadn't we? That hadn't all been fake. I hadn't just imagined it.

One of the sliding wardrobe doors was mirrored. Out of habit, I turned my back on my reflection as I got out of the top half of the jumpsuit, then pulled the elasticated waist down over my hips and stepped out of it. I only ever looked at myself when I was dressed. Not when I wasn't. There's no point looking in the mirror when you know it's going to show you something you don't want to see.

I left the jumpsuit on the floor and pulled on the duck-egg blue dressing-gown. It was big enough to envelop myself in and comfortingly soft. Then I took a towel and the basket of toiletries Rob had left for me through to the bathroom. Closed the door, but didn't lock it. No point when there was no one else in the house to burst in.

The bathroom had a mirrored cabinet mounted on the wall next to the towel rail, above a glossy grey storage unit. The cabinet was a little too high, an oversight on Rob's part. Georgie, who was shorter than me, would just about be able to make out her head and shoulders; I could see my reflection from the chest upwards and the window behind me, reaching up into the eaves.

Anyway, I could live with that. Full-length mirrors were what bothered me. The body, not the face. The face was unmarked. If that was all you had to go on, you'd never guess what had happened to me.

I stripped off and got into the shower. It was good and hot. I soaped myself and breathed in the lily-of-the-valley perfume of the toiletries Rob had chosen. He liked delicate scents, and had never been keen on anything too out-there and in-your-face, or too aggressively sexy.

He'd wanted me to look good, but he had never wanted me to stand out. And on the whole, that had been fine by me. Especially once Georgie had come along. I had been desperate to be the kind of mum who passed muster, who was easy for other people to approve of.

Back in the bedroom, dressed and with my hair towelled dry, I picked the jumpsuit up off the floor and held it up to the window to examine it, as if it was evidence of something or had been left there by somebody else.

There was a tear in it that I hadn't noticed before. It was in the gathered fabric just below the waistline. It was about an inch long and slightly frayed at the edges, which were jagged, as if someone had forcefully ripped it or hacked at it with blunt scissors.

It could have happened when I fell outside the house, or when I tried to smash Rob's windscreen. Or earlier. I'd dressed for my birthday lunch in a hurry, having spent too long on my hair and make-up – Rob had been downstairs, restless and ready to go, and he'd already called up twice to remind me when our table was reserved for.

What did it matter? The damage was done. It didn't mean anything. There was no reason to believe it was some kind of message or reminder, or a mysterious act of sabotage. That kind of guilty paranoia would get me nowhere.

I hung the jumpsuit in the wardrobe and closed the mirrored door, and went back downstairs to find myself a microwaveable meal for one.

The house was still silent but it might as well have been screaming at me to escape. I made it through half a pasta bake in front of *Murder, She Wrote* on the TV and made myself wash up before putting on the sandals I'd spotted in the bottom of the master bedroom wardrobe and hurrying out.

Quarter of an hour later I was sitting in the courtyard garden of the Fox and Hounds, nursing a small white wine, breathing in the scent of wisteria and trying to ignore the spectre of Rob sitting next to me, lounging like a bored child.

I'd never been here before, with him or anyone else. It was the only pub on Fox Hill, a place that people from Kettlebridge sometimes drove to for lunch if they wanted to walk in the woods afterwards. It didn't have much of a reputation for its food, which was probably why Rob had never booked it for us. He liked to go to new or sought-after places, not village pubs reliant on locals who wanted to be able to get home on foot after a few too many.

Would he have taken Chloe out? Chancing it, asking for corner tables in places where they were unlikely to be spotted or recognised, enjoying the risk? She'd have been nervous, and he'd have encouraged her, and afterwards she'd have hurried to the car and then they would have sat there and held hands and grinned at each other ruefully, mischievously, like companions in crime.

I'd let him down. I had wanted too much. I should have seen it coming.

Back when Georgie had just started school and we'd settled in Kettlebridge, he had been working so hard, so constantly, week in, week out and often weekends too. When he came home it was obvious he needed me to be there for him. To feed him, listen to him, encourage him, sit on the sofa next to him drinking red wine. And I had ignored him. There were other things I wanted, and there was only so much time. Three hours, maybe four, between cleaning up after dinner and bed.

But was I really just trying to prove myself to him all along?

I had signed up for a history degree with the Open University and I was determined to see it through. The minute Georgie was asleep, I settled down at my laptop, leaving Rob alone in front of the TV. By and by he'd come to me and say, *I'm going to turn in*, and I would say, *OK. I won't be long. Just a little bit more to do…*

Back then, Rob hadn't been making the kind of money he made now. I was planning to train as a teacher after getting my degree, and I assumed we'd need the salary I'd be able to bring in. I imagined a future in which Rob and I would be more or less equals. More equal than we'd been since I jacked in my job and left my dad and sister behind to move in with him. And more equal than we'd been when Georgie was little. It had been down to me to change the nappies and sort out the childcare, all the more so because having her had been my idea...

He hadn't even wanted to have a baby. I'd had to talk him into it.

How could he possibly justify trying to keep her now?

I could just jump in the car and drive to where Georgie was staying and get her. Surely I could find some way of persuading them to release her to me? I didn't know the staff members who were running the trip all that well, but I was staff too. That would be enough, wouldn't it? As long as we kept on moving afterwards... If I did that, I would never be able to come back...

A shadow fell across the table in front of me and I looked up to see Tony Everdene looming over me, holding a pint of lager and smiling his small, wary smile. His expression was apologetic, as if he was worried that I might think he was pestering me, and he looked every inch the off-duty solicitor in a neatly ironed short-sleeved polo top and jeans.

Ah, the flirty neighbour. He doesn't look like obvious stalker material, I imagined Rob saying. *Though probably they never do.*

'Hello, again,' Tony said. 'I didn't expect to see you again quite so soon – I wasn't sure if it was you. Are you waiting for someone?'

He didn't seem like someone Rob would have gone out of his way to hang out with, but then, who *did* Rob hang out with? There were people he knew from the gym or cycling, who he might go out for a drink with once in a while. But close friends, friends he could confide in, who he might confess his secrets to? There were none of those, and hadn't been for years. We'd moved a few times when Georgie was little, and there was always a new house to do up, but it wasn't just that. It was hard to nurture friendships when there were things you just didn't want anybody to know...

I had never thought of him as lonely.

But still... No wonder he had fallen for Chloe.

Tony was still waiting for an answer. I made an effort to pull myself together. 'I'm here on my own,' I said. 'How about you?'

He shook his head as if this was a very unlikely suggestion. 'No, no. Just killing a bit of time. I always pop in here at this time of the week, while the girls are at bell-ringing practice.'

'Bell-ringing practice?' Surely no father of bell-ringing twins could be a potential stalker. 'That seems like an unusual hobby.'

'It is, I suppose. One of their friends in the village got them into it. We're not churchgoers or anything, but that doesn't seem to matter. I think they're keen to have new recruits. It seems to be a dying art. The girls haven't been let loose on a Sunday service, though. They tell me there's good pocket money to be made out of ringing at weddings, but they're not that proficient yet. It's quite a skill, apparently.'

'I'm sure it is.'

'Keeps them out of trouble, for now anyway,' Tony said with a slight, humorous grimace. 'One of these days I'm sure they'll throw up their hands in horror and refuse to carry on going. I'm actually surprised they haven't already.'

'Well, they might,' I said, remembering the dance lessons that Georgie had insisted on dropping as soon as she was adolescent and self-conscious. 'Do feel free to join me, if you'd like,' I added, waving a hand at the seat opposite me.

The imaginary Rob I'd summoned as a companion rolled his eyes. *Really, Stella. What is this? I thought you were planning to abscond with Georgie. How's getting drunk with the overly friendly neighbour going to help?*

'That's kind of you,' Tony said, but made no move to sit down. 'If you're sure.'

'I'm sure,' I said. 'But if you'd rather just have a bit of time to yourself, I won't take offence. I know peace and quiet can be hard to come by. Family life tends to crowd it out, doesn't it?'

You hypocrite, said phantom Rob, shaking his head in disbelief. *You can't bear to be alone. You're terrified of it. That's why you're here.*

'There is something to be said for a bit of time out,' Tony admitted. He put his pint down on the table and settled into the chair opposite me.

I said, 'How old are your girls?'

'Fourteen.'

'Same. My daughter's fifteen in October.'

Talking about our children. Safe, common ground wherever two or more parents were gathered. I could cope with this, surely. I'd managed it plenty of times before.

Tony said, 'So did your other half send you to check out the local?'

'Oh… no. He's not planning on living here.' I drew a deep breath. 'We seem to be in the process of separating. I found out he's met someone else.'

I appeared to have struck a chord. He stiffened and stared down at the table as if it was an effort to collect himself sufficiently to say the right thing. Then he looked up and said, 'I see. I'm really sorry to hear that. It must be a very difficult time for you.'

It was really peculiar having someone feel sorry for me – and not in a patronising, let-me-tell-you-how-to-fix-it way. It was a heady experience. I was torn between wanting to play down what had happened – after all, what right did I really have to somebody else's compassion? – and wanting more of it. Much more. It felt so close to being understood and forgiven.

'It's been a bit of a shock,' I said, and then – because sympathy can be seductive and it turned my head to feel that someone was on my side – 'Also, it's actually my birthday today.'

Tony's eyebrows went up. 'You mean you found out about this – about your husband's other person – today?'

'I did,' I said. And then: 'She's my daughter's maths tutor.' Why had I told him that? But suddenly it was hard to hold back. It was the show of sympathy – I couldn't resist it. 'I'm actually the one who recruited her. My daughter doesn't know yet, though. She's on a trip at the moment. Back Saturday evening. Rob – that's my husband – wants us to sit down with her after she gets back and explain everything. Or at least, explain the version of things that he wants her to know.'

Yeah, right. You'd know all about being selective with the truth… You do know that people in glass houses aren't supposed to throw stones. That was phantom Rob, listening with one eyebrow raised at my hypocrisy.

But Tony just said, 'I see.' Then he steepled his fingers and peered at me gravely over the top of them, in exactly the way I would expect a lawyer to do. 'I'm sure you really don't need me to tell you that you should seek professional legal advice.'

'Rob wants us to meet a mediator tomorrow to kick things off.'

Tony frowned slightly, like a patient teacher confronted with a pupil who is stubbornly resistant to learning. 'Far be it for me to tell you what you should do, but you might want to consider postponing that until you've had a chance to talk to someone. Something else you might want to bear in mind is that sometimes possession really is nine-tenths of the law. If you leave a property, that can be taken to reduce your claim to it.'

'I had heard that. I suppose it makes sense. If you give something up, why should you get to keep it?'

Tony looked as if he wasn't sure whether he'd heard me correctly. 'You must have had quite a shock. Is there anyone who could give you some support? A friend? A family member?'

I thought of Mum and how keen she'd been to move me on. 'Not really.' I pulled a face. 'The thing is, even after everything that happened today, I still can't bring myself to hate him. My husband, I mean.' I lowered my voice, as if Rob might overhear. I could picture him smiling, waiting for me to acknowledge him. 'I still think about him all the time. It's like he's with me, you know? In my head. I find myself imagining what he'd say. Talking to him. Maybe it would be easier if I *did* hate him.'

'If you don't now, it's possible that you will. If there's anything that's going to make you hate someone, it's being involved in litigation against them.'

'Can you really hate someone if you understand their point of view? Because in a way, however I might feel about it, I can understand why he did what he did.'

Tony looked at me in consternation. 'It's all very well being able to see the other person's point of view. But it doesn't necessarily help if it obscures your own.'

'Tony, I'm a forty-year-old part-time working mother of a teenage girl who's just been dumped by her husband. I don't *have* a point of view. Not one that anybody else cares about.' I finished my glass of wine and set it back down on the table. Could I get another one? How would that look? What would it do to me? I was already light-headed. 'Do you mind if I ask you something? It's kind of a legal question. Nothing to do with me and Rob.' This wasn't true, strictly speaking, but Tony didn't need to know that. 'It's just something I've always wondered.'

Tony's face took on the cagey, slightly haunted look of the professional faced with a layperson who wants to pick their brains. It wasn't all that often that acquaintances asked for my advice about schooling or education, but when they did, my reaction was probably much the same.

'You can certainly ask,' he said, 'but I can't promise you an answer.'

I leaned forwards. Suddenly it didn't matter what he thought of me, if he felt sorry for me or liked me or was attracted to me, or thought I had a screw loose and was coming on to him. And equally, I didn't care if he was my good new neighbour or a creep. I just wanted to know.

'If a person has done something wrong, and their lawyer knows it, the lawyer just has to keep quiet about it, right? Isn't that client privilege or something? And then the lawyer still has to defend the person, and can't let on?'

Tony let out an infinitesimal sigh. 'I'm not a criminal lawyer,' he said, 'but I can tell you it doesn't quite work like that. Client privilege doesn't mean you can confess to a crime and the admission just disappears as if it never happened. In that situation, there are limits to what the defence can do. You can't ask your legal representatives to lie for you, basically. Or if you do, you have no right to expect them to agree.'

'But what if it wasn't exactly a crime?' I persisted. 'What if it was something you ought to have done and had promised you'd do, but you hadn't followed through? I mean, there lots of things that might arguably be morally wrong, but aren't actually crimes. Or that aren't crimes now, but might have been once upon a time. And then there are things that would have been considered absolutely the right thing to do in the past, but suddenly aren't acceptable any more. If something can be right one day and wrong the next, maybe it's just that people's attitudes changed and so did the rules. Maybe then it's just a matter of timing, and nothing to do with right and wrong at all.'

Tony stared at me in dismay. I let out a small laugh and shook out my hair, as if the question had been some kind of joke that had fallen flat. 'I'm sorry,' I said. 'You didn't come here to talk shop.'

Phantom Rob folded his arms and shook his head. *No more drink for you. You've already said too much. What is this, confession time?*

I got to my feet. 'Anyway, I should probably be getting back.'

Tony finished his drink and stood up too. 'I'll come with you.' Then, on seeing my surprise: 'Unless you'd rather I didn't, that is.'

'No, no, do come, by all means…' My voice trailed off. 'But don't you need to collect your girls?'

'What? Oh, no – not tonight. They're going back to their friend's house. Birthday sleepover. I only really came here out of habit. Because it's what I usually do at this time of the week.'

Was it strange that he hadn't mentioned this before? I decided it wasn't. After all, he hadn't changed his story. He just hadn't gone into the details before, and why should he? It hadn't been relevant.

We made our way back along the main road of Fox Hill – such as it was, with its lone convenience store and pub – towards the turning onto Fox Hill Lane. Rob's presence seemed to fade away, as if we'd left him behind in the pub. An elderly couple who were walking towards us smiled and nodded at Tony and glanced at me as if I might or might not have some kind of special significance, then passed us by.

'I take it this is the kind of place where everyone knows everyone,' I said.

'I suppose it is. By sight, anyway.'

Then he started talking about bell-ringing again. What safer topic could there be? He told me that different peals had names and that there were plaques in the bell tower commemorating occasions when – decades or even centuries ago – the bell-ringers had rung particularly long or complicated sequences to celebrate jubilees and the ends of wars. He was just telling me that there was a novel set in the world of bell-ringing, a detective murder mystery, as we approached the end of Fox Hill Lane and the white façade of Gamekeeper's Cottage came into view.

Perhaps he'd realised I hadn't been paying much attention. He stopped talking and the conversation abruptly dried up.

'I really wish I had something to read. There's nothing in the house,' I said, and immediately wondered if that sounded like an invitation, or if he might take it to mean more than I had intended.

'I could lend it to you, if you like,' he said.

'What? Oh, you mean the murder mystery. But they say you should never lend a book. People always forget to give them back.'

'But I know where you are,' Tony countered. 'Why don't I pop it round to you now? It won't take me a minute to find it.'

I hesitated. 'You must have well-organised bookshelves,' I said.

'Absolutely. Alphabetical, by author. I insist on the twins doing the same,' he said with mock seriousness, then, 'Only kidding. But I do know where it is.'

'Well, if it's no trouble…'

'None at all. Anyway, what else are neighbours for?'

He went off into his house, and I walked on towards Game-keeper's Cottage.

As I stood on the front doorstep and rummaged for my key I suppressed a shudder. A quite unreasonable shudder. Nothing was going to happen to me here – nothing worse than what Rob had already done. *He* was the one to be afraid of, not my kindly, stuffy, book-loving neighbour.

This time my key turned in the lock much more easily, and when I stepped into the entrance hall the atmosphere seemed expectant, as if the house had been watching and waiting for me and was pleased to have me back.

Chapter Eight

I just had time to check my appearance in the bathroom mirror – not too wild – before Tony showed up. The buzzer for the side gate sounded like an actual bell, a small one or one at a distance, with a low, silvery tone. Another Rob touch: modern, but with a nod to authenticity. I dashed downstairs to let Tony through and opened up to find him on the doorstep, holding a paperback copy of *The Nine Tailors* by Dorothy L. Sayers in one hand – it had a black-and-white picture of young men pulling bell ropes on the cover – and a cardboard egg carton in the other.

'Here you go,' he said. 'I thought you might like some eggs as well? We have more than we can eat.'

I took the book and the egg carton from him. Offerings on a summer evening. Under other circumstances, I would have been touched. As it was, I was too overwrought to feel anything more than token gratitude. Still, I managed to remember my manners: I might have been in the process of losing my mind, but I wasn't so far gone as to take kindness for granted.

'Thank you. That's very thoughtful of you. So you keep chickens?'

'Yes. It was the girls' idea, I hasten to add. Not mine. They're called Charlie and Lola, after the children's books. Except obviously they're both female.' He grimaced. 'And Charlie is actually Charlie II. Charlie I got a prolapse and had to be put out of her misery. I always assumed that laying eggs was quite straightforward, at least compared to human reproduction, but it seems it isn't always quite as straightforward as all that.'

I could have just thanked him and shut the door. He was still on the other side of the threshold, and there wasn't any need to let him in – he'd already done what he had said he'd come to do. But instead I loitered. Perhaps I wasn't quite ready to be alone in the house.

'My daughter always wanted a pet,' I said. 'Cat, dog, anything. We never let her. My husband was dead against it.'

'Well, she's very welcome to pop over and see Charlie and Lola sometime if she would like. I mean Charlie II and Lola.'

'That's nice of you. Thank you.'

I had to reciprocate. I had to offer him something more than just words. I said, 'Would you like to come in? You might be interested to see what my husband's done to the place.'

'Well, if you're sure I wouldn't be intruding.'

'No, no. Anyway, it won't take a minute.'

I withdrew into the hall to make way for him. Tony squared his shoulders as if stiffening his resolve, and stepped in.

*

I didn't lead him upstairs to the bedrooms – I hadn't gone quite that far in losing sight of what was appropriate – so it didn't take long for me to show him round. We started with the kitchen. He looked around with narrowed eyes, as if so much whiteness was uncomfortable to take in, though the evening light was more muted than the sunshine had been when I first saw it, and to me it seemed bright but not dazzling. Perhaps I was just getting used to it.

I put the book and the carton of eggs down on the worktop next to my handbag and said, 'There. A few more bits and pieces, and it'll almost start to look as if someone lives here.'

He said something in reply, but I wasn't listening. I had flicked open the lid of the cardboard carton and was looking at the eggs he'd brought me; a perfect half-dozen, each one speckled in a slightly different way, one with a tiny white tail-feather clinging to it.

I felt a brief spasm of fellow feeling for poor Charlie I, the hen for whom things had gone so badly wrong, and whose life as a layer had come to an untimely end. The eggs in front of me and my hands hovering near them came into very sharp focus. At the same time everything I could hear blurred into one, a soft, rushing stream of distorted sound like being underwater. Then I pulled myself together and closed the egg carton and looked up at Tony, who was watching me as if he wasn't at all sure what I might do next.

'I'm sorry,' I said. 'I wasn't following. What did you say?'

Tony shook his head. 'Oh… nothing.' He turned away from me and looked conscientiously around, as if someone might be quizzing him on the details later. 'It certainly is quite a transformation.'

'It's what my husband does,' I said. 'Buys places, does them up, sells them on. And sometimes he knocks them down and starts over.'

Tony winced. Obviously he was thinking that Rob was treating me like one of his properties, cutting his losses and moving on to a new investment. But I didn't want Tony feeling sorry for me here. Not yet, anyway. It was too intimate, more so than in the pub. I turned my back on him and walked abruptly out of the kitchen back across the hall, and he followed me.

The living room looked even emptier and lonelier than I remembered, with its small grey sofa and flat screen TV and expanse of wooden floor, and its empty fireplace.

'It's not exactly cosy, is it?' I said, and turned round to find Tony standing right behind me.

He said, 'When we were in the kitchen, did you really not hear what I told you?'

I put my fingers to my temples and rubbed them. 'I think I may have kind of faded out a little. I'm sorry, I didn't mean to be rude. Is it too late to ask you to tell me again?'

Tony shrugged. He didn't look wounded; he looked resigned. 'No harm done, and there's really no need for you to be sorry. It's still as true now as it was five minutes ago. I may have put it in a slightly roundabout way, but what I was trying to tell you is that my wife and I aren't together any more. I do understand what a shock to the system it is.'

'Oh!' I stared at him in horror. How could I have not taken that in?

Always the way. You never mean for things to go wrong. But they do. Just like you never meant to hurt anyone. But you did, whether they know it or not.

Rob again. His voice in my head had exactly the same dry disillusionment with which he'd spoken to me in the hall before walking out and leaving me there on the floor. *You're a shadow of who you used to be. You're history, babe.* I could see him like an apparition, standing behind Tony at arm's length from us both, leaning against the frame of the door that led back to the hallway.

I fixed my attention on Tony. He was watching me very closely, as if I was something he might be able to make more of but not if he was too quick to show his hand.

'I'm sorry about your wife,' I said.

Without even intending to, I had somehow moved closer to him. Close enough to be grabbed or struck. A little frisson of fear ran over me. A kind of electricity, not all that different to the kind that makes your hair stand on end. Not all that different to desire.

I stepped forward again, and so did he, and then I put my mouth very close to his and the little dance was completed. Our lips made contact and I felt something moving through me and out of me that could have been a shudder of despair or a little gasp of hope, or both. And then we kissed.

*

It wasn't the kiss itself that was shocking. No fireworks went off, no arrows landed. It was as tentative and exploratory as any encounter between two animals who aren't yet sure whether they might be enemies or friends or who might dominate whom, and don't quite dare to find out – like two dogs in the street who are both still on the lead.

The shock was that he wasn't Rob. Rob always kissed with intent, as if he was on stage one of the project cycle that led to full, satisfying sex and felt impelled to move on sooner rather than later. Tony Everdene kissed as if a kiss was just a kiss. I could feel his lips curving into a smile before we broke away.

'That was… unexpected,' I said.

'In a good way, I hope.'

Tony didn't look at all embarrassed or unsure of himself. He looked amused and intrigued, as if he did this kind of thing all the time and was wondering how far I would go. As if he wouldn't stop me if I didn't stop myself.

I turned away and went over to the window at the front of the house and pulled down the plain white blind. The room dimmed. Without the glimpse of woodland on the far side of the lane it was even more clinical. Like a cubicle on a hospital ward after lights out.

Tony said, 'I don't think you have to worry too much about what the neighbours think when you only have one neighbour and he's already with you.'

'Other people come down here sometimes. You said you had to be careful about your bike.'

'True, though I don't think opportunistic thieves would be particularly interested in what you're doing in your living room. Do you have a bicycle?'

'No.'

'Well then, like I said, nothing to worry about.'

We kissed again, and then we were on the sofa and his hands were on me and I was breathing faster. I couldn't believe what I was doing but that didn't seem like a good reason to stop and anyway, I was beyond being surprised by what I was capable of. It was as if something was unspooling, moving towards a conclusion that wasn't inevitable but would be reached sooner or later if nothing intervened to stop it.

And then whatever it was that was unwinding hit a snag and came to a halt, and I grabbed both his hands and pushed them away.

Everything slowly came back into focus. The bare room, dim but not yet dark. The white walls. The drawn blind. Tony Everdene sitting at the other end of the grey sofa that still smelt new, watching me.

'I think that's what's known as a visceral response,' he said.

I glanced down at myself, pulled down my top and picked a stray hair – one of his – off it and dropped it on the floor.

'I'm sorry,' I said. 'I think it's all a bit soon.' I folded my arms across my chest and stood up. 'After all, my husband only dumped me at lunchtime, and it hasn't even got dark yet.'

He stood up too. 'I may be wildly off the mark here, but I don't think that's what stopped you. I don't think it was anything to do with him. I don't even think it was anything to do with me. I think it was something to do with *you*.'

And Rob was back in the room as if he'd been there all along, still leaning against the doorframe, looking on in amusement.

He's right, isn't he? I'm the only one who's seen your scars. And now I don't want you any more.

'Look, I don't want to feel embarrassed every time I walk past your house,' I said. 'Can't we just forget this ever happened?'

He paused as if to give this possibility due consideration, then shook his head.

'I think not,' he said. 'I won't forget, anyway. I must say, I don't particularly *want* to forget. I don't see why either of us should be embarrassed. But we can pretend it didn't happen, if you like. Anyway, I'm sorry too. I hope you don't think I was taking advantage. In my defence, it isn't every day that a woman who looks like you falls over in front of my house.'

'I don't think a defence is needed,' I said. 'I'm not accusing you of anything.'

'No. Not yet.'

'What do you mean? What could I possibly have to accuse you of? You've been nothing but kind to me.'

He looked regretful, as if a golden opportunity had just slipped through his fingers. 'I should go,' he said. 'Feel free to call round if you need anything. Or even if you don't. I hope you enjoy the book. And the eggs.'

'I'm sure I will,' I told him, and showed him through to the hall.

Instead of heading off he stood there looking at me. His expression was sharp and speculative and he wasn't smiling at all. My heart rate shifted up a notch, but all he said was, 'I hope you'll be all right here. Cheerio, then. Good luck.' Then he stepped through the front door, which I'd opened for him, and out onto the gravel.

He didn't look back. I held on for a moment to see if he would. I don't know what I was waiting for: a wave, maybe, or some other sign of acknowledgement. But he didn't so much as glance over his shoulder.

You screwed that up good and proper, didn't you?

Rob again, lurking in the empty hallway behind me.

If that was your attempt at getting your own back, I'd say it fell pretty flat. Sum total of your fightback so far is a damaged windscreen and an abortive fondle on the sofa. It's not much, is it?

But we kissed, I said under my breath. Then there was nothing for it to retreat back into the empty house.

Chapter Nine

Eighteen years earlier

The first time I ever talked to Rob was at Brickley Museum. We were in a light, high-ceilinged upstairs gallery, surrounded by a press of other people and big screens displaying blown-up black-and-white photographs and rather gloomy paintings. In the next gallery there were recreations of homes from different eras, from seventeenth-century dark wood and tapestry to florid Victorian drapery and wallpaper. Right from the start, our relationship was surrounded by other people's houses.

The event was the launch for an exhibition about domestic interiors, and I was writing it up for the local paper. I'd been a junior reporter long enough not to be anxious about what I was doing. The story would be a few paragraphs at best, ideally with a quirky opening paragraph and a big picture, and I didn't have to file my copy till lunchtime the next day. The photographer had already been and gone, and I'd shaken hands with the local dignitaries and done my bit to represent the paper. It was time to start edging towards the exit so I could slip away. There were plenty of chores to do back home, as there always were.

I'd noticed the tall, good-looking, fair-haired guy before. Not with lust, particularly. I'd just clocked him. *Oh, look at him. Bet he fancies himself.* He was wearing a dark-blue suit that he looked perfectly at ease in. Whenever I saw him he was talking to someone different. More than once it was a woman, or group of women, who looked happy to have cornered him.

As I made my move he caught my eye. Or maybe I caught his. He was standing with his back to the nearest painting, a big dark picture of two women sewing by a fireplace while an old man lay dying on a chaise longue next to them. The painting was all shadows and shades of red and the sunlight was very bright. I had to squint a little to see him.

Then the movement of the group of people behind him propelled him towards me, like one small sea creature pushed towards another by the current. Or maybe he actually wanted to talk to me.

Well, you were meant to mingle at these things, weren't you? Small talk didn't come that naturally to me, but I'd learned to make the effort. It was all part of the job – schmoozing, building a network of contacts who might give you useful information later on. I had begun to realise it was a part of the job I wasn't particularly good at. Still, I'd never get any better if I didn't work at it.

We introduced ourselves to each other, but even before he told me who he was I'd read the name label pinned on the lapel of his suit and knew he worked for the estate agents who were sponsoring the event.

Someone came by and topped up our glasses with slightly warm white wine. We carried on chatting and the sun carried on shining. He didn't make an excuse to move on, and I didn't attempt to break away either. I began to feel a little hot. Maybe the temperature in the gallery was rising. He held my glass of wine while I took my jacket off and folded it over one arm. As I took my glass back I realised that he was really taking notice of me. He was definitely interested. Carnivorously interested.

When the crowd had thinned out and I said I really ought to go, he pulled a face as if that was a shame. He fished a business card out of an inner jacket pocket and I accepted it, and he took my empty glass while I rummaged in my bag for one of mine. He dumped my glass on a passing waiter's tray and took my card and tucked it away in his jacket pocket – he did all of these small social manoeuvres as smoothly as a conjurer who knows exactly what the outcome of the trick will be. Then he asked me if I'd like to go out for a drink sometime.

I was flattered, naturally. After all, he was very good-looking. Charming, too. But I was wary. A flirty chat at a launch was one thing. Dating was quite another. I had enough problems already, and no time. So I said no.

He shrugged and smiled and said, 'Well, you can't blame me for trying.' And I shrugged and smiled too, and turned on my heel and left him there.

I felt light-hearted, light-headed even, with barely a pang of regret. It had been perfect. The perfect encounter. To meet, to chat… to smell the promise of something more hanging in the air… and then to walk away. That was how powerful I felt, knowing that he had wanted me and I had turned him down.

As if I was somebody who could say no any time I chose to. Who could afford to look a gift horse in the mouth. A man had stood and watched me go, and I had been the woman disappearing into the mystery of her own separate life…

Then he rang me at work and talked me into it.

'I'm sorry to bother you like this, out of the blue. It's just that I've been thinking about you, and I really would like to see you again, and I guess I must have messed up somehow without realising it, but I thought… if this doesn't seem too crazy… I couldn't let it go without asking you again.'

'Asking me what?'

'Whether I could buy you a drink. Friday evening, six o'clock. Just one, after work. Unless you're busy?'

I hesitated. How long was it since I'd been out on a Friday night? 'OK,' I said.

He exhaled. 'Thank you. Honestly, you wouldn't believe how much I practised what I was going to say on this call. It was embarrassing. I'd never normally do something like this. I mean, ringing someone out of the blue after meeting them at a do.'

Later on, I found out this wasn't true. He'd dated plenty of girls, and picked them up pretty much anywhere. It was easy for him, looking the way he did. They didn't usually say no.

But at the time, I chose to believe him.

He told me where to meet him – not at a pub, as I'd expected, but at the front of Brickley's biggest department store, the one Mum had once worked in. I always thought of her whenever anybody mentioned it, and then I thought of her leaving: the big suitcase by the front door, her new brown suede-look trousers, the taxi outside in the road. Not the taxi Dad drove, which was still parked on the driveway. *Keep an eye on Molly for me*, she'd said. The worst part of it had been that she'd looked so happy to be leaving.

I said, 'Where are we going after?'

'Surprise,' he said. 'Come dressed for cocktails. I'll take care of the rest.'

Then he hung up, and as I put the phone down I realised that the clacking of the typewriter on the desk opposite mine had gone silent. My colleague Jan had been listening into my conversation. This was unusual, because she was desperate to leave Brickley behind for a job on Fleet Street and generally treated junior staff like me with bored indifference.

She said, 'So where's he taking you?'

'I don't know. I'll find out on Friday. How did you know it was a date?'

She rolled her eyes. 'Oh come on, please, it was obvious. I've never heard you sound like that on the phone before. Anyway, I hope he doesn't disappoint.' Then she yanked her copy out of the typewriter, leaned over the piece of paper with a sigh and a swoosh of hair and started counting up the words.

I had only a vague idea of what dressing for cocktails might mean, and my wardrobe definitely didn't cover it. I was tempted to splash out on something new, but my salary didn't go far and I had bills to cover at home, especially as Dad wasn't in a great way and wasn't working much, plus I had a car to run. In the end I found a petrol-blue batwinged top and matching skirt in a charity shop that looked almost as good as new. I figured wherever we were going would probably have dim lighting, so hopefully it would pass muster.

And the lighting *was* dim, and even though it was so early in the evening the bar was busy enough to take the edge off my self-consciousness. Rob had picked a place I would never normally have gone into because it looked too swanky and too expensive – all mirrors and gleaming surfaces and velvet upholstery, with dark red and dull gold on the walls. But as we waited at the bar I decided I liked it. It gave the evening a sense of occasion, as if just being there was enough, whatever else happened or didn't happen.

He insisted on paying for our drinks, and I let him. After all, as he said, it had been his idea to come here. Then he spotted a free table and nabbed it for us before another couple could get there.

'You can't hang around in a place like this,' he said to me as they gave us baleful looks and shuffled off to find somewhere else to sit. 'No prizes for coming second.'

He flashed me a quick, bright smile that had just a hint of self-deprecation in it, as if he knew he might sometimes get up people's noses but really, when it came down to it, he didn't care. I'd never seen anybody manage to be arrogant and charming at the same time before. There was something about that mix of self-awareness and thick skin that was very hard to resist, but at the same time I found myself wanting to resist it. To not be bowled over. I smiled back, but I was beginning to wonder how much I liked him.

I asked him about his day, and that was all the cue he needed to start telling me about his plans. He put me to shame, because although I'd once thought of myself as ambitious I'd realised, since starting work, that perhaps I wasn't. Or not enough. I liked reading and I had thought I might be good at writing but after a couple of years of reporting on parish council meetings and bonny baby competitions I knew I wasn't a newshound.

Anyway, I'd only decided I wanted to be a journalist because Mum's boyfriend sold advertising for a sister paper of the *Brickley Mail* in Ashdale, which was about ten miles north of Brickley on the Oxfordshire border, and was more moneyed and more rural. In my more cynical moments, I resented Mum for seeming to be pleased with herself for having traded up, in terms of her address at least. Lee never hesitated to point out that most of the hacks on his paper earned less than he did, but he also spoke about them with grudging respect.

I wasn't sure I was good enough to be successful. Rob had no such doubts, and had already decided his current job was not for him. 'I'm not going to be an estate agent all my life,' he said. 'I'm going to go into business for myself.' He told me about the property market: hotspots, predictions, interest rates, mortgages – all things I'd never paid much attention to. Looking in estate agents' windows only ever served to confirm that buying my own place was out of reach. But Rob didn't see it that way. He saw it as a kind of game that he was determined to win.

I didn't listen to all of it that closely. I was watching him, though. He was good-looking, there was no doubt about that. But a little voice in the back of my head was saying, *What are you doing? If you don't get out now, he's going to eat you alive...* There was an intensity in the air, like a premonition, but I couldn't tell if it was a premonition of doom. Or maybe it was just the heady combination of strawberry daiquiri and other people's perfume and smoke.

Then a girl I recognised from school recognised me and came over to say hello, and the spell was broken.

I introduced her to Rob, only just remembering her name in time. Connie. Connie Feldman. She looked from me to Rob and back again as if trying to figure out what he was doing with me. I asked about her baby and she fished a blurry photo out of her handbag and proudly showed it to me before heading off to the exit, where her boyfriend was impatiently waiting for her.

'She dropped out of school to have the baby,' I said to Rob after she'd gone. 'She was only seventeen. She seems happy, though.'

'Well, she would tell you that, wouldn't she?'

Rob stretched out and angled his arms behind his head. He seemed on edge, as if the interruption had spoiled the evening for him in some way. 'People with kids always have to make out it's great. They only moan about it to each other.' He brought his hands together, interlaced his fingers and flexed them so that his knuckles cracked. 'Personally, I think there are other things you can do with your life.'

'Yeah, well, it would be kind of weird if you were sitting here telling me you wanted a baby. Since we only just met.'

He let his hands drop. 'True.'

'I mean, I'm not crazy about the idea either, believe me. I looked after my kid sister quite a lot when she was little, so I don't think I idealise what it's like.'

'Everybody idealises having kids. There are whole industries built on myths about family life.'

'That's true, I guess. But having said that, I like having a sister. I mean, I wouldn't be without her.'

The next getting-to-know-you, small-talk question was an obvious one: *Do you have any brothers or sisters?* And yet I hesitated to come out with it. I had the strangest sense – almost as if I could hear an echo of what he was thinking – that he knew what I was about to ask, and was willing me not to. *Please, no, not that. Everyone asks, sooner or later, and I still never quite know what to say…*

I said it anyway. Smiling brightly, leaning forward across the table, doing my best to be engaging. But he didn't smile in response. Instead he leaned back and folded his arms. 'No.'

'Oh. OK.'

'And before you ask whether I was a lonely only, I wasn't. And that's rubbish anyway, in my opinion. Did you know that only children actually tend to be over-achievers compared to people with siblings? No offence, of course.'

'None taken.'

'As if it's actually possible to be an over-achiever anyway. No such thing.' He was warming up now, as if he was enjoying sounding off on the subject. 'What is this obsession with having to hand down your genetic material, anyway? It's ridiculous. I don't know why people can't see what a sham it all is. You've got one life and you should live it for yourself, not give it up to a bunch of screaming kids who are probably going to hate your guts in a few years' time anyway.'

'Sure. Right.'

'The whole thing's just designed to guilt-trip people. As if not reproducing yourself enough was some kind of crime. That was what my mum always used to say. It drove her nuts. I used to see the way other women spoke to her sometimes. Kind of sympathetic but snide at the same time. Making out she'd fallen short somehow. Anyway, that's women for you. Always carrying on as if having babies is the be-all and end-all.'

'I don't think women *do* do that,' I said. 'Not these days, anyway.' Why did I feel as if I was defending myself? But I did, and it seemed important to make a good case. As if I had something to prove, and might be penalised in some way if I didn't. 'Women want all kinds of other things besides babies. Like careers, for a start. What does your mum do? Does she work? Mine used to, but she stopped when she broke up with my dad and moved in with her boyfriend. She says she gave up her job when she met a man who could afford to keep her in a style to which she was completely unaccustomed.'

'No, my mum doesn't work,' Rob said shortly. 'She's dead.'

My stomach lurched as if someone had just hit the button in a lift and we were going down much faster than anyone could have expected. The room seemed to swim around us. The only still point was Rob's face, and his expression of disgust.

I'd made him talk about a subject that he probably preferred not to discuss with anyone, let alone with a near-stranger who he'd met once and asked out on a date. If I had thought this was the way to get closer to him, I couldn't have been more wrong. All I had achieved was to push him away.

'I'm so sorry,' I said.

'Not your fault. Obviously.' He finished his drink. 'Actually, it was my dad's.'

I stared at him. I couldn't quite believe my ears. He looked back at me with a very faint hint of a smile, as if my confusion gave him some kind of minor satisfaction.

'It's all right, don't worry, you're not having a drink with the son of a murderer. He didn't actually kill her. Not as such. The baby did that. And she chose to go ahead with having the baby even though she was getting on a bit by then and she wasn't in brilliant health, and she knew it might be risky.' He leaned forward. 'You want to know what happened. Don't you?'

'Only if you want to tell me.'

'OK, look, I'll make a deal with you. I'll tell you, but you have to promise me that we don't ever have to talk about this again.'

I nodded. 'Sure. I mean, if you're comfortable with that.'

I was actually a little frightened of him. Or maybe of what he was about to tell me. And I could already feel the weight of that promise of silence. I could see that I would go along with it, and that from his point of view this would bring the evening back under control and make it possible to carry on. But at the same time I knew it would snuff something else out.

'I'm actually not comfortable with it,' Rob said. 'I don't think it's the kind of thing anyone could be comfortable with, unless they were a sicko. You're not a sicko, are you?'

He seemed to expect an answer. I said, 'I don't think so.' I was beginning to feel squeamish.

'I know some people just love gory details,' Rob went on. 'I guess people like that might take a macabre interest in gynaecological disasters. Just like they rubberneck at the aftermath of car crashes.'

'I'm not rubbernecking,' I said. 'You don't have to tell me. Only if you want to.'

'I know I don't have to, believe me. I never usually talk about this.'

So he *did* want to tell me. Suddenly I felt absurdly privileged. We barely knew each other and already he trusted me enough to do this. I had never realised how intimate it would be to know something about a man that was painful, maybe even dangerous, and that he didn't find easy to share.

I said, 'What happened?'

'She had pre-eclampsia and a placental abruption. Basically, she lost a lot of blood, she lost the baby and then we lost her. You could call it a tragedy, I suppose. Or you could just call it biology. Tragedies happen, that's the thing. They're not just on some stage somewhere. And modern medicine can work miracles, but even now it can't fix everything and it can't bring back the dead.'

All I could think of to say was to tell him how sorry I was. He leaned back again and said, 'You asked what she did for a job. She worked in a typing pool and then she had a clerical job inputting data into a dumb terminal. That's what she did right up until a month before she died.'

I said, 'When did it happen?'

He shrugged impatiently, as if this was irrelevant. 'When I was fifteen.'

I opened my mouth to speak and he said, 'Don't tell me you're sorry again. It really doesn't help, believe me.'

'Your dad... how is he?'

He shrugged. 'Not great. Carrying on. I drop in on him every now and then and he puts up with me for a while and then makes it clear he'd rather I left. We were never that close. Anyway, there we are, that's my sob story. It's not like I needed a reason not to want kids. But now you know why I feel how I feel about it. So, now that's out of the way, same again?'

I blinked at him.

He said, 'I meant your drink.'

'Oh! Sure.' I got to my feet. 'I'll get them.'

'No you won't. Sit down. Least I can do, after all that.' He stood up. 'Your challenge is to think of something else to talk about when I get back. And never to bring all that up again.'

He went off to the bar. He really did seem to have shrugged off what he'd just told me. Or perhaps he just wanted to show that he hadn't let it get the better of him. Everything about him was confident and poised, from the way he moved to the efficiency with which he caught the bartender's eye, paid for our cocktails and carried them back without spilling a drop. You never would have guessed that he'd just been confiding in me about such a distressing subject.

As he returned I was gripped by a sudden impulse to get up and walk away from the smoke and glitter and noise of the bar and into the night. To escape from whatever it was we'd just started.

But then he put down my glass in front of me and grinned and said, 'So did you think of something to talk about?'

'I did. I wanted to ask you where you would most like to live,' I said.

He started telling me about the property market again and I was riveted, even though I wasn't really listening. I could quite happily have sat there and watched him for hours. I knew then that it was already too late for me to walk away.

Chapter Ten

The book Tony had brought me smelt musty and old, and the print was challengingly small. I had just finished the first chapter, and had taken in almost nothing, when the buzzer sounded again.

Tony.

It had to be. Besides Rob, who else knew I was here?

I pressed the buzzer and a familiar, impatient voice said, 'Good grief, it's like Fort Knox round here. Well, are you going to let me in or what? I won't be a minute. I've got something for you. Something you wanted. Well, you said you did.'

My spirits lifted instantly as I let her through and opened up. It was Mum. On reflection, she must have decided she wanted to help me after all.

*

'I won't come in,' she said. 'I'm parked just outside on the lane – I hope that's all right. I figured I wouldn't be in anybody's way, not out here.' She rummaged in her handbag and brought out a slip of paper and passed it to me. 'Here you go.'

The piece of paper had been torn off the bottom of a page of a lined notebook. Mum had written the address out carefully, all in capitals. There was a phone number, too.

'You mustn't say anything to Lee about it,' she said. 'He'll only worry about the effect it might have on me, and that's the last thing he needs. Anyway, that's where Molly is. So now you know.'

'So… you're in touch with her?'

'Yes. Obviously. In a very minimal way, I am.'

'Then... how is she?'

'She's not married, she doesn't have any children and she moves around a lot. Beyond that I don't know. She won't see me. She doesn't want to meet. She just lets me know where she is.'

'Does she know about Lee?'

'She does,' Mum said bitterly. 'She knows all about how ill he is. And she doesn't care. She won't come and visit him, not even to say goodbye. Not even if it was just her and us, and we never breathed a word about it to anyone else. That's how bad it is. It's downright cruel, in my opinion. She's a bad egg, Stella, and that's the long and the short of it. I'm sorry to sound harsh, but there it is.' She shook her head. 'My own daughter. I'm sorry to say it, Stella, but I think there's something wrong with her. There has to be. Probably there always was.'

'But you stayed in contact. That could only have been because both of you wanted to.' Molly hadn't chosen to stay in touch with me; she'd as good as told me that was the last thing she wanted.

'I thought it was better to know where she was than not to know,' Mum said. 'I'm guessing she felt the same way. I'm sorry it's come to this, Stella, because I can see what's going to happen. You'll start imagining that maybe everyone could get together and it could all be out in the open and everything would be lovely. Except it won't be, and that's just a daydream. If you do reach out she's only going to rebuff you. She isn't interested. She doesn't want to know. And if you ask me it's a jolly good thing that she does feel like that. Because let's face it, you've got troubles enough.' She sighed. 'As have we all.'

'But Mum... You're making her sound like a monster.'

'Well, I wouldn't go quite that far,' Mum said.

'I mean... she was very young when it all happened... and she hadn't had the easiest time of it.'

'Yes, well, she was still old enough to know better. We don't need to make excuses for her. Look, I know you're not going to want to take my word for it. You'll want to see her for yourself. Maybe then you'll come to your senses and sort something out with Rob. Just promise me you'll put Georgie first. She's going to be hurt and confused enough as it is – what's the point in giving her something else to fret about? She's such a sensitive child. If it all comes out, especially right now with your marriage coming unstuck at the same time, it'll be completely overwhelming for her. And given what's going on with Lee, I think we've all got enough to cope with.'

She glanced back at her car as if half expecting to see someone descending on it to give her a ticket. 'I have to go,' she said. 'I told Lee I was just popping to the supermarket. Just try to be sensible, won't you? Remember, your number one job is to protect Georgie. She comes first. I'd say your sister should come a pretty distant last. Anyway, I must get on. I have a dying husband to get back to.'

And with a final reproachful look she turned and headed back towards the road. She pressed the exit button and walked through the gate briskly and with dignity, a woman who had completed one mission and was on her way back to carry on with another.

Everybody I'd met who knew her now seemed to admire her. It hadn't always been like that, though. It might as well have been several lifetimes ago, but there had been a time, after she left us for Lee, when our neighbours had felt sorry for Dad and Molly and me, and had responded to any mention of her with pursed lips and sighs of disapproval.

The gate shut silently behind her. I glimpsed her car turning in the lane, and then I was alone again.

Half an hour later the slip of paper was still sitting on the little round kitchen table in front of me, and I still hadn't phoned.

Molly's address surprised me. She was living in an upmarket part of London, and I'd never had her down as a city girl or as someone who'd have the money for an expensive area. When she was little she'd been in love with the idea of living in the country, and drew endless pictures of the sheep and goats and chickens she would keep. And I had daydreamed about having money and space and a wonderful husband who would take care of everything…

What if Mum was right, and I should just leave Molly be?

If I called her out of the blue, she might hang up. And even if she didn't, it would be easy for her to turn me away.

If I turned up at her place, surely she'd at least hear me out?

But what if she slammed the door in my face? Or just wasn't in?

She didn't want to be found. She'd made it very clear that she wanted a clean break. And maybe she was right. Maybe it had been easier that way. The clean break was a dividing line and on one side of it was Molly and the sequence of events that had ended with her walking away and choosing to be forgotten. And on the other side was everyone and everything I still had, and the rest of my life.

Except now all that was slipping out of my fingers too… apart from this house.

Dare you, Rob might have said. *Bet you don't have the nerve.* I could picture him sitting on the other side of the table, watching me as if I was an experiment.

It was a Thursday night: she might well be in. It was still a reasonable hour to call. But if I left it any longer it would be getting late…

I picked up my new phone and rang her number. It rang and rang. And then someone answered. All she said was hello, but I knew it was her.

*

My heart nearly burst out of my chest, but I couldn't let that stop me. I had to press on, to tell her what was happening and prepare her for what might follow. There was no formula I could rely on and the exact right words would never come.

'Molly. That's you, isn't it? It's me. Stella. Mum gave me your number. I hope you don't mind me calling you out of the blue. How are you?'

'Yeah, I'm all right. Mum called me and told me you might ring.'

Her voice was soft and slow, almost drawling, and husky. As if she smoked, or had just been sleeping.

'She did?'

'Yeah. She told me why, too.'

Across the table from me, imaginary Rob smirked.

'You mean she told you about Rob.'

'Yeah. That's tough. I'm sorry.'

'Did she say he basically threatened to start telling Georgie stuff if I don't go along with exactly what he wants?'

'Yeah. She did.'

'Sounds like you had a good long talk about it. I didn't realise. She didn't mention it to me.'

'Actually it was all a bit rushed. She didn't want Lee to know she was calling me.'

'Oh. I see.'

I waited for her to ask how he was. To say something, anything, that acknowledged how ill he was and what Mum was going through. But she didn't. Instead she said, 'The thing is, about you and Rob… if you don't mind me being blunt… what do you expect me to do about it?'

I don't know what I had expected. Maybe tears or recriminations. Or bitterness. But definitely not this. And I hadn't expected Mum to go behind my back like that, either. Though perhaps I should have done.

'I thought I should warn you,' I said.

She sighed. 'This is your family and your problem. Nothing to do with me. It's up to you what you tell Georgie about what we did. I'm not going to help you come clean. If that's what you thought, forget it.'

My hands had started shaking. 'Is that what you said to Mum?' My voice sounded wobbly, as if I was about to break down crying.

Molly hesitated. 'Sure.'

'What did she say? She must have tried to persuade you.'

Molly sighed again. 'Did she hell. She rang me to ask me to tell you to back off. She thinks you ought to give Rob what he wants and not rock the boat. But then, she always did have a spot soft for Rob. Look, I'm sorry to be the one to break this to you, but Mum just wants all this to go away.'

'I don't believe it. You must have misunderstood.'

'You can't count on her to stick by you when the chips are down. I don't know how you've got this far without figuring that out. She really does care about Georgie, though.' She said this lightly, as if it was an interesting weather phenomenon that she had spotted in the distance. 'I guess she's mellowed in old age, maybe. She's quite the devoted grandmother.'

'Georgie *is* pretty special. Though I say so myself.' My voice sounded very small, as if I was offering up a last line of defence. I cleared my throat and tried to speak more boldly. 'I know maybe now isn't the right time… but I just wondered… do you ever think you might like to meet her?'

'Stella, you're not listening to me. I am not going to be brought back into the fold like some kind of prodigal sister. Not for you, not for Georgie, not for anyone. I don't want to meet her. Not ever. If you tell her about me you should tell her that too. And if she has any sense she'll leave well enough alone.'

'You do know about Lee, don't you?'

'Yeah. Mum told me. Sounds like it's been tough on her. Who'd have thought that she'd end up nursing him?' She said this quite lightly, as if we were discussing people she barely knew. 'Anyway, she really doesn't want him upset. Which might be something else to bear in mind.'

'He's dying, Molly. Will you not go and see him, just to say goodbye?'

There was a long silence. 'No,' Molly said finally. 'I don't suppose he'd want me to, either. No, me paying Lee a deathbed visit would definitely be a big mistake. And Stella, don't call me again, OK? Not ever. I do wish you well. I'm even going to wish you a happy birthday. See? I remembered. But I can't help you with Rob and Georgie. You're just going to have to sort something out without me.'

And then she finished the call.

Across the table from me, imaginary Rob folded his arms and shook his head.

Told you so.

I sat with my head in my hands for a while. Then I got up and rummaged in the drawers for a corkscrew and took a bottle of white wine out of the fridge and a suitable glass out of the cupboard. I settled on the sofa in front of the TV and started drinking, and kept going till the white living room blurred at the edges and turned dark.

Chapter Eleven

I found myself sitting in a car with my dad, heading down a straight, fast country road through woodland. I knew immediately that I was dreaming, because he'd been dead for years.

Vivid as he was, he would vanish. I was glad to see him again, but I was sad and scared too because the gladness was almost inextricable from missing him. And I was reminded all over again of the hole he'd left in my life, even though – all the time I'd lived with him and after I had left home too – I had taken him for granted. Been frustrated with him, even. He'd been a melancholy presence in the armchair in the living room, tired out after a long day driving the cab, resigned to Mum having walked out on him.

Poor old Dad. You might have described him as a broken man. I'd wanted him to fight back somehow, to show her, to wrestle some happiness from the fate she'd consigned him to – the role of the abandoned husband, the cuckold who's left with the kids, and who's too bruised and exhausted and downhearted to even think about meeting someone new. I'd wanted Dad to be heroic somehow. I hadn't realised that just sticking it out was a kind of heroism all of its own.

And now I was sitting next to him and he was driving, and I had been here before and knew how it ended, both for him and for me.

'Rob dumped me,' I told him. 'You probably wouldn't be surprised. I know you didn't really like him. I got the impression you thought I rushed into it. Maybe you were right. I hadn't known him all that long before I jacked in my job and moved in with him. It just seemed like long enough at the time.'

He didn't respond. It was as if he couldn't hear me. I decided to keep talking anyway. What other chance would I get?

'I know you were hurt,' I said. 'Maybe you thought I did it because I was desperate to leave home. I was ready to go, it's true. But you can't blame me for that. I did carry on helping with the bills and money and stuff. And you know I came back to see you.'

Still nothing. He was oblivious. He didn't even seem to be aware that I was there.

The trees along the sides of the road were midsummer green and the sun was still high in the sky, even though it was early evening. It was that day again. My birthday. We were fast approaching a turning point, speeding towards it as if it had never happened and was perhaps not irrevocable.

And I had no choice. I knew it just as clearly as I knew my dad was dead and I was dreaming and we were both heading for disaster. There was absolutely nothing I could do.

The steering wheel was so close – but I couldn't move to grab it. The brake pedal was somewhere under my dad's feet but I couldn't reach that either. Dad wasn't going too fast, anyway. I had never felt as safe in a car as I did when I was with him. He was always steady, always calm. He never swore. If other people were erratic, he just gave them as much space as he could. Nobody panicked him. Anyway, he drove for a living. He knew what he was doing.

'Slow down, Dad,' I said, but he didn't hear that either and I knew it wouldn't make any difference.

I don't know whether I saw the movement at the edge of the road before he did. He had spent a lot more time on the road than I ever would, and his reflexes should have been faster. But I had the advantage of hindsight. I knew what to look out for.

And there it was – the small stir of a shadow among the shadows. Then the deer stepped forward into the light, as beautiful and terrible and unexpected as something from a fairy tale.

Dad immediately swerved to avoid it. Time went slow and silent. The view of the road ahead skewed as if reality was stretching and morphing into a strange new form and the trees were rushing to meet us. Then the world exploded into noise and breaking glass and crumpling metal and everything went dark.

*

When I surfaced I was in a hospital bed. I was sitting propped up and my elbow was in plaster. There was darkness all around me, stretching for miles. I knew I was still dreaming and tried to shake myself awake. I did not want to relive what was coming next. But I couldn't move. It was as if I was paralysed.

There was no one else nearby except the consultant who was standing at my bedside and looking down at me. I could see the tiny hairs in his nostrils, the lines around his watery green eyes. He was slightly balding and freckled, with scrappy ginger hair. A small man with the power to give big news. News of life and death, and everything in between.

I knew the news wasn't good. I could tell from the way he was looking at me and how careful he was to maintain eye contact. He was trying to treat me with respect and to acknowledge that I was a person as well as a patient. At the same time, he wasn't in a position to spare me.

He began to speak, but what he said was hard to follow. Odd phrases cut through the haze. *Punctured lung… pierced intestines… elbow fixed with metal pins…*

Then he leaned down and whispered something in my ear.

You may never have a child of your own.

Tears began to stream down my face. The consultant had vanished. I was completely alone. Every inch of me was swathed in bandages with only the tiniest of gaps for my eyes and my mouth, and I couldn't move and couldn't breathe…

My head jolted back and I found myself gasping for air on a sofa in a strange empty white room.

The lights were on and there was a book on the sofa next to me and a glass and a mostly-drunk bottle of wine on the floor. The TV was muttering away. Otherwise it was very quiet – the dense quiet of the middle of the night in the countryside, in a place surrounded by trees. There was no sound of movement in the house or outside, not even the distant hum of traffic.

Fox Hill. I was in the middle of nowhere, exactly where Rob wanted me to be. This was it. This was what I had to wake up to. I was completely alone. I couldn't even conjure up the spectre of Rob to torment me.

My head was pounding and my mouth tasted as if I'd been poisoned. I got to my feet and took the bottle of wine and my glass through to the kitchen. It was glaringly white, and every step jarred.

I washed up, tipped what was left of the wine down the sink, drank some water and turned off the TV and the downstairs lights. After all, no one else was going to. When everything was tidy I went slowly and carefully up the stairs to my brand-new single bed.

Chapter Twelve

The next morning, in natural light, the kitchen looked a little less stark. Less like the backdrop for a nightmare. But the nightmare wasn't over, and I still couldn't see any way out of it.

It was going to be a cooler day. Plenty of clouds, maybe even a little light rain. I opened the window over the kitchen sink to look out at the square of garden with its artificial grass and was just in time to see a fat ginger-and-white cat slink across it before leaping up and over the fence and out of sight. Then I heard a cawing sound overhead, something between the shriek of a battling cat and the complaint of a gull fighting for scraps, but thinner and more bloodless.

A frisson ran down my spine. The sound was as eerie as something from prehistory, like standing stones or old wells, reminders of a time when people lived off their nerves and superstitions and believed in sacrifice. I found my keys and unbolted and unlocked the back door, and went out barefoot.

A milky sky, grey with pale patches of blue. There was dew on the green plastic grass. I hoped Georgie had been warm enough in the night and that she had slept well in her bunk bed. It might strike her as chilly when she got up, but she had plenty of layers she could put on and no doubt she'd soon be distracted by the excitement of whatever activity they were planning to do that morning, and by the adventure of being away from home.

Then I imagined Rob and Chloe together, peacefully sleeping. I was almost certain they'd be at her flat. She'd have cream-coloured bedding, maybe patterned with scattered sprigs of flowers. Light would be seeping in from around the edges of the blind and the room would be bright and quiet, apart from their steady breathing.

He'd be on the left-hand side of the bed, as usual, on his side facing her, as still as if he was dead. It probably wouldn't have occurred to her that I also slept on the right. She'd be on her back with one arm outstretched, blissfully oblivious to the alarm clock ticking away the last few minutes of their rest...

Well, they might as well enjoy it while they could.

I looked up and saw the dark shapes of two birds of prey wheeling above me. Red kites. A pair. They'd been reintroduced to our area some years before after almost dying out, and had become a more common sight, especially by the roadside as they fed on carrion. But I had never seen two together. They must be nesting somewhere nearby.

It seemed you couldn't get away from couples, even if there were no humans in sight...

Back in the kitchen, I rummaged through the cupboards and drawers. It was well equipped – Rob hadn't skimped. There was a black marble pestle and mortar for grinding spices, heavy enough to bash in someone's skull, and an array of knives in a wooden block, their handles tilted towards me.

I remembered the cracked glass of Rob's windscreen, and his and Chloe's horrified faces behind it.

Had I really done that? I had. Was I capable of doing something like that again? I'd done it once, so the answer had to be yes...

Rob had left a small portable radio in an otherwise empty cupboard. I put it on the worktop and plugged it in, and worked my way up and down the frequencies through snatches of pulsating music and fuzzy chatter. Eventually I landed on a discussion about honeymoons, and turned it off.

I broke a couple of the eggs Tony had given me into a bowl and whisked them until they frothed. The mixture was yellower than shop-bought eggs would have been, and thicker. I tipped it into the frying-pan and stirred it till it cooked, and once I'd eaten it my queasiness vanished.

Suddenly it became clear to me what I was going to do, and then it seemed inevitable that I would do it. I felt wonderfully calm, as if somebody had just comforted me. Why had I never realised before that it was indecision that was the problem, and when you made your mind up there was nothing more to be frightened of?

I cleared up and went upstairs to dress in one of the outfits that Rob had picked out for me – the dark trousers and the shirt patterned with a small print of green leaves.

I could almost have been any normal person on any normal morning, getting up and going to work. Except I wasn't due back in at school till Monday. Would that happen? Would I ever stand in front of a class again? It seemed a remote prospect, like old age or death.

Handbag. Keys. Lock up. I stepped out of the house onto the gravelled front garden. And then I saw it.

An unmistakably flat rear tyre on the driver's side.

How could I not have noticed it before? It must have happened the day before, on the way here from Kettlebridge... how could I have been so oblivious?

I swore. Not quite under my breath. Then there was the sound of throat-clearing somewhere nearby. Tony Everdene's face appeared over the hedge between our houses, peering at me as if I might be about to do something dangerous or unpredictable.

He said, 'Is everything all right? I'm sorry to intrude, but I couldn't help overhearing you just now. It sounded as if you might be having a spot of bother.'

'Oh, it's nothing too serious,' I said. 'Just a flat tyre.' I tried to smile as if I could very easily take this kind of thing in my stride. 'It's just really bad timing. There's something I need to do in Kettlebridge first thing, and now I'm going to have to call someone out and it'll probably take forever.'

'Well, I'm afraid I'm not particularly handy when it comes to fixing flat tyres myself, but I can certainly offer you a lift. I'm just about to head that over that way myself. I can drop you off in town if you like.'

I hesitated. He didn't look as if he was dressed for work. But then, maybe even solicitors didn't wear suits these days.

'Sure,' I said. 'I'd love to have a lift, thank you.'

I went out through the pedestrian gate and approached Tony's house for a second time. He opened the passenger door of the big family estate car and I climbed in and slid it shut. He got into the driver's seat next to me and suddenly we were very close, closer than we had been since we'd kissed.

Had that really happened? It seemed so unlike the kind of thing I would ever normally do…

But it had. And I had recoiled. *Visceral response*, he'd said. Did I owe him an explanation? Was that what he was thinking as I sat here next to him?

How very cosy, Rob might have said. *But are you really sure this is a good idea? You're not, are you? You know there's something fishy about him. But you're all for just ploughing on regardless, aren't you?*

Tony said, 'So how was your first night in your new home?'

'Oh. Fine, thanks. Though I'm not sure it's home, really. But a new place, I guess.'

Would he have noticed that I'd had a visitor? I decided not to mention Mum. How could I when I didn't want to think about why she'd come, and how Molly had rebuffed me? Instead I said, 'I guess your daughters are going straight to school with their friend, are they?'

'What? Oh, yes. Yes, they are. Your daughter's back from her trip soon, isn't she?'

'She is.'

'Will she be coming back here? I'm sure the twins would love to meet her.'

I hesitated. 'I don't really know what's going to happen, to be honest with you.'

'I'm sorry,' Tony said. 'I don't mean to pry. By the way, you need to put your seatbelt on.'

'Oh yes, of course.'

I strapped myself in and he reversed out of his driveway into the road, then set off along the lane and turned onto the main road that would take us back to Kettlebridge.

The woods began to thin out and then we were heading between open fields. It was quiet and hazy. I remembered coming this way with Rob the day before, and how disorientating it had been. If anything, I was further from finding my bearings now than I had been then.

'Here's an idea,' Tony said. 'Let's play a game. Ask me a question and I'll answer, and then you can answer it too. Then I'll ask you something, and we'll go through the same routine. If one of us chooses not to answer, the other has won. How does that sound?'

'Fine by me,' I said. It might seem odd if I refused. Or was it odd to agree? I seemed to have lost my compass for how to behave.

'OK. You start, then. It can be as nosy or as abstract as you like, but remember, you have to answer it too.'

What did I want to know about him? What was I willing to tell him about myself? I said, 'You're a solicitor. Have you ever knowingly broken the law?'

'"Knowingly" is an interesting choice of word,' he said. 'Not knowing you've broken the law is no defence, by the way. But anyway, I might have taken one or two illegal substances once in a while, back when I was a student. It's no defence to say that pretty much everyone I knew did the same, and I'm not the only one who went on to become a lawyer. There, that's my confession. You?'

'Never. Neither knowingly nor deliberately.'

'Good,' Tony said. 'You'd have put me in an awkward position, from a professional point of view, if you'd confessed an actual crime.'

'Why, would you have reported me for it?'

'I suppose it would depend what it was. I would have encouraged you to report it yourself first, of course. Anyway, now it's my turn. Have you ever made a promise you didn't keep? I mean a really important promise. One with the power to make a big difference to someone else.'

I could just lie. It wouldn't matter. He probably wouldn't be able to tell. He might not ever find out.

'Interesting choice of question,' I said.

'That's not an answer,' Tony observed.

I stared straight ahead. Kettlebridge would come into view any minute now. We were nearly there. What did it matter if I played along or not?

'My answer to that is yes,' I said.

'Is that it?'

'I just told you I once broke a promise. That's it. You never said I had to give details.'

'I'm not sure that's within the spirit of the rules.'

'Then I think the game is over,' I said.

Tony sighed and reached out to turn on the radio, and the sound of a violin concerto filled the car.

All the rest of the way I thought about the promise I'd broken. I had said I would tell the truth when the right time came. But then the time never came, and I didn't go looking for it. And so we had carried on living a lie, right up until the point when Chloe had come along and turned Rob against me, and threatened to wreck everything I had done my utmost to protect.

One advantage of having lived, until very recently, in the same small town as my husband's mistress was that I knew exactly what her daily routine was. We taught in different schools, but they were less than a mile apart. Every Monday to Wednesday morning our paths crossed as we walked to work, me on my way from Fairfield Road, her coming from her flat near the town centre. I was part-time, she was full-time, and as I didn't work Fridays, we wouldn't normally have coincided today. But as long as she'd spent the night at her flat as usual, I was in with a good chance of catching her. She wouldn't half be surprised when I did.

I'd never mentioned bumping into Chloe to Rob. Before I'd found them in our bed together, it hadn't seemed particularly noteworthy – back then she was just the maths tutor I'd hired for Georgie who happened to be a newly qualified teacher at one of the neighbourhood schools. Rob had let her into the house a couple of times and knew her to say hello to, but that was it. Or so I had thought.

It was a gamble. If I was wrong – if Rob gave her a lift, or if she'd gone back to Fairfield Road – I would miss her. But I was pretty sure I wouldn't. She and Rob must have been in the habit of meeting at her flat. It was probably a kind of comfort zone for the pair of them. Otherwise I'd have caught them out before.

I had told Tony that I had broken a promise. And I had, and I hated myself for it. But what about all the promises that Rob had broken? He hadn't shown so much as a flicker of regret or guilt or doubt. So much for his marriage vows… He'd obviously decided they were expendable, and I was too…

Tony and I had said an awkward goodbye over the plaintive melody of the violin concerto he'd put on after our conversation dried up, having failed to find anything else to say to each other after I'd opted out of the little game he had suggested. He had dropped me off at the side of one of the main roads into town before pulling back out into the early morning traffic, which wasn't too bad as yet but would soon begin to build towards the chaos of cars, bikes and schoolchildren that marked the beginning of the school day.

Chloe, like me, preferred to make an early start so she could arrive well before her students. If anything, she was even more

punctual than I was. If I was ever running even five minutes late,
I wouldn't see her.

She ran like clockwork – maybe that was something else Rob
liked about her. She'd come round every Saturday morning on the
dot of ten to teach Georgie algebra and geometry at the dining
room table, and she'd smiled sweetly and carried on as if butter
wouldn't melt in her mouth, and all the time – for how long? – she'd
been sleeping with Rob on the sly. But perhaps she hadn't wanted
to arouse my suspicions. Perhaps she had been tormented inside,
even if she'd looked perfectly well and rather pleased with herself.
Or perhaps she was so in love with Rob that nothing else mattered.

At least I knew she was a creature of habit. That was useful.
From everything I knew about her she was, in the main, a quiet,
conscientious, steady sort of young woman, who worked hard and
turned up on time. The kind who, usually speaking, preferred a
quiet life. Not someone who'd be the life and soul of the party, or
who would have got through lots of boyfriends and see Rob as just
another kind of experience to share with her friends. He'd chosen
well from that point of view: she'd be likely to be discreet.

For a man who claimed not to have a lot of time for teachers, Rob
certainly seemed to have an awful lot to do with them in his personal
life. First the wife, then the mistress. Or was that even part of the
attraction – that Chloe in some way reminded him of a younger, less
compromised version of me? Did she even know how disparaging he
sometimes was about our shared profession? Had he ever said to her,
'Those who can, do – those who can't, teach?' I was willing to bet he
hadn't. But he'd said it plenty of times to me. Sometimes being married
to him had been like doing one-to-one lessons with a recalcitrant
teenager – the type who is determined to get a rise out of you.

Chloe wasn't the type you'd expect to have an affair with a married
man – she didn't seem in the least like a scarlet woman – but maybe
that was why she was exactly the type who would. After all, I had
been quiet and steady and conscientious too, once upon a time.

If Rob had turned my head, it wasn't so hard to understand how he could have turned hers. Inside every quiet girl was a passionate romantic trying to get out…

I could almost foresee the glimmering of a possibility that one day I might feel sorry for her. If Rob had brought out and indulged her inner wild girl, the chances were that eventually he would also crush it, however little he intended to. After all, he'd crushed me. And I had let him. Perhaps, in the end, I had felt safer that way. Maybe I believed it was what I deserved.

If he really did move her into Fairfield Road as his live-in girlfriend, it wouldn't be long before he started expecting her to know which dry cleaner to use, and to warn him if the town centre was going to be closed to traffic on a Saturday morning. Which was, actually, some kind of very small, mean, hollow satisfaction. What an old witch I had turned into, imagining the future of the lovers and cackling, 'It'll never last…'

Would I bump into them? Together? Separately? In the supermarket, the town centre, out walking? It seemed inevitable that I would.

Would I learn to grin and bear it? How could I? How could either of them expect me to?

People would know. Our neighbours, my students, their parents. Everybody would know. Georgie would know…

Apart from a few dog walkers and a couple of children making their way into school in time for breakfast club, there was next to nobody around. I crossed the green where a medieval manor house had once stood, its ruins long since demolished. Then I made my way into the narrow strip of old woodland that had been left undeveloped to either side of the stream that ran through the north of the town on its way to join the Thames.

I'd been here countless times before, often with Georgie, whether it was to come to the neighbouring playground or just for a stroll. The place was soaked in memories of her childhood, of times when it had just been the two of us, walking and talking, noticing things, pointing them out to each other. The thought of Rob wrestling all that from me, and installing another woman in my place, made me feel... it wasn't rational, and it wasn't fair, it wasn't even personal... it made me feel like someone who might be capable of doing things she really ought not to do.

The path through the little wood was tarmacked and lined with streetlamps, and flanked by the garden fences of people's houses along the best part of one side. It was a pretty tame wood, a baby wood, quite different to the wilderness on Fox Hill – you could glimpse rooftops through the trees all around. Various minor paths crisscrossed the undergrowth and lead to the stream, and there were a couple of crossing-points that people – probably kids – had made: old branches laid down that you could walk across when the water was shallow, or piled-up rocks that could serve as stepping-stones.

You would assume it was safe. As safe as anywhere. Or at least, that was what Chloe would think as she hurried to work, wanting to believe Rob's bland assurances that I had now been dealt with and she had nothing more to fear from me.

To my right, the garden fences gave way to an open field that was used for football matches and the playground I'd often taken Georgie to, until she outgrew it. On my left the trees were thinning out. Then I came to a bridge over the stream and the path that Chloe – if I knew anything at all about her – would be heading towards any minute now.

I didn't want to give her the chance to duck away and avoid me, so I walked right to the end of the path. To my right was the stream, with an overgrown coppice beyond it. To the left was a grass verge planted with trees, with a fence on the far side, running parallel to the path, marking the boundary of gardens of the neighbouring flats. Once you were on the path, there was nowhere to escape. It was as good a spot as any for an ambush.

The path led to a turning circle that was at the end of a quiet residential road, with the stream running on behind a block of garages. I'd be able to loiter to one side here, out of sight, and pounce on her. She wouldn't know what was coming until it was too late.

I settled down to wait next to the low wall that ran along one side of the turning circle, in an overgrown spot partly concealed by two tall elder trees festooned with ivy. Sometimes I'd seen teenagers lurking here, smoking and exchanging gossip, but it was presumably too early for them to congregate and there was no one else around. There might be passers-by, possibly people I knew at least by sight or well enough to acknowledge, but none of them would think anything of me being here. They'd assume, correctly as it happened, that I was waiting for someone.

A helmetless kid cycled past, followed by an elderly lady with a little dog, who recognised me and looked as if she would have quite liked to stop and exchange the time of day but was pulled away by her impatient pet. And then I saw Chloe, walking along the path the way I had just come.

She didn't look at all like a marriage wrecker. She looked like a nice, sweet, young, possibly silly girl – as most women surely are once upon a time – walking along a path by a stream in the dappled shade of the overhanging trees on a summer morning that wasn't yet sunny but might become so. She certainly didn't look like someone any reasonable person might wish to do actual bodily harm to. Which was pretty much what I had attempted the day before.

I had to try to talk to her... even though she almost certainly wouldn't want to speak to me. I had a question for her, and she was the only person who was in a position to answer it.

My heart was in my mouth. I drew back as if I could vanish into the shade of the elder trees, or maybe just let her go past in peace and not accuse her or attack her or anything.

She looked so innocent. And in the end, what had she been guilty of, other than wanting something that was out of reach? I knew all about that... and about the kinds of distortions and accommodations you could find yourself making after you'd got what you'd set your heart on.

Now she was close enough to call out to, but she still hadn't seen me. Maybe she wouldn't recognise me. That happened sometimes, when you saw people out of context. I felt pretty far removed from Mrs Castle of Fairfield Road, who had paid Chloe for maths lessons in blocks of ten and always made her tea in the same mug, with little kittens on it, when she came round on a Saturday morning.

And she was no longer Chloe the likeable maths tutor, either.

I don't know which happened first: her finally seeing me, or me calling out her name. She froze in the centre of the turning circle, and I stepped forward out of the shadows and walked towards her.

Chapter Thirteen

She looked shiftily from side to side. Perhaps she was hoping to spot someone she could call on for help. But there was no one.

'Morning, Chloe,' I said pleasantly. 'I was hoping I'd find you here. I just have one question for you, and after that I'll leave you alone.'

'I don't think I can tell you anything,' she said, folding her arms. 'I know you and Rob have some difficult things to sort out. But that's nothing to do with me and it wouldn't be right for me to get involved.'

'But you *are* involved. You could hardly be *more* involved. You can't get out of it that easily. And you certainly can't get out of it in the morning and back into it at night. It's an affair, not a pair of pyjamas.'

Chloe bit her lip. She was wearing an Alice band – an actual Alice band! – and a white blouse with a Peter Pan collar and a cotton skirt that was striped red, white and pink, like the dress that Milly-Molly-Mandy had worn in the books that my sister had liked to have read to her when she was a kid, especially because she shared a name with the heroine. Chloe was literally wearing a hat-trick of references to children's books. You'd have assumed she was a primary school teacher rather than someone who was going to spend most of the day ahead telling misbehaving teens to be quiet and pay attention.

I was still angry with her, but standing here like this, at such close quarters to her – to the woman my husband had chosen over me – had the unexpected effect of making me even angrier with *him*.

The old fool... I never would have thought I would think of Rob that way, that dispassionately, but really... He must have promised her the moon – but did he even believe himself that he meant to try to deliver it?

'I don't think Rob would be very happy if he knew you were doing this,' Chloe told me.

She said his name as if it had magical properties – as if he was a genie she could summon, and who was about to suddenly appear and swagger nonchalantly towards us to rescue her. Her hand went to her necklace, which had her name picked out in gold, and I knew at once that he must have bought it for her.

I'd have expected him to think that name necklaces were tacky. But maybe she'd asked for it. Maybe, because it was still early days, still the honeymoon period of their romance, he thought anything she wanted was charming and adorable. Maybe, even if he did privately think it was tacky, he wouldn't have dreamed of saying so to her, would instead just have allowed himself to enjoy her taking pleasure in it...

Name necklaces were a thing because of Carrie Bradshaw in *Sex and the City*. Chloe probably thought of Rob as her own personal Mr Big, who had begun the process of extricating himself from his unhappy marriage and was now about to become her joyous ever after.

And what did that make me? The wrong wife. The mistake. The one who you might sympathise with a little but who was a loser in the end, who was just there to be envied, betrayed, discarded and written out. If Chloe had ever felt guilty about what she'd done, she hadn't felt guilty enough to stop.

'As Rob isn't here, I guess it doesn't matter too much one way or the other what he might think,' I said.

'This is harassment,' Chloe said. 'I need to get to work. And you need to leave me alone.'

'Just one question,' I said. 'More a word of warning, really. Knowing my husband as I do, I think it's something you might want to be aware of. I remember what you told me about your baby nephew, how much you enjoyed spending time with him. And then there was that time you said you thought maybe you should've trained to work with little kids rather than older children. I remember it because I saw the look on your face and I recognised it, and I think I know what it meant. So that's why I'm asking you if you've ever thought that you might want children of your own one day. No, it's all right, I don't expect you to tell me. I think I can guess the answer, anyway. But if you're really serious about Rob, you might want to discuss it with him. It's always good to be clear about what you're getting into, don't you think? Because what you're going to find is that he's dead set against it. Of course, you might be absolutely happy with that. But if not, well… perhaps the two of you don't have quite as much of a future as you might like to think.'

She frowned as if I'd said something embarrassingly wrong. Not quite the reaction I'd expected. It didn't seem as if I'd touched a nerve.

'Look, between you and me, he never really wanted kids. He made that plain right from our very first date,' I said. 'He came round to the idea of having Georgie once we knew she was on the way, and he adores her now, obviously, but he's always been absolutely adamant that one is enough. I am the mother of his child. His only child. And I'm afraid that however he feels about you – or whatever he's told you he feels about you – that isn't going to change.'

She raised her eyebrows, pursed her lips and gave her head a little shake, like someone about to ask for the manager to make a complaint. 'This is really none of your business. Now please, let me pass.'

'You've made it my business. I don't know how much time the two of you have actually spent talking, but how well do you think you really know him? Has he told you about his family, for example? Have you asked him about that? Because it seems to me that things between the two of you must have moved pretty fast. You might want to slow down and take a look around before you get into something it might not be easy to get out of.'

'I think *you* need to talk to him,' Chloe said. 'You're meant to be meeting him later, anyway, aren't you? Perhaps after that.' She smiled at me as if she was willing to try to be reasonable. 'Look, I know things are bound to be difficult between us now, but maybe they won't always be. I always really enjoyed teaching Georgie. I'm sorry not to be able to carry on, but I'm glad I had the chance to get to know her. I'll send you a cheque to refund you for the rest of the lessons you'd paid for in advance.'

'Don't,' I said. 'I won't cash it.'

'It's money I owe you,' Chloe said.

'You owe me a lot more than that. And don't you dare talk to me about Georgie like that. As if you weren't… getting up to things with her father all the time you were coming round the house making out you just wanted to help her.'

Chloe's eyes flashed. Touchy. People never liked being reminded about what they'd done wrong.

'Get out of my way,' she said.

She moved to step round me, but I blocked her.

'I haven't finished with you yet,' I said.

She let out a groan of frustrated rage, like a stroppy child told for the umpteenth time to do something she really doesn't want to do.

'Just leave me alone, Stella,' she said.

She raised her hands as if to ward me off or perhaps shove me out of the way. Then, in a light, instinctive, protective gesture, she folded both her arms across her body.

And that was when I saw it. It was just so obvious… once you knew.

The tender way he'd spoken to her. The bluntness and haste with which he'd cast me out. The way she was standing her ground, so sure of herself and of him and the new life they were going to create together. Because the new life was already there, in secret. That was why sweet little Chloe was being so staunch and so ruthless.

And that was why I was really here. Not to tell Chloe a few home truths. It was too late for that. I was here to find out what else she and Rob had been keeping from me.

The air rushed out of me as if I'd been winded. The scene in front of me began to blur: Chloe, the trees, the rushing stream. The turning circle seemed to be spinning under my feet.

I said, 'You're having his baby. Aren't you?'

It didn't sound like an accusation, or a reproach. It sounded almost admiring, as if I had found it in me to pay her tribute from the depths of defeat.

I could see her toying with the idea of denying it. She and Rob must have agreed that no one could know. At least not yet. But she wasn't afraid of what he might say if she went ahead and told me I was right. Obviously she didn't know him that well yet. Not well enough to be apprehensive about how he'd react if she didn't try to stick to what they'd planned.

She couldn't have seen the side of him that he usually took good care to keep hidden. And maybe she never would. Maybe that wasn't him. Maybe he had only been like that because of me…

Her eyes met mine. She looked much more proud than sorry.

'He's happy about it, then,' I said.

She gave me a rueful smile. 'We both are,' she said.

They were both happy and they both wanted this baby. There it was, and there was nothing I could do about it. She was absolutely sure that she had him, and she saw a future with him. I was just a bit of unpleasantness that had to be got through first.

Yes, she felt bad for me, a little, but that didn't change anything. It made about as much difference as a hanging judge briefly wondering what it would feel like to be a condemned man walking towards the scaffold. And then delivering his sentence.

'It's very early days,' Chloe went on. 'Hardly anybody else knows yet. So I'd appreciate it if you'd keep it to yourself.'

A first-time mother-to-be… Of course she would think nothing else really mattered. It was only natural.

'Chloe… how far gone are you?'

'Not three months yet. I only found out a couple of weeks ago.'

'Congratulations.'

It came out as a whisper. Not menacing. Just weak. If only I didn't feel as if I was about to lose my balance and fall, the way I'd done outside the house in Fox Hill…

I drew breath and tried to compose myself. My surroundings came back into focus. I managed to say, a little more loudly, 'I'm sorry for what I did yesterday. When I smashed the windscreen. I must have frightened you. I never would have done anything like that if I had known.'

She grimaced. 'That's no excuse. I'm telling you, Stella, you need to stay away from me from now on. Otherwise Rob's really going to give you something to be sorry for. If you want to carry on seeing Georgie, I suggest you get a grip and learn to be grateful for what you've got.'

With that she moved round me and walked briskly on. I didn't try to stop her. I knew she was right. I'd been willing to tackle Chloe, but I couldn't fight a baby. Especially not a baby that Rob actually wanted.

I turned to watch her go. She was a neat, dignified figure in her striped skirt and summer blouse, making her way purposefully onto the road and out of sight.

A mother who was approaching with a little girl in a gingham dress gave me a nervous look, the way you do when you are out with your child and see an adult who you aren't too sure about, and decide to give a wide berth. I had no idea how much she would have heard, or how much any passers-by might have picked up. I had been oblivious. But maybe it was just the expression on my face that scared her.

I wasn't angry any more. Not with Rob, not with Chloe, and not with their baby, who was as blameless as it was possible to be. All I wanted to do was burst into tears. I could feel my face contorting with the effort not to give into the childish urge to start bawling.

All that sweetness, all that love… the new baby, who would look a little bit like him and a little bit like her… that new life. Someone else had given Rob the gift he had always maintained he never wanted. And he wanted it now, even though he had declared from the start that he had no intention of trying to give it to me.

Chapter Fourteen

Sixteen years earlier

The *Brickley Mail* didn't include a photo of the wreck of Dad's taxi with its report on the inquest, the way it sometimes did after a crash. I never knew whether that was out of consideration for me, given that I'd worked there not so very long ago, or just because the editor thought the other images they had would work better. But anyway, I was grateful for it.

The byline on the news story was Jan Flashman. My old colleague still hadn't made it to Fleet Street. I'd been conscious of her, on and off, in the public gallery at the inquest, pale and serious, listening intently and scribbling in her notebook. But mainly I had been aware of Rob sitting next to me, calm and composed in his dark suit. Him being there was what had got me through it. He was the only person there I could reach out and touch, and he was the only one who seemed real.

I'd lost so much... Dad, my health, my strength. Confidence, not just in myself but in my body and my future...

In my nightmares, the consultant told me I might never have a child of my own. That wasn't quite what he'd said, but I had been told that the damage that had been done to my Fallopian tubes in the accident meant it was very unlikely I would conceive naturally. I hadn't realised that the idea of being able to do something, of potential, could matter so much, and yet that you might only realise how much it mattered when it was taken away.

Before the accident, I'd been more concerned about *not* getting pregnant... I had never really thought that hard about having children, or wanting them. On the whole, it just seemed like something other people did. Older, settled people, who had money and houses that weren't wrecks they'd bought to do up. If people my age had babies it was usually unplanned, like that girl from school Rob and I had bumped into on our first date.

And yet now I noticed pregnant women, women with pushchairs and prams and toddlers, everywhere I went, and it always cost me the same dull pang that was composed of a mixture of sadness and anger and longing. Almost like a kind of love that might never find somewhere to go, or be returned.

I felt scarred and broken and wrecked and doomed, and I hated myself for having survived when Dad had died. At the same time I was passionately, guiltily grateful for still being alive. Life was precious. I had always known that in theory, but now I really believed it. And yet I knew how frail it was, too. I knew it could stop at any moment – it could be yanked away from you or anyone you loved in the time it took for a deer to step out onto the road.

I was numb and haunted and afraid of almost everything. At the same time, I somehow kept going – I got up in the morning and got moving, I was polite and considerate to people, I kept myself presentable. I tried my best because I knew it was what was expected of me. I had to be someone who coped – I'd been that person when Mum left, and I clung to behaving like that person still.

The only person I could safely lean on, who didn't need me to be strong, was Rob.

My sister hadn't come to the inquest. Too upset, and anyway, she was only sixteen. Mum and Lee were no-shows too. Mum hadn't even come to Dad's funeral. Still, they had invited me and Rob to stay for the duration of the inquest, and had put us up in the second and smaller of their two spare rooms. The other was Molly's now. That had been settled before I had even got out of hospital, before I'd even got so far as putting it to Rob that maybe she could come and live with us.

I was obviously in no fit state, anyway. I had expected Lee to be unenthusiastic about taking Molly in – I'd even been prepared to be angry with him about his attitude. It would have been a relief to lose my temper with someone. But whatever his thoughts on the subject were, he had managed to keep them to himself. It seemed that in the aftermath of a tragedy, even Lee was capable of putting his usual bluntness and sarcasm aside.

Tragedy. That was what the newspaper called it. *Daughter survives tragic crash after dad swerves to avoid deer.* I knew Jan Flashman wouldn't have come up with the headline. One of the sub-editors would have done that. It was odd to think of Jan going back to the office after the inquest to sit opposite the desk that had once been mine, consulting her notes, hammering away at her typewriter and pausing to fiddle with her split ends when she got stuck, the way she always had done. People might have interrupted her to ask *How was it?* and she would have answered them briefly and tersely, and they would have backed off. She'd have wanted to get on.

I was grateful for her focus now. I knew she would have taken it seriously. It was a comfort, in a way, to think of someone else dwelling on what had happened, puzzling over it, being absorbed by it the way I had been for so many months. Even if, in Jan's case, she would have been preoccupied for it only for as long as it took her to write her report. And then she would have moved on to something else.

I was mentioned by name:

Mr Cooper's daughter Stella, 24, was seriously injured but has since made a good recovery. Miss Cooper, who now lives near Bristol, was formerly a reporter on this newspaper and was visiting Mr Cooper to celebrate her birthday when the fatal crash happened. Mr Cooper, who had worked as a taxi driver for many years, was taking his daughter back to his home in Brickley after a day trip to Grovewell Park in Oxfordshire.

Jan had found an expert on road safety to give her a quote about the dangers of wild animals, who had warned that even experienced drivers could be caught unawares. I was quoted too, thanking the passing driver who had stopped to call the emergency services and paying tribute to my dad. There was no mention of my sister. As it wasn't a formal obituary, the story didn't end with a list of names of other close relatives who Dad had been survived by. So there had been no dilemma about whether or not Mum should be named and included. Instead, the final line was a comment from the coroner, passing on his condolences to the family after the tragic end to what should have been a happy day out.

The day out had been my idea and I'd suggested it because I'd felt guilty about having moved away to be with Rob. Still, the coroner wasn't to know that...

It was so rare for me to spend any time alone with Dad, or to see him outside of the house... to go out anywhere. Molly had been at school. It had seemed like the ideal opportunity. And it had been good, even though we didn't quite know what to say to each other... though that didn't seem to matter. You don't necessarily have to talk when you're walking through beautiful gardens with someone. As we got into the car to come back, I had even said that we'd have to do it again sometime...

That had turned out to be the very last thing I'd ever said to him.

Alongside Jan's report, the newspaper printed a shot of the woodland along the stretch of road where the accident had happened. Next to it was a picture of Dad, which I'd provided them with. He was dressed up in a shirt and tie, looking a bit hot and uncomfortable and smiling nervously. They'd cropped out the other half of the photo, which had Mum in it, wearing an off-the-shoulder magenta top and matching lipstick.

I didn't have that many pictures of him – he'd always been very camera-shy. I'd taken this one a few years before Mum had left, on one of the occasions when she'd nagged him into taking her out for dinner. I had no idea if she'd see it, or remember. Or what, if anything, she would feel if she did. Anyway, I liked it. It summed up how I thought of him. He looked mild-mannered and put-upon, and as if he didn't quite know what was going to hit him next but expected that something would.

Tragic crash. It was a sad story, the kind that is intended to make newspaper readers shudder and count their blessings. I'd written up similar stories for the paper myself, and talked about them with whoever was around, at the water cooler or on the way out of the building at home time. *Makes you think, doesn't it? It could happen to anyone.*

But it hadn't happened to anyone. It had happened to us.

Physically, I had been told I had made a good recovery. I had a metal pin in my elbow and scars on my belly from surgery and broken glass. Six months had passed between the accident and the inquest and the scars had barely begun to fade. I still hadn't let Rob see them. He could hold my hand, he could hug me, but in bed at night I recoiled from him and turned away. Once or twice he had asked when I thought I might be ready and I had not been able to answer him.

I wouldn't have expected Rob to be so patient. After all, this was not what he'd signed up for. He'd wanted a lover and a companion, not an invalid to look after. And he'd been so good. He'd spent hours in the hospital at my bedside, and when I was discharged he'd been there to take me home. He'd been there for me when I was sorting out the funeral, and at my side during the ceremony itself. He'd helped me and Molly go through Dad's stuff, pick out what each of us wanted to keep and dispose of the rest. He'd even organised someone to clean the place before I said goodbye to it for the last time and handed the keys back to the landlord.

And then there were all the hours he'd spent driving me to and fro between Brickley and the West Country… I still hadn't got back behind the wheel. I couldn't imagine that I ever would.

I knew I couldn't expect him to wait for me forever. But still, I couldn't bring myself to give him the body I couldn't get used to myself, and that I shied away from looking at in the mirror. And so we had gone on living on borrowed time, with Rob being there for me and me pushing him away.

I read the newspaper cutting about the inquest sitting at the cheap kitchen table we'd bought when we'd moved into our new house in a village near Bristol, just before the accident. The house was Rob's second purchase and to start with it had been in an even worse state than the first. I hadn't been able to help much and looking after me had slowed Rob down, but he hadn't complained. It now had a watertight roof and the wiring had been redone, but the kitchen extension was still just a plan on paper, the garden was a wreck and every single room needed work.

Rob poured out coffee and put a mug next to me, then went upstairs. I turned to the letter Molly had enclosed with the newspaper cutting. It was written in purple ink in large, careful handwriting. *I think this is what you wanted. I hope you are feeling better. We're all looking forward to seeing you at Christmas.* It was a very short note but I got the feeling she'd written it out several times and didn't know what to say. That was one of the things Dad's death had done to us: it had left us at a loss for words.

Anyway, she seemed to be all right. Maybe even better than all right. She'd settled, she was managing to be happy. She'd just finished her first term at the sixth-form college in Ashdale and had told me she liked it there. Mum said she had a boyfriend, though she hadn't brought him home yet.

For her, life was moving on and opening up. Which was right and healthy. She couldn't be expected to be sad all the time. She wasn't damaged or scarred like me. She wasn't stuck like me. There were no constraints on her future. Surely all of that meant I didn't have to worry about her any more. She was Mum's responsibility now. Sometimes, in my more grudging moods, I thought that was how it should have been all along. And I seemed to be incapable of summoning up the energy to worry about her anyway.

I put the letter and the newspaper cutting back in the envelope and Rob came closer and dropped something on the kitchen table. A paper wallet. I opened it and saw airline tickets inside.

'They're flights to the Canary Islands,' he said, sitting down on the chair next to me. 'I thought it might be a good time to talk about going away. How about it? I hope you're not going to say no to Fuerteventura in January.'

Just for a fraction of a second, I felt angry with him. Could we really afford it? Why hadn't he asked me first? And then, if we'd agreed on going away, why couldn't I have helped him choose where? Because yes, the sunshine would be lovely, but what was I going to pack for the beach? There was no way I could wear a bikini now...

But I'd never have been able to figure out where to go, let alone deal with the travel agent and find the best price and book it. It was as much as I could do to cope with getting up and getting dressed each day and keeping daily life ticking over. It was astonishing how shopping and cooking and keeping on top of the housework seemed to use up all the time I had.

He'd taken the decision out of my hands and had picked somewhere and we were going. Maybe it would be far enough away to leave behind everything I wanted to forget.

I was suddenly overwhelmed with gratitude. I flung my arms around him and began to cry.

'I have to say that's not quite the reaction I expected,' he said, withdrawing slightly. 'I hoped you'd be pleased.'

'I am,' I said, and then I kissed him. For a moment he seemed to be unsure about whether to break off or not. Then he kissed me back, and I began to think that perhaps everything would be all right.

*

By the time we flew out to the Canary Islands we were lovers again.

We had an apartment to ourselves in the hotel. The floor was tiled red, the walls were white and the sun streamed in. The centrepiece was an enormous bed. Otherwise it was sparsely furnished and impeccably clean. There were no distractions, no worries. Nothing to focus on but us. It was like living inside a pleasant dream, but I couldn't help but feel that it was some kind of test for the two of us. That made me uneasy, because I couldn't tell for sure whether we were making the grade or not. Or maybe it was Rob who was testing me in some way, and I would only find out the outcome once we left.

Inside or out, we were surrounded by space. There were sand dunes stretching from our windows to the horizon and we walked on volcanic beaches where the sea broke on black rocks. After sundown the sea was black too and the sky was clear and starry, but it was still mild when we strolled down to the village in the evening and wandered round the steep cobbled streets and white square buildings that overlooked the cove.

The days of the holiday passed in a blur of blue skies and balmy air. It was strange to feel the sunshine on my arms and legs and face, the parts of my skin that I was willing to expose. So luxurious it seemed too good to be true, and I couldn't quite believe I deserved such cosseting. I was dazzled. It was as if I'd been rescued. As if Rob and the sun had brought me back to life.

We were as close as we had ever been, and as tender. And yet I couldn't help feeling that he was still waiting for something.

On the very last morning, I woke up to find him propped up on his elbow and looking down at me.

'You're beautiful when you're asleep,' he said.

I pulled a face. 'What, not other times?'

'Of course other times,' he said seriously. His hand wandered down to the hem of my vest and crept upwards to caress the scars on my belly. 'You know, I've been thinking about us, and about the future. You're everything I could ever want. Everything I need. You're perfect.'

I could almost hear what he was thinking but not saying. *You probably can't have children and I don't want them. Yes, you're perfect. For me.*

He moved his hand to my hair and brushed a strand out of my face. 'When I heard about the accident I was terrified I'd lose you. I never want to feel like that again. You know I'm not a believer, but I prayed for you to come back to me. And now you have.'

Only two people – Rob and Mum – knew what the consultant had told me after the crash about the likely impact on my fertility. Rob and I had never explicitly discussed it. He had said only that he was sorry and that I should concentrate on getting better. I was grateful to him for recognising it wasn't something I wanted to talk about, and for leaving well enough alone, and that had become part of the gratitude I felt for him all the time, mixed with disbelief that he had actually decided to stick by me when so many other men surely would have decided to turn tail and flee.

Mum's reaction had been more brusque. 'Well, it's not the end of the world, however it turns out. You could save yourself a load of bother. It seems to me the big question is how Rob feels about it. If he's not fussed, the two of you could have a very nice life together without having kids. And I don't think you have too much to worry about, because he's clearly devoted to you. I can't imagine it'll make that much difference to him.'

I had not been sure this was true. I was afraid it might not be, and I was afraid it might be, too. Because what if I *did* decide I wanted to have children one day, and to explore the options that were open to me? Or what if I decided that I was content to live my life with Rob and without children, but Rob changed his mind – and set his sights on someone who didn't come with the difficulties I now presented, who could conceive his baby just like that?

I had learned to put all these thoughts aside so that I could concentrate on what it took to get me through from day to day. The one thing I was sure of was that I couldn't bear to lose Rob.

He said, 'I think we fit together pretty well, don't you?'

He seemed to expect an answer. I said, 'We do.'

'We should be together always. You and me, just like this. Just the two of us. We don't need anyone else. Do we?'

He was looking me straight in the eyes, as if seeking reassurance, or perhaps just so he could be sure I meant what I said.

I shook my head. 'We don't,' I said. 'You're everything I want. You're everything I need.'

And then he asked me to marry him, and I said yes.

Chapter Fifteen

The meeting with the mediator was due to take place at eleven, so I had nearly three hours to kill between my confrontation with Chloe and whatever kind of ordeal was to follow. Plenty of time to brood. I spent it walking aimlessly round the riverside gardens that had been planted on the site of Kettlebridge's former abbey, of which literally nothing remained, although there was a Victorian folly – part of a roofless tower, a crumbling wall – that looked like an authentic ruin.

I couldn't begin to understand it. How could he have been so quick to want a baby with Chloe when he had been so profoundly reluctant to have one with me?

More than reluctant. He had been dead set against it. When we got back home from the holiday in the Canary Islands he had been even more explicit about it. Clarifying the terms of the deal, just to make sure.

You do know how I feel about children, don't you? You know I don't want them. I mean, I don't want them at all. I don't want to fiddle round with test tubes and all of that, and I don't want to bring up someone else's child.

Somewhere, some part of me had felt, briefly, crushed and resentful. He was giving it to me straight, and that was supposed to be a good thing, wasn't it? And yet, it seemed as if he was saying that what I wanted, and what I might want one day, didn't matter to him – or at least, not as much as having his own way on this. He was telling me, essentially, *Take it or leave it…*

I had tried, tentatively, to express how I felt. *But Rob... what if you feel differently in a couple of years' time? What if I do? The doctor said it would be difficult for me to conceive. But not impossible...*

I won't change my mind, he had said, and the way he looked at me made my blood run cold. *Have you changed yours? Because I'm not sure I can take this. You wavering like this, saying one thing one day and something else the next. Not when it's something so important.*

I'm sorry, I had said to him. *I was being silly. Like I said, you're all I want. Forgive me?*

Now, all these years and a daughter later, I was facing the loneliness and uncertainty I had been so afraid of. Life without Rob. And yet that was as nothing compared to the prospect of life without Georgie.

The lawns that stretched to the river were as pretty as a picture postcard, with brightly painted narrowboats chugging slowly by and tall poplars shading the children's paddling pool. A stream ran along the boundary of the grounds, and was busy with ducks squawking over bread thrown by passers-by. I'd come here often with Georgie for picnics or walks. We had been happy here. Rob hadn't often joined us, but on the rare occasions when he did, he'd seemed happy too...

Once we had her, he had learned to love her.

People could change. Even people like Rob, who was always so sure of himself and so adamant about his decisions. I knew that. He'd shown me that before. But I'd never expected him to use that capacity to change to fall in love with someone else, or to try to take Georgie away from me. Or to threaten to tell her the truth, which, given how she might react to discovering that we had deceived her, might very well turn out to be another way for me to lose her.

I bought a coffee from the kiosk by the paddling pool and sat on a bench by the riverside and watched the water sliding by.

It was hard to believe, but once this had been a scene of violence and destruction. The medieval townspeople had not been at all keen on the monks, unsurprisingly given that on one occasion some of them had been forced to dig up their dead, years after interment, and re-bury them, after paying the required fees, in abbey-approved graves. Eventually the townspeople's resentment reached such a pitch of outrage that a mob gathered at the abbey and burned it to the ground, forcing the monks to choose between the flames and the risk of drowning in the river.

There was a lesson for Rob. Rules lead to rage, and the powerful never seemed to know when they had gone too far. It was too late to tread gently when the fires had already been set. And it was never wise to put people in a position where they had nothing left to lose.

The peace was interrupted by a particularly irritating ringtone. Typical – even out here by the riverside, there was bound to be a mobile going off. Then I realised it was my new phone and scrabbled to answer it.

It was Rob.

'Hi. Good morning. You're up, then.'

It sounded as if Chloe hadn't spoken to him yet. Probably just as well. Presumably she was busy in classes and hadn't had a chance to call.

'Yeah. I'm up. What do you want?'

'Can you give the mediator's office a ring and tell them you're not coming to the meeting under duress?'

'But I *am* coming to the meeting under duress. Aren't I?'

There was a brief pause. I knew exactly what he was thinking: *just get her into the room, get the ball rolling. The sooner this is over, the better.* And also: *for Chloe's sake… the baby… I just have to get through this.*

When would the baby be due? Soon after Christmas? Georgie had arrived in the autumn…

'It's over, Stella. Can't we just agree to move forward with the minimum of disruption to everybody? Particularly Georgie?'

'I'll be there,' I said. 'Don't worry, I wouldn't miss it for the world. After all, we have a lot to talk about.'

'Stella…'

'What?'

'Are you OK? You sound… odd.'

'Of course I'm not OK. I haven't been OK for years. You know that. It was why you wanted to marry me,' I said, and ended the call.

The office of Kettlebridge Family Mediation was in a creaky old house off Gull Street, the traffic-clogged thoroughfare that ran east to west across the centre of town. At one time, the rule of the monks had held sway to the north of it, while the marshy land to the south had been a haven for gamblers, drunks, prostitutes and all other kinds of illicit behaviour. Gull Street had marked the limits of the law. It seemed as good a place as any for me and Rob to face up to the lines we'd crossed in our marriage, though they never did seem like lines once you were on the other side. Lines were supposed to be clear and easy to abide by, and they weren't meant to turn into traps.

Somehow, even though I'd been in town all morning, when it came to it I walked through the swing doors at the front of the office building five minutes late.

Which could only mean that part of me didn't want to do this at all. Didn't want to confront Rob, and was scared of what I might find out if I did.

Inside the office building there was a corridor stretching straight ahead and a door marked 'Reception' open to the left. It wasn't exactly top security… it seemed like an angry spouse would just be able to walk in off the street and cause mayhem, if he or she chose… but maybe the rooms where meetings took place were somewhere upstairs, behind locked doors. Or the building might be such a warren that you'd have run out of steam by the time you tracked down whoever it was you were angry with.

I went through to reception, which was completely empty. There wasn't even anybody at the desk in the corner, though there was a sheaf of A4 papers and a half-drunk cup of tea next to the keyboard. There were a few assorted uncomfortable-looking chairs and a large, framed art deco poster of the Riviera on the wall for anyone stuck waiting to look at, if they didn't fancy leafing through one of the tired-looking copies of *Homes & Gardens* sitting on the corner table next to the whirring standing fan.

If there was actually nobody here, wouldn't I be justified in just walking out again…?

I didn't sit down. Instead I hovered by the reception desk and tried to picture Georgie at the Whitelark Outdoor Education Centre, perhaps readying herself to swing forward on a zip wire strung between wooden towers, or climbing on hay bales. She'd been so lucky with the weather, which was bound to switch from sunshine to storms sooner or later. The whole thing could have been a washout. At least she'd be able to enjoy herself before coming home.

A stressed-looking middle-aged woman in standard office wear came through the doorway in the corner behind the desk and said, 'I'm so sorry – can I help you?'

'I think we must have spoken earlier. I'm Stella Castle, here to meet with my husband, Rob.' I attempted a smile. It felt all wrong. 'Well, he's still my husband for now.'

What was I doing? Was I really trying to make light of my own break-up in order to ingratiate myself with a stranger who wasn't having a particularly good morning? It was astonishing how powerful the instinct to play nice was.

'Ah… yes. Do take a seat, Mrs Castle. I'll let Jane know you're here.'

She sat down at the desk, pressed a switch on the phone and announced my arrival. I sat down too and stared up at the Riviera poster. It looked like heaven. The woman in a white dress looking down at the sun-soaked view, the old convertibles lined up at the roadside, the beach, the palm trees, the blue sea...

Holidays could be a lifesaver. I knew that. The question was, what did you do with your life when you got it back?

Rob had asked me not to book anything for this year, as he was so busy and really couldn't get away... He'd muttered something about seeing how things stood in July and then booking a sunshine break for October half-term. He probably hadn't wanted to be too far away from Chloe, and to miss out on whatever arrangement they had for seeing each other. And then he'd decided to get rid of me.

It suddenly hit me that Rob and I would never take Georgie on holiday together again. All of that... All that shared history, from the first bucket and spade to taking her to see the Mona Lisa... all gone.

I bowed my head and massaged my temples with my fingertips. My head felt as if the base of my neck was shooting rays of pain into my skull. I wasn't going to be able to do this – to face Rob, to challenge him, to make sense of everything.

To tell the truth...

'Mrs Castle? I'm Jane Herring, the mediator.'

I looked up and saw a woman with long, curly hair and large plastic-framed glasses that made her look slightly owlish. I could only hope she was wise. She had three little ladybird brooches pinned to the front of her lavender-coloured blouse, which seemed like a sign of quirkiness, but you could be quirky and wise, couldn't you? Or maybe she was genuinely eccentric, and Rob was in such a rush to get rid of me and shack up with Chloe that he'd gone and booked us an appointment with the battiest mediator in town.

'Do call me Stella,' I said, standing up and offering her my hand to shake.

Her touch was light and cool. I had to resist the urge to hold onto her tightly and pump her hand up and down to show I meant business. Like a man determined to be taken seriously. Was hers the kind of hand that could pull you up and out when you were under water, or drag you to safety when your life was going up in flames behind you? It didn't seem like it. It seemed like a hand that would discreetly push tissues in your direction and then, later on, present you with a surprisingly large bill.

Jane led me along the narrow corridor and up a flight of stairs to a meeting room and there was Rob, waiting, sitting at one side of a large round table (obviously chosen to facilitate non-combative discussions), with a wiped-clean whiteboard to one side of it in front of several shelves of books. The room had something of the atmosphere of a school library and the whiteboard made it look as if Jane was about to teach us a lesson, which perhaps she was. Judging by the rows of textbooks about law and child psychology and social work, it was going to be a sobering one.

Rob was casually dressed in an ironed shirt and chinos – he was one of those men who somehow looked as formal when he was dressed down as he did in a suit. He looked tired. But he didn't look worried. Not in the slightest. He looked hopeful, as if he'd seen the light at the end of the tunnel and was sure that he would get there.

'Don't stand up,' I said, though Rob had made no move to get to his feet. I gestured towards the chair on the other side of the table, facing the whiteboard. 'I take it I'm meant to sit here?'

'Certainly,' Jane said, 'if you feel comfortable with that.'

'Well, I wouldn't say comfortable exactly. No, comfortable is definitely not the word for how I feel about any of this.'

'Stella,' Rob said, 'would you just sit down?'

I sat. Jane took the chair nearest the whiteboard, crossed her legs and studied us both as if waiting for one of us to make a start.

Rob said, 'I mean, if we can't even sit down together, we're not going to get very far, are we?'

He'd addressed this to Jane, like a schoolkid appealing to Miss about something someone else had done wrong.

I said, 'Rob, I am in the room, you know. I don't think you have to talk through the mediator about absolutely everything. I mean, if we can't even talk to each other about sitting down, we're not going to get very far, are we?'

Jane's eyebrows went up. Rob looked down at his knees and his jaw muscles tightened fractionally. Jane wouldn't have noticed, but I knew he was holding his tongue. Which made a change.

'I'm sorry. I'll try not to be sarcastic,' I said to Jane. 'I know it's aggressive. Not a constructive way to enter a negotiation. It's just that it's been a rather challenging twenty-four hours. I mean, this time yesterday, I was getting dressed to go out for my fortieth birthday lunch with my husband. And since then I've found out rather a lot about him that I didn't know.'

I glanced at Rob and was pleased to see that he looked slightly unsettled. Jane cleared her throat and said, as if she wasn't quite sure whether it was a good idea, 'Go on?'

'Well, for starters, he told me he doesn't love me any more, doesn't want me and plans to divorce me. I also discovered that he plans to move me out of the marital home into a creepy little cottage in the middle of a wood. And he seems to be under the impression I'm going to let him hang onto our teenage daughter, though he has indicated that he's willing to let me have her at weekends, which I imagine would give him the chance to relax and recover from all that weekday parenting by spending quality time with his new girlfriend. Jane, you must see a lot of separating and divorcing couples, so you might be able to cast some light on this: was there ever any man of a certain age who ditched his wife for a woman who was actually older than her? I suppose there must be a few examples, but they're the exception that prove the rule, don't you think? Still, that's the power of love. Love is blind, especially when it comes to clichés.'

The room went quiet. Rob started jiggling his foot so his shoe tapped against the table leg, as small and irritating a sound as a dripping tap. I could just about make out the sound of the traffic in the street below and the faint hum of the air conditioning over the rasp of my breathing and the pounding rhythm of my blood. Was this the build-up to a panic attack? Or was it just heartbreak?

Jane said, 'I don't know if you had the chance to read any of the information about the service we offer here, Stella? I have plenty of spare copies of the leaflet if you'd like one to take home with you. Alternatively, if you have access to the internet, you'll find some useful information on our website.'

'Yeah, yeah, I read the leaflet. Rob left me a copy of it in the kitchen drawer of the house he wants me to have. I get it. You're the closest thing there is to DIY divorce. You're the fastest, cheapest way out of a marriage, as long as a couple can actually stand to be in the same room together. Which we can, can't we?' I gestured towards Rob, who was still staring down at his knees. 'I mean, look at us. Not quite the best of friends, but we're within arm's length of each other and we're not actually trying to kill each other. Not yet, anyway. But as I said, it has only been twenty-four hours. Give us time.'

Rob looked up. 'Are you going to let her get away with this?' he said to Jane.

'I never let anybody get away with anything,' Jane said. 'I can't. I'm not in a position to. I'm not a judge. You may yet find yourselves in front of one, but you are not there now.' She swung round and plucked a leaflet from the plastic magazine file standing at the end of the bookshelf behind her, then unfolded it and spread it out on the table in front of us. 'This might help us to focus,' she said. 'It's a very simple summary of what this process can achieve.'

I glanced down at the text, which was familiar from when I'd glanced at it the day before, though this time different words jumped out at me... *voluntary... confidential... impartial...* and then the list of bullet points about what mediation was not: *counselling... therapy... a chance to bully the other partner... reconciliation...*

'Well, it's not going to achieve anything if Stella hasn't come here in the right frame of mind,' Rob said. 'I can see that she's just here to make a mockery of the whole process.'

Jane adjusted her glasses and peered at us as if she wasn't at all convinced about what she was seeing. 'Mediation certainly has the best chance of success when both parties have had time to prepare emotionally and are ready and willing to take part,' she said.

'Then surely it's doomed to failure,' I said. 'Unless you split up a decade ago and have moved on so far you don't care any more.'

'I'm not going to wait a decade for a divorce,' Rob said. He still wouldn't look at me. 'Jane, I'm sorry. I can see that this is a mistake. I'm afraid I've been misled. Stella clearly isn't ready to embark on this process in this way.'

'But Stella is here,' Jane pointed out gently. 'Which must mean that she has something she wishes to say. Or hear.'

I stared at Rob and willed him to meet my eyes. But he just folded his arms and fixed his gaze on the whiteboard, as if waiting for class to begin.

I said, 'I suppose congratulations are in order.'

That got his attention. He turned to me and his mouth opened. He said, 'What?'

'I'm just a little bit confused. Perhaps you can help me understand. You always used to be so clear about it. You didn't want children. That changed when Georgie came along. But you didn't want any more, and I respected that. I understood it. I'm not complaining – I was happy with it too. But now you've met someone else and you're having a baby with her. It's a remarkable transformation, Rob. I've tried to figure it out. Could just be the march of time, of course. A change of attitudes. A case of the ticking clock. Maybe you're amazed at how easy it was, and it all just seems different this time round. Or maybe you love her more than you ever loved me. Anyway, I thought I'd ask. You see, it really is amazing what you can find out when you start talking.'

Jane Herring started to say something about how she could see we had things to discuss but felt it would be beneficial for us both to save them for a more appropriate forum. Rob cut across her: 'When did you talk to her?'

'This morning. On the path by the stream. She was on her way to work. I always see her there. Anyway, I was obviously going to find out sooner or later. Sooner's better, don't you think? At least I know a bit more about where you're coming from. That's an essential part of any negotiation. As you've always said yourself. You know what, Rob, we've been married long enough for me to think you could never really surprise me again. Turns out I had that wrong. I take my hat off to you. For my fortieth birthday you managed a blinder.'

'I'm afraid that if we're not going to be able to focus on a discussion I can support, it might be for the best if we drew this meeting to a close,' Jane said.

'Actually, we're just getting started,' Rob told her. He fixed me with his coldest stare. 'You're going to regret this, Stella. I told you to leave her alone.'

'Oh, come on. I think she quite enjoyed telling me, actually. She seemed pretty pleased with herself. Anyway, we're all family now, aren't we? Though maybe you haven't had a chance to think that through yet. There's the issue of how it might affect our daughter, for example. But that can wait for another day, can't it? Or at least, I guess that's what you thought.'

'I'm not going to take any lectures on parenting from you,' Rob said. 'You're a liar and a cheat, and you know it.'

We were interrupted by the faint but unmistakeable sound of a default Nokia ringtone. It was coming from my handbag. My phone. I rummaged for it and just had time to see 'Mum' on the screen before the call went through to voicemail.

'I'm sorry. I have to listen to this,' I said to Jane. 'My stepfather's got terminal cancer. He could have taken a turn for the worse. I need to find out what's happened.'

'Do what you need to do,' Jane said, 'but afterwards, I suggest we wrap this up. I don't think we're going to make much progress today.'

'You're not kicking us out of the room, are you? Because I paid for this session in advance. I think we have the room,' Rob said.

'No, I'm not "kicking you out of the room",' Jane said. 'I just think it might be better if you left.'

Even she was beginning to sound exasperated. Their voices faded as I dialled the number for voicemail and held the phone to my ear.

It wasn't Mum calling. It was Lee.

Rob said, 'What is it? Is everything all right?'

One glance at him was all it took to tell me that he didn't hate me completely, in spite of everything. He looked exactly as he sometimes had when Georgie was a baby and teething and had been crying most of the night, and he had to get up and be on it and do a site visit in the morning. Tried to the limit. Impatient. Bad-tempered. But he didn't look as if he didn't care.

I listened to the message again. Both Rob and Jane fell silent. The room wavered around me as if it was about to dissolve and then settled back into place. I drew a deep breath.

'It's bad news. My mother's dead,' I said, and called Lee back.

Chapter Sixteen

Lee didn't want me to go to the house, but I did anyway. Rob drove me there, which was in itself a turn of events so strange that it felt as if I'd slipped into a parallel existence, one that connected to the old life in Fairfield Road but had nothing to do with the last twenty-four hours. Only the new clothes I was wearing were proof that he really had taken me to Fox Hill.

I watched Rob driving and was grateful not to have to be the one concentrating, remembering when to turn and monitoring the traffic. I wasn't sure I'd still be able to do it. I wasn't sure I'd ever be able to do anything. At the same time, a small voice in my head reminded me that I would have to manage on my own again sooner or later, and probably sooner. *This is only temporary. It's just a respite. It doesn't change anything. He still doesn't want you. He wants to be with Chloe, and he's having a baby with her.*

Everything was as vivid as a hallucination, and seemed as ephemeral. It was as if my surroundings had become unstable and might be switched for something else at a moment's notice. I had forgotten what the shock of a death can do to you: how it makes you feel unreal, like an imposter in your own life.

'This is good of you,' I said to Rob as we left Kettlebridge behind and passed through the fields that separated it from Critchley, where Mum and Lee's house was.

A tractor pulled out in front of us. Rob grimaced, slowed down and started to look for an opportunity to overtake, but there was too much traffic coming the other way.

'Stella, for what it's worth… I'm sorry. Really, I am.'

'Thank you.'

'You know I was fond of her. I admired her, actually. She had guts, and you always knew where you stood with her.'

Nowhere, if that was where she wanted you to be. I didn't say so, though. I said, 'She was fond of you, too. She once told me that if she'd had a son, she'd have wanted him to be like you.'

He cleared his throat. 'I'm not going to make a big deal of it right now, but you shouldn't have gone up to Chloe like that. You really are going to have to leave her alone from now on, OK?'

That seemed like a conversation from a thousand years ago. Did it still matter? I supposed it did. 'Fair enough,' I said. 'I promise I won't do anything like that again, and I'm sorry, and you can tell her that from me. If it's any consolation, I think I was the one who came off worst. She seemed absolutely fine.'

'She wasn't meant to tell you.'

'She didn't. I guessed.'

He shot me a quick sideways look. 'Really? If you don't mind me asking… how did you know?'

He sounded pleased with himself, too. Unbearably so. Under other circumstances I don't know how I might have reacted. Violently, perhaps. As it was I was still too shocked by the phone call I'd answered in the mediator's office to be anything more than numb.

'She looked smug,' I said.

He didn't answer for a moment. Then he said, 'This is why I didn't want you to know just yet. I knew it would upset you.'

'Well, thank you for your thoughtfulness. Protecting me from upset has obviously been very important for you over the last six months or so.'

'It hasn't been that long, actually.'

'Oh, spare me.'

'Stella, neither of us set out for this to happen. It just… happened.'

'Indeed. I'm sure it was a miraculous surprise to you. Given what I saw when I walked into our bedroom yesterday, it's obviously a wholly astonishing outcome.'

'Does it really have to be like this? Do you have to be so—'

'What? Bitter? I think I'm being remarkably restrained, actually.'

Rob took the turning for Critchley, away from the tractor we'd been following. It pottered steadily off into the distance, trailed by the queue of traffic that had built up behind us. The open fields we'd been passing through gave way to neat rows of houses. We were nearly there. There wasn't long left for me to be angry with him. At least not while he was a captive audience.

'I'm not going to ask you if you were being careful,' I said. 'It's pretty obvious you weren't. Or at least, you weren't being as careful as you could have been. I'm not even going to ask you when it started. I don't care. I don't want to think about it. It'll only make me want to murder you.'

Rob exhaled between his teeth. 'That's a little excessive, don't you think?'

'Only if I actually did it. As a thought-crime I'd say it's understandable. We wives tend not to take kindly to our husbands replacing us with younger models.' I sighed. 'Look, in a way, I don't blame you. She's young. She's sweet. And I don't suppose she's got any scars.'

'I wasn't trying to replace you,' Rob said stiffly. 'It wasn't like that.'

'Rob... I really don't want to know what it was like.'

'I don't think I could tell you, anyway,' Rob said. 'But I'll tell you something. I'm in love. And suddenly everything makes sense. I mean, I get it. I feel alive like never before. I feel young. Everything's brighter and more real. I mean, it's amazing. It's like magic. Can you really not find it in your heart to be pleased for me?'

Another silence. A longer one this time. I thought about what he'd said and about how I had once felt like that about him. He was telling me that he had never been in love before. Not with me. Not with anyone. So perhaps he was right and I should feel happy for him. Or perhaps he was wrong, and he had felt like that for me once and it had died over time and he had forgotten.

Perhaps what he felt for Chloe would die one day too. But whether it did or whether it didn't, it would be nothing to do with me. Regardless of whether or not he loved me or ever had, he had decided he didn't need me any more.

He was waiting for me to answer.

Maybe he thought I might be about to give them both my blessing. Even after everything that had happened. Even after me losing Mum. The only person left in the world who I loved and could be close to was Georgie, and he had threatened to try and take her from me. But if he needed a response from me, maybe I wasn't quite so powerless after all.

He was in love. By definition, that meant he hadn't been thinking clearly. Perhaps it was time for me to do a little of his thinking for him.

I said, 'You and Chloe must both be very excited about the new baby. Of course you are. That's only natural. But you know what to expect. Chloe doesn't. Have you thought about what it's going to be like for her looking after a newborn and Georgie too? Because you're away a lot. You always have been. And you work late pretty much every weeknight. Don't tell me you're going to do it all differently this time and be a more involved dad, because I won't believe you. You run your own business. You can't step back.'

'Chloe's very good with kids. I'm sure she'll cope just fine,' Rob said. But he didn't sound sure. 'Anyway, she's very fond of Georgie.'

'Yes. She told me that, and I believe her. So she'll want the best for her. And I'm sure you do too. And Rob, you know what that is. I want Georgie living with me during the week. That's non-negotiable. You can see her at weekends. As for the house, and the money… I guess that's up for discussion. You're going to need to sort somewhere out for you and Chloe and the baby. And for Georgie, when she comes to visit. We'll have to see.'

'Stella, this isn't a great time to talk about this.' He sounded almost crestfallen. He knew I was right.

'It's as good as it's going to get. You just missed the turning, by the way. It was the last left.'

Rob swore under his breath, pulled in by a corner, reversed and headed back. I said, 'I don't think we should tell Georgie yet. I mean about you and Chloe and the baby. Obviously I'm going to have to tell her about Mum. It's going to be a lot for her to take in.'

'Let her finish the trip,' Rob said. 'Tell her about your mum when she gets back. As for everything else… I don't know. I guess I could talk to Chloe about it.'

The idea of him consulting his girlfriend rankled, but I managed to stop myself from objecting. Better for him to think he was holding back out of the goodness of his heart than to feel as if he'd been browbeaten into it.

This time he found the turning and pulled up outside the house. There was no obvious evidence of disaster. It looked much as it had looked just yesterday: neat, quiet and net-curtained.

'You seem weirdly calm,' Rob said. 'I think you must be in shock. Would you like me to go in with you?'

I hesitated. And then I realised I *did* want him with me. I didn't want to go in there alone.

'All right. Thank you.'

He followed me as I got out of the car and went to the door.

It took Lee a while to answer the bell. He looked dazed and ashen. Still, he drew himself up tall and regarded us both with a hint of challenge.

'There you are,' he said. 'I know you're sorry that I'm the one who's still here, but you can't always get what you want, can you?'

I said, 'Is it all right if we come in?'

'Oh, yes. I suppose there's going to be stampedes of people coming round the place. Women, mostly. Women love this kind of thing, don't they? Calling on the bereaved. Well, if they bring food I don't mind. Who'd have thought that your mother would beat me to it? Anyway, you'd better come on in and inspect the scene of the crime.'

He turned and withdrew into the house, and we followed him into the sitting room, where a plump blonde woman was sitting unhappily on the sofa. I recognised her as Rose, the neighbour Mum had occasionally trusted to keep an eye on Lee.

There was a sense of space and hollowness in the room, as if a large, central piece of furniture had been taken away, or as if the curtains had been removed for washing and the acoustics had suddenly changed because there was nothing there now to soak up and dampen the sound of speech or any other noises. But the curtains were still in place and the centre of the room looked just as it always did. Empty. There had never been a rug or a coffee table there, so why were my eyes drawn to that central space as if something familiar was missing?

'That's where it was,' Lee said. 'That's where all the drama happened. The CPR, and all that. Rose, you can hop along if you want. You've done more than your fair share of sitting in on misery today. Thank you for waiting with me. I hope it wasn't too tedious for you.'

Rose sniffed, wiped her cheeks and stood up. She'd obviously been crying, and probably trying not to. She said, 'Just let me know if you need anything.'

'I will,' Lee said. 'Chin up. It's not the end of the world. At least not for us.' He settled heavily into the armchair he favoured, which had a high back and faced the TV. 'What's the worst that can happen? Well, you and I know the answer to that, don't we, Rose? We just saw it. But the dead can't complain. And if you're not dead yet, what have you got to complain about?'

Rose didn't move. She appeared to be struggling to think of something suitable to say. Lee said, 'You'd better get on home, Rose. I have new visitors to entertain, as you can see. You'll be all right to let yourself out, won't you?'

Rose murmured that she would, and shuffled out. A minute later I heard the front door opening and very softly closing behind her.

Lee said, 'She's got a soft spot for me. Could you tell? Unluckily for her, I'm not going to make old bones. I mean, older bones. There's a bottle of whisky in the kitchen. I'd like one of you to go and pour some of it into a glass for me and bring it here. You can help yourselves too, if you like.'

'I'll pass,' Rob said. 'But do you want one, Stella?'

If I started drinking now, I had no idea how long I'd manage to keep a grip. I said no thank you, and Rob went off to the kitchen and I sat down on the sofa.

'Before you ask, I don't know when we'll be able to have the funeral,' Lee said. 'Like I said on the phone, the coroner's got her. Unexpected death. Has to be looked into, apparently. Procedure has to be followed. Even though they know it was her heart that went.'

'I'm going to have to tell my sister,' I said.

Lee shrugged. 'If you want. It's not exactly as if they were close. Pam thought the best thing was to have as little to do with her as possible. I can't say I disagree. You do know the only contact they had was the annual Christmas card? Which Pam always hid. Didn't want anyone asking any awkward questions. You included. Do you know where she is?'

'I do.'

'Well, I don't want to see her. I don't suppose she much wants to see me, either. So maybe you could politely hint that she should stay away.'

'Lee,' I said, and then stopped as Rob came in with a glass of whisky and handed it over, then sat down next to me but with a safe distance between us.

Lee raised the glass, observed the way the golden-brown liquid caught the light, and then quickly drank a couple of mouthfuls before resting it on the arm of his chair. 'Thank you,' he said. 'I didn't like to ask Rose. She's one for doing everything properly. You can tell which one's her house, even the weeds grow in rows. I'm not sure she'd be down with letting the terminally ill widower have exactly what he wants, when he wants it.' He sipped a little more whisky and sighed. 'If you want to know anything about what happened to your mum, or have me go over it again, you'd better ask now. I'm getting increasingly decrepit, as you know. I'm liable to forget.'

It was on the tip of my tongue to ask him why he hadn't called me earlier. I could have seen her, one last time. Waited with them both till her body was taken away. Would I have sensed her presence still, as if she hadn't yet gone? Would it have been a way to say goodbye? As it was, the room felt both as if something essential was missing and as if she might walk back in at any minute.

Part of me felt I should have been there – that I should have been the next of kin, not him. And yet I knew that was just wounded pride. It would have made no difference to Mum, anyway: it was too late.

I said, 'Did she look… peaceful?'

Lee turned and fixed me with a look and said, 'She looked dead. She wouldn't have wanted you to see her. She was a very proud woman. You know that. Remember her however you want to remember her, but don't remember her as something covered up on the floor waiting to be taken away.'

He turned away, leaned back and closed his eyes. 'I'm going to miss her,' he said. 'I wish they could have carted me away and had done with it.'

I bowed my head. I was suddenly conscious of Rob sitting next to me and was unexpectedly grateful to him for having been a son-in-law that Mum could approve of. Yes, they'd gone behind my back, and she'd been willing to take his side over mine. But now that didn't seem to matter as much as the fact that for so many years she'd been proud of him. And, by extension, of me.

In spite of everything, this was easier because he was here.

I'd always avoided being on my own with Lee. Never really knew what to say to him, even after all these years. It wasn't that we didn't get on. We'd always been capable of sitting in the same room and having a conversation. It was just that, left to our own devices, we probably wouldn't have chosen to. That awkwardness wasn't about to be washed away by grief. It was still there, like an off-key note in a sad song.

Maybe it was right that Lee was the one who had been with her and not me. If anyone had been the love of her life, it was him. I had thought that I had made my peace with her leaving us for him long ago. It was a surprise to learn that there was still enough of that old hurt left for this new one to bring it back to life.

Chapter Seventeen

Rob insisted on giving me a lift back to Fox Hill. I didn't resist. I was gripped by panic, but not about him. Out of all the things I could have obsessed about, I had homed in on Molly.

Under the circumstances – especially given that she'd just told me she never wanted to hear from me again – how was I going to tell her that Mum was dead?

As we made our way along Fox Hill Rob overtook a cyclist in a familiar blue-and-yellow top. Tony Everdene. Rob passed him a little too closely and he glanced reproachfully at us as we moved ahead. As Rob pulled in by the gate to the cottage I turned and saw him labouring into view behind us, coming up the home stretch of the hill.

I said, 'I don't think that's the way to endear yourself to the neighbours. Did you see the look he gave you?'

Rob switched off the engine. 'What are you talking about? Oh, you mean the guy from next door. Did he give me a look? I didn't notice. Wouldn't have been the first time. I used to see him every now and then when I came over to check up on things, glowering at me. He's just the type. Lives to disapprove and complain. He's introduced himself, then, I take it?'

'Actually, he's been very helpful.'

Rob swivelled towards me. 'He has, has he?'

For no good reason, I felt myself blushing. He was expecting me to, and I couldn't stop myself.

'I fell over in front of his house,' I said. 'You abandoned me in a very impractical pair of high heels. I didn't get very far in them. My phone had died and I was going to get the bus, and he invited me in and called me a taxi. He was very nice, actually. And then I had the flat tyre I told you about, and he gave me a lift into town this morning.'

'I see.' Rob frowned. 'I assumed you'd got a taxi. Was it really wise to get in a car with a stranger?'

'Well, he's not really a stranger, is he? He's my neighbour. The neighbour you chose for me, remember?'

'So he's been sniffing round, has he? Well, he didn't waste much time.'

'Come on, Rob, he's married. Some people actually take their vows seriously, you know.'

'Right. And did you meet his wife? Because all the times I've been here, I've never seen her.'

We glared at each other. Rob said, 'Who knows where she is? Might be under the patio. Or in that big chest freezer in his garage. Just saying you might want to ask him.'

'And you actually want me to live here? You might want to brush up on those sales skills.'

I got out of the car just as Tony pulled up and dismounted behind us. He left his bike on the pavement and came over.

'Hi, Stella.' He glanced at Rob, who was now standing beside me and bristling like a cat who's been stroked the wrong way. 'Morning.'

'Hi. This is Rob, my husband.' I gestured towards Rob, who didn't smile. 'Rob, this is Tony. I know you've seen each other around, but I don't think you've met properly yet.'

'No. I haven't had the pleasure,' Rob said.

Neither of them made any move to shake hands. Tony said, 'That's a big car you have. You might want to be careful. It's a narrow lane. My girls like to cycle, too.'

'Thanks for the tip,' Rob said. 'I'll bear that in mind. And thanks for giving my wife a lift this morning. I gather she appreciated it.'

He said *my wife* with a slight but unmissable emphasis. Tony blinked and said, 'No problem. I was heading that way, so… no big deal.'

He glanced across at his bike as if he was about to step back and collect it, then thought better of it and turned to face me.

'Are you all right then, Stella? Do you want any help taking care of that flat tyre?'

'Actually, I'm going to take care of it,' Rob said. 'We don't need any help, thank you.'

'Good. Well, let me know if you need anything,' Tony said with a final glance in my direction, and beat a retreat.

Rob gave me a look that was a mixture of triumph and irritation.

'I guess he's not *that* keen,' he said, just loudly enough for Tony to hear as he wheeled his bike up his garden path. 'Would you fix us some lunch? Sandwiches or something would do. It's been a long morning.' He tapped in the code on the keypad next to the pedestrian gate. Mum's birth date. I knew then that I was going to keep it like that. 'Unless you object?'

Did I object? Could I? He'd come to see Lee with me. He was going to fix my tyre. Everything would be easier if we could be amicable. Wouldn't it?

Or was this just a different way of him reasserting control?

He was having a baby with another woman.

But he was still Georgie's father. Without Rob, there would have been no Georgie…

'Fine by me. One good turn deserves another,' I said, but the gate had swung open and Rob was already walking through.

When Rob came in from putting the spare tyre on I had the sandwiches ready and waiting.

'Almost like old times,' he said as he washed his hands at the kitchen sink.

'Almost.'

He dried his hands on the hand towel and came over to sit opposite me. He looked as immaculate as ever. He'd managed to change the tyre without getting so much as a smudge of oil on his clothes. I wondered what Chloe would say if she knew he was here, helping me with my car, about to eat the food I'd prepared for him.

'I didn't expect you to wait for me,' he said.

I'd waited for him because I thought he'd say something sarcastic if I didn't, which was what he usually did. But I decided not to tell him that. I didn't want to criticise him. If this was some kind of ceasefire, I wasn't ready for either of us to break it just yet.

Instead I said, 'I didn't expect us to end up having lunch together today.'

He glanced at me. 'No.' Then he took a bite out of his sandwich. 'Not bad.'

I'd tried to make it the way he liked it: cheese with just a little bit of mayonnaise and a slice of ham. It should have had lettuce as well, but that was one of the things he hadn't provided me with.

He said, 'Did you try and get in touch with your sister?'

'I called her. No answer.'

My sandwich tasted odd and I suddenly felt like retching. I wasn't sure I was going to be able to finish it. I took a couple of deep breaths. Rob was watching me with something not a million miles removed from concern. The sick feeling receded and I was able to carry on speaking.

'Mum came round here last night to give me her number. It was the last time I saw her. I called Molly and she pretty much told me to get lost. It turned out Mum had spoken to her already and told her to say I should just go along with whatever you wanted.'

Rob tried a mouthful of the coffee I'd made for him and pulled a face. 'Ugh. Long-life milk.'

I imagined myself picking up my own cup of coffee and throwing it in his face. The day before, I would have been angry enough to do that. Or would I? Was it ever going to be possible for me to hate him the way I should? He had touched me so gently once. He had stroked my scars.

'You really did line all your ducks up in a row, didn't you?' I said. 'Considering you can't have had that much time to get all this together.'

Rob shrugged. 'You didn't change the code to the gate,' he said. 'Some might say that subconsciously, that means you don't mind me knowing how to get in.'

'Don't push it,' I said. 'Anyway, I thought you hated all that psychological stuff. Though maybe that's only when it's applied to you.'

Did Chloe know that about him? Did she know how he liked his sandwiches yet? But maybe he would be different with her. Maybe all of us were different with different people, and all it took to change was to attach yourself to someone new.

Rob gave me a flickering half-smile. 'Just like old times,' he said.

I'd only had a few mouthfuls of my sandwich but I couldn't manage any more. He was still busy chewing. There wasn't much that put Rob off his food.

'Mum gave me Molly's address,' I said. 'She's living in London. I'm going to go there and try to see her.'

Rob stopped eating, paused, swallowed, and set down what was left of his sandwich on his plate.

'I'm not sure that's a good idea,' he said.

'Why not? The worst that can happen is that she isn't there or doesn't answer the door, in which case at least I've tried to tell her in person and I can leave her a note. Then I can come back and spend the night with Lee.' I had felt that Lee shouldn't spend his first night in the house without Mum on his own, and had persuaded him to agree to me sleeping over.

Rob sighed. He leaned back and folded his arms. 'I had somebody do a little bit of digging,' he said.

'What? You mean you hired a private detective or something?'

'Something like that,' he said. 'Your mum asked me to see what I could find out, so I obliged.'

'You should have told me.'

'Well, maybe, but it's a bit late to say that now, isn't it? And anyway, what good would it have done? Let sleeping dogs lie. That was what your mum said, and I have to say I think she was right. Look… Molly's a volatile person. Unstable. Unpredictable. There have been mental health issues… drink and drug use… problems with the police. A caution for being drunk and disorderly, complaints from neighbours about antisocial behaviour. And bad relationships. Everything you'd expect, really.'

'I don't care. She still deserves to know her mother's dead. And she ought to hear it from me. Besides, I can't believe you're really that concerned about her, given that you were willing to drag her into your little plot to blow up our marriage.'

'You're the one who dragged her into it. Your mum only got in touch with her because you'd been asking about her. I never thought you'd consider making contact with her. I guess you called my bluff. You surprised me, Stella.'

'Well, I'm glad to hear I'm still capable of a few surprises.'

'Anyway, I'm not concerned about her. I'm concerned about you. I don't think you should do this. How are you even going to get there? You're in no fit state to drive. I don't think you'll be safe on the road. If you are going to insist on going, I think I should take you.'

'And what do you think Chloe would have to say about that? How do you think she would feel about you being here?'

'Look, she knows. She's fine with it. I already called her.'

'When?'

'Just now, outside in the garden, after I'd finished changing your tyre. I thought she should know about Pam. Look, she understands that I have a family and I have responsibilities. She wants me to do right by you and Georgie. She's always said that.'

I got to my feet. 'You do not get to do that,' I said. 'You can't use me to keep Chloe in line. You can't play us off against each other.'

Before he had time to come up with a response I was walking out of the house. Rob followed me. 'Stella, where do you think you're going? That is a ridiculous suggestion... I was talking to you...'

I pressed the exit button by the pedestrian gate, stood back and gestured to him to go through.

'It's time you left, Rob. If you don't, I'm going to scream blue murder. And I think you know my attentive neighbour will be round here the minute he hears me. Maybe he is a psycho, maybe he isn't, but he doesn't like you much and right now that puts him on my side. I don't know, maybe the two of you could cancel each other out.'

'You're making a big mistake,' Rob said. 'This conversation is not over.'

He stalked through the gate, got into his car, turned at the end of the lane and accelerated away. The gate closed and it was mercifully quiet. I became aware of the birdsong, the blue sky. The ginger-and-white cat I'd seen in the garden first thing in the morning – which seemed a lifetime ago – slunk in through the gate, eyed me warily, then decided I could safely be ignored and pattered off across the gravel towards the back garden.

Life was going on all around me, oblivious and unstoppable. It made my heart ache to think that Mum wouldn't see that blue sky, or any blue sky again. Knowing that seemed to make it more vivid, as if I was trying to take something from it to give to her, even though it was too late now to try to give her anything.

But it wasn't too late for the rest of us.

I wanted very badly to call Rob and apologise and thank him for everything he'd done and tell him that I was wrong and he was right. But instead I turned and went back into the house. I rinsed his plate and mug and wondered if that would be the last time we'd ever eat alone together. And then I began to get ready to leave.

Chapter Eighteen

Molly's neighbourhood turned out to be surprisingly chi-chi, with grand, sweeping Victorian terraces that had been meticulously restored as well as rows of cosy-looking two-up, two-down back-to-back houses from the same era, equally well-kept. Desirable, as Rob would have said. There were shabby-chic interiors shops and boutiques selling handbags at monthly-salary prices, and florists and cupcake bakeries and, naturally, estate agents. It didn't fit with what he'd told me about her. I wouldn't have minded living there myself.

Being lonely here would be different to being lonely in Fox Hill. Wouldn't it be easier to live alone here without being lonely at all? You would always be able to go to places where there were other people around and none of them knew you and, by and large, they would leave you alone: galleries and markets and museums and shopping malls, parks and multiplexes and cafés.

People thought of the countryside as safe because of the lack of crowds, but safety was really just a matter of chance, wherever you were. Chance, and who you got close to. Like anywhere.

The roads near the Underground station had been busy with rush hour traffic and pedestrians, but as I headed towards her address it became quieter until finally I was standing in front of her house, and there was no one else in sight.

It was Victorian and terraced, like most of the other property round here, but a little bit more run-down than its neighbours. The red paint on the front door was peeling, and there were weeds springing up between the paving stones in front of it. There was a row of buzzers next to the front door, all yellowing and old, but no names, only numbers.

I crossed the weedy front garden, rang the top buzzer and waited. She wouldn't be in. It was a fool's errand…

Suddenly Rob was at my shoulder, looking on with a supercilious smile. *You see? I told you this was a big mistake.*

I willed him to vanish and pressed the buzzer again. Then I heard a familiar voice.

'Hold your horses. You don't have to wear it out. Who is it, anyway? Because this had better be good.'

'Molly… It's Stella. I've come because I've got news for you. Bad news. It's about Mum.'

There was another silence. The silence went on for a little while and then a little while longer. I tried pressing the buzzer again, but there was no reply.

Was this going to be it? Would she just leave me here, and wait and see how long I'd hang on before I gave up and went away? Was that really how she felt about us now?

Mental health issues… drink and drug use… problems with the police.

Rob again. But he shouldn't have gone nosing round in her affairs like that. She had made it clear she wanted nothing more to do with us. Hadn't she earned the right to be left alone? Wasn't it the least she deserved?

Suddenly the door swung wide open and there she was.

Molly.

Thirty-two now, but she still looked like a doll. Big eyes, snub nose, big forehead, round cheeks, dark eyes. I'd forgotten how petite she was. Her wavy hair was coloured platinum blonde and even though it was barely evening she was wearing a long pink shiny dressing-gown patterned with splashy blue and purple flowers, which instantly reminded me of all the bright colours and pretty things she'd loved when she was little. She had pink fluffy slippers on, too. It looked as if I'd interrupted plans for an early night.

She wasn't smiling.

'You'd better come up,' she said.

I stepped in and she closed the front door behind me. *Well, this is what you wanted,* I heard Rob say as I followed her through the communal hallway. *Don't blame me if you're frightened. Given what you did to her, I'd say you've got good reason to be.*

We went up several flights of stairs covered with well-worn carpet and came to a halt outside the door to the top flat. She unlocked it and ushered me in, then closed it behind us, bolted it and slid a chain across the door to secure it.

'I've learned it pays to be cautious,' she said.

I found myself in a generously proportioned attic room that had been turned into a treasure trove of drapes, rugs, pot plants and fairy lights. Underneath all that it looked as if it hadn't been refurbished for at least a couple of decades, though someone – Molly, maybe – had slapped a coat of fresh white paint on the walls and ceilings.

There wasn't much furniture: a small, white-painted bookcase, a futon-style sofa that Molly had covered with a pink-and-white striped cotton throw and a mismatched table and chairs. Earlier in the day it might have been uncomfortably hot. It was still warm now. The window was open wide and the air smelt very faintly of incense-scented joss sticks and traffic fumes.

'So tell me,' Molly said. 'What happened?'

I told her. Her face glazed over as if it might be about to crack. And then we both stood there looking at each other as if neither of us knew what to do next. It was as if all of our shared past was right there in the small distance between us, making it solid and impossible to cut through.

Once more I was conscious of Rob, as if he was lingering in a corner of the room and studying us with something approaching pity. *You see? She's shocked and upset, but she doesn't want any comfort from you. You're the last person she would turn to. She knows she's more likely to find what she needs at the bottom of a bottle. Or from some man who doesn't love her. Anywhere but from her sister.*

Molly clasped her hands together and let out a long breath that was almost a sob. Then she turned her back to me.

She said, 'I just need a moment. Sit down if you want. But then I'm going to have to ask you to leave.'

Then she hurried out of the room and closed the door behind her.

I held my breath and waited to hear the sound of crying, or things breaking, or anything. But there was nothing.

After a while I let myself perch on the futon sofa. It was as hard and unyielding as it looked. Imaginary Rob swung round one of the mismatched chairs and settled on that, crossing his legs and jiggling his ankle as he always did when he was angry and waiting.

Look what you've gone and done. I told you to leave her alone. She's vulnerable. She always was. You took advantage of her, and now she probably thinks you're back to finish off the job. But all those years you were busy playing happy families, you were quite willing to pretend she didn't exist. Yes, you forgot all about her. It was easier that way, wasn't it? And you know what the really sad thing is? She thinks she was better off without you.

'I never forgot her. How could I? I could never forget my own sister,' I said out loud as Molly came back in.

She looked startled, but she'd obviously decided what to say and do in advance and wasn't about to be put off. I couldn't smell drink or smoke. She looked a little paler than when she'd let me in and it was possible that she'd been crying, but I couldn't be sure. Perhaps she was just shocked. Perhaps she didn't really care. And if that was how she felt, could I blame her?

'Thank you for telling me about Mum,' she said. 'But you shouldn't have come all this way. I'll see you out.' She went to the door and undid the chain.

I stood. 'Will you come to the funeral?'

She actually shuddered. I was glad she had her back to me so I couldn't see the disgust on her face. 'No. No way.'

'Can I at least send you the details, when it's arranged? In case you change your mind.'

'I won't,' she said. 'I know it sounds harsh, but it's how I feel. It's like I said to you on the phone. It's nothing to do with me.'

The bolts were sticking and she had to yank them. Her hands were trembling. Finally she got the door open and held it for me to go through. She looked resolute but not far from the edge of something, like a parent who is being pushed to the limit but is still doggedly sticking to the boundaries.

'I'm sorry,' I said. 'I didn't mean to make things worse.'

She shook her head impatiently. 'You haven't. You coming here is nothing, OK? It makes no difference. When you've gone it'll be like it never happened.'

I followed her downstairs and we came to a halt in the communal hallway. I said, 'So you're all right, then? You're settled? This seems like a nice area.'

'It is,' she said. 'I'm OK. Really I am. You don't need to feel guilty about me.'

On impulse, I rummaged in my handbag for the leather holder I used for my credit cards, took it out and flipped it open. 'Would you like to see a photo of Georgie? I have one here,' I said, and held it out to her.

She was horrified. She didn't even glance down at it. Instead she held up her hand to stop me.

'You aren't my family any more,' she said. 'All that is over with.'

I withdrew. I was mortified, not for myself but for Georgie, and for Molly too.

'I'm sorry,' I said. 'I just thought…'

Molly shook her head. 'Like I told you, I'm not interested. I really don't want to know.'

I put my credit card holder back in my bag and zipped it up.

'Rob met someone else,' I told her. 'He's having a baby with her. That's why he wanted to get rid of me.'

Molly grimaced. Her hands flew up to her mouth and she clenched them and then let them drop. As a kid she'd always bitten her nails, much to Mum's disgust and regardless of what Mum painted them with. They were bare now and so short there was nothing there to bite.

'He really did a number on you, didn't he?' she said. 'And I always thought he was one of the good guys. Just goes to show how much I know.'

'So… are you seeing anyone?'

Molly managed an incredulous smile. 'Does it look like it? What are you going to ask me next – how many times a week I have someone else in my bed?'

'No, of course not, I just… I don't mean to pry.'

'I get it. You want to know if I'm happy. And I am. Though maybe you find that hard to believe. You should worry about yourself, Stella. You don't have to worry about me.'

'You never wanted to have another child?'

She froze, but only for an instant. Then she opened the front door and pushed it wide. She was looking at me in a way that left me in no doubt about how far I'd gone in crossing the line of what was tolerable for us to talk about. She was still holding back, but she wasn't far off grabbing hold of me and shoving me out.

'Get out, Stella,' she said. 'Get out and don't come back.'

'Molly, I'm sorry, I didn't mean—'

'I don't talk about that stuff,' she said. 'I don't talk about it ever. You have no right to try and make me to. All I want is for you to leave me alone. Surely that can't be that hard for you to understand.'

'OK,' I said. 'I really am sorry, Molly. I won't bother you again.'

I couldn't bring myself to look at her as I stumbled out and walked away. I heard rather than saw her close the door behind me. My heart felt torn in two and my eyes were hazy with tears.

The whole meeting had taken barely quarter of an hour. It felt as if years or decades had gone by, long enough for everything to have changed completely, but the summer evening outside was just as bright as it had been when I went in, as if no time had passed at all.

Read the room, Stella. That was Rob, pacing alongside me. *How does it feel, to come so far for so little? You see, it's much too late. She didn't even want to look at the photo. She doesn't want to know. She hates you. In all seriousness, given what happened, what else do you expect?*

I clamped my hands over my ears to silence him. A passer-by gave me a startled look. I sped up my pace and began to sweat, even though the day had cooled.

This is what it had come to. Neighbours expressing polite concern. Strangers looking at me as if I was mad. Maybe this was what they meant when they talked about hitting rock bottom. But it also seemed quite possible that I still had some way to go.

I managed to find my way back to the nearest Underground stop and get on the right train. I was grateful to Rob for having suggested that it wouldn't be a good idea to drive. As it had turned out, he was right. Hopefully I'd have pulled myself together by the time I made it back to Oxfordshire.

At Paddington station I found myself studying my reflection in the mirror above the washbasins in the ladies' and wondering who exactly I was staring at.

But I had to pull myself together. There was Georgie to think of... Georgie, who would be back tomorrow evening, tired but happy to be home and excited to tell us about her trip. Georgie, who didn't know anything about any of this. And then there was Lee. I had promised I'd go back to the house tonight and stay with him. I'd have to make sure he'd eaten... eat something myself, if I could... find some sheets for the bed in the spare room... sit and watch TV with Lee until it was time to try to sleep.

And then there was work. I was due back in on Monday morning, and I hadn't even told the head what had happened yet. I would be entitled to a few days off, and she might let me take more time if it was unpaid. But did I want to make myself seem dispensable at a time when my marriage was about to fall apart, and I was likely to need my income more than ever? It was only a month till the end of term. It might be manageable. It might even be better to try to keep going… the job might be a respite, a reminder of something like normality – a part of my life that still had its old familiar structure, where I still knew what to do and how to behave.

Maybe Rob would let me stay in the spare room at Fairfield Road for a week or two while I sorted out Mum's funeral, for Georgie's sake if not for mine. I'd probably be going to and fro to keep an eye on Lee anyway, maybe sleeping over there some of the time if he needed or wanted me to. I'd be busy. Too busy to stop and think. Which was the best way, wasn't it? Because if I stopped, I might not be able to carry on at all.

Chloe might be willing to tolerate the idea of me staying on in the house with Rob as long as I tolerated him slipping away to see her now and then. I got the feeling the rush to get me out and kick-start divorce proceedings had come from him rather than her, anyway. She might even have found it slightly overwhelming. Rob could be, when he decided he wanted to take charge of your life…

We would say goodbye to Mum without Molly there, and I would probably never see her again. Rob and I would sort something out. We'd have to, because the baby would come whether we did or not. We'd make a deal. Georgie would be sad but she wouldn't be shattered. Life would go on, the way it usually did. I would keep finding reasons to put off telling her the truth that Rob had threatened me with. And maybe she would never find out…

You did promise that you would tell her, years ago. Rob's face floated in the glass next to mine, superior and condemning. *You're very bad at keeping your side of a bargain. Still, I guess it's only human nature to want what you can't have. And then to want other people to believe you've got it.*

The mirror was curved, set in a wall that was almost perfectly semi-circular. I could see my back view, too, reflected in the full-length mirror that stretched round the other side of the round space behind me. No Rob. He was miles away, probably curled up on Chloe's sofa, having just finished a cosy little TV supper for two. Looking through the book of baby names. Asking about her family so he could make a good impression on them when they met. Thinking about anything but me.

Next to me two young women were touching up their make-up and talking loudly about what they were planning to do that evening and who might be there. They were behaving the way people who are with friends in public spaces often do, as if no one else was there.

It cost me a pang to hear them, and suddenly I was envious. They were so free. That camaraderie, that sisterliness. I'd been so busy trying to keep up appearances, playing the part of the wife and mother, I hadn't even let myself see how much I missed it.

The woman standing next to me said to her friend, 'We ought to really let our hair down. You deserve to have a bit of fun.'

'Let's see,' the other woman said, spraying herself with perfume so strong it made me cough and prompted me to move on, out of the round windowless underground room with its mirrors and candy-striped paper and harsh overhead lighting, past the turnstile and up the stairs to the station concourse.

*

Rush hour was coming to an end and the sky was just beginning to fade beyond the dirty glass of the vaulted roof high overhead. My train was already waiting at the platform but the carriage I boarded was almost unoccupied. I settled at an empty table seat and a few minutes later I was on my way, rattling through the city back towards the green countryside that I had come to think of as home.

I'd done this journey several times with Georgie, though not if Rob was around because he always preferred to drive. We'd gone to see Santa in Selfridges, the dinosaurs in the Natural History Museum and London Zoo – little trips I hoped she would remember, and look back on with nostalgia. I'd always loved sitting on the train with her, with her seriously studying the view out of the window as if it was important to take note of every passing thing.

There was only one stop on the way: Brickley, where Molly and I had grown up. Going through it was as close as I ever got to going back. The next stop after that was Barrowton, where I'd get off and pick up my car to drive over and stay with Lee.

At Brickley station, there was no one much waiting on the platform. It was too late for crowds. But a couple of passengers came into my carriage, and a woman with a child chose the two seats opposite me as a good place to settle.

The child was a girl, about eight years old, with carefully plaited hair. Before settling into the seat that the woman pointed out to her she gave me a fastidious, wide-eyed gaze, as if to say: *If I have to I will, but if it was down to me I wouldn't be anywhere near you.* Then the woman muttered something to make her hurry up and she dutifully squeezed round the far side of the table between us and sat down.

I tried to catch the girl's eye and smile at her – *I'm not that bad, honestly, I'm perfectly normal and nice* – but she decided not to humour me and instead focused pointedly on the iPod she'd just retrieved from her bag.

She was responding to me as if I was a weirdo. The creepy sort of adult that children were warned about.

I heard Rob's voice in my head just as clearly as if he was sitting next to me at the table, observing me with the detachment of a scientist engaged in field research.

You see? She can tell there's something wrong with you. She knows you've done something. Or rather, to be accurate, she senses that there's something you've left undone that you ought to have done. She can smell the guilt on you. Children and animals are clever like that. They're hard to fool. They pick up on what's unsaid.

I closed my eyes and thought of Rob with Chloe, his arms round her, his hands on her. Perhaps stroking her belly the way he had once stroked mine. I remembered my mother in the mortuary and Lee alone in his armchair, smoking because he didn't really care any more whether he lived or died, the TV on in front of him but unwatched.

Then I pictured Georgie toasting marshmallows on the campfire as the sun set and the hills around her faded from view, watching the flames and the shadows. Maybe she'd be thinking about coming home tomorrow. I knew she would be looking forward to it, however good a time she'd had. But then, when she got back, I was going to have to tell her about Mum…

And finally I pictured Molly, back in her white-painted flat in her flowery dressing-gown, curled up on the sofa that she'd covered with a pink-striped throw. Would she be drinking a glass of wine? Smoking? Sipping hot chocolate? Reading? Weeping? Laughing at a TV programme, having put all thoughts of her family out of her mind? On the phone to a lover, or a friend?

I didn't know. I had no right to know. She wanted nothing more to do with me, or with any of us. And if she got her way, I would never know any more about her than I knew now.

Chapter Nineteen

Fifteen years earlier

When we got back from the Canary Islands the first person I wanted to tell about the engagement was Mum. I rang her with Rob sitting right next to me on our old yellow sofa in the kitchen, which was just close enough to the phone point in the hallway for the cord to stretch. That was where I always called from, usually with Rob nearby. It didn't bother me that he could hear what I was saying. It wasn't as if I had anything to hide from him. Especially not now that we were getting married.

We spent a lot of time in that kitchen because it was the only room in the house that was warm. There was plenty of work to do on the house still and before we went away I had felt despondent about it, and guilty about having taken so long to recover from the accident. But since our return everything seemed bright and full of possibilities. The rotting window frames and peeling wallpaper and barely warm radiators struck me as minor inconveniences, little challenges that would soon be overcome.

'She might deafen you from there,' I said to Rob as I pressed the buttons on the phone to call her. There weren't many numbers I knew by heart. Hers was one and Dad's had been another.

He carried on turning over the pages of the free property paper, scanning the listings the way he always did, even though we were nowhere near being ready to put the house on the market and trade up.

'She won't shriek,' he said. 'She's not the type.'

'I think she'll be pretty pleased.'

He seemed to be in no rush to tell his dad, but I told myself it didn't mean he was having doubts. It was just that they didn't get on. His dad wasn't in brilliant health – he'd been having kidney problems – but that seemed to make Rob even more reluctant to have anything to do with him.

Rob's unsympathetic attitude to his dad was a sharp contrast to the attention he'd lavished on me since the accident, and once or twice I had tried to suggest we should do more to stay in touch and offer support. But Rob had bitten my head off in response and accused me of nagging, and I wasn't about to press him on the subject now.

It wasn't a reflection on Rob's character – I knew how caring he could be. If Rob hadn't been so busy looking after me, perhaps he'd have had more energy to spare…

Mum was the one who answered the phone, as usual, which was a relief to me because I still found it awkward making small talk to Lee. He always said, jokingly (it was the kind of joke he made), that one of Mum's many jobs was to be his secretary. She'd given up her job at the department store when she moved in with him, and hadn't done any paid work since. I sometimes wondered if she missed it, but I never asked because I knew she wouldn't admit it even if she did.

'Mum? It's Stella. I've got news for you.'

'Stella? Is that you? Sorry, I can't hear you very well. We've got people round.'

Quite a few people, judging by the chatter and music in the background. One of the things Mum had gained when she threw in her lot with Lee – apart from a bigger house and more leisure time – was a more active social life. On several occasions down the years I'd gone round there and found myself sitting in a corner while they and their friends got tipsy and danced, knowing that Molly, who went to bed early because she was so much younger, was probably trying and failing to sleep in one of the spare rooms upstairs.

'You're going to have to speak up,' Mum said. 'You got back all right, then?'

I turned and grinned at Rob. I felt like I was presenting Mum with a prize.

'Rob's asked me to marry him!'

'What?'

I said it again. She squealed. I held the phone out so Rob could hear and grinned at him.

'Oh, Stella, that's wonderful news! Congratulations!'

When I put the receiver back to my ear I could just about make Lee's voice somewhere close behind her, booming and jokey, demanding to know if Rob was going to make an honest woman of me. Mum ignored him. 'Have you got a ring yet? When's the big day?'

'No ring yet. I don't have a date yet either, but Mum, we want the wedding to be really small. It's going to be a registry office do, and we're thinking we might just ask you and Lee and Molly and Rob's dad. We're going to save the money to spend on the house.'

I wanted to explain that part of the reason Rob wasn't keen on having a big do was that he didn't have any close family who would come, apart from his dad who he wasn't even that bothered about inviting. But I couldn't bring myself to say any of that with him sitting there. Maybe she would figure it out, anyway.

'Oh, well, you know I'm not going to get hung up on all that mother-of-the-bride stuff,' Mum said.

'As long as she doesn't expect us to pay for it, she can have as big a do as she likes,' I heard Lee say in the background.

'We're certainly not expecting you to pay for it,' I said.

'Oh, ignore him. He's probably worried that you're going to give me ideas,' Mum said. Even though she'd been living with Lee for years, they'd never married – at least, not yet. I got the impression Mum would have liked to, so could only assume that Lee wasn't keen. The only time the subject had come up when I was in earshot, he'd said something about a man who marries his mistress creating a vacancy. Mum had pointed out that you had to be married to have a mistress in the first place, and Lee had just said, 'Exactly.'

'We want to do it sometime this spring,' I said. 'We don't see any point in waiting.'

Mum relayed this point to Lee. He said, 'He hasn't got her in trouble, has he? Do I hear the pitter-patter of tiny feet?'

My heart sank. After the high of the holiday, it was a shock to realise I could still be crushed just like that. Lee didn't know about that aspect of the consequences of the accident. I was glad Mum hadn't told him – he was capable of being even more tactless when fully informed than he was when he was ignorant. But still, I could have done without pregnancy speculation at that particular moment.

Was that what everybody was going to think when we told them we were getting married quickly and quietly? Oh, well, what did it matter?

'Don't be silly, Lee,' Mum said. Then, to me, 'I would get your sister to come to the phone, but she's out somewhere with her awful boyfriend. Anyway, she can barely bring herself to put two words together at the moment. I know people go on about teenagers, Stella, but I don't remember you ever being like this.'

I had to suppress the reflex answer that came to mind. *At Molly's age I couldn't afford to be like that because you had just left us. And even if I had been, you wouldn't have been around to notice. Besides, she lost her dad six months ago and she's had to move house and start sixth-form college somewhere new, so cut her some slack...*

Instead I just said, 'We're not going to have bridesmaids or anything like that. You don't think she'll mind, do you?'

Mum snorted. 'She's well past the bridesmaid stage, Stella, believe me. Pink is over. Her idea of a nice dress is something you'd see in a horror movie on someone who just came back from the dead. Anyway, I'm going to have to go. We'll drink a toast to you.

Congratulate Rob for me, won't you? And congrats to you as well! The future Mrs Castle! What a catch!'

Just before she hung up I heard Lee bellow something I couldn't make out, and Mum burst out laughing. Then the line went dead.

I put the phone back in its cradle. 'I didn't get the chance to speak to Molly. She was out with her boyfriend. Seems to be going through a bit of a rebellious teen phase.'

Rob took the phone from me and set it down on the floor.

'Everyone has to grow up sometime,' he said. 'You worry about her too much. When I'm your husband, I'm going to forbid you to worry about anything. Especially your little sister. And I think you'll find I have ways of making you do as I say.'

He put his arms around me. 'Maybe now would be a good time to start,' he said.

He started kissing me and the jangling effect that my family always had on my nerves – the side-effect of grief and guilt and love – began to dissipate. By and by I forgot about Molly completely, just as he had said he wanted.

The following Saturday Rob woke me with breakfast in bed and told me to dress for a walk. The living room floorboards were only half-sanded and it was unusual for him to want to go out somewhere if it meant leaving a task in the house unfinished, so that gave me an inkling of what might be on the way. He also wasn't much of a rambler. Walking was too slow for him, and when we attempted to go out together he tended to get impatient with me for not keeping up. I'd been trying to build up my stamina since the accident, but I was still some way off Rob's level of fitness.

He drove me to a local beauty spot, a cliff-top wood beside the River Avon. As we made our way along a path through the trees I was conscious of him looking out jealously for passers-by, as if he wanted us to have the place to ourselves, or was planning to do something and didn't want anybody else around. By and by he steered me towards a bench with a view of Clifton Suspension Bridge and sighed with relief on seeing it was free.

'Good. Let's sit here. You must be tired.'

'I'm not too bad.'

We settled down and I rubbed my mittened hands together and watched the plumes of our breath rise and mingle in the air. I was glad of the respite, but didn't want to stop for long. I could feel the cold from the bench soaking through my coat and trousers, setting off a dull ache in my bones.

It wasn't just the elbow that had been broken in the accident that hurt. My old injuries seemed to send out faint pangs that radiated across my whole body, like a subdued distress call.

'This is beautiful, isn't it?'

Rob was rummaging in his pocket. Then a woman crashed through the undergrowth nearby and he froze and exhaled in exasperation.

The woman saw us but didn't acknowledge us. She was clearly looking for someone, and seemed agitated. 'Polly? Polly, where are you?'

Then a little girl in a blue coat came barrelling out of the trees and rushed into the woman's arms.

'Mummy! I thought I'd lost you!'

The relief on the woman's face was so intense it made me shiver. She embraced the child and then started scolding her and lead her away.

Rob said, 'You'd think people would learn to keep hold of their kids.' His hand went back into his jacket pocket and he brought out a small green velvet-covered box. 'I wanted to give you this,' he said, flipping it open. 'I know we've done this already, but just to make it official – Stella, will you marry me?'

It was a diamond ring. The jewel was as clear as ice, but even in the watery January sunlight it flashed with primary colours. I took it out of the box and slipped it on. It fit, of course. I held my hand up so we could both admire it and said, 'You know the answer's yes. But this is huge. Can we really afford it?'

Rob stiffened as if I'd laughed at him and thrown it back in his face. The day instantly seemed to darken. 'I wouldn't have got it for you if I couldn't afford it,' he said. 'Don't you like it?'

'I love it,' I said quickly. 'It's dazzling. I just can't quite believe I deserve it.'

Rob softened, and the day was sunny again. 'You idiot,' he said. 'I'll be the judge of that.' He embraced me and kissed me, and I couldn't tell whether I was giddy with joy or with relief.

That evening he drove me over to Ashdale so we could go out for dinner with my family. I understood without him saying so that he'd wanted me to have the ring to show off to Mum.

When we parked outside the house I said to him, 'Before we go in, there's something I should tell you.'

He turned to me with a frown. 'Stella, don't do this. Don't spring stuff on me when we're just about to celebrate our engagement.'

'It's nothing bad,' I said quickly. 'At least, I don't think it is. It's just that Mum rang the other day and told me that she'd had a bit of a chat with Lee. I think she thought it would help him to avoid making tactless comments. You know what he's like, always putting his foot in it. Anyway, she told him we probably won't be having any children. Because of what happened in the accident. But don't worry, I don't think it'll come up. Molly knows too, apparently. Mum told her a little while ago, but she said it barely seemed to register. That's teenagers for you, I guess – too wrapped up in their own stuff to pay much attention to anyone else. Anyway, I'm sure Molly won't say anything, and Lee's under strict instructions not to mention it. I'm sorry, I know I should have told you before. I think you were out running or something when she called, and then what with one thing or another it just slipped my mind.'

That wasn't strictly true. I hadn't forgotten. I just hadn't wanted to bring the subject up. It seemed so humiliating, somehow. For Lee to know that about me. About us.

'Hang on a minute,' Rob said. 'So your mum told Lee and your sister that you can't have kids because of the accident? Why didn't she just tell them that we've decided we don't want them, and we plan to have a perfectly happy life without? I don't see why she needed to go into any details. It's not like we need an excuse.'

We stared at each other. I had anticipated that he might not be all that comfortable with what Mum had done. But I hadn't expected this. I felt as if an abyss had opened up between us and I was about to fall into it.

'Well, you know, we're not trying for a baby but we're not not trying, and they said it was very unlikely I'd ever conceive but it's not totally impossible and miracles do happen, so…'

'That wouldn't be a miracle,' Rob said. 'That would be a disaster. I told you, Stella, it's not what I want. If you don't understand that, you don't understand me. And if that's the case then I can't see that we have any kind of future together.'

Tears came to my eyes. The baby we might have together was suddenly so real to me I could see it and feel it in my arms. A sweet, still, sleeping little thing, looking like him and like me. I knew it was very unlikely… I knew he didn't want it… but if it just happened… wouldn't he change his mind?

Rob reached out and touched my lips with his fingertip as if to shush me. 'I'm sorry,' he said. 'I shouldn't have been so sharp with you. It's just that I can't bear feeling that we're not in this together. I need to know that you want me as I am, feeling as I do. I need to know that I'm enough for you.'

How could he be worried that he wasn't enough for me? It should have been the other way round.

'Of course you are,' I said. 'More than enough.'

He frowned. He looked kind and patient, like a good teacher. 'Are you sure? Because you know this isn't the kind of thing that can be taken back later.'

'I want you, Rob. I can't imagine my life with anyone but you.'

He rewarded me with a small, sad smile. 'That's how I feel. Look, I'm glad we had this chat. It's important to be sure. I do worry about you, Stella. You know how much you mean to me. How important you are to me. And it seems to me that what they said – about how you're very unlikely to get pregnant unless you have treatment – well, for your sake, I really think that's a blessing in disguise. If there was some weird fluke and you *did* get pregnant, I'm not sure it would even be a good idea for you to have the baby. I mean… since it happened… you're not exactly robust, are you? The accident took its toll. And not just physically. I know how profoundly it's affected you. I see it every day. I just need you to trust me, and let me look after you. From now on, it's the two of us against the world. Right?'

A tear ran down my cheek. As I rubbed it away, the hard glint of my diamond ring caught my eye through the gloom, lit up by the yellow glow of the nearest streetlamp.

Rob took both my hands in his. He looked into my eyes as if something might be hiding there and it was imperative for both our sakes that he should find it and overpower it.

'We don't need to be embarrassed about our choices,' he said. 'We don't have to defend them or explain them to anyone. We just have to be sure about what we want, and about each other. OK?'

I nodded. 'OK,' I said, and my voice sounded like a little girl's.

Rob leaned forward and pecked me on the forehead, as if absolving me of something. 'Good. Now let's go do this.'

We got out of the car and went up to the house, and I readied myself to smile and enjoy Mum's excitement. But I couldn't quite shake the feeling of having lost an argument, and of having signed up to something I was going to regret.

*

Mum came to the door to let us in, and cooed excitedly over the ring as we stood in the hallway. Molly was nowhere to be seen. Neither was Lee. The living room door was ajar and I could hear the whine of motor racing and the patter of commentary. Mum took our coats and hung them over the banister post, and we went through into the living room to join Lee, who was alone in front of the TV. Still no sign of Molly.

Lee got up and said, 'Hello, lovebirds. I hear congratulations are in order.'

He turned to Rob first and shook him by the hand, then pecked me on the cheek. He smelt strongly of cigarettes. Then he turned down the volume on the TV a little and sat down in front of it again. He made no move to switch it off. The rest of us remained standing.

Mum checked her watch. She said, 'I would offer the two of you a drink, but I don't think we have time.'

I said, 'Where's Molly?'

Mum rolled her eyes. 'Still getting ready. If we rented the bathroom to her by the hour, we'd be rich.'

'What about her boyfriend? Isn't he meant to be coming?'

'Jason?' Mum made a small noise of disgust. 'She broke up with him. Which is a good thing, if you ask me, but she's been carrying on like they're Romeo and Juliet gone wrong.'

'That's the whole point of Romeo and Juliet, you daft woman,' Lee interjected. 'She'll get over it. Young girls like her go from one to the next. Nothing upsets them for long. They just have to get used to the idea that not everyone's going to treat them like a princess. Anyway, him not coming means one less mouth to feed.'

'Well, I think she really needs to pull herself together,' Mum said. 'Especially as we've got something to celebrate.'

'If she's not ready by seven, we'll have to leave without her,' Lee said. 'If we lose our reservation you ladies will have to cook for all of us, and I don't suppose you'd like that.'

'No, we certainly wouldn't,' Mum said.

Lee reached for the packet of cigarettes on the side table next to him, took one out and lit it. 'Last one,' he said, with a meaningful glance at Mum.

'I think there's still some in that carton we got from Duty Free. I'll go and see if I can find it,' Mum said, and went off to the kitchen.

Rob sat down at the end of the sofa next to Lee's armchair, with a good view of the TV. When the doorbell rang neither of them looked away from the motor racing. A cupboard door banged in the kitchen and Mum called out, 'Could somebody get that? Whoever it is, tell them we're not interested.'

Rob glanced at me. 'Stella—?'

'Yes, might as well make yourself useful,' Lee said.

I went out and opened the front door to a greasy-haired, disconsolate-looking boy about the same age as Molly, who was carrying a cardboard box with a couple of records and an odd-smelling black jumper in it.

'Molly's stuff. She wanted it back,' he said. He thrust the box into my arms and immediately turned on his heel and sloped off into the darkness.

I shoved the door shut and carried the box upstairs. I paused for a moment to listen at Molly's bedroom door but couldn't hear anything. Then I knocked and said, 'It's me. Stella. Can I come in?'

A moment later the door opened wide and there she was with black eyeliner smudged halfway down her cheeks from rubbing her eyes, looking resentful as only someone interrupted during a good cry can be.

I stooped to put down the box on the floor. I knew better than to try and hug her – she was too upset to be ready to be comforted. I said, 'They want to leave soon. Shall we go freshen up?'

Molly shrugged. She was wearing a creased emerald-green T-shirt and black jeans, an outfit Mum would probably disapprove of, but I wasn't about to suggest she get changed. Since she'd started at sixth-form college she'd taken to wearing clothes she found in second-hand shops, which were usually rust-coloured or dark, but her bedroom was still done up in pink and lilac, the colours she'd loved when she was younger, just as it had been when she was living in Brickley with Dad. I wondered how long it would take her to ask if she could paint the walls black.

'Sure,' she said. 'Nice ring, by the way.'

'Oh. Yeah. Thanks. I'm terrified of losing it.'

'I bet.'

In the bathroom, I touched up my lip gloss and Molly soaked cotton wool in make-up remover and wiped her face. Looking in the mirror, I thought that perhaps we didn't look as different as Mum had always said we did. You could definitely tell we were sisters.

I wondered whether she might say anything about what Mum had told her about the aftermath of the accident. But she didn't. I didn't know whether she was being tactful because she thought I wouldn't want to talk about it, or whether she was so preoccupied with her own unhappiness that she'd clean forgotten.

'Do you want to try some of this?' I said, holding out my lip gloss. She shook her head and I put it back in my handbag. And then I spotted the bruise on her arm.

She immediately yanked her sleeve down and turned to me with an unexpectedly forbidding stare.

'What are you looking at?'

'Did Jason do that?'

She lifted her chin and glared at me just as she had sometimes done when she was little. Mostly she'd been biddable and well-behaved. She could be left alone to play with her dolls for hours on end, which Mum sometimes sighed and said was something to be thankful for. But every now and then she'd shown an unexpected stubborn streak. Especially with me. She didn't do it so much with Mum. She seemed to have decided that what Mum wanted from her was for her to be as good as invisible.

'It's none of your business,' she told me.

'Molly, he should never have treated you like that. It's not acceptable. If I'd have known about that when I saw him just now…'

'It was an accident,' she said. 'I bruise easily. You know that. I always have. Every time I hurt myself when I was a kid, it looked worse than it actually was. Anyway, I've finished with him, so he can't do it again, OK? I'll see him around at college, I guess. But apart from that, I'm never going to see him again. So don't say anything. Especially not to Mum. She'll just say it's my fault for being stupid, anyway. You know what she's like. She thinks I should never have gone out with him in the first place.'

'There's no way it's your fault,' I said.

Molly said, 'Don't say anything. If you do, I'll do something even worse to myself. Or I'll run away and you'll never know what happened to me. And that'll be your fault. You have to promise me.'

I hesitated. She was probably right about what Mum would say. 'I won't tell Mum.'

'You get the ring and I get the bruise,' Molly said. 'At least one of us gets to be happy.'

'You can be happy too,' I protested, but Molly just said, 'I'm going to get changed,' and walked out.

I found out later that she started seeing Jason again soon after. But by then it was much too late to intervene.

Chapter Twenty

Twenty-four hours had passed since I'd stood on Molly's doorstep and tried the first in the row of buzzers, hoping that she'd answer. I was worn out but wide awake. I'd spent a mostly sleepless night in the spare room next to the bedroom that Lee and Mum had shared, and then had come back to Fairfield Road to thrash out an interim agreement with Rob, get a new key cut so I could still come and go, and prepare for Georgie's return. And now the time had nearly come, and I was about to see her again.

According to the notice on the whiteboard outside the school entrance, the coach was running late. That was par for the course – I couldn't remember there ever being a time when one of these trips had got back when it was meant to. Not that I was bothered about that. I was so grateful to be there, waiting. I couldn't ever remember a time when I had looked forward to seeing Georgie so much.

I trudged back to the side road across from the school where I'd parked and got back into the car to wait.

Of course it'll be lovely to have her back. You're going to have to tell her Grandma's dead, though, aren't you? And that's just the beginning. Because then there's the parental break-up, and moving house, not to mention the new little half-sibling on the way. Sure, Chloe and I have agreed to let you off the hook until after the funeral. But then she's going to have a lot get to grips with. And once that's all in the open, do you seriously think you'll suddenly discover such an appetite for truth-telling that you'll want to carry on with more?

Even though Rob had agreed to let me pick up Georgie on my own, I couldn't shake the feeling that he was there with me, like one of those intruders in the backseat who shows up in films to attack the driver.

People said it was hard to talk to children about death, but so far it had not been difficult with Georgie. Rob's dad had passed away when she was little, and she had accepted that in a matter-of-fact way, much as she would have done if we'd told her he had moved house or gone on holiday – though she had barely known him, so it was very different to Mum…

But still, she had not seemed to be frightened by the idea. In her primary school science lessons they'd taught her to categorise the world into things that were alive, dead or never alive, and tasked her with designing a poster at home to show she'd understood. She had sat there quite happily at the dining room table drawing gravestones in the column for the dead, and I had felt slightly squeamish about what she was doing, frightened even, as if she was innocently invoking some kind of curse.

She had been puzzled by my reaction. *Am I doing it wrong, Mummy? No, no, you're right, the dead are dead…*

Once, when she was six or seven, she'd spotted a tiny bird lying on the garden path, frozen to death. Its talons had been curled up in a way that reminded me of newborn fingers, of Georgie's clinging on to mine all those years ago: that combination of frailty and strength of will. *I will hold on.* We had dug a miniature grave in the back garden and ceremonially buried it. *It will go back to nature now*, I'd said. Georgie had been wrapped up warm in her red hat and scarf and mittens, her breath forming clouds in the cold air. She'd looked sombre but satisfied, as if being part of nature made everything all right.

No, in the main death had not been hard for us to talk about. Birth, though, that was another matter…

My phone beeped. At last: a text message from Georgie.

Nearly there! Just outside town, should be with you in five minutes XXX

She'd sent it five minutes ago…

And then there it was, finally – the coach making its way down the main road, which was visible from the cul-de-sac where I'd parked, then pulling into the semi-circular driveway in front of the school building.

Georgie wasn't a little kid any more… It wouldn't do to be uncool and make a fuss of her in front of her schoolmates…

I got out of the car and ran across the pelican crossing to join the other parents who were waiting in front of the school, at a polite distance from the coach so as to give space for the students' backpacks to be unloaded from the luggage store underneath their seats.

One by one, tired-looking teenagers were emerging from the coach and going over to their parents… I couldn't see her at any of the windows… where was she?

And then there she was… her fair hair glinting in the sunlight, a smallish, slimmish girl in an old hoodie and jeans and dirty trainers coming slightly hesitantly down the steps, as if she wasn't sure I would be there or wasn't confident that she wouldn't trip.

It was always like that with Georgie. She never threw herself into anything. She watched, and waited, and sometimes you even forgot that she was observing everything and taking it all in. Then she would say something that floored you and you'd realise all over again what an idiot you'd been for taking her for granted.

She picked up her rucksack and came over to me.

'Hi.'

'Hi. Good times?'

'Yeah, pretty good.' She suppressed a yawn. 'Tired, though. Did you have a good birthday?'

'Yeah, not bad. Missed you, though. Dad took me out for lunch, which was pretty nice except none of it was as tasty as the cake you made me.'

'It was a good cake, wasn't it?'

'It was a good cake.'

And then (swivelling her eyes to check who was in earshot, and dropping her voice): 'I missed you, too, Mum.'

Which she almost instantly followed up with: 'Dad too, of course' – looking worried, as if she might have been unfair to him. She was always like that: it was very important to her to be even-handed. She had always shared out praise and other kinds of affirmation between us as if we were a couple of kids warring for her attention, and she was the weary lone parent meticulously ensuring that we had as little as possible to squabble over.

I said, 'Shall I take your backpack?'

Once again, a quick sidelong glance to check whether anybody might have heard, and a frown of rejection. 'No, thanks. I can manage.'

She got the backpack onto her shoulders and we started walking towards the pelican crossing. Everybody was moving slowly, weighed down with bed rolls and sleeping bags and luggage of varying degrees of practicality, trudging towards the road and over it and fanning out along the pavements and across the green towards waiting cars and houses. The sun had begun on its downwards track towards the horizon and bathed everything in the long soft light of a bright summer evening. It was idyllic: the gentle evening and all those homecomings, all those kids who were glad to see their parents and all those parents who were glad to get them back, the usual squabbles and niggles forgotten in the sweetness of being reunited after absence.

And this was it, everything I had longed for and treasured most, to be the mother of a daughter and no different to all the others. Nothing to see here, nothing to be ashamed of, nothing to disclose. Knowing it was all about to change made me want to hold onto it so badly it was like being squeezed until you feel yourself begin to crack. Except it was me who wanted to tighten my grasp until nothing that was precious could get away from me.

*

Once we were in the car I said to her, 'I'm really sorry to have to do this, Georgie, but I have some sad news to tell you.'

Her posture changed instantly. Her eyes widened and she stiffened as if trying to steel herself.

'What is it? Is it Lee?' She had always called him that – he had refused point blank to be Grandad. He had always claimed that it made him feel too old, and since you were only as old as you felt, he'd rather just be Lee. And then he had usually made a joke about how in fact you were only as old as the *woman* you felt, while Mum looked on and smiled indulgently and I did my best not to meet Rob's eyes.

'It's not Lee. It's Grandma. She had a heart attack this morning. It was very sudden and very quick and she didn't feel any pain.' (From what Lee had told me this was not true, but I wanted to soften the details.) 'An ambulance came and they tried to save her but they couldn't. It was her time to go.'

Her time to go. Was that consoling? I didn't actually find it comforting at all, the idea of there being a time, as if it was something fixed yet invisible to you until it happened. Like a sentence that had been suspended but no one was going to let you know how long for.

Georgie was rigid with shock. She was staring at me as if I'd just morphed into somebody she didn't recognise.

'But she wasn't ill,' she wailed, and then she burst into tears.

I started crying too. I put my arms around her and held her closely and my tears ran down into her hair and hers soaked into the shoulder of my T-shirt. I thought of the promise I had made her years before, when she had found that dead bird and I had explained what death meant, that I would be there for as long as she needed me. I wondered if she would remember it, and if she would always still want it to be true.

And underneath all of that, I heard the word I'd heard echoing in my head and my heart the first time I ever held her, reverberating through my blood like a pulse or the rhythm of a drum: *Mine.*

Mine. Georgie was mine and I was hers. And every inch of me felt alive and needed and ashamed.

Chapter Twenty-One

Seven years earlier

I always did my best to help Georgie with her homework. Rob expected me to make an effort, and we both wanted her to do well. I didn't want her to be the child who went into school with a collapsing model Tudor house or sagging papier mâché volcano. But one day her teacher set her a project that I didn't want to help her with at all.

She brought home a piece of A3 sugar paper and a note asking everyone in the class to create a family tree over the half-term holiday, complete with names and photos. The family trees would be displayed on the classroom wall and all the parents would be invited in one afternoon before the end of the school day to look at them. Their attention was meant to reward the kids for their efforts. But for me, the idea of our family being put on display like that was a nightmare.

Maybe there were some proud parents who would think it was a brilliant idea, but didn't they realise how difficult this kind of thing could be for some of us? People who had family members they were estranged from, or who it was painful to remember…

The idea was to introduce the kids to the idea of genetics by showing them how physical characteristics were inherited. I understood that, but I cursed the teacher for her good intentions.

Still, there was nothing for it but to make a start. Full biographies weren't called for. Names were, though. And photographs.

I enlisted Rob's help. Like me, he had his doubts.

'Do we really have to do this? Can't she opt out or something?'

'It'll seem weird if we do.'

'Well, this stuff is your department, Stella. If you think you can handle it, I guess it's fine by me. I'm not wild about the idea of a bunch of people rubbernecking at my mum and dad. Still, I guess it's homework and Georgie needs to do it. I'll see what I can dig out for you.'

The following day, late in the evening after Georgie had gone to bed, he came up to me when I was studying at my laptop in the dining room and put a small, white-rimmed photograph down on the table next to me.

It was old. Older even than Rob, maybe. It looked faded and nostalgic. The colours were sweet shades of pastel, like flavours of ice-cream – hazelnut, vanilla, strawberry, pistachio. The shadows had the sepia tint you see in prints made from film rather than from a digital camera.

He wasn't in the picture. It was just them, his parents as a young couple standing on a beach. His mum was a pretty blonde with flicky hair and one hand draped over his dad's shoulder. His dad had a drooping moustache and the kind of low-key grin that goes with a swagger and good times. They were both facing away from the camera, squinting at the sun, and the light falling on their faces smoothed the details of their features as if they had been partially erased.

All you could really make out was their expressions. They were at the seaside somewhere, and they were both smiling. They were the picture of happiness.

But pictures could be deceptive. There were plenty of photos of me and Rob where we looked just as happy, like a couple who had nothing to hide and never would.

'It's a lovely photo,' I said, and Rob grunted.

'You'd better find somewhere you can make a colour copy of it. I want it back, and I don't want you wrecking it by putting Sellotape all over it,' he said, and walked away.

After that I had everything we needed, apart from a picture of Molly.

I chose one of her from around the time when I'd left home to live with Rob, before Dad had died. There she was at fourteen in a peach-and-white patterned top and a bit too much turquoise eyeshadow, smiling shyly up at the camera as if she wasn't sure anybody would ever find her pretty. She looked as if she was waiting for someone to pay attention to her but didn't dare assume that they would.

When we made a start on the project I was nervous about what Georgie might ask. Would she want to know what Molly looked like now, or where she lived, or what she did? Would she want to meet her? Would she ask why we never saw her...?

But Georgie showed no particular curiosity about the individual pictures. She was more worried about making sure she drew straight lines to connect them up. It was only when we'd finished the family and all the pictures were named and stuck in place that she pointed to Molly and said, 'Is she dead, too?'

We were standing side by side at the dining table, looking down at the piece of pink sugar paper which had books on either side to weigh down the edges and keep it from curling up. There they all were, a network of faces joined up by the lines Georgie had marked in pencil first and then gone over carefully in black felt-tip. Rob's parents. Mum. Dad. Lee. Molly. Me and Rob.

Then there was a big, smiling picture of Georgie, the only child. She was the focal point of all of it, like a princess.

'No, Molly isn't dead,' I found myself saying. 'But we don't know where she is.'

Georgie frowned. 'Why don't we know? Is she lost?'

'She didn't want to see us any more. It was her choice. It's sad, but it happens sometimes.'

'Like breaking friends?'

'No… Yes. A bit like that. There's nothing we can do about it. It's just how it is. We aren't ever going to visit her and she isn't going to visit us.' Then, in a sudden burst of inspiration: 'I think she lives very far away, anyway. Once she sent me a postcard from Italy. She always wanted to travel. I think she just kept on moving.'

I hoped this would satisfy her. If someone was travelling all the time – which sounded exciting – it was fair enough that they wouldn't turn up to eat Brussels sprouts at Christmas.

She pursed her lips thoughtfully and seemed to be about to give up on the subject. Then she said, 'Did she ever see me?'

'Once. When you were very small,' I told her.

And then I couldn't bear it any more. I removed the books on either side of the family tree and rolled it up and put an elastic band round it.

'Anyway, that's done, finally,' I said. 'You can put it in your bookbag ready to take to school. I'd better get on with making dinner. Otherwise there will be nothing to eat when Daddy gets home.'

It sounded sharper than I'd intended, as if I was ticking her off. As if I'd accused her of asking too much of me. Of wanting something I couldn't give her, and keeping me from all the other things I had to do just to keep our lives ticking over.

I swept away and left her there staring at nothing, as if trying to comprehend what on earth she could possibly have done wrong.

Chapter Twenty-Two

'I'm so sorry for your loss,' Rose said, shaking my outstretched hand and then clasping it in both of hers. Behind her, another cluster of mourners came in. The timing at the crematorium was tight, and we had just five more minutes in the waiting room before the service was due to begin. I'd hoped to greet everybody before we went in, but there was no way I was going to manage it.

Still, it didn't matter. People would understand. I could catch up with anyone I'd missed at the reception afterwards. And Mum would have been pleased to have a respectable turn-out. She had cared about that kind of thing. I knew Lee didn't. He had said to me rather bluntly that he didn't see much point in spending out on the funeral, and he didn't care if he was just tossed into a hole in the ground when his turn came.

This was a goldfish bowl of a room, with a glass wall facing out onto the garden of remembrance, and it was warming up as more people arrived. I was beginning to feel slightly faint. It was a sweltering July day with a hint of thunder in the air, building towards the heat of noon.

Better pull myself together. I was the one who had organised all this, and it was down to me to make sure everybody else got through it all right and there weren't any upsets or disturbances.

Probably just as well, really, that Molly hadn't come.

But would Mum have wanted her there? Perhaps…

And would Rob keep his end of the bargain? We'd agreed to maintain a façade of togetherness for Georgie's sake, at least until after the funeral. It had helped that we'd barely been in the house at the same time. I'd been going back and forth to keep an eye on Lee and working, too, and Rob had often been away, sometimes genuinely for work, sometimes because he was spending time with Chloe. But I had always been conscious that our time as a family at Fairfield Road was coming to an end.

Soon it would be the end of term, and the summer holidays would begin. Georgie would have to be told what was going on. Then she and I would move out and take what we wanted with us, and Rob would move into Chloe's flat, and the house on Fairfield Road would be put on the market and sold.

I suspected Georgie had seen through our pretence anyway. She'd spotted me coming out of the spare room one morning, and every now and then I had caught her giving me worried looks, as if she had something on her mind and was trying to figure out whether it was safe to ask me about it.

But all that was a problem for another day... Right now, I had Mum's funeral to get through.

'Your mum was such a strong person,' Rose said, giving my hand a little extra squeeze and then releasing it. 'You must miss her terribly.'

'I do,' I said. 'I'm very grateful to you for all your help over the last couple of weeks. You've been a lifesaver. I know we all appreciate it.'

'Oh, it's nothing. I'm glad to be able to help. Thank goodness you have such a supportive husband. It must make such a difference. I know Pam thought he was wonderful. We were always hearing about her marvellous son-in-law.'

'Well, that's very kind of you to say.'

I wondered if Rose would change her mind when she spotted what Rob was up to. He was standing by the exit that led from the waiting room to the chapel, talking to her twentysomething daughter who worked as an optician in Kettlebridge and who was probably the most attractive young woman in the room. She was hanging on his every word, and gazing at him with a mixture of sympathy and admiration which he was no doubt lapping up.

What would Chloe make of that if she was here? I was irritated myself, and I was the one who had already lost him.

Anyway, it was none of my business…

Actually, I thought he looked tired and very slightly the worse for wear. Maybe the responsibility of impending fatherhood was getting to him. Or maybe she was giving him grief about us waiting until after the funeral to tell Georgie we were separating.

Either way, though, he could have had the decency to stick with Lee and Georgie rather than letting himself get sidetracked into a funeral flirtation.

Lee was sitting on one of the chairs lined up along one side of the waiting room, facing the garden of remembrance. He looked shell-shocked. I got the impression he'd decided to try to get through the occasion by taking in as little of what anybody said as possible. Georgie was next to him, looking very pale in her white blouse and black skirt. She was giving a reading later, and although she'd practised endlessly she was still nervous about it.

'So… you're coping, are you?' Rose looked anxiously up at me.

'Yes, I think so. Lee's not keen on the idea of carers going in. But's that all right, as we're managing OK for now. The hospice is sending a very nice lady round to talk to us once a fortnight. That's about all they can do for now. They won't take him in to look after him till right at the end.'

'Well, I think you're doing marvellously. You all are.' Rose glanced across at Georgie and grimaced sympathetically. 'Your Georgie was the apple of your mum's eye, you know that, don't you? My goodness, she was a proud grandma. "She's my prize," she said to me once. I think she really felt that. Your little family gave her so much joy. I hope that can be a comfort to you. Anyway, you will let me know if you need anything, won't you? I'm always very happy to pop in on Lee.' She leaned forward confidingly. 'I'm not sure he's always happy to be popped in on. But it's better to grumble than to give up and let it all wash over you, don't you think?'

I murmured my agreement. Rose withdrew with a final encouraging smile and I turned to greet another local friend of Mum's who had been waiting her turn at a discreet distance. Someone from the Kettlebridge bowling club. Mum had got into bowling a few years ago, and had been fiercely competitive. Like Rob, she always played any game to win...

There were plenty of people here who'd got to know Mum since she and Lee moved to Critchley, but nobody from before. None of the guests who'd once come to the drunken parties she and Lee had thrown in Ashdale. Nobody from her life with Dad in Brickley. Even though she'd been sociable, she had not been one for staying in touch. I hadn't been able to find any contact details for friends or family from before she was married to Dad, and Lee had discouraged me from even trying: 'She always said the best thing about her childhood was forgetting all about it.'

Did Molly find it easy to leave people and places behind when she moved on? Or did she ever look back and wish she could have stayed?

Annabel, the humanist celebrant who was going to lead the service, came over to speak to me and Mum's bowling club friend withdrew.

'How are you doing?' Annabel said. 'All set?'

'I think so. As ready as I'll ever be.'

I'd chosen Annabel to lead the ceremony because I'd liked the sound of her voice on the phone and Lee wasn't fussed who did it as long as it wasn't religious. She was a wiry, unflappable person, and mercifully diplomatic. She'd driven over to Critchley to take notes about Mum's life to use in her introductory remarks, a meeting which I had dreaded beforehand but had got through without too much difficulty, especially once Lee had dozed off. Annabel hadn't turned a hair on hearing that Mum had left her family to be with Lee, or that I had an estranged sister who wasn't planning to come to the funeral. Nor had she pressed for any details about why.

Of course, there was plenty I hadn't told her. But this was not the time. My worst nightmare would be to be exposed in front of these people. I'd had actual nightmares about it, dreams in which Annabel stood up in front of all Mum's sympathetic friends and neighbours – people from the bowling club and the charity shop where Mum had volunteered, regulars from their local pub in Critchley – and told them that I was a liar and a fraud. And then all their expressions had turned to shock and disgust. Rob had folded his arms and looked on with one eyebrow raised, as if to say, *I knew this day would come. You're for it now, aren't you?*

In my nightmare, the angriest of all had been Georgie, who had sat there next to me listening soberly as Annabel explained exactly what I had done. And at the end of it all, when Annabel had finished, she had turned to look at me and stared at me as if I was a stranger, and got up and walked out without a word.

'I think they're ready for us to go in now,' Annabel said. 'Would you like me to get people moving?'

'Thank you, Annabel,' I said. 'Yes, let's go.'

We filed in and took our seats. I was in the front row between Lee and Georgie. Rob had extricated himself from his heart-to-heart with Rose's daughter, and was sitting on Georgie's other side. The coffin was in place on a plinth in front of us. Closed casket. Mum hadn't specified, but I was pretty sure that's what she would have wanted. *I don't want people staring at me if I can't open my eyes and stare back! Imagine the shock you'd have if I did!*

The introductory music I'd chosen was playing. It had been hard to figure out what Mum would have wanted, and in the end I'd gone for classical music that I hoped she at least wouldn't have objected to. She might have said it was boring, perhaps. I wasn't really listening to it, so perhaps that was why I picked up the sound of the door opening and someone else slipping in.

I wasn't the only one who noticed. There was a general stir, and not just because of the eddy of cooler air she'd let in or because she was only just in time. She would have stood out whenever she'd arrived.

Her hair was cropped and platinum blonde, and she was wearing big black sunglasses and a loose, filmy black dress. She looked as if she'd stumbled into the wrong funeral. I almost thought she might turn and walk out again, but she didn't. She sidled into a free seat at the end of a row and took her sunglasses off.

Molly.

Rob caught my eye and hissed, 'What is she doing here? I thought you said she wasn't coming.'

Georgie said, 'Who? What are you talking about?'

But there wasn't any time to attempt an answer. The introductory music faded out and Annabel took her place at the lectern facing us. Georgie bowed her head over her printed order of service. She was checking through the reading she was going to give. Lee stared straight ahead and upwards at a fixed point in the middle distance, as if he hadn't registered Molly's arrival. Perhaps he hadn't. Perhaps he really was past caring.

Annabel began to speak. Her voice would have been soothing if I hadn't been acutely conscious that Molly was listening to it too. She'd turned what I'd told her about Mum into a tribute that drew attention to certain aspects of Mum's life and smoothed over or ignored the rest, the way a flattering portrait does. Difficult childhood, taken into care, married at eighteen. Two daughters. I had asked her to mention Molly. The name seemed to linger after she'd said it, like a tune you half-remember and can't place. But Annabel had already moved on to Mum finding love with Lee and eventually marrying again. Becoming a valued member of her local community in Critchley. A devoted grandmother. A cherished wife.

It was a story full of omissions. And why shouldn't it have been? Surely the bereaved should have the privilege of editing their memories of the person they'd lost until they came up with a comfortable version of the truth?

Would it hurt Molly to hear it? To be named, but not properly acknowledged? Or was her life separate enough now for her to be indifferent about how she featured in Mum's eulogy? I actually felt angry on her behalf. And yet there was nobody I could be angry with apart from myself.

I was giving the first reading. It was a poem, not too long. I'd practised it with Georgie. I wasn't particularly nervous about it, not as far as I was aware. But when I went up to stand by the lectern, I was so violently conscious of Molly sitting there listening to me and watching me that I couldn't speak.

She didn't look angry or vengeful. There was no need to be frightened, at least, not yet. But still… she was *there*. And she knew exactly what I'd done. She'd been part of it. She remembered it. And she knew how far I'd fallen short of what I ought to have done, and how badly I had let my daughter down by failing to tell her the truth.

What else could I expect from Molly beside judgement?

The sight of her hurt my head like an alarm going off. I had to close my eyes and force myself to concentrate. When I opened my eyes I made an effort not to look up again, but to fix my attention on the words in front of me on the lectern. They swam briefly around each other and then came back into focus. The ground under my feet seemed to be moving or undulating, as if it might be about to collapse. Or maybe it was me who was on the brink of falling.

I gripped the lectern and managed to make a start. My voice sounded like someone else's. High, wavering and hollow. Surely that couldn't be me? My hands were trembling. I couldn't help but see that people were looking up at me aghast. Yes, they felt sorry for me, there was sympathy, but nobody wanted to see this, someone losing the plot, making an exhibition of herself, getting choked up…

Lee was stony-faced, as if he thought I was letting the side down. Georgie looked anguished, as if my humiliation was her own. But

Rob was watching me with cold detachment, as if I was absolutely nothing to do with him.

How could I be? How would someone like him ever get mixed up with a woman who was making such a mess of things?

Somehow his disapproval steadied me as nothing else would have done. My voice became mine again and I was able to rattle off what was left of the reading and come away from the lectern and return to my seat.

Then it was Georgie's turn.

Another poem. She stepped up and began to read in her clear, slightly hesitant, best-and-loudest voice. Brave girl. Good girl. She was doing what I had just failed to do, and staying composed. But I couldn't bring myself to look at her. The sound of her voice seemed to form a perfect arc connecting her and Molly, and I was sure that everybody else in the room must be conscious of it too.

Then she had finished and was settling into her seat next to me again.

She gave me a frightened little look. I managed to say, 'Well done.' There was more Annabel. More music. I wasn't crying. I was at my own mother's funeral and I wasn't crying. My heart was beating louder than it ever had before but no one else showed any sign of hearing it.

Then it was Lee's turn to go up to the lectern. I could barely make out a word he was saying. My heartbeat drowned all of it out.

He sat down again and I forced myself to turn round and try to catch Molly's eye, to smile at her and show that she was welcome. To prove to myself that I could take her presence in my stride.

But the place at the end of the row where she'd been sitting was empty. She had already gone.

Chapter Twenty-Three

Twenty-four years earlier

The day Mum walked out on us, I stood in the hallway and watched her as she prepared to leave. She was wearing a brand-new outfit – confident, new-life clothes. A red jumper, brown suede-look trousers, high-heeled boots. She put her raincoat on in front of the full-length mirror, carefully tied the belt at the waist and fluffed out her hair. Then she said, 'Keep an eye on Molly for me, would you? I'll be in touch.'

She fluffed out her hair one last time, picked up the big suitcase and stepped out of the front door. She turned to give me a wave before she got in the waiting taxi, as if she'd won a prize holiday out of the blue and was delighted to be off. Then she was gone.

As I closed the door behind her I had a sick feeling in the pit of my stomach. I couldn't kid myself. I knew it was final. She wouldn't be back.

I turned round and there was Molly in her pale pink nightie with her hair in a mess, coming down the stairs.

'Was that Mummy? Did she go to work early?'

Why soft-soap it, or hold back? She had to know.

But I couldn't bring myself to tell her straight away. Instead I just passed on what Mum had said to me. 'She's gone away for a bit.'

Molly's face puckered up as if I'd just told her something incomprehensible and tasked her with unravelling it. 'But when's she coming back?' And then, as an afterthought: 'Why didn't she say goodbye to *me*?'

'I guess she was in a rush,' I said helplessly.

Molly frowned. It was beginning to make sense to her, but not in a good way. 'Did she take a suitcase?'

'Yeah, she took a suitcase.'

'Which one?'

I told her. It was the biggest, the one Molly and I shared when we went away for a week. Too big for a short trip, even for Mum, who liked to have scope for a lot of outfit changes.

It was then that Molly knew she'd been abandoned. It was much worse seeing her realise it than it had felt to figure it out myself. First of all she was horrified, as she might have been if our house had suddenly burst into flames. Then she screwed up her face and turned and ran away from me up the stairs to her room. A minute later I heard her crying.

I felt about a million years old. I trudged up the stairs and sat next to her on her bed and stroked her hair and tried to comfort her. I had to try. If I could make Molly feel better about it, maybe I would feel better about it myself.

We'd see Mum again soon, I told her. It would all be all right, she'd taken that suitcase because she liked to have a lot of clothes, more than she could possibly have time to wear. I would have said anything to stop Molly crying. It was like pushing a huge rock uphill: she'd quieten and maybe even almost move towards a smile, and then it would hit her again and she'd start weeping afresh.

I didn't know whether Dad could hear. He often slept in after he'd been working late in the evenings. Anyway, he didn't come in and I didn't ask him to, and part of me wasn't surprised that he didn't appear.

After what felt like a very long time – though it was probably only ten minutes or so – Molly agreed that it was time to get up so as not to be late for school, and came downstairs with me so I could make her some breakfast.

And I felt better too. I'd helped her, I'd comforted her, and now I was going to make sure she went to school on time on a full stomach and was properly dressed in her uniform, with her teeth brushed and her hair done. And nobody would even be able to tell that anything had happened.

Mum had gone. I didn't yet know why or where. But maybe it wasn't the end of the world. Maybe we could find a way to carry on without her. Mum had asked me to keep an eye on Molly but I was going to do more than that. I was going to look after her. And if I could do that – if I could make this OK for Molly – maybe it would be OK for me too.

If I had known then that years later Molly would walk out of Mum's funeral before the end, I might not have been surprised. I would have taken it to mean that even as a grown-up, Molly would still be angry. That she'd never get over Mum leaving us without saying goodbye to her. She was so little at the time. I'd have reasoned that being so young might make it harder, rather than easier, to forgive and forget.

But if I had known that Molly would slip away from Mum's funeral without so much as saying a word to me, I wouldn't have believed it.

After Mum had gone, when I was sitting on Molly's bed and stroking her hair and trying to soothe her, it didn't feel as if I was telling her lies. It was more as if I was telling her a story. We were both characters in the story and so were Mum and Dad, and in the story Mum came back and everything worked out and in the end all of us were happy.

We'll see her soon, I told her. *She'll be back.*

It might not have been true, strictly speaking, but it worked. It distracted her and it comforted her, just as all the stories I'd read to her had done down the years, whether they were about Cinderella or Milly-Molly-Mandy or the Faraway Tree or the Famous Five. And it felt as if the bond between us was unbreakable, and as if that was all we needed to pull us both through.

Chapter Twenty-Four

The reception after Mum's funeral passed in a blur of sympathy and well-meant comments. It was all as inconsequential and senseless as a dream. Eventually, after an hour and a half, the only mourners left inside the pub were me, Rob and Georgie. Lee had gone out for a breath of fresh air, or so he had said. It was time to pack away. It was over.

The finger buffet had been picked clean. All that was left was a few sausage rolls on a napkin in a bowl, some bread rolls and a small residue of salad. The pub manager offered to box up anything we might want to take home, but I told her not to bother. 'We've done pretty well,' I said. Was it the right kind of thing to say? It would have to do.

Rob said, 'Are we ready, then?'

He was standing at a slight distance from me, as if whatever was wrong with me might be contagious.

'Yeah, I think so.'

Ready for what? I had no idea. Ready for life without Mum? Ready to lose my mind? Ready to forget? Because I would forget. I knew that because I had been through it with Dad after the accident and I knew how it worked. By and by all I had left of her would be memorabilia, a blurry impression of her appearance and mannerisms and the way she'd talked. And the way she'd made me feel. That longing for everything to be easy between us, for her to be pleased with me and for me to be happy for her.

I said a final thank you and goodbye to the pub manager, who wished us all well and said again that she was sorry for our loss.

Georgie was hovering nearby, waiting to leave. She looked exhausted, and as if tiredness was the only thing that was keeping her from tears.

'All right, love,' I said. 'All done now. We can go.'

Lee was outside in the pub garden, smoking. As we approached him Rob said to me in a low voice, 'Can't you do something to get him to give up?'

'Under the circumstances, no, I don't think so. It's his life and he knows there's not much of it left. And it's his wife's funeral.'

'Great. Now my car's going to stink of cigarette smoke.'

'You're the one who insisted on driving.'

'Just as well I did. You don't seem entirely with it, if you don't mind me saying so. And I don't think it would have helped anybody to have Lee commenting on your driving all the way to the crematorium.'

Lee stubbed out his cigarette. 'Party's over, is it?'

'It is,' Rob said. 'Time to get you home.'

Lee stood up. 'You could have done with a bouncer on the door to keep out the riff-raff,' he said.

Was that a reference to Molly? I didn't reply. It seemed like the best thing to do was to pretend that it was just some kind of joke.

Lee settled into the front seat of the car, and Georgie and I sat in the back. Georgie fell to biting her nails. When I gently pointed out what she was doing in the hope that she would stop, she folded both hands in her lap and turned away from me so she could stare out of the window.

We set off back to the house. Not far to go. We'd be there any minute. It was nearly over.

There was silence in the car, and it was into this silence that Georgie spoke.

'Do you know who the blonde lady was?'

Nobody responded.

'She came in just before it started and sat at the back,' Georgie added helpfully.

More silence. Incriminating, painful silence. And Georgie was still waiting for an answer.

Obviously it was down to me to tell her. Rob was concentrating on driving. And it wouldn't help anybody if Lee decided to share his opinions on the subject.

'That was Molly. My sister,' I said finally.

Was?

'We weren't expecting her,' I went on. 'I mean, I got in touch with her to tell her when and where it was, and to give her the option to get involved.' That didn't sound too bad. That sounded reasonable. 'I guess she changed her mind at the last minute.'

Another silence.

Then Georgie said, 'You mean, that was my aunt.'

'Yes. That's right.'

'Why do you think she didn't stay?'

A small animal scurried across the road ahead of us – a badger, by the look of it. Rob hit the brakes and swore under his breath. Usually he would have minded his language with Lee and Georgie around. Clearly he was feeling the pressure.

I remembered the deer appearing at the side of the road and Dad swerving to avoid it. The final moments before the car hit the tree, when the collision had become inevitable and everything went slow and silent before the crunch.

'I don't know,' I said. 'I guess she wanted to come and pay her respects, and once she'd done that, she felt it was time for her to go.'

'I would have quite liked to meet her. I mean, she's my aunt. My only aunt. Do you think we'll see her another time? Like maybe we could visit her or something, or she could visit us?'

'I don't know about that,' I said slowly.

'Well, maybe we could ask?'

Georgie said this as if she wasn't expecting an answer, as if she was suggesting something that was perfectly obvious but – for reasons to do with inexplicable grown-up intransigence – hadn't been considered. 'Where does she live, anyway?'

'In London, for now. But I think she likes to move around quite a bit. I mean, she could take off again any time.'

'That sounds exciting,' Georgie said, and sighed. 'Anyway, I guess she didn't care about Granny all that much. It seems kind of harsh to say she wasn't coming, even if she did change her mind. I mean, it seems like they didn't get on.'

'Bit of a cheek her turning up like that, if you ask me,' Lee said. 'Making her entrance. Stealing the show. Not that it really bothers me, but Stella, in my opinion it would have been better if you'd just left well enough alone. Anyway, I don't imagine she'll bother coming to *my* funeral, so you should all be spared the awkwardness of seeing her again.'

'It wasn't that awkward,' Georgie said, blithely ignoring Lee's reference to the prospect of his own death. 'It was mysterious. Everyone was wondering who she was. I heard Rose and her daughter talking about it at the reception.'

'I'm not sure it's very nice for people to gossip about the mourners at a funeral,' I said.

'At least it gave everyone something to talk about,' Lee said. 'Besides you getting stage fright, I mean.'

I'd almost managed to kid myself that it hadn't gone that badly. The image of everyone staring up at me came back as vividly as if I was still stuck there in front of the lectern, unable to speak.

'Look, every family has a black sheep,' Lee said. 'Some families have nothing but. Rose will probably ask me about it, and I'll tell her to mind her own business, and then she'll give up and talk about something else. There's a controversy about parking in our road, for example. Someone using up too much space with too many cars. I ask you. People will always find something to get het up about.'

'But I'm not het up,' Georgie protested. 'I just want to know what's wrong with her. Because you're all behaving as if she did something awful. I mean, I guess cutting yourself off from your family *is* awful… but why did she do it? Was there a big row or something? Because it seems like none of you want to talk about it.'

The silence that followed that remark was the heaviest and most deadening of them all. It was cut short by Rob pulling over. We had arrived.

'I hope *my* parking won't cause any controversy,' Rob said.

'Car's a bit big. Probably just as well you're not round here all that often,' Lee said.

'I'll come in with you, Lee,' I said. 'Help you get settled.'

'No need. Still, if you must. I wouldn't want you to feel troubled in your conscience about me.' He turned to look over his shoulder at Georgie. 'Your aunt wasn't much good,' he said. 'I wouldn't bother about her too much if I was you.'

He made it along the path to the house without needing to lean on my arm for support. Once he was settled in his chair in front of the TV he said, 'You should get on home. You'll only clatter about so I can't hear the telly. Women always seem to struggle to just stay sitting down. I don't suppose I'll come to any harm, anyway. I've got my panic button if I get panicked, and you can't really go wrong if you don't move from in front of the idiot box. It's actually the healthiest place to be.'

I told him I'd be back later, and left him there with the TV remote on the arm of his chair. The channel he was watching was showing the last scene of *Goodbye, Mr Chips*, which I wouldn't have thought was Lee's cup of tea at the best of times, let alone today. Surely the last thing he would feel like watching was the end of the life of a childless widower? But perhaps when you were so close to the reality of passing away, the movie version was just a diversion like any other.

The doctors had given him a rough estimate of the time he had left some months ago, and he had outlived that, a feat he was particularly proud of because he didn't have a lot of time for doctors and enjoyed proving them wrong. Did he have any regrets? He had always seemed to live life on his own terms, and to enjoy it – and to enjoy winding other people up whenever the opportunity presented itself. I didn't know whether he had ever wanted children. As I knew from my own experience, it was unwise to make any assumptions about why or how things turned out for people the way they did.

By the time he'd got together with Mum, it had seemed to be a given that they wouldn't have a baby. She'd been well into her thirties by then, not too old in theory, but I doubted whether she would have had any appetite for going back to nappies and broken nights. She had made one or two remarks that suggested he'd been a busy bachelor before they started seeing each other. She had been proud that after his history of 'stringing along' his girlfriends – as she had put it – she had been the one who had finally tamed him and persuaded him to settle down.

I went back to the car and got into the passenger seat next to Rob, who set off for Fairfield Road. None of us said a word the rest of the way home.

That night I cooked steak for Rob and myself and something made out of Quorn for Georgie. My food tasted slightly off, the way food does when you were unhappy when you prepared it. But the others didn't seem to notice. Or perhaps they were just being polite.

How many more times would I cook for the three of us? We had eaten so many meals here. Now it was nearly all over, and Chloe was waiting in the wings. Probably Rob was thinking about her. She'd want him to call, to say how the funeral had gone.

Well, it could have been worse. Stella was in a bit of a state. Messed up her reading. But anyway, none of that matters, darling. The only thing that matters is that soon you and I are going to be together all the time. How soon? Very soon, very soon, I promise you. Of course I want it all out in the open. You think I don't want everyone to know that we're together now? That you're having my baby? Don't you know how proud I am?

As soon as he'd finished he pushed his plate away, yawned, stretched, said he needed to check his emails and withdrew to his office at the end of the garden. But he didn't look particularly eager. He had the slightly defeated posture of someone who's just been scolded, or expects to be.

Georgie, who was never a fast eater, was still picking at her food. Rob shouldn't really have left the table before she'd finished, but why worry about table etiquette when we had neglected so much else?

There was a clattering sound as she dropped her knife and fork into her plate. It made me jump, and she stared at me as if she was disturbed by how easy I'd been to startle.

Her eyes were clear and blue. People sometimes said how like Rob's they were. But he was watchful and guarded, and her gaze was trusting and direct. That was how you could be when you had nothing to hide.

'Mum, I probably shouldn't say this… I hope you don't mind… I know it's been an awful day for you and everything, but are you and Dad getting on OK?'

I couldn't quite believe she'd asked. Would Rob be angry with me for answering without him there? Probably. But she was giving me a chance to at least acknowledge that there were difficulties. I could do that much, surely.

'No,' I said. 'The honest truth is we've been having some problems. We're still talking to each other, obviously. But some of the things we're talking about aren't very nice.'

Georgie's face crumpled. 'Are you going to get a divorce?'

'I shouldn't really talk to you about this without your dad here,' I said. 'We need to sit down with you, all three of us together…'

'Are we going to be able to carry on living here?'

'We?'

'Yes. You and me. I mean… I can't really live with just Dad, can I? He's never around. I mean, look at how often he's been away in the last few weeks. I'd basically be looking after myself.'

Every instinct told me to tread carefully. Rob had come round to the point of view that Georgie should live with me during the week, but he was capable of changing his mind, especially if he felt I'd jumped the gun and cheated and then somehow defeated him. Even his love for Georgie might not be enough to overcome his powerful hatred of losing.

'I shouldn't talk to you about this without him here,' I said. 'All I can really say for now is that you're the most important person in the world to us.' Was that still true for Rob? Now he had Chloe, and a new baby on the way? 'We want to do this as amicably as we can, and so that it causes as little disruption for you as possible.'

Her eyes filled with tears. 'I know you will. I mean, I know you'll want to. I just wish you didn't have to.'

And then she put her head in her hands and sobbed.

'Georgie… shh… I'm so sorry… I really can't bear to see you cry.'

That was true. I couldn't. I was beside myself. I moved close to her, stooping so that I could embrace her, willing her to let me embrace her and comfort her properly.

She looked up at me and her face was slick and shiny with tears. She said, 'I know this is silly… I know you'll tell me it's not my fault… but I can't help but think that if I'd been better in some way then both of you would have been happier and none of this would have happened.'

'You're right about one thing. It's not your fault,' I said. 'If it wasn't for you, I'm not sure we would have lasted for as long as we did.'

I straightened up and cradled her head against my belly and her tears soaked into the fabric of my jeans. I thought of the jumpsuit I'd worn on my birthday and the little jagged tear I'd found in it when I hung it up. I thought of the clothes Rob had left for me, and the bathroom mirror in Fox Hill that was too high for me to see my scars. I thought about how lucky I was to be here and to be holding my daughter and to be alive.

Georgie looked up at me again, and I touched the tears on her face and brushed them away with my thumb.

'It will all be all right, I promise,' I said, and she looked reassured. As if she believed me. That was how much she trusted me.

I smiled down at her and suggested finding something to watch and curling up on the sofa together. But all I could think about was the time when she was little and had suddenly developed a sense of herself as a person with a past, who had a history that she didn't remember.

She'd asked to see pictures of herself as a baby. Well, that wasn't a problem. She'd looked through them carefully, turning the pages as if she was reading a very important and precious storybook. And then she'd asked if there was one of her in my tummy.

I told her there wasn't. I didn't have any scans to show her. I did have a photo that had been taken a few weeks before she was born. But it was too intimate. Too exposing. I had chosen to keep it to myself.

The picture was all pregnant belly, sideways on, glistening slightly from the shower, with an arm across the breasts. There were faint pink stretchmarks towards the underside of the bump, close to the hips. Otherwise the skin was pale and smooth and unmarked. There was no face, no hair. Just the belly and that glimpse of arm. It was almost anonymous.

Georgie had never seen me naked and I had never let her see my scars, although she knew I had them. I was always careful to keep myself covered up, and she knew why. *Mummy has scars. She doesn't like anybody to see them, except for Daddy when it's quite dark.* She accepted my attitude to being seen as part of me, as if it was just another feature that I couldn't have changed even if I had wanted to.

If I had shown her that picture she might not have started asking questions, and even if she had, I could probably have found a way to fob her off. But I had been afraid she would remember and want to see it again later, when she was older. And then it would have been harder to lie.

I had taken that picture myself, from the other side of the bathroom. Recording the moment. The baby who was soon to come out into the world.

If I had shown it to Georgie and she had gazed at that pregnant belly and asked where the scars were, I might have told her the truth there and then. As it was, I could only imagine what she might think if she were to find the photo by chance and then realise that the body in it wasn't mine.

Chapter Twenty-Five

Fifteen years earlier

It was Mum who told me what had happened and what Molly planned to do.

I called her the day after we got back from honeymoon, expecting to have a conversation about the sights we'd seen – the Hollywood sign, Venice beach, the stars on the Walk of Fame – and to hear about Mum's latest plans to renovate her house and whatever Molly had been up to. I expected to hear that Molly had been staying out late, sleeping in, perhaps seeing someone new. I did not expect to hear that she was pregnant. And the very last thing I ever would have expected to hear was that Molly wanted to give her baby to me.

'She only told me because she'd stopped going to college and I wanted to know what she was planning to do with her life. She's nearly five months gone, and she's absolutely determined to go ahead and have it,' Mum told me. 'Jason doesn't want to know. Which is probably for the best, really. Anyway, it's hardly a surprise. It seems like something went on between them after we all thought they'd broken up. But it's well and truly over now. I mean, it was – even before this happened. Or that's what Molly's told me, anyway.'

She sounded beleaguered, as if she couldn't quite believe that Molly had ended up in this situation after only a relatively short time in her care. And at the same time there was a scandalised, gossipy, rather detached tone to her voice, as if she was talking about some other family's troubles.

Molly... pregnant. My little sister, who was barely more than a child herself...

I said, 'Is she all right...? I mean, how is she?'

'She seems to be fine, physically at any rate. Fit as a fiddle. She's like me – I always carried well. But she's refusing point blank to stay here. She wants to come and live with you and Rob. Then she wants to hand it over to you to adopt.' She paused. 'Lee thinks it's a good idea. For her to stay with you, anyway. He's not at all keen on her being here. As for the rest of it, he just says it's women's business and he doesn't want anything to do with it.' She sighed dramatically. 'It's been quite a stormy couple of days, I can tell you. Once or twice I nearly rang you at the hotel. But then I thought I ought to let you enjoy your honeymoon, at least. Anyway, I managed to persuade Molly that I should be the one to tell you what's going on. It's hardly ideal timing, is it? I really am sorry to have to hit you with all this when you've barely had time to unpack.'

'No, that's all right,' I said. 'I'm glad you told me. You're right to have told me.'

Even though I believed I ought to share everything with Rob, I was glad he wasn't in the house. He'd be back any minute, though. He'd only gone into the village to the newsagent's to get bread and milk. But for now I was by myself in the kitchen.

There was so much still to do. The walls were brown where they'd been replastered but not repainted. The rain was streaming down the new French windows we'd put in to open out from the extension into the tiny back garden, which needed to have a new patio laid and was currently knee-deep in weeds.

But this could be a house with a baby in it. Right there on a mat by the sofa, rolling and gurgling while I got the supper ready. *My* baby.

I knew that this was what I wanted. It was as clear as everything else I could see, as real as the rain running down the glass or the unpainted plaster on the walls. I wanted it so much that I was immediately terrified it wouldn't be possible, and that either Rob would say no or Molly would change her mind.

'A baby can put a heck of a strain on a marriage,' Mum said. 'And your marriage is very new, and I know you and Rob have talked about this and decided you aren't too bothered about having kids. Molly seems to be absolutely convinced you'll say yes. But I have tried to explain to her that you would be quite within your rights to say no.'

After the night when Rob and I had gone over to Ashdale to celebrate our engagement, I made a point of telling Mum that we were both quite content to live out our married lives as a family of two. I knew how important it was to Rob for us to present not having children as a choice we were both happy to make. I had done my best to convince myself that this was the case. But now that wasn't how I felt at all. I wanted to say yes to Molly. But would Rob agree?

'It would be a huge thing to take on,' Mum was saying. 'You're going to need to think about it, and I don't think you should feel under any obligation, unless it's actually what both of you want. That's why I thought I should be the one to talk to you. To make it easier for you to say no.'

'I'll have to talk to Rob about it,' I said.

There was a sharp little inhalation of breath at the other end of the line. 'So you really might do it?'

'What are you going to do if we say no?'

'Well, that's really up to Molly, isn't it? If she's old enough to get herself in trouble, she's old enough to figure out the rest. My advice to her would have been to get herself sorted out in double quick time and forget all about it. But she seems to be convinced that the two of you will want the baby. She says she wants something good to come of it. But if you don't want it, and if she's still determined not to stay here… well, I suppose we could try and find her somewhere else to live. But that's going to cost, and what employer is going to want her?'

'We'll take her in,' I said immediately. Though surely that would make it almost impossible not to take in her baby too, if that was still what Molly wanted us to do. And what if Rob said no? 'We've got to be very careful with her,' I went on, sounding more sure of myself than I felt. 'We have to make sure she's got a roof over her head and she's OK. Her and the baby. I mean, if she still wants to go ahead and have it. It's her choice. She has to be free to change her mind. She might decide she wants to look after the baby herself. There's no reason why she shouldn't. I mean, there's the money side of things, but we could help her with that. But anyway, the last thing we want is for her to run away or do something stupid.'

'I think the way she sees it, she's going to hand this baby over to you and then take off and go gallivanting around the world and living whatever kind of life she wants. I have to say, Stella, she's not exactly taking responsibility for what she's done. She just wants *you* to take responsibility for it.'

'Mum, she's only seventeen years old and she recently lost her dad. I don't think it's very helpful for us to judge her.'

'That's all very well, but let me remind you, I wasn't that much older than she is now when I had you. I think I'm allowed to have an opinion. I'm just concerned for you, that's all. And I'm sure I don't know why you're talking as if you think this is *my* fault all of a sudden,' Mum said huffily. 'I've done my absolute best by your sister, as much as I could do. It hasn't been easy for me, dealing with all of this. It's different when you have a husband to consider. You'll find that, I'm sure. Whatever you decide. Anyway, I did try and warn Molly. I told her to go and get herself on the Pill. But then it seems she stopped taking it when she and Jason broke up, and then when they got back together she forgot all about it. Until it was too late. The problem is, Stella, she's not like you. She's got no common sense. Never has had.'

'I know it's not your fault, Mum. I didn't mean to imply it was.'

'You do want this baby,' Mum said. 'Don't you?'

I hesitated. She sounded pleased. Clearly, she wanted me to want it...

'But I can't be sure about Rob,' I said.

Mum sighed. 'Well, I have to say I can see why he might not go for it. I mean, for you this is your niece or nephew. It's family. You can't expect him to feel that much of a connection. You've got to put yourself in his shoes. How would you feel if he suddenly produced a baby from somewhere and expected you to love it?'

'But Molly *is* family. For both of us. Isn't that the whole point of being married? We're all family now.'

Mum made a clucking sound with her tongue. 'Then heaven help him. Still, he doesn't have anybody else, does he?'

'Not who he's close to.'

'Well, do you think he'll come round?'

'I don't know.'

'You're going to be in a fix if he doesn't, aren't you? I suppose we all will. I mean, in a way, it is the most obvious solution. You're much better set up to be a mum than Molly is, anyway.'

'Mum! You shouldn't say that.'

'Why not? It's true. You're the one with the house and the husband. I know you haven't been in brilliant shape since the accident, but you seem ever so much better than you were.' Mum fell silent, as if she was ruminating. Then she said, 'You should let me talk to Rob.'

'Oh, Mum, no.'

'Why not? We've always got on. And he lost his own mother, didn't he? That makes a difference. I think he's more appreciative than he might be otherwise. I know it's the standard thing for young men not to think all that much of their mothers-in-law, but I've always felt that Rob's been very respectful towards me, actually.'

'But the way his mum died is part of the problem. He's really squeamish about medical things. And birth. Almost phobic.'

'Well, this way he's got an excuse to stay away from all that, hasn't he? It's not as if *you'll* be the one doing it. Anyway, she'll probably pop it out in two seconds flat. I never had any trouble with that side of things myself. Nor did my mother. You know she had eight children by three different fathers. Never in labour more than a few hours with any of them. One thing the women in this family don't have a problem with is breeding. In the main, anyway.'

It was so unusual for her to mention her own mother that I almost forgot to be stung. It didn't seem to occur to her that I might be hurt, because after a brief pause she ploughed on: 'So how about I call back a bit later on, and have a chat with him?'

'Mum, no. I need to do it. I think I just need to be honest with him. Put my cards on the table. See what he says.' But I was suddenly increasingly and sickeningly convinced that he would say no.

'Well, if you go into it like that he'll say no for sure. You sound all angry and defensive already. If you turn this into a battle of wills, you'll lose. And if he says you have to choose between the baby and him, you'll lose them both. The powers that be prefer you to be married if you want to adopt. Or so I've heard. They're traditional types, judges.'

'So what do you think I should do?'

'You're a woman who's got a man and wants a baby,' Mum said. 'Do you really imagine you're the first woman in the history of time to have to use a little persuasion?'

'Oh no, I don't think it should be like that. We should figure out what to do together.'

'That's all very well when you want the same things,' Mum said. 'Don't say I didn't warn you.' And then she hung up.

I went over to the French windows and looked out at the rain falling and the wreck of the garden. It was the strangest thing. I actually felt as if I was pregnant myself. I touched my hand to my waist and it seemed to me that I was already beginning to swell.

The ghost of something new was growing inside me and there was nothing I could do to stop it.

Then I heard Rob's key turning in the door.

He came in and dropped the shopping on the table and kissed me. 'I've missed you,' he said.

'You were only gone for ten minutes.'

'Longer than that. Anyway, it was too long.'

We carried on kissing. The rain carried on falling. I felt shameless and brazen. I didn't even care about my scars. My body felt powerful, like the body of someone who could change things and make things happen. One thing led to another right there on the sofa. When we had finished he looked into my eyes as if he couldn't quite believe what I'd done to him, and I knew there would never be a better time to ask for what I wanted.

I didn't tell him straight away. Instead I fixed us scrambled eggs and coffee for brunch while he lounged on the sofa and leafed through the newspaper. The rain had stopped and the sun had come out, and in the suddenly bright light he looked tired and slightly punch drunk. I spotted a rainbow high above the back fence through the window over the sink but didn't call him over to see it. I had learned that there were times when it was best just to leave Rob to himself, to think whatever he was thinking or leave him to think nothing at all.

As he sat down at the table he said, 'I'm good for nothing now. You've worn me out. But look at you! You look positively radiant. I feel like I've just had an encounter with a vampire.'

'I don't think they operate by day.' I put his plateful of food in front of him.

'A mutant vampire.' He squirted a dollop of ketchup on the side of his plate and prepared to tuck in.

'Mum rang while you were out,' I said casually.

He didn't pause, or freeze. He showed no signs of detecting that anything untoward might have happened. Instead he put a forkful of eggs and toast into his mouth, chewed and swallowed.

'That's the stuff for the troops,' he said. 'I think I'm reviving. How is she?'

'Oh, she's fine. Considering. Molly's pregnant.'

He set down his fork. '*Pregnant?* How did that happen?'

'The usual way, I guess.'

'Was it the greasy, long-haired lout ex-boyfriend?'

'Yeah.'

'Seems the type.'

'Not that you ever actually met him.'

'Never wanted to. And I think I want to even less now.' He studied me for a moment. 'Stella... what *is* this?'

I speared another forkful of food. 'What do you mean?' I said, sounding not very convincingly innocent.

'Well... you said she's pregnant. You didn't say that she's pregnant and she's going to have an abortion. And you don't seem upset about it. And why is it that I feel like I've just walked into some kind of ambush?'

I chewed, swallowed, and smiled. I set down my knife and fork. 'You're good,' I said. 'You're very good.'

'I know you, Stella. Don't forget that. No one else will ever know you the way I do.'

'The funny thing is, I don't really feel I know you,' I said. 'Not well enough to predict what you're going to do, or how you're going to react. I think you're always going to be a little bit of a mystery to me.'

He looked pleased at this. 'That's good, isn't it? Surely it would get boring otherwise. To tell you the truth, I can't predict what I'm going to do next myself half the time.'

'When you saw me the first time – when we met at the opening at Brickley Museum –what was it that made you want to talk to me? I mean, me in particular. There were lots of other women you could have talked to. So why me?'

He grinned. 'Who says I wanted to talk? Sometimes men are very simple, Stella. It's women who make them complicated.'

'Mum asked me if it might be possible for Molly to come and stay here for a bit,' I said. 'I don't think they're getting on very well.'

Rob let out a groan. 'Ah, now we're cutting to the chase. Are you kidding me? Seriously? We just got back from honeymoon and now we have to babysit your pregnant little sister?'

'I know. I'm really sorry. The timing is awful.'

'You mean you actually want to do this? You want her here?'

'Please, Rob. I'm sure she'd stay out of the way. We have to help her. I don't think I could live with myself if anything happened to her.'

'You said you wanted her to stay for a bit. How long are we talking?'

We sat there and stared at each other. Neither of us made any move to eat any more of our rapidly cooling scrambled eggs. I said, 'I haven't actually spoken to her yet. But Mum says she wants us to have the baby.'

Rob said, 'OK.'

'I mean that Molly wants us to have the baby. And Mum seems to think it might work out. I know we talked about all this before and I get how you feel about it, and I know what we agreed. And you mean everything to me. You know that, right? But this means something to me too. It made me think about the future. Just a daydream, really. In twenty-five years' time, when we're fifty. What it would be like to have a son or a daughter to be proud of. And the thing is, Rob, you'd be good at it. You'd be really good at it. Being a dad, I mean. I know you would. And I think you'd enjoy it. It'd make you happy. It'd make both of us happy, and it's not that we couldn't be happy without it. But it'd be a different kind of happy.' I put my hand on my heart. 'I've got to tell you, Rob, it's what I want. For both of us.'

Rob picked up his knife and fork. 'You really don't listen sometimes, do you? I said OK.'

I gaped at him. He said, 'I can see how much you want it. If I don't agree I'm never going to hear the last of it.'

'But Rob—'

He set down his fork and held up his right hand to stop me. 'I wouldn't do that if I were you. Don't question it. Just take it. Before I change my mind.'

That shut me up. Rob put his knife down too. He said, 'I'm telling you now, if Molly's sick in the house I'm not going to clear it up. And she doesn't get to put her choice of music on in the morning. Maybe not ever. She can wear headphones. I'm not going to be changing any nappies, either. And we're not having another one. Not by any means. Even if they figure out how to clone babies in a vat. This is it. We're going to have an only child. That's the deal.'

I got up so fast and so clumsily that my chair toppled over behind me. Rob grinned at me. His eyes were a little wet – but that never happened. He never cried. I rushed over to embrace him and draped myself around him and squeezed him tight. He patted my arm cautiously, almost sympathetically, as if I was an overexcited child who had just opened a present I really, really wanted, and he was thrilled to be the giver of the gift but at the same time couldn't help but be slightly wary.

Maybe he already knew what I had yet to learn: giving someone what they want is no guarantee that they'll carry on loving you, or stay happy. Or even continue to be grateful.

A week or so later Rob drove us to Bristol station so we could meet Molly off the train. We found a parking spot near the taxi rank, where it would be easy to spot her when she came out. It was pouring with rain again and I kept wiping the windscreen to stop it steaming up. I was scared of missing her. I didn't trust her to be able to spot us, or even to remember what make of car we had. Also, part of me didn't really believe she'd ever turn up.

How could she possibly go through with what she said she intended to do? In a way, wouldn't it be better for her to realise sooner rather than later that she couldn't? It was just too much. To go through the whole of the pregnancy, to give birth, and then to hand her baby over to us…

I wanted to believe she could do it and at the same time I didn't want to let myself believe. Because if she *did* change her mind… which she would have every right to do, right up until when the paperwork had gone through the court system, which could take more than a year, maybe even a year and a half… what then?

Then I spotted her through the streaming rain, coming out of the glass doors at the front of the station. She looked exactly like what she was: a kid who wasn't tough, but who was trying to appear to be. You never would have guessed she was pregnant.

She was wearing a leather jacket that might have seen better days, but not recently, and faded jeans and heavy black boots. She'd brought hardly anything with her – a brown duffel bag that she was carrying on her back. That was it. She was striding along as if it was important to look determined, as if acting as if she was sure she was doing the right thing would help to convince her that she was.

My heart seemed to sink and lift at the same time. I got out of the car and waved at her. 'Molly? Molly! Over here!'

She saw me and in spite of everything, broke out into a grin. She picked up the pace and hurried towards me, and finally she was running and it crossed my mind to tell her to slow down, be careful, but then it was too late and she was close enough to hug.

She was still so small…

The rain was drenching us. I pulled back and said, 'We'd better get in the car.'

I was about to usher her into the passenger seat, but she went round to the back. Rob turned and gave her a bright but awkward smile. 'Hi, Molly. How are you?'

Molly seemed disconcerted to suddenly find herself an object of interest to him. He never usually paid her much attention.

'Fine, thanks,' she muttered. She folded her arms across her chest and wriggled down in her seat like a schoolkid in the back row trying to slouch down out of the teacher's line of vision.

'I'll take it slowly,' Rob said, starting the car.

'Honestly, I'm fine,' Molly said. 'You don't have to have to do anything differently on my account.'

Rob set off. I turned back to Molly and beamed at her, willing her to relax and be happy, or as happy as she could possibly be.

'We had a new boiler put in yesterday, so there's plenty of hot water if you want a bath,' I said.

This had very nearly not been the case, and Rob and I had come close to having a row about it. We almost never argued – I couldn't remember the last time we had quarrelled about anything – but I had ended up yelling at him. *This is my pregnant teenage sister who's planning on giving us her baby! We can't make her boil the kettle for her bath!*

Rob had looked me up and down with a coldness that I was so unused to that it shocked me into shutting up. *You're not the pregnant one*, he had said. *You've got no excuse for getting hysterical.*

'That's nice,' Molly said indifferently. She was staring out of the window, watching the rainy city go by. She actually did look happy. That was the surprising thing. Or maybe it was more relief at having finally got away from Ashdale.

'I hope you'll like your room,' I said. 'It's the only room in the house that's actually finished.' I had talked Rob into giving up the bedroom we'd been sleeping in to Molly. 'I painted it for you.'

'That was nice of you,' Molly said. 'What colour?'

'Pink. Like your old bedroom.'

She gave me a wry smile. I suddenly realised how tired she looked. 'You don't think I'm maybe a bit old for pink?'

'We can change it if you like,' I said. 'You can have whatever you want.'

'Within reason,' Rob interjected. He was not keen on pink, which had almost prompted another row.

'I got some vitamins for you. And plenty of fruit,' I said. 'And there's lots of nice walks we can go on. Plus there's a yoga class in the village hall that we could try.'

Molly sighed. 'Don't take this the wrong way, but are you going to be like this the whole time?'

'Like what?'

'You know. Fussing. Painting my room pink like the one I had when I was a little girl. Feeding me up. Mothering me. I mean, I'm OK, you know? I've got through it so far. I know it might be hard to believe, but I am capable of making my mind up about my own body, and I do know what I'm doing.'

She said this surprisingly fiercely. I said, 'OK. I'm sorry.'

'I mean, I appreciate it. Believe me. But you two are seriously going to have to relax a little bit, or you're going to drive me crazy.'

We had made it out of the city centre, and the traffic was easing. Before long we'd be on the quiet back road that led to the village and then I'd be ushering Molly into the house that would be her home too, where – if all went according to plan – she would spend the rest of her pregnancy. And then the baby would arrive and then...

Rob said, 'Molly, don't take this the wrong way – and I know you and Stella have talked about it already – but are you really sure you're certain about this? Because it's a big thing.'

'Yes,' Molly said. 'I'm sure.'

'Thank you, Molly. I think I needed to hear that,' Rob said. He was still keeping his eyes on the road. 'Maybe Stella needed to hear it, too.'

But I didn't believe her. Not entirely. It just seemed too good to be true. And I carried on feeling that way right through to the final weeks, when Molly was moping round the house, big and fretful and bored and tired, napping on the sofa at odd hours of the day and neglecting the little household chores that Rob had encouraged me to ask her to do, just to keep her occupied.

By then Molly seemed to have lost interest in almost everything but the Danielle Steel novels she liked and her favourite brand of ice cream. But I knew she was scared. I was too, and I was sure Rob was, though I didn't ask him about it. He wouldn't have wanted to discuss it, and I would have struggled to reassure him, and anyway, what could we do? Nothing but wait and hope and look after Molly as best we could. The birth was like a wall looming up in front of us that only she could get through.

All the books I'd read said that first-time mothers usually gave birth after their due date. Molly wasn't interested in the books, though I had managed to persuade her to go along to a couple of hospital antenatal classes. 'I won't be late,' she said, and she turned out to be right. She went into labour in the wee small hours of a cold October morning, just two days after her due date. It was fast, too. Fast and rough. When Rob drove us through the night to the hospital she was rigid with pain and fear in the backseat next to me. She wouldn't take my hand to hold: 'The way this feels, I'll break it.'

She had always said she didn't want us there at the birth. 'That's the bit I need to do on my own. And no offence, but I'm not sure I want you seeing me like that.' So we sat it out in the waiting room. As the minutes ticked by the old fear that she would change her mind came back to me. It was as comforting as a bad habit, easier by far to think about than what might or might not be happening in the delivery room. The longer we sat there the more convinced I was that she would never, ever give her baby up. How could she? Why should she? By the time we were finally allowed onto the postnatal ward to see her I had already prepared what I was going to say to her when she broke the news.

She'd wanted to help me, she had meant to help me, but in the end, it had not been possible. She'd set out to do something and then found that what she needed was to do something else. I would have to give up on my chance of motherhood. I'd come so close, and it was already over.

I hadn't told Rob any of this. Until we knew for certain, what was the point in making him suffer? Though maybe he wouldn't suffer. Maybe deep down, he would be relieved. After all, he had only signed up for this because of me…

And at the same time I was giddy with elation, because Molly and the baby had made it through.

She was sitting up in her hospital bed with the baby in her arms, supported by the pillow on her lap. The baby was a tiny, featureless bundle, cocooned in pastel cotton. Molly looked exhausted and tender and I felt like an intruder. I hesitated, not wanting to go any closer. She was holding the baby. She was a mother now. She'd earned it. How could she give it up?

But then she looked up and smiled and said, 'Did they tell you? It's a girl.'

Her voice sounded hoarse. She must have screamed. They'd given her gas and air, but nothing else. How could she go from that, just a few hours ago, to this?

'They didn't say. That's wonderful. Congratulations,' I said. I sounded croaky, too.

'Congratulations to you, too,' Molly said. 'Come on, come and meet her. Don't be shy.'

Rob put his hand on the small of my back and nudged me forward. He stood back by the curtains of her cubicle, which were partly open to let the light in through the window at the end of the ward. I moved forward and sat down on the side of the bed. Molly said, 'Look at her. Isn't she perfect?'

And I made myself look, and she was.

Her face was tiny, smaller than the palm of my hand, just about visible between the little cotton hat I'd bought for her and the cloth she'd been wrapped in. But I could see enough to know that she looked like Molly. I wouldn't have thought it was possible for a newborn to have such a strong resemblance to an adult, but there it was – the cheekbones, the jawline, the slant of her downy eyebrows. I couldn't see anything of Jason there at all. Though perhaps when he was a boy Jason had looked quite different to the surly young man I'd met on my mother's doorstep.

'She was crying, and then she had a feed. Took to the bottle just like that. One of the midwives swaddled her and she went off sleep, good as gold,' Molly said. 'Would you like to hold her?'

I stiffened. 'I don't want to wake her.'

'Go on, Stella,' Rob said. 'You should try.'

Molly told me to take the pillow from her lap and shift it onto mine, and to hold my arms the way she was holding hers, arranged so as to form a cradle with the right hand facing upwards to cup the baby's head.

'I have a name for her, by the way,' she said.

'You do?'

I knew without looking at Rob that he would be bristling at that. We had drawn up a longlist of possible names and a shortlist of five favourites for a boy, five for a girl. Molly, who had been both stoic and distracted in the later weeks of pregnancy, had seemed happy to leave it up to us. We had never agreed on her having the final say.

'She's definitely a Georgie. Georgina Lydia Castle. That'll do, don't you think?'

Molly glanced up at Rob as if checking for approval. He said, 'What do you think, Stella?'

'Works for me,' I said, too mesmerised by that small sleeping face to turn around.

Then Molly very gently and carefully transferred her into my arms.

I was conscious of the morning light pitching in, bleaching the blue cotton of the cubicle curtains and the sheets on Molly's bed, touching us with brightness. And I was conscious of the weight of the moment. Georgie was so light. But there was so much future that came with her, day after day and month after month stretching into the invisible distance, and all of that was what Molly was giving me.

I'll look after you, I found myself saying to her. I realised I hadn't spoken out loud. The words were in my head, but as clear as a public promise. *You're safe with me. I'll never leave you. I will make sure you know who you are. I will tell you the truth. I will live up to you...*

She was just right. We fit together like something that was meant to be, like the proper end of a fairy tale.

Her eyes flickered open. She looked a little crabby, like a person with a bad hangover who is not at all sure about facing up to the day ahead. Her mouth puckered as if she remembered the bottle she'd been given and was dismayed that it had gone. Her eyes widened. They were a deep murky blue, the colour of the sky reflected in the distant sea on a cloudy night.

I knew she couldn't focus yet and wouldn't be able to see me. Her vision was as hazy and opaque as her eyes. But her gaze seemed to reach out for somewhere to settle, and to find my face. I heard Rob sigh. Even though he hadn't held her yet, she had touched him too.

A year and a half later I met Molly at the waterfront in Bristol and we sat together on a bench and watched the sun go down. The reflected light played on Molly's face and tinged it blue, as if she was cold or frozen.

It was a mild spring evening but she was huddled inside her coat, an old blue-and-green tweed thing that looked and smelt as if she'd picked it up in a charity shop somewhere. Underneath she was wearing a black jumper and jeans. She didn't have any make-up on and she looked very pale, all the more so because she'd had her light-brown hair cropped and dyed peroxide blonde, or (which seemed possible) had cut and coloured it herself.

I didn't want to be out too late: I was conscious of Rob back in the house, minding Georgie, desperate for me to get back and take over. It had been a long road and we had come to the end of it. The adoption had been approved. Georgie was ours.

It had been Molly's idea to meet me here, and she'd given me the impression that there was something she wanted to say. I asked how she was: she said offhandedly that she was fine. She asked how we were and seemed to pay little attention to my answer, which should have been my cue to back off. But when I got onto the subject of Georgie, I found it hard to stop.

'We've got safety stuff everywhere,' I told her. Where did the urge come from to prove myself to Molly? It was as if I felt I had to assure her I was living up to the responsibility of mothering in her place. Almost as if I still couldn't really believe that Georgie was mine. 'Stairgates, socket plugs, door stoppers, plastic corners on the coffee table. It's not quite the look Rob was going for, but there we are. He says that when we get buyers round it'll help to sell the place as a family house. He wants to find somewhere else to do up, though I can't say I fancy the upheaval.'

'Yeah, well, he thinks he can make money that way, doesn't he? He seems to know what he's talking about. I'd go along with it if I were you. After all, right now Georgie's pretty portable, isn't she? It's not like you need to get her settled into school and stuff.' Molly sighed, laced her hands together and stretched out her arms and hands till her knuckles cracked. The sound set my teeth on edge. 'I've got itchy feet myself. Let's face it, there's nothing to keep any of us here any more, not now all the paperwork's done and dusted. It's time to move on.'

She'd been living across the border in Wales, about a half-hour train ride away. She worked in a bar, went to clubs and parties and festivals, and had a loose crowd of friends who, as far as I was aware, had no idea that she'd had a baby. Up until then I'd been able to kid myself that she was more or less happy.

'Molly… are you planning on going somewhere?'

She'd mentioned a couple of times that she wanted to go travelling, though she'd always been vague about what she had in mind. She had always maintained that once the legalities of the adoption process were completed, she was going to take off. I had tried to make it clear to her that there would always be a place for her in our lives, but on the face of it, I'd accepted that she meant what she said. After all, it was her right to vanish if she wanted. But at the same time part of me hadn't been able to believe that she would cut off contact completely. Not forever.

And another small, mean, insecure, shameful part of me loved Georgie jealously and wanted her to be mine and to love me best of all, and was afraid that one day, whatever her intentions at this stage, Molly might be a threat – a rival for Georgie's affections. Another mother, one she might discover one day and prefer to me. I very rarely allowed myself to think like that, but when I did, it seemed to me that the more distance we could put between us and Molly, the happier and safer we would be.

Molly folded her arms and sighed exaggeratedly, as if I was being particularly dumb. Her expression was pained and hard at the same time, as if every bit of the gentleness and softness that had once been part of her nature had been used up.

'Like I've always told you, Stella, what I want is a clean break. I know you've talked about staying in touch and sending photos and stuff, but I don't want any of that. Georgie's yours. That's it. Now I go off and live my life, and you and Rob and Georgie live yours.'

'I get that's how you feel now, Molly. I respect that, really I do. But the door is open, right? I'm Georgie's mum, but you're her birth mother and you're my sister. That makes you a pretty important person in Georgie's life, however much or however little you want to see of her. I mean, you know, we're going to tell her about you.

We have to. We owe it to her, and to you. We're so grateful to you. You've given us so much. And she has to know who she is and where she comes from. I promised her that in the hospital, the first time I held her. I looked down at her and I said to myself that I would take care of her and be truthful with her. No nasty surprises, like when Mum left without telling us.'

Molly sighed. 'Don't bring that up. Mum leaving is nothing to do with it. This is totally different. Look, just don't make a meal of it, OK? Tell her as little as you can get away with. She doesn't need anything from me. And I don't see why she would ever want anything from me. Apart from maybe to see what a narrow escape she had. You're her mum. Why would she want another one?'

'We can't second-guess how she might feel. And it's her right to know.'

'Oh… *rights*,' Molly said contemptuously. 'Inside a family there's no such thing as rights. Look, this is how it is. I am not going to change my mind. Ever. If she does come and look me up in the future she is in for a nasty surprise, because I will refuse to see her. I didn't want to keep her. I couldn't keep her. I wanted you to have her and now you do. Make the most of it. Be happy. I know you and Rob will love her, and that's what really matters – who does the loving. But that isn't me. The only loving thing that I get to do in all of this is to give her to you. And now that's done, there's no reason for me to have anything to do with any of you. Especially not her.'

'Molly… I don't want you to feel you have to stay away from me and from Mum because of Georgie.'

'You're just saying that because you think you have to. Because you think it's the right thing to say. Maybe you still feel like you have to try to look after me. I don't know. But you don't, not any more. I'm an adult now, and you've got someone else to look after.'

'I really don't want to lose you because of this.'

'Well, that's just tough, Stella, because you already did.'

She turned now and stared at me. She looked blazingly angry, as if I'd wronged her or colluded in someone else wronging her. As if hurting me now was her only chance of revenge.

'Come on, get real. What else did you expect? How else did you think this was going to turn out? I told you all along, all I want from you now is for you to leave me alone.'

She got up and started walking away. I ran after her and grabbed her by the arm. 'Molly—'

She shook me off so forcefully I stumbled and nearly fell.

'Get lost, Stella,' she said. 'I don't care about any of you any more, and I don't want you to care about me.'

'Please let's not say goodbye like this,' I said. 'Let me at least give you a lift to the station.'

'You just don't get it, do you?' I could see her reaching for something more she could say, something so unforgivable that I would finally find it possible to let her go. 'You're such a hypocrite. You kid yourself you're trying to do the right thing, but you want what you want, the same as anybody. And you already made your choice. You chose Georgie. I'm just a footnote. And do you know what, I don't blame you. Because sometimes I think that if I could have chosen between you and Dad, you wouldn't be here today.'

I stared at her. 'That is a vile thing to say.'

She sneered at me. She looked almost unrecognisable, a million miles removed from the little girl I remembered – ruthless and brutal, someone who didn't care any more what she said or who she hurt.

'Sometimes the truth is over-rated, right?' Then she managed a bitter half-smile. 'If he'd been the one who survived, none of the rest of this would have happened,' she said. Then she turned and walked away.

This time I made no attempt to follow her. I stood and watched her till she rounded the corner of one of the big waterfront buildings and disappeared from sight. I was too shocked to cry.

And then I thought of Georgie waiting for me back home. Georgie, who was so innocent, so affectionate, so untouched by all of this. So like Molly had been when she was little. The way her chubby little arms would reach up for me, the solid, comforting weight of her as I swept her up into an embrace…

I started walking. Slowly at first, and then more decisively. I had to concentrate, remember where I'd parked, find the way back home. I'd only recently started driving again – Rob had gently suggested that I should, because what if he was away sometime and there was an emergency and I needed to take Georgie to the hospital? Once I'd thought of driving as something I needed to do for Georgie's sake, I had found it possible to try.

One step at a time, that was the way to do it. One step at a time, and don't look too far ahead.

I was back just in time to supervise Georgie's bath, and it was easy to put all thought of Molly aside. I didn't call her, and our phone stayed silent. I didn't tell Rob what had happened till I'd put Georgie to bed, and we were both sitting on the sofa with a glass of wine.

He picked up the TV remote and said, 'How did it go with Molly, by the way?'

I gave a tiny shrug. 'Pretty badly, actually.'

He put the remote down. 'What do you mean? What did she say?'

'Oh… nothing she hasn't said before. It's just that now it seems more final. She really doesn't want to have anything to do with us. And if Georgie ever comes and looks her up, she's going to tell her to get lost.'

Rob exhaled. 'I see. Well, that's not so bad, is it? I don't suppose Georgie ever will look her up, anyway. Why would she, if she doesn't even know Molly exists?'

'But she has to know.'

'I won't tell her if you don't. And your mum and Lee won't tell her, either. The only person who's got a bee in her bonnet about giving Molly her dues is you. Everybody else is quite happy to write her out. Even the lady herself.'

'But Rob… we can't do that to Georgie. We have to tell her about Molly. If she finds out we've been lying to her – and she almost certainly *will* find out eventually – she'll be shattered. She'll feel she can't trust anybody about anything. She'll never forgive us.'

'But this isn't about Molly,' Rob said. 'This is about *us*. All three of us. Her life will be what we make of it. We're the ones who get to tell her what her story is. That's what being a parent is, isn't it? Your sister had the right idea. It's time for a fresh start.'

He leaned forward and kissed me. His hand snaked up under my jumper to caress my scars, and suddenly my whole body went limp. I could feel my willpower draining away, and resurfacing only as the need to please him and keep him close.

He broke off again and withdrew his hand and stared at me with his eyebrows raised, as if I'd provoked him and he'd indulged me but now it was time to get serious.

'There's really no rush to tell Georgie anything, is there? She's still tiny, anyway. And she knows who Mummy and Daddy are. That's enough for now, isn't it?'

'Yes. Yes, I suppose it is.'

'Good girl.' He studied my face. 'Molly really upset you, didn't she? What else did she have to say?'

As I remembered the parting words she'd flung at me I felt a sob rising in my chest, but suppressed it.

'She said that if she could have chosen, Dad would have been the one who survived the crash, and I would be dead.'

Rob shook his head in disgust. 'That's a terrible thing to say. Can't you see how much better off Georgie is without her? Molly's toxic. Forget her. I don't ever want to hear her name again.'

I began to cry. He embraced me again, and by and by he led me up to bed and I forgot even about Georgie, and only thought about him.

*

I didn't hear anything from Molly. It took me a couple of days to get in the right frame of mind to call her, and when I did I found the line had gone dead.

I didn't tell Rob what I had in mind. I knew he would have discouraged me. I waited for him to go off on a house-hunting trip. Then I took Georgie with me in the pushchair and caught the train across the border to Wales, and took a bus to the house Molly had been living in.

It turned out to be a fruitless journey. A shifty-looking young man came to the door and told me Molly had moved out, and had left no forwarding address.

I called Mum from the phone box at the station before catching the train back. I was dimly aware of passers-by looking at me strangely. I must have looked a sight – crying down the line with the receiver jammed under my chin, brushing my tears away with one hand and jiggling the pushchair to keep Georgie happy with the other.

Mum said, 'She told me she was going to leave, too. Don't worry. We'll hear from her. If you think about it, Stella, isn't it for the best?'

I didn't tell Rob where Georgie and I had been. I didn't like lying to him, but I knew that if I explained he'd be angry with me. Concerned, yes, but angry too. His anger wasn't hot: it was cold. I only saw flashes of it, every now and again, but that was enough for me to know I couldn't bear it. And why risk it, when there was nothing to be gained?

Mum was right, as it turned out. A postcard from Molly arrived a few days later. It seemed conclusive, and when I showed it to Rob he was pleased, as I had thought he would be.

It came from Italy, and she'd written on it, *This is just to let you know I'm fine. Better than fine. I'm having the time of my life. I can't tell you how good it feels to leave my family behind.*

Rob said, 'You know your mum thinks Molly's missing something, and I have to say I think she's right. We're well rid. Now can we please just get on with the rest of our lives? Because you and I have got a house move to plan.'

I didn't say anything. I hid the postcard away with the photo I'd taken of Molly's pregnant belly shortly before she went into labour, and did my best to forget.

Chapter Twenty-Six

'I'm so glad Dad told me about him and Chloe and the baby,' Georgie said as we approached Fox Hill. 'It makes me feel like he trusts me, you know? Like, he trusts me to be able to deal with it.'

'We both trust you,' I said, feeling slightly sick. Because yes, we trusted Georgie, but how was she going to feel when she found out she couldn't trust us? 'You've coped with all this brilliantly.'

Georgie took a moment to reply, but I could tell she was pleased. 'I mean, it's weird. I said that to him. But if you can be all right about it then I can be all right about it, I guess.'

'I think I can be all right about it.'

'That's good,' Georgie said encouragingly, as if she was the mother and I was a kid who had done better than expected in a test.

I hadn't been there when Rob told her about Chloe and the baby. He'd taken her out to see the latest *Star Wars* film – his idea rather than hers. He was geekily enthusiastic about the whole franchise, which reminded him of his childhood. He'd broken the news to her over milkshakes and burgers afterwards, and later he'd told me gleefully how well she'd taken it, as if this was some kind of vindication of everything he'd done. I hadn't bothered to point out that she was probably just trying to please him. It would only have led to another row.

'You don't have to put a brave face on it, though, Georgie,' I said. 'I mean, if you feel unhappy about it, or angry, that's OK too. It's a lot of upheaval. A lot of change.'

Georgie shrugged. 'I get two new bedrooms,' she said. 'Also, it's pretty round here.' She was taking in the fields to either side of the road, then the trees gathering along the verge as we came to the woods.

'It's not particularly exciting,' I said, wondering if it would be awkward when we bumped into Tony Everdene again.

'I don't care about living somewhere exciting. Also, Mum, you don't have to apologise for it in advance, OK?'

'OK. But also, you can be honest with me,' I said. 'Tell me if you hate it. I wasn't sure about it myself when I first saw it. If you don't want to live here, we can look at other options.'

'I promise I'll tell you what I think,' she said.

I sneaked a glance at her in profile. She looked serious and composed, and was studying the road ahead as if it might hold answers to questions she had been mulling over but wasn't about to ask.

If only Rob could have put off his mid-life crisis by a couple of years, till she had safely left home…

We were deep in the woods on Fox Hill, and coming to the end of the lane. The cottage was in sight. As I slowed down to stop I glimpsed Tony Everdene in his driveway next door, opening the door of his car. I hadn't seen him since he'd offered to help with my flat tyre on the day of Mum's death. There was a tall, long-haired teenage girl next to him – one of the twins, presumably. She was leaning down to stroke the ginger cat I'd seen in the garden on my first morning in the house.

I opened the gate and drove through to park on the gravel. The gate shut behind us and I turned to Georgie and said, 'First impressions?'

'So far so good,' Georgie said.

We got out of the car and I put my key in the front door and turned it. It opened easily, and we stepped through into the white space of the hall with its black-and-white chequerboard floor. It was very quiet and the air was still and heavy, as you'd expect given that it had been closed up and empty through the July weeks of summer heat while I'd been sorting out Mum's funeral and living between the spare room in Fairfield Road and Lee's spare room in Critchley.

'Are you going to give me the guided tour?' Georgie said.

She stepped forward without waiting for me to reply. Her hair shone like liquid in the bright light coming through the open front door, and the breeze rushed in and riffled it. As she disappeared into the kitchen I experienced a moment of blind panic, as if she'd vanished for good. Then I pulled myself together, closed the door and followed her.

'I like the kitchen,' Georgie said, looking around with her hands on her hips. 'It's surprisingly spacious, actually – bigger than you'd expect from outside. You know, it's almost as big as the kitchen at Fairfield Road.'

I couldn't help but be touched by this attempt to weigh up the merits of the house in terms she must have heard Rob use to describe other properties. Although she did sound wistful when she mentioned the old house. Still, it was inevitable that she'd make comparisons, given that we'd lived in Fairfield Road for so long that she barely remembered the various places we'd moved into and out of before.

We moved on through the sitting room – 'Nice big telly,' Georgie commented, and tested the sofa. I banished the thought of Tony embracing me in exactly the same spot.

The sound of our footsteps on the floating wooden staircase was softer and less noticeable than I remembered. Having someone else there – someone I wasn't scared of, or anxious about – made the whole house feel different. Less echoey. Less isolated.

But when we walked into my bedroom – or rather, the one that Rob had decided should be mine – I did a double take at the sight of a strange woman and girl drifting towards us.

It was just me and Georgie reflected in the mirrored wardrobe, that was all. I was taken aback by how apprehensive I looked: I was literally wringing my hands.

Georgie was looking down at the single bed.

'Who's that for?'

'It's for me,' I said. My chest felt tight. 'We'll bring over your bed from Fairfield Road. If we decide you're happy to come here, of course.'

'I think it's fine. I don't know what you're so worried about,' Georgie said.

She went out to the bedroom I'd earmarked for her – the one overlooking the garden at the back of the house – and I followed her.

'I could have my desk here, by the window,' she said. Then she studied my face anxiously. 'Honestly, Mum, I like it. I really do. The place just needs a bit of colour on the walls, that's all. But we can make it nice. I'm sure it'll work out.'

I tried to look as if I was pleased that she was pleased. But I couldn't get Rob's voice out of my head.

She's trying to tell you that everything's going to be all right. But she doesn't know, does she? She won't look at you that way when she knows.

I might have been in the process of separating from him, but I still seemed to take him with me wherever I went. And much as I hated hearing what he had to tell me, this time I feared he was right.

A week or so later, I went back to Fox Hill by myself to measure up and check that the bedroom furniture Georgie wanted to bring with her would fit. I was determined to make sure that come moving day, everything would go as smoothly as possible.

It was an August day of torrential rain. I'd never seen Fox Hill in such gloomy weather. A great pool of standing water had collected in a dip by the turning for the village, and the woods were rain-lashed and dripping.

I took the road slowly and carefully enough to annoy a driver behind me in a 4x4, who roared angrily past me at the earliest opportunity. My heart was hammering. I was always extra jittery when driving in bad conditions. It was a relief to get inside in the dry, with the rain pattering on the roof and streaking the windows.

It didn't quite feel like home yet. But it would. I went upstairs and got out my tape measure and notebook, and was absorbed in adding arrows and numbers to the rough floorplan I'd drawn when the doorbell rang.

But who knew I was here? Nobody. Only Rob and Georgie and Chloe knew about this house. I'd told Lee about it, but he probably hadn't taken any notice.

Rob had taken Georgie to the cinema and as far as I knew Chloe was at her flat back in Kettlebridge. Besides, she wouldn't have any reason to track me down. I'd been perfectly civil to her when we'd last met in passing, and she'd got everything she wanted. Hadn't she?

As I went down to answer the door I lost my balance, lurched forward and only just saved myself from crashing headfirst down the stairwell. I caught my breath and went down to press the intercom in the hallway.

'Stella? It's Tony Everdene, from next door. I wondered if I could have a quick word?'

I hesitated. Then I buzzed him in and opened the door, but not very wide, and he approached and stopped on the step.

He was holding a big black umbrella, which wasn't really enough to protect him from the rain. My nerves began to dissipate. It's hard to feel anxious about a doorstep chat with someone who obviously feels awkward about coming to see you, and is getting soaked into the bargain.

'Look – you're getting drenched,' I said. 'Won't you step in?'

But he shook his head.

'No, no, I don't mean to take up your time. I just noticed your car there, and I saw you and I think it must have been your daughter here a week or so ago as well, and I wondered if you were getting ready to move in.'

'Yes. We are. Just me and Georgie. My husband is moving in with his girlfriend. Ex-husband. I mean, he's not an ex-husband yet. They're having a baby together.'

I imagined Rob just behind me, looking on in amusement. *That's right, get him up to speed. You're still wearing that diamond ring I got you, though. And your wedding ring. But he isn't wearing his. And he wasn't last time, either, was he? Well, not everybody does, not all the time. It's not like it's a legal obligation. Probably best not to bother if you want to try and pick up random passing women. But anyway, why don't you ask him about his mysterious wife?*

'It sounds like you've had a difficult time,' Tony said.

'I know Rob was maybe a bit... brusque when you met him. I'm sorry.'

Rob would have snorted at that. *Of all the things you have to apologise for, I'd say my behaviour is pretty much bottom of the list. Anyway, I didn't want him sniffing round you and can you blame me? Just look at him. He's shifty. There's something not quite right about him. No wonder he's attracted to you.*

Tony shrugged. The rain was blowing against his back, soaking into his hair and trickling down to his collar. He said, 'I got the impression he wanted to be the one to help you.'

'I guess he did,' I said. 'I still have your book. I must give it back to you sometime.'

'I'd actually forgotten about that. Please, don't trouble yourself. Feel free to keep it.'

'I saw your daughter, by the way. One of your daughters. She looks like you.' I hadn't particularly thought this at the time, but it seemed like a reasonable thing to say.

'Yours looks like you, too,' he said.

Many people had said that to me over the years, and it had got to the point where I didn't really think anything of it. I knew it was true, and I agreed. Georgie was my daughter and she looked like me. Well, why shouldn't she? We shared a lot of genetic material, after all. More than I shared with anyone else now living, other than Molly...

Then Tony and I spoke at the same time.

He said, 'I was actually a bit concerned, because—'

I said, 'It's nice that our girls are about the same age—'

Then both of us stopped. I took in the pelting rain, and his uncomfortable but resolute expression – as if he had felt obliged to come here for some reason that he wasn't particularly keen to acknowledge, and would much rather have been at home, playing solitaire or reading important biographies or whatever it was he did with his spare time. When he wasn't cycling, or waiting for his daughters to finish bell-ringing, or supporting them in other similarly wholesome pursuits.

He said, 'I honestly don't want to bother you, Stella. I'm sure you're busy. I just didn't want to pass up the opportunity to speak to you. To try and explain myself, after what happened. I mean, you're probably not interested in my explanations…' He gave me an awkward little half-smile.

'Tony, please, you really don't need to explain anything.'

He drew himself up a little straighter. 'I'm afraid I do,' he said. 'Since we're as good as neighbours now. If I don't, sooner or later someone else will tell you. Or you'll end up saying something to my girls. Or your daughter will. And then all of this will be even more difficult. I should have told you at the beginning, but we are where we are. Look, when we met, when you came into my house, you saw a picture of my wife with my girls…'

'Yes…'

'My *then* wife, I should rightly say. She passed away two years ago.'

'Oh, Tony… I'm so sorry.'

'We were already divorced,' he said flatly. 'She died of cirrhosis of the liver. She drank herself to death. Anyway, I thought you should know. Pretty much everyone else round here does. And I probably should have told you too. It's just that, every once in a while…' He grimaced again. 'It's really lovely not to have to explain.'

'You didn't owe me an explanation, Tony. You really didn't have to say anything at all.'

'When you drove past the other day you looked at me as if you thought I'd done something really terrible,' he said. 'I may be a monster. My wife certainly thought so, at least some of the time. But I don't think I'm the kind of monster you might think I am.'

'I don't think you're a monster at all.'

But I *had* wondered if he might be. When you're conscious that you're not quite what you seem, or quite what you ought to be, it's hard to trust anybody else. And I always had Rob's voice in my ear to contend with, mocking me, reminding me of everything that was wrong with me...

Tony sighed. 'And now you feel sorry for me. Well, I suppose it's an improvement. Anyway, good luck with the move, Stella. If I can be of any help, please, do just let me know.'

I imagined Rob breaking into spontaneous applause. *You see, Stella, that's how you do it. That's how you come clean. Other people can find the courage to do it, so why can't you?*

'Thank you for telling me,' I called out, but Tony didn't turn back. He trudged towards the gate, hit the exit button, waited patiently for the mechanism to open it and then withdrew out of sight.

Chapter Twenty-Seven

I had started off intending to do it by the book – and at the time, I thought Rob felt the same. Throughout the adoption process, when the social worker from the local council talked to us about what the future might hold, we had repeated our commitment to being open with Georgie about the circumstances of her birth. When she started asking questions, we would give her answers – but answers with an age-appropriate level of detail, answers that were the truth but not necessarily the whole truth. We would not wait – as adoptive parents from twenty or thirty years before had done – for her to be old enough to understand. We understood that the latest research showed that sharing the truth as early as possible was associated with the best outcomes for the child. That was how the social worker put it. What she meant was: *it's better for Georgie if you tell her, and tell her early. Don't put it off.*

There had been plenty of opportunities to tell Georgie about Molly down the years that followed, presented to me like little gifts one after the other. It wasn't even as if we'd had to sit her down and formally explain it to her. Though we could have done that, too.

Again and again, the moment had passed, and I had let it. The truth was too painful, too difficult. It came with scars, with memories of the silence before the crash and the shock of the collision and of Molly, the last time I had seen her, telling me she wished I had died. And Rob seemed more than happy to carry on leaving things as they were.

So many missed chances. Conversations about other families, about orphans, about parents who were not who or what they seemed...

Conversations about stories. All those princesses who had lost idealised mothers and were stuck with real ones, who weren't really their mothers at all. Snow White, Cinderella, Sleeping Beauty... you name it, there I was, right at the heart of the story but wearing a hideous disguise, waiting to receive my just desserts at the end. The bad mother, the deceiver, the one who was willing to go to great lengths to turn the direction of the story her way: doomed to fail, and to be banished or burned or laughed at, or to vanish in a puff of smoke, or some other suitable form of punishment. That was part of the point of the fairy stories, to expose me and then dispose of me...

All those unwanted children growing up in homes where they didn't belong. Stories that Georgie had listened to wide-eyed, counting her lucky stars that she was safe at home with her mother.

And the questions...

How many babies could you have? Was she going to have a little brother or sister? Where did babies grow? Where did they come out? How did they get there? And then (tactfully, with a delicate expression of distaste, not wanting to press for details about something that was obviously not altogether proper, but needing to know): 'Is that what happened with me?'

Yes, you grew in your mummy's tummy and then out you came and you cried so loudly it gave your daddy a headache!

Explaining the mechanics of birth to her made me feel queasy. Not out of squeamishness... but because I hadn't done it. I had dreamed about it... I had imagined it... But it wasn't me who had gone through it. And that made me shy away from the whole topic as if I didn't think it was something that ought to be discussed.

Once she wanted to see our wedding photos, and I showed her a few and then she quickly lost interest, as you do when you're young and are shown photos of the past that you're not in. She must have noticed Molly, who was wearing a too-big puffy-sleeved dress with a splashy print of pink and purple flowers and little white lace shoes, and smiling at the camera from behind a too-long fringe. But she didn't comment or ask who it was, and I didn't tell her.

She never asked to see her birth certificate. Perhaps that might have forced it out of me, but then again, it might not. It would have reminded me that I shouldn't keep avoiding the truth. But even then I might have improvised some way to fob her off.

I would have hated myself for doing it. But I would have done it anyway, the same way I hid my scars from her and everyone but Rob.

In my dreams, I told Georgie about Molly over and over again. The conversation turned out so many different ways. She told me she had always known. She walked away arm-in-arm with Molly, without a backwards glance. She told me she hated me and wanted to live with her dad instead. And she told me it was impossible to love a liar and vanished into thin air.

It's insidious the way lies mount up. Almost like an addiction. The more you tell, the more you need to keep on telling, and the more ways you find to persuade yourself that the time hasn't quite yet come to stop. I knew I needed to open up to Georgie. I had to confess what I had hidden from her. And yet now I had seen Molly and knew for sure that she hadn't relented – that she would rebuff Georgie if Georgie ever sought to get in touch with her – I was even more scared of having that conversation. All it would lead to for Georgie was rejection and a dead end. She wouldn't just find out that I wasn't who she thought I was. She would also have to face up to the brutal fact that her birth mother wasn't even willing to meet her.

Still, the clock was ticking. Mum's funeral was over. Rob and I had formally separated and Georgie and I had moved into Fox Hill. Georgie knew about Chloe and the baby that was on the way. She was even a little bit excited, and nervous, at the prospect of having a sibling, though she was trying tactfully not to let on, in case her feeling that way about it might upset me. As if she felt it was one thing for her to show me that she was coping and taking it all in her stride, but quite another for her to actually be positive about it. I was grateful to her for being so sensitive. And at the same time I wondered if it was healthy for her to be quite so wary of hurting my feelings.

And then one quiet afternoon I got a phone call out of the blue from Rose, and knew at once from the shaky tone of her voice that it was bad news about Lee.

I was in my bedroom, hanging up the clothes I'd just washed and rather sketchily ironed – I'd got sloppy about that kind of thing now I was living apart from Rob – when Rose called me on my mobile. As she began to tell me what had happened it was hard to focus. I was distracted by the sound of Rob's voice in my head, as clear and inescapable as if he was in the room with me.

Here we go again, then, Stella. He's gone, and you're going to have to let Molly know. And after that maybe you'll finally find the guts to tell Georgie the truth. You're still here. There's still time. And if you don't, one of these days it'll be too late.

Chapter Twenty-Eight

Rose told me she had gone in, as she did every day, to water the pot plants – Mum had been fond of them and had built up a collection, and Rose had taken it upon herself to keep them going, knowing that Lee was indifferent to their fate either way. He had given her a key to the house so he wouldn't always have to get up to let her in.

'He was in that chair of his in front of the TV, same as usual,' Rose said. 'I wanted to think he was still dozing. But when I looked at him I knew.'

She'd already called out the doctor to certify the death. I thanked her for all she had done, and promised I'd be over there as soon as I could. As I ended the call a flash of movement caught my eye on the far side of the room, but it was only my reflection in the mirrored front of the wardrobe.

I went over to close the wardrobe door. There was the jumpsuit I'd worn the first time Rob brought me to Fox Hill. The date outfit, with its jagged tear. I probably really should get rid of it. I couldn't imagine that I would ever wear it again.

Georgie had been out for a run and was in the shower; I could hear her singing over the sound of the water running, though I couldn't make out the tune. More bleak news for her. Another piece of her childhood unravelling…

I left a brief message for Rob to let him know, and asked him to call me back.

Should I have cried? My whole body felt heavy, as if the power of gravity had been turned up and was pulling me down. The sun was still shining but I wouldn't have been surprised if there was a storm brewing: there was a weird electricity in the air.

The shower stopped and I heard a door open, then footsteps, then another door closing.

My legs suddenly felt weak. I was tempted to lie down on the new-smelling carpet Rob had installed, just to feel something solid under me. Instead I forced myself to knock on Georgie's bedroom door and tell her that I needed to speak to her.

She was sitting at her desk, looking through a box of nail varnishes. She was wearing her big fluffy blue dressing-gown, which was patterned with cat footprints, and she smelt faintly of strawberry shampoo. The picture of well-adjusted adolescence. Her room was tidy in a way that teenage rooms are not traditionally supposed to be, with numerous mementoes of childhood – things she'd made at school, or knick-knacks she'd been given – carefully arranged on various surfaces. Things she prized. Georgie was like that. It made me uneasy sometimes. It was almost as if she wanted to remind herself who she was – as if, at some level, she suspected that there might be something more, or different, to who she was than she knew.

She turned round as I came in, took in the expression on my face and said, 'What's wrong?'

'It's Lee. Georgie, I'm sorry to have to tell you this, but he's gone.'

She got up and came over to hug me. 'Oh, Mum, I'm sorry.'

'I'm going to have to go over there,' I said. 'It might take a while to sort things out. I've rung your dad to let him know. I couldn't get through to him, but I've left him a message. I thought he could come and get you.'

That was how I usually referred to Rob now. *Your dad.* And maybe he and Chloe did the same for me. *Your mum.* Though they might have some other, unkinder way of referring to me when Georgie wasn't around.

Paranoid. That's what you are. That's what a guilty conscience does for you...

'Maybe I could go next door for a bit, till Dad shows up,' Georgie suggested. She had got to know the Everdene twins over the last few weeks since we'd moved in, bonding over her interest in their cat – she'd always wanted a pet and never been allowed one, because Rob was vehemently opposed to anything that might create mess or result in scratched upholstery.

Rob would probably hate that. Georgie spending time in Tony Everdene's house. But he had no right to hate it. Anyway, it was his fault for not being around.

'OK. Good idea,' I told her.

I left her to get dressed and went next door to speak to Tony, crossing my fingers it wouldn't be inconvenient for him to take her in. The car was in the driveway and the lights were on, so they were definitely home.

Tony came to the door wearing an apron with what looked like a splash of tinned tomato on it. When I explained what had happened he asked if Georgie would like to come over for dinner.

'That would be brilliant. Unless Rob's here before then, of course.' I checked my watch. 'Which seems unlikely. As long as you're sure there's enough food for her to have some. I wouldn't want the rest of you to go short.' I hesitated. 'She doesn't eat meat, by the way.'

'My girls are the same. I'm making vegetarian spaghetti Bolognese. There'll be plenty to go round.'

'Then I'll bring her over in a minute. Thank you again! Thank you so much! I'll return the favour sometime. You're a lifesaver!'

And so Georgie disappeared into the Everdene house, and I drove off through the woods to see Lee for the last time.

Rose couldn't get out of there fast enough. She offered to stay with me, but she could barely hide her relief when I thanked her for everything she'd done and told her not to worry, and insisted she go home. She made me a cup of tea and put it on the occasional table by the sofa with some biscuits she'd found in a cupboard somewhere, and then she left.

I checked my phone and saw I had a rather curt text from Rob.

Sorry about Lee. On my way to get Georgie.

She'd barely have had time to eat her spaghetti Bolognese.

He must have sprung into action as soon as he got my message. Was that a sign of how much he still cared about us, even though he had Chloe now and a new baby on the way? Or maybe it was just a measure of how much he hated the idea of being beholden to Tony.

My tea seemed to have cooled quickly, as if there was some kind of unusual chill factor at work in the house. I drank it anyway, though I hadn't thought I would want it. It wasn't as if Lee going to mind.

Everything was very still, very quiet. The carriage clock on the mantelpiece kept ticking while time stretched out and simultaneously stopped.

It was too late to be afraid. The event to be afraid of had already happened. There was something in the room that wasn't exactly calm, but was at least an absence of torment, as if Lee had been suffering much more than he had let on or than any one of us had realised, and now all that was over.

There was no sense at all of him left. No presence. Just stillness. At the same time he was right there, still sitting in his favourite chair. Rose hadn't moved him. She'd covered him up with an old bedsheet patterned with tiny sprigs of lilac, because that's what you do after someone has gone. You feed the living, and you cover the dead.

The exact same room where Mum had passed away. Almost unchanged, though perhaps less immaculately tidy. The same knick-knacks, the same framed photographs. I would have plenty of time now to reflect on how Lee had not given me the chance to sit like this with her. Had not wanted me there, when it came down to it. But here I was, with him.

She had loved to hear him tell the story of how they'd met. He'd gone to her counter at the department store in Brickley, asking for advice about perfume. She'd sweet-talked him into busting his budget, and he'd asked her to giftwrap his purchase for his girlfriend and then told her to keep it.

'Sold – hook, line and sinker,' was how he liked to describe it when he told the story. Which didn't sound romantic, exactly. It sounded as if she'd trapped him, or as if he'd trapped her. But maybe the truth was quite different, and not something that either of them would want to share.

Anyway, she had been happy with him – much happier than she had been with us. That much had been blindingly obvious. Meanwhile Dad, who was nearly twenty years older than her anyway, had seemed to age another twenty as soon as she'd gone.

The first time I had met Lee was also the first time Molly and I had set eyes on Mum after she left us to move in with him. I'd been struck by how young Lee was, compared to Dad – he was much closer in age to Mum, whereas Dad had been turning silver-haired for as long as I could remember. We'd gone out for Chinese, and Molly had picked at her food while Lee barked out occasional sarcastic remarks and Mum looked pained, as if we weren't enjoying ourselves nearly enough. The meal had come to an abrupt end after Molly turned pale green and rushed off to the toilets to be sick.

I was jolted back to the present by the sound of the doorbell ringing. I rushed to answer it, expecting to see the doctor. But instead it was Rob, smiling slightly as if he was pleased to have had an unforeseen opportunity to surprise me. He took advantage of my confusion to walk right in, and closed the door behind him.

*

'So this is where it happened, is it?'

I followed him into the living room. He was standing at a cautious distance from Lee's armchair and looking down at him, as if he half expected Lee to jump up, throw his sheet off and announce that it was all a big practical joke.

'Rob, where's Georgie?'

'I left her with Chloe.' He flashed me the sheepish-yet-arrogant smile that meant he thought he was probably going to get away with something, but was prepared to brazen it out if not. 'They're fine. They're going to watch some TV together. Anyway, it's good for them to have some time to bond.'

'Why did you do that? You could have just left her with the Everdenes.'

He pulled a face, as if he was offended by my reaction but, under the circumstances, was going to cut me some slack. 'You made it pretty clear you wanted me to get her, pronto,' he said.

'Well, yes, but I thought she would be with *you*, not dumped on Chloe. You just did that because you've decided you don't like Tony.'

'I don't especially, no. But also, I got the impression you didn't want to impose on the neighbours any longer than necessary. And I thought you might like some company, even if you couldn't bring yourself to say so. I take it the doctor hasn't been yet?'

'No, he hasn't,' I said, sitting down on the sofa again.

'I guess they're not going to rush for a dead man. Got enough trouble taking care of the living. So you've just been sat here, have you? And then you'll have to wait for the undertakers to turn up, I suppose. Enough to drive you round the twist. I thought you might welcome some company.' He approached me and surveyed the sofa as if he wasn't quite sure he wanted to sit down on it. 'I know I'm not ideal. You'd probably much rather have Tony Everdene to snuggle up with in your hour of need. But here I am. After all, I am still your husband, technically. And at least I'm alive.'

'Rob, I don't think you're being very respectful.'

'Oh, come on. What's respect? Sitting round moping? He wouldn't have wanted that. He'd have laughed at you.' He gestured towards Lee. 'Did you know that if you looked at him now, his face would probably be all smoothed out, as if he was young again? It's one of the things that happens.'

'I don't want to look,' I said.

'No,' Rob said. 'I don't either.'

He came closer to the sofa and sat down beside me.

'It's awfully stuffy in here.'

'Well, open a window if you want.'

'I suppose it's just…' He gestured towards Lee again. 'Claustrophobic.'

'Rob, what are you doing here?'

'I told you. I didn't think you should be alone. I'm here to support you. And we can still be friends, can't we? We were married for a long time. All that surely can't disappear just like that.' He clicked his fingers. The sound seemed very loud, as if he'd dropped something and broken it.

'That's not how you were talking a couple of months ago.'

'That's not how *you* were talking a couple of months ago,' Rob said.

I shifted slightly along towards the end of the sofa. He was sitting just a little too close for comfort. I said, 'What does Chloe think about you coming here?'

'Well, it's a mission of mercy. She can hardly protest. Anyway, it's good for her and Georgie to spend time together. You know Georgie likes her.'

'She does,' I conceded.

Rob yawned and stretched. 'I have to say, though, we could do with a bit more space. The sooner the better. But between you and me, I think she's got unrealistic ideas about what we can afford. And we haven't even had a decent offer on Fairfield Road yet. I keep getting pointed little comments about how we might be in a better position if I hadn't been quite so generous to you.'

'Am I supposed to feel sorry for you because your girlfriend resents me?'

'You could try to sympathise. It's not easy, you know.'

'What's not easy?'

Rob sighed again. 'This whole pregnancy lark. Sometimes she can really be quite hormonal and moody and difficult. Selfish. I mean, I understand she's tired. But she can't expect me to wait on her hand and foot all the time. I mean, women have been doing this stuff for centuries, and I'm sure not all of them have been given foot massages and had their dinner made for them. Probably hardly any of them, come to that.' He glanced at me. 'I have to say, I don't remember your sister being quite this bad. Though I suppose she wasn't working.'

'You know what, Rob?'

He turned to me hopefully. 'What?'

'I actually don't sympathise with you at all.'

'Oh.' He looked deflated. 'Well, that's a little brutal. Still, I suppose you ladies like to stick together, at least some of the time. Have you told Molly about Lee yet?'

'Not yet. I will do, though.'

'I've been wanting to talk to you about that, actually. About Molly. Have you been in touch much? Since your mum's funeral?'

'I've called her once or twice. She's been quite hard to get hold of. Why?'

'Did you ask her why she ran out like that?'

'I just asked if she was all right. She said she was sorry and it had all been a bit much. I couldn't get any more than that out of her. She just rang off.'

Rob shook his head. 'You see? Erratic. I still feel that Georgie's better off without her.'

'Rob, not so long ago you were threatening to tell Georgie all about her.'

'Do you really have to keep bringing that up? Let's just try and keep on moving forwards, shall we?' He gestured towards Lee again. 'Life is short. Let's try to make the best of it. I just wanted to check that you weren't planning on doing anything about all that without talking to me first. That's all. I wouldn't want you to just suddenly tell Georgie about Molly on the spur of the moment. I really think we need to take a unified approach.'

'You know what? I'm not surprised Chloe's fed up with you.'

'Oh, don't drag Chloe into this. She's got nothing to do with it.'

'Into what?'

'Into this. Us.'

I wasn't aware of him having moved, but suddenly he seemed to be just inches away. He gave me a lazy smile. 'Come on, Stella. Be honest. I know you think about me. I think about you, too.' He tapped the side of his head. 'I hear you in here. I have whole conversations with you. After all the time we've spent together, and everything we've been through, it would be strange if I didn't. I don't think there's anything wrong with that.'

'There's plenty wrong with it.'

'I'm just being honest. Which, let's face it, is not your forte. You know what your problem is? You just can't bear the idea of being bad. Even when you want to be.'

His face was close enough to touch or to slap. For a wild moment I thought he might try to kiss me. But no, that was impossible. Not here, in this room with its shut-in air and old furniture and Lee's body in the armchair in front of the TV.

'I think you're controlling and a bully,' I said.

His smile broadened as if I'd given him a compliment. 'Women only say things like that to men they secretly like.'

I couldn't move. I wanted to and at the same time I was mesmerised. He leaned forward, very slowly, so that his mouth was almost on mine. Our lips touched, but barely. The slightest possible contact, as light as a feather or a leaf. He withdrew just as slowly, keeping his eyes on me.

'You're looking at me as if you hate me, but it's only because you used to feel something else,' he said.

The doorbell rang, and I leaped up as if someone had stormed in to accuse me of something and had caught me red-handed.

I said, 'That must be the doctor. Rob, you should go. It was good of you to check up on me. But I expect Georgie and Chloe will be wondering where you are.'

'They know exactly where I am,' Rob said. He was standing too. 'When are you going to stop pretending?'

But I had no answer to that. I already hated myself for just having sat there and let him do that to me.

I opened up and let the doctor in. Rob expressed his condolences and said he'd be in touch, and strolled out into the evening as if nothing at all had happened.

Chapter Twenty-Nine

I finally rang Molly once I got back to Fox Hill, about half past nine that evening. I knew it was a little late to call, and I thought her reaction might be curt, and it was. She said, 'Thanks for telling me. But I won't be coming to the funeral.'

'Would you like me to send you the details? In case you change your mind?'

'No, because I won't. Not for him,' she said, and rang off.

I sat there on the grey sofa Rob had chosen for me, looking up at the brightly coloured print that Georgie and I had picked out to hang on the wall, and thought about what Rob had said to me.

You know what your problem is? You just can't bear the idea of being bad.

He had a point. Maybe. But why did I always let him get to me?

I picked up the phone and called Molly back.

'Look,' I said, 'I'm really sorry to keep bothering you like this, but hear me out, just for a minute, OK? When you turned up at Mum's funeral and saw Georgie, I felt like there was a connection there. You must have felt it too and I'm sure Georgie did. She was asking about you afterwards. Now I know I screwed up. I know I should have found a way to tell her years ago. I know I have to do it. I think maybe meeting you again would help to make it easier. If that's still something you might like to do.'

But she just sighed. 'Before we talk any more about this, Stella, there's something you should know.'

She told me she had applied for a job in the south of France, helping someone she'd met through an art class run a holiday lodge in the foothills of the Pyrenees. If she got it she'd be leaving soon, and she'd be away for six months at least, maybe longer. She had already started looking for someone to take over the lease on her flat.

She didn't seem to be in a rush to get off the phone. Maybe, because she knew she was going to be leaving and had told me so, it was easier for her to spend longer talking to me.

'Molly, if that's what you want that sounds wonderful.'

'I think it's what I want. It's not always easy to tell.'

'Do you think there might be anything you would like of Mum's? All her stuff is still there. Lee didn't get rid of it. You could come and have a look sometime, if you wanted.'

There was a small, dead silence at the other end of the line, as if she might be about to hang up on me again. Then she said, 'I'd actually really like to look through the old photo albums. Assuming Mum kept them somewhere. I think she would have done, because *you* were in them.'

'Molly…'

'I don't have that many photos of me as a kid. I remember those albums – I can picture them. But my memory might have played tricks on me. It would be interesting to see them again.'

'If I find them I'll set them aside so you can look through them. Anything you want, it goes without saying, you should take.'

'Good. Well, that's settled then. But as for this business of meeting Georgie…'

Suddenly she went quiet. I could hear her breathing, but I had no idea what she was thinking.

She had always been so clear that she wasn't interested. This was the closest she had ever come to hesitation. Maybe it was easier for her to consider it now because Mum and Lee had both gone – though why should that be the case? She might have fallen out with them both when she was younger, but she had repaired her relationship with Mum to some extent, at least enough to send her a Christmas card every year.

Was it because Rob and I weren't together any longer? That certainly made it easier for me, though he wouldn't be too happy when he found out that he'd been kept at arm's length from all this…

'No pressure,' I said. 'Think about it and let me know.'

'I will. But can you wait? Please don't say anything to Georgie just yet.'

'All right,' I said. 'Let's stay in touch, though. Don't go disappearing again.'

'I won't. Oh, and Stella?'

'Yes?'

But whatever it was, she couldn't quite bring herself to come out with it. Instead she said, 'Go easy on yourself. You don't sound too good,' and ended the call again.

Lee's funeral passed by in a blur of greetings and regret – regret because I couldn't, hand on heart, say I had loved him, which made me sad because he had been such a big part of Mum's life for such a long time and that made him family. True to her word, Molly didn't show. Rose came, along with her daughter and a few other local people who had been friends of Mum's, plus a handful of Lee's old drinking buddies and colleagues. Others made their excuses. He didn't seem to be as connected to people in the village as Mum had been, but then, he'd been less active socially, especially as he had got older and had begun to suffer from increasingly poor health – and had got, if anything, more saturnine and misanthropic.

Rob brought Chloe along. He was stiff and formal with me, as he'd been every time we'd had cause to speak to each other since the day of Lee's death. Chloe was now conspicuously pregnant in a demure black wrap maternity dress. She blushed and smiled when I asked after her health and I felt so guilty about having let Rob kiss me that I could barely bring myself to look at her. I knew she would probably misinterpret my behaviour and conclude I still resented her. But perhaps that was for the best. I saw Rose's daughter casting slightly wounded looks in Rob's direction, and wished that all of us could have managed to be oblivious to him.

Georgie spent the night after Lee's funeral with Rob and Chloe, in the spare room at Chloe's flat. The next day, when I came to pick her up, it was Rob who answered the door. He said, 'They're just finishing watching a film. Is it all right if I have a word?'

I said, 'We can talk if you want, but is it going to take long?'

'No, shouldn't think so.' He looked up and down the road. 'Look, can we do this somewhere else? Maybe we could sit in your car.'

'No way,' I said.

He sighed. 'It's like that, then, is it? All right. Let's walk.'

We made our way across the main road and into the park just north of Gull Street, a quiet space circled by a path and edged by trees that were beginning to turn vivid colours. There was a family group playing a game of rounders and a couple of dog walkers, but nobody who was close enough to overhear us. Anyone who knew us might think we were the perfect former couple, negotiating a new relationship that allowed both of us to keep our dignity while going our separate ways.

'I felt we hadn't really caught up for a while,' Rob said. 'I just wanted to check that you're all right.'

'I'm fine, thank you. And you?'

'Oh, don't be like that. I can't bear it when you get all defensive on me.'

'I'm not being defensive. I'm fine.'

He grimaced as if he didn't believe me. 'How's work? You're coping with everything, are you?'

We were now just a week into the autumn term, and already I was weirdly exhausted, as if I was running on empty, so much so that I had wondered if there was actually something physically wrong with me. Objectively I knew the fatigue was just a reaction to everything that had happened that summer, not to mention the question of how and when to tell Georgie about Molly. But I wasn't about to admit any of this to him.

'Like I said, I'm fine,' I told him.

'How did things go with Molly? You must have spoken to her.'

'I did. She might be moving to France.'

I probably should have told him that she and I had talked about the possibility of meeting. But I knew that in one way or another, he would just make it more difficult.

'Oh. Really? Well, I suppose that solves that problem, doesn't it? Anyway, I thought you might like to know that Georgie hasn't mentioned her,' Rob said. 'She's probably pretty much forgotten about her. So I don't think you're going to have any difficulties there.'

We had come to the clearing where a fork in the path led to the tall stone column from which a statue of Queen Victoria looked down across the park. When we first moved here Rob had helped Georgie climb up and stand on the top of the pedestal that supported it, which was about chest height for an adult, high enough for me to be uncomfortable seeing her up there. But she had thought it was a great adventure.

That was what dads did, wasn't it? Encouraged kids to be bold. He was a good dad, whatever he'd been as a husband…

'I was rather hoping you'd call me,' Rob said. 'I've been wondering how you are. You do know you can call me anytime, don't you?'

'I'm not going to do that, Rob.'

We came to a standstill and faced each other. He said, 'So that's the game we're playing, is it?'

'It's not a game.'

He reached out his hand and rested it on my arm. 'Stella, come on. Be reasonable. I'm trying to make things right here.'

I shook him off. 'You still think you can do whatever you like with me,' I said. 'But you're wrong. I'm going to go and get Georgie and take her home.'

I turned and began to walk rapidly back along the path the way we had come, almost colliding with a startled jogger as he came round the corner past a tall bank of rhododendrons.

Rob hurried to catch me up. 'Stella, I think you've really got the wrong end of the stick here. All I want is for us to be able to be friends.'

'Then I'm sorry, but you're going to be disappointed.'

'I don't see why. Plenty of other people manage it.'

'Because we're no good for each other. Not any more. And that's the truth.'

'Now you're just deliberately misunderstanding me,' Rob said plaintively.

I didn't answer, and he settled for trailing behind me the rest of the way back to Chloe's flat.

A couple of weeks later, Molly called me out of the blue on a beautiful Sunday morning. She said she was thinking of getting on a train to Oxfordshire, and was I free to meet? She'd been thinking about Mum and Lee's house, which she had never been to. She'd like to see it, if it wasn't inconvenient. And the old family photo albums, if I had them to hand.

I said, 'The albums are still there, in the house. When would you like to come?'

'No time like the present. Are you free today?'

I could tell from the sound of her voice – the mixture of nerves and recklessness – that she'd been building up to this for a while, and had suddenly given into the impulse to ask me.

'Sure,' I said. 'I'm free.'

'Good. Thank you.' And then she said, 'I don't know how you'll feel about this… if you don't think it's a good idea, we could leave it… but perhaps I could come back to your place afterwards, just for a bit. You know. Say hello to Georgie, if she's around. As an aunt. No drama. Just, you know… contact.'

It was testament to the influence Rob still had over me that I hesitated.

If I expressed any doubts about this, she might never ask again…

But then I said yes.

Chapter Thirty

A few hours later I found myself sitting in my car in one of the four spaces allocated for pick-ups from Barrowton station. There was a big sign right in front of me warning that you shouldn't wait for longer than twenty minutes. I'd already been there for twenty-five. No sign of her. I was trying to read to pass the time but not a single word was going in.

There was a knock on the window next to me and I looked up and there she was.

She was wearing a purple coat with a black dress printed with purple flowers underneath, and she'd dyed her hair a new coppery shade of red and was carrying a bright red handbag to match. She waved at me through the glass and I waved back. I got out of the car to greet her and we pecked each other on the cheek like a pair of grand old ladies. She was smiling, but at the same time she seemed agitated and overwrought, although she was clearly doing her best to hide it.

'You look colourful,' I said as we settled into the car.

'Not too colourful, I hope. The purple coat is vintage, as they say these days. Which makes me feel old, because it used to be just second-hand.'

'I can't have you feeling old, Molly. That makes me feel *really* old.'

'I'll always be your little sister, though. No matter how ancient we both get.'

'You'll never be ancient. It's not possible.'

'I feel it sometimes,' Molly said. 'I got the job in France, by the way. I'm leaving next month.'

Was that why she had rung me up that morning? Because she knew for sure that she was about to leave?

As we set off I congratulated her about the job and asked her a little more about it – where she'd be living, what exactly she would be doing – but got the feeling she didn't want to talk, or perhaps didn't even know all the details herself. Then she fell to examining her fingernails, which she'd painted bright red to go with her lipstick and accessories, and I focused on the road ahead. Things left unsaid seemed to hang in the air between us, and there was no space left for small talk.

When we got to the house in Critchley I unlocked the door with the key that had been Mum's and turned to glance at Molly before I pushed it open. Her face reminded me of myself in the mirror on my first day in Fox Hill. She looked like somebody who has just been cast loose and isn't at all sure where she's fetched up.

I said, 'Are you sure you're OK?'

She didn't say yes or no. Her mouth twitched as if she wasn't sure whether or not she could trust herself to speak. Then she said, 'If we're going to do this let's get it over with,' and went on through.

Inside the house she walked quickly from room to room, taking in the brown carpets, the knick-knacks, Lee's favourite chair in front of the TV.

'It's smaller than I thought,' she said. 'Smaller and more normal. Like any nice, normal couple could have lived here.' She barely suppressed a shudder. 'It's stuffy, isn't it?'

'It's closed up pretty much all of the time. I try to air it now and then, and one of the neighbours still comes round and waters the plants. If you see anything you want, by the way, do just let me know. You're welcome to take anything you can carry now, or I can put a sticker on it and send it on to you later.'

'A sticker? You have stickers? Like for good behaviour?'

'Just to avoid confusion. See this? Rose the neighbour has taken a shine to this.' I pointed out a copper-topped side-table with a ficus plant standing on it in a flowered china planter. There was a discreet sticker on the copper surface next to the planter, with Rose's name written on it.

'You *are* organised. So I'd better not take a shine to Rose's table, then?'

'Well, you would take precedence, obviously. If you really did want it, I'm sure Rose could choose something else.'

'Don't worry, I'm just teasing you. I don't want anything. I especially don't want that table. I just wanted to have a look around. Thank you for humouring me.'

'The house isn't on the market yet. I'll let you know how it goes when it is. Half of the value of the place is yours. That's how Mum's and Lee's wills were set up. It's all to be split evenly between the two of us.'

'Oh… really? That must have been Mum's idea. I didn't know she'd done that. I wouldn't have expected Lee to sign up to it. I guess she wore the trousers in the end, right? Well, good for her. But anyway, I don't want it. I'm not even going to be here. You'd better give the money to Georgie.'

'That's not quite how it works. As an executor of the will, I have to make sure you have your share. What you choose to do with it is up to you.'

'OK. Whatever.'

'Would you still like to look through the old photo albums?'

She shrugged. 'Sure.'

She'd sounded so keen when we had discussed doing this before that I was taken aback by her indifference now. She settled gingerly on the sofa, as if she didn't really want to touch anything.

An image of Rob right there in the same place came back to me as if he'd just decided to join us. His face had been so close to mine, and he'd fixed his gaze on me as if I mattered more to him than anything in the world. And then, his mouth on mine. Almost a kiss. Would that be the last time anyone would ever touch me like that? I pushed the thought to the back of my mind, brought the albums over from the table where I'd put them aside and joined Molly on the sofa.

There were three albums in all, charting Mum and Dad's life together from their wedding day to my sixteenth birthday, which was when they abruptly ended because Mum was the one who had compiled them and soon after that she had moved out to be with Lee.

She had left the albums with Dad, and after the accident Molly had taken them with her to Mum and Lee's house. I had found them in the bottom of a chest of drawers that Lee had refused to let me sort through after Mum passed away. The rest of the chest of drawers had been filled with her clothes, and it had occurred to me that she might have put the albums there because she was worried that otherwise Lee might come across them and throw them out.

I opened the first and oldest album on my lap and pushed it across so that its spine was between us. We'd shared books like this long, long ago, when Mum used to ask me to read to her.

'You turn the pages when you're ready,' I said. 'There's no rush.'

The first picture was of Mum and Dad together on the street outside Brickley registry office, just after they'd tied the knot. He was grinning from ear to ear and she seemed just as delighted and shockingly young. She had the kind of joy on her face that goes with embarking on something dizzyingly new, the expression you see on babies taking their first steps and kids at the top of slides and teens on fairground rides.

It was so strange to see them that way, as if time had been rewound and they'd been given the chance to have theirs over again, and were so caught up in the loveliness of the present moment they had forgotten it wouldn't last.

I remembered the photo, and I wouldn't have expected to be moved by seeing it again. I had thought that the events of the last few months had given me some kind of immunity, where I couldn't feel and respond to loss any more even if I wanted to. I had been constantly busy, organising and arranging and keeping going, and at the same time I had been in some kind of deep freeze that was also a long slow panic, repeated day after day. Grief had been like a light up above the ice I was buried in, something I could see but not feel. But I began to feel it then. It was seeing them both at a time when they'd been free that did it: free of mistakes and disappointment and betrayal. Free to be happy.

Molly kept turning the pages and I appeared, a baby frowning and crying and learning to smile, and then trudging round with dolls and ribbons in my hair. Then Molly showed up as a newborn – smaller and thinner than I had been, with an unlikely quiff of brown hair and dark eyes that were unexpectedly thoughtful, as if she was pondering the world's injustices and wasn't at all sure that she wanted to stick around to witness them more closely. And next there was the first photograph of me holding her, except I wasn't looking the camera but down at her, the serious little baby in my arms.

And I looked thrilled. Ridiculously thrilled. I had exactly the same big-joy grin that the camera had caught on our parents' faces the day they got married, the grin that meant it was the beginning of a great new adventure. There was nothing forced or self-conscious about it. I looked as if I'd won the biggest prize in the universe. A couple of pages further on I didn't look quite so pleased – perhaps it had just been a bad day, or maybe I'd begun to realise that new babies cried and slept a lot and couldn't actually play with you or do much that was exciting. But at the beginning, I'd reacted to her as if she was a long-promised miracle that had finally been dropped into my arms.

Mum had said, *You seemed so keen to have a little sister, we thought we ought to oblige.* And I had liked that version of events because it made it sound as if I'd conjured Molly into being, as if she were a genie I'd summoned by performing the right magic trick to make my wishes come true.

'Are you sure you're all right with this?' I said to Molly. 'When we came in you looked like you were having second thoughts.'

'No, I'm all right. Let's do the second album.'

Mum had been working at the perfume counter in the department store by this time, and there were several pictures of her in her uniform, heavily made-up and, to my surprise, looking slightly nervous. There were bucket-and-spade holidays, birthdays, Christmases. We looked happy, as happy as any family.

Molly paused for a long time over a photo of me at about eleven and her at about three, playing schools. I was the teacher, naturally, standing importantly by the mini blackboard that had once been one of my favourite toys, and which had been handed down to her although I wasn't above commandeering it. Molly was one of my pupils, along with a large teddy bear and a foolish-looking giraffe.

The third album recorded my teenage years, when Molly had been at primary school. There I was in blue eyeshadow and novelty jumpers, suddenly self-conscious and watchful. The resemblance to Georgie was striking. Dad appeared in the pictures less and less, and looked increasingly tired and disgruntled.

But then Molly came to a summertime picture of me and her playing in the garden together, with me pointing the hosepipe at her feet as she laughed at the spray.

She was about seven in the picture, and she looked wildly happy. The grass was soaked, and the water was flying up into the sunshine and Molly's hair was dripping. It was Dad who had said it was all right for me to play with the hosepipe to entertain her. Mum usually stopped that kind of thing if she saw it, and came up with some pretext or other to do with the risk of Molly slipping and hurting herself, or the potential damage to the lawn.

I had always suspected, maybe unfairly, that Mum didn't want us to have unbridled fun. She always had to remind us that happiness could have consequences. Also, while she'd been keen for me to help out as a kind of babysitter, I had sometimes wondered how bonded she really wanted me and Molly to be. Us playing together like that had felt like joining forces, almost an act of defiance.

'I would like that picture,' Molly said. 'Can I have it to keep?'

'Sure you can.'

I very carefully peeled back the sticky plastic covering it, took it out and passed it to her. She held it carefully, not wanting to smudge it with her fingertips, and studied it as if it was something precious that had been taken away from her and that she had never expected to get back. She looked as if she was trying to commit it to memory in case someone robbed her of it again.

'You can take more of the pictures if you like,' I said. 'You choose however many you want.'

'No point. I don't like to have too much stuff,' Molly said, setting the photo carefully down next to her on the sofa. 'I don't believe in putting things in storage, and I'm going away soon anyway.'

'If there's anything you want I can look after it for you,' I said.

I had only meant to be helpful. But it sounded as if I'd made a false promise, almost a kind of threat. The words lingered, growing heavier and more ominous, taking on echoes of other times and other places.

Molly gazed at me bleakly. 'That's what you do, isn't it?' she said. 'You look after the things I can't keep.'

'Molly, I—'

But she shook her head. 'You still don't get it, do you? I really did want you to have Georgie. I was grateful that you were willing to take her. You were the only person I could turn to.'

'I guess Mum was pretty hard on you.'

'Mm. She was.'

She turned to the last pictures in the album, which were from my sixteenth birthday. I hadn't had a party, though a couple of school friends had come round for tea and cake. Mum looked as if she could barely bring herself to get close enough to Dad to be in the same photograph, and Dad was obviously trying, and struggling, to get into the spirit of things and be properly cheerful.

The rest of the pages were blank. Molly closed the album and pushed it towards me, and I took it from her and put it back on the pile at my feet. Then she picked up the picture of us playing together in the garden and stared at it again.

'That's why I could never hate you,' she said. 'You were kind to me.'

'Molly…'

She picked up her handbag, put the photo away inside with shaking hands and got to her feet. The composure she had maintained so far had gone. She looked as if she didn't know whether to run away, start throwing things or burst into tears.

'I should hate you, at least a little bit,' she said, staring down at me. 'Look at everything you have. The house. The job. The daughter. The life. As for your marriage, that might have gone south now but you had a husband long enough for him to have made a difference. When all's said and done, at the time it would have been hard for you to adopt Georgie without him, and he did provide for you when she was little. And what about me? I'm a thirtysomething renter who drifts from one place to the next and never settles down for long. I don't have a career. I'm single and childless. I don't own anything of value. I should be jealous of you. But I'm not. It's impossible for me to be. I can't even resent you.'

I stood too. 'If you did I wouldn't blame you,' I said.

Molly shook her head. 'You stuck around so you could look after me. Mum told me that, you know. She said she asked you if you'd like to go with her before she left, and you said no.'

'She shouldn't have told you that.'

'Yeah, well, we were in the middle of an argument at the time. I guess she would probably have said I was being difficult. It was when I was living with her and Lee and I'd started seeing Jason and she didn't approve. She accused me of doing it to spite her. I said

I had no reason to care for her opinion and she said it was totally predictable that I was hanging out with a thug and what a shame it was that I couldn't be more like you. So then I said of course you were totally perfect and all that was missing was the grandchild, and she blew her top and said there wasn't going to be a grandchild. That was when I found out you probably weren't going to be able to have children. And then she told me about you having decided to stay and look after me when you could have gone off with her. Which I think she said both to remind me how great you are and to make the point that she was quite happy to leave me behind.'

'Well, she shouldn't have said that. And if she was bigging me up, I think it's pretty clear that I don't deserve it.' I reached out and put my hand on her arm. 'There was no way I was going to leave you. I loved you. Love you. I have missed you. I do understand why you felt you had to get away from us all. But I don't want that to ever happen again.'

'But you don't understand,' Molly said.

'I'm sure I don't. But I want to, and how can I if you don't tell me? What is it I don't understand?'

'It's not your fault. I didn't tell you. I lied. It wasn't Jason who was Georgie's father. It was Lee.'

Then she put her face in her hands, crumpled down onto the sofa and burst into tears.

Chapter Thirty-One

It was as if all the air had been sucked out of the room and time had stopped. It was still exactly the same fussy, familiar space: the occasional tables, the china figurines and family photographs, the ferns and ficus plants, and Lee's favourite chair still in front of the TV. But the walls and ceiling might as well have just collapsed around us and left us surrounded by debris and plaster dust.

Molly wasn't in a single one of the pictures on display. And now I knew exactly why she had decided she had to leave. Why she had never considered keeping Georgie for herself. And why she had wanted to cut us all off and never look back.

Lee had always been so harsh about her. So dismissive. He'd spoken about her as if she was nothing. Worthless. And I hadn't challenged him. I'd accepted it. Not because that was what I thought of her but because it was what I expected of him. It was just how he was. That was what I had thought.

And he had done that to her.

The minute he stood up to speak at Mum's funeral, she had walked out.

How could I not have known?

There was a picture of Mum and Lee right there in pride of place next to the carriage clock on the mantelpiece, posing for the camera on their wedding day. Lee in a suit, looking pleased with himself. Mum every inch the glamorous older bride in a shiny cream-and-gold dress and crimson lipstick. I remembered that picture being taken. Rob and I had been standing to one side with Georgie, who

I'd talked into wearing the flowery dress Mum wanted her in, even though she was secondary school age and too old for it. No Molly. By then Molly had been long gone.

Seeing Mum and Lee together like that, smiling for the camera, made me feel sick. There were images of them as a couple everywhere, laughing, sipping cocktails, celebrating. The pictures seemed to crowd round us, Molly weeping on the sofa and me standing by her, frozen with shock. Mum being oblivious, and Lee carrying on as if he'd done nothing wrong, as if there was nothing to know.

He'd fooled us all. All that memorabilia was like evidence at a crime scene, dating back for years and years. I wanted to knock everything down and smash it all. To cut him out and burn up what was left of him, till there was nothing left but ashes.

Other, remembered images presented themselves... Molly with her bruised arm in Ashdale on the night of the dinner to celebrate my engagement to Rob, crying upstairs, not wanting to come down. Then Molly at the station with her duffel bag, pregnant and grateful to get away, determined never to go back. Molly passing her baby over to me, giving me her blessing. And later: Molly at the waterfront, surly and cold, finding something cruel to fling at me so I would let her walk away.

And further back than that, the times when it had been possible for Molly and me to be happy together. All those moments that had been captured in the albums she and I had just looked through. Me spraying her with the hose in the back garden, playing teachers with her, holding her when she was a baby...

All these years we'd been apart I had missed her without always being conscious of it, and at the same time I had been disorientated, as if something was out of kilter or off key and needed straightening out. I had put this down to my failure to tell my daughter the truth about her origins. Perhaps Rob had been part of it too, with his knack for dominating me and shaping how I thought about myself and everything else. But what if I had also always been aware – without ever having been able to put it into words – that there was something Molly hadn't told me?

And now I knew. I had not been the only keeper of secrets in our family, and the secret Molly had been burdened with all these years had driven her away.

I forced myself to move, and sat down next to Molly and tentatively reached out to put my hand on her shoulder. She flinched and shrugged me off.

'Don't say I should have told you,' she said. 'I didn't mean to tell you today. I couldn't tell anyone, not while Mum was still alive. I just couldn't. It was easier just not to see any of you. To cut myself right out of the picture. I wasn't even going to stay in touch with Mum… but then, it was just a Christmas card once a year and letting her know when I changed address, and we both knew it was never going to be any more than that.'

'I hate him,' I said. 'I'm sorry he's dead because if he wasn't I could kill him.'

'No, don't say that.'

'Why not? It's true. He did that and he just got away with it his whole life long. And I was so blind and stupid that I didn't see it. Molly, I'm so sorry. I failed you. I should have protected you. You should never ever have gone to live with them after the accident. You should have been with me.'

'For goodness' sake, Stella. That never could have happened. You were a wreck.'

'But all the same…'

'You can't look at it like that. That's part of what it does. You put blame on yourself and that isn't where it belongs. Believe me, I know. It's what always happens.'

She drew in a big, shuddering breath, straightened up, reached for her handbag and rummaged in it but didn't find what she was looking for. I passed her a tissue from mine and she took it and gave me a quick sidelong glance that was almost an attempt at irony, as if she was being self-deprecating about not having been organised enough to come equipped with tissues of her own. As if I might think slightly less of her for it, or see it as typical for her not to have everything she needed.

'I wasn't expecting to cry today,' she said, and blew her nose. 'I thought I could keep a lid on it. I can't tell you all the things I've done to try and stop myself hating him. I mean, I even tried to convince myself that I quite liked him, though I'm not sure I ever did. And, you know, he didn't need anybody defending him. I defended him, in my head, all the time. I still do. You know… anything, any bit of an excuse that might make what he did seem a little bit less bad. I mean, you know, like he wasn't married to Mum at the time. Though they had been together for a long time. And he didn't hurt me… not that much, anyway… It didn't happen that often… If I'd been better at taking the pill, then I wouldn't have got pregnant…'

'Molly, I don't know if you have talked about this to anyone before, but if you ever have, I hope they said what I'm going to tell you now. You have to know that what he did was evil and wrong, and it wasn't your fault.'

Her breathing was steadier now. She opened her handbag, stuffed the tissue I'd given her in it, took out a small round mirror and held it up to inspect her reflection. She ran her fingers under her eyes to wipe her smudged mascara away and put the mirror back in her bag.

'I used to get drunk sometimes and tell total strangers,' she said. 'People at parties, if I decided I liked the look of them. I didn't go into specifics. I mean, I don't think I did. I can't really remember. Anyway, I could manage that. It was you I couldn't tell. And you know what? The people I did tell, they were shocked but no one was ever that surprised. Everybody knows that things like that happen. They know that it's the kind of thing other people do. They know it unless it's their own family, right under their noses.'

'I should have known.'

'But it was good you didn't know.' Molly turned to face me. She looked defiant now, as if she was determined to show me that whatever might have happened to her back then, she was no longer someone who anyone could victimise. 'I was able to protect you, and to protect *her*. Georgie. Because if it wasn't my fault – and I do know it wasn't, I tell myself that all the time – then it sure as hell wasn't hers.' She grimaced and shook her head. 'I thought I could handle it. I thought I could get away with coming here and not telling you... I thought I was in control of it by now. I mean, usually I don't think about it any more. It's like something that happened to someone else, that could never happen to me now. And I hate talking about it. Hate it. I never wanted to accuse him. What was the point? Mum wouldn't have believed me unless I could prove it. What would that have achieved? It would only have made things worse. I mean, if ever a woman had put all her eggs in one basket, it was her with him. And I don't know what *you* would have said. I don't know if you would still have wanted the baby. How could you and Mum have ever seen each other again if you'd taken on the baby I had with her boyfriend? She would never have forgiven you. And I honestly think she would have blamed me. That was the one thing I really wouldn't have been able to bear. I couldn't risk it. No, it was much the best thing for everyone for me to just keep quiet, bide my time till I knew Georgie was safe with you and then leave.'

'Molly...'

She looked very young suddenly, a teenage girl again, innocent, trusting and unharmed.

'I would have wanted Georgie whatever,' I said.

As I said it, I realised it was true. I would have wanted Georgie whatever the circumstances, as long as Molly wanted me to have her. And if that meant a rift with Mum and Lee, so be it. Rob, though... it might have changed how he felt about it... without him, the adoption might not have been approved...

It would have been a different world. Different lives. But here we were, with the darkness and the lies and the good things that had endured and survived in spite of everything.

'Molly… did Lee know?'

'No. I didn't want him to know. I thought it was safer. I wasn't sure what he would have done. Do you remember the time when you and Rob came round to the house after you were engaged, and you saw the bruise on my arm? That was Lee. That was what he did when I threatened to tell Mum. Anyway, it stopped soon after that.' She straightened up and stretched. 'You know what? You saved me. I was so happy to come to live with you and Rob and to know that I could make you happy too. It made me feel so strong, that I could do that. It was like being invincible. I felt like I could do things nobody would believe. But the time I felt strongest of all was when I walked away.'

In the silence that followed all I could hear was the quiet tick of the carriage clock on the mantelpiece. I thought of all the times Mum must have dusted it, and brought Lee drinks as he watched TV, and vacuumed around his feet. All the care she had given him, having absolutely no idea what he had done and what he was capable of.

The room seemed to darken even though the light hadn't changed, as if something viscous and shadowy had pooled overhead and was slowly dripping from the ceiling. Then Molly reached out to grip my hand and the room was once again just as it had been before: dim in the watery sunlight and crowded with old possessions waiting to be cleared.

'Listen to me,' she said. 'You can't tell Georgie. Don't even think about telling her. This is why I never wanted her to know about me. I felt like the less she knew, the better… It's only now he's gone that I feel like it's safe for me to meet her. But she must never know that he's her father. All it will do will hurt her. She doesn't need to know that about herself… that she came out of something like that. Someone like him. Who could sleep with a teenage girl who'd just lost her dad, in the house he shared with her mum. And then just carry on as if nothing had ever happened. He lied and he kept on lying. He even married Mum in the end, and she never knew. But now he's gone, and Georgie never has to know either. There are times when the truth is good and there are times when it's even more important to be kind. And this is one of those times. That way this stops here.'

'But, Molly…'

Could ignorance ever be a blessing? How would Mum have reacted if she had known about what had happened between Lee and Molly, or that Georgie was Lee's child? And Lee had not known that Georgie was his either… but might he not have suspected? If he had still been alive to accuse, would he have denied everything? I could see that Molly was in some way dependent on the belief that he had not known, as if that made his treatment of her easier to put behind her…

Molly's grip on my hand tightened. I looked into her eyes and saw how desperate she was for me to agree. I said, 'All right. I will never tell Georgie who her father is.'

'You have to promise me. I know you and your conscience. Don't mess up. This is a secret that's only safe if you keep it. And I won't be easy in my mind unless I know for sure that you can do it.'

'I won't tell her.'

'Good.' She released my hand. 'You know, the strange thing is that now you know, I do feel better for having told you. Well, perhaps not better. But relieved. It's like something's been lifted.'

In spite of my shock at what I'd just heard, I felt that too – as if some form of pressure that I'd never registered before had been released, and gradually it was becoming easier to breathe.

'I'm sorry about the way I left,' Molly said. 'When we met at the waterfront that time, I didn't mean what I said. I was just like, I don't know, I had to throw something at you. To make you leave me alone. I was trying to hurt you. But it wasn't true.'

Because sometimes I think that if I could have chosen between you and Dad, you wouldn't be here today. If he'd been the one who survived, none of the rest of this would have happened.

'It doesn't matter what you said,' I said. 'There have been times when I felt like I didn't deserve to be the one who got to live. But here we are.'

Molly got to her feet again. 'We should go. I don't want anything else from this house. You can burn the lot as far as I'm concerned.'

'You still want to do this? You want to go to Fox Hill?'

Molly drew herself up as tall as she could and folded her arms. 'Stella,' she said, 'Georgie is the one good thing to have come out of this family. So yes. I won't stay long. But I would like to go and see my niece.'

I didn't have it in me to feel anxious about her meeting Georgie, not any more, not after what she'd just told me. All that old fear and guilt, all that darkness, belonged right here, in this living room where Molly had disclosed what Lee had done to her. And here was where we were about to leave it. It was time to go home.

I locked up and drove us both away. I wanted only to put distance between us and the house where Mum and Lee had both lived and died, and Molly must have felt the same. It was as if its shadows were spilling out and following us, as if they wanted to lay claim to us and draw us back in and keep us there. As if such a thing was possible. As if something or someone there believed that was where we belonged, and wasn't yet ready to let us go.

But then the road began to rise towards Fox Hill. Trees gathered along the verges as if standing sentinel, ready to ward off anyone who wasn't welcome. I thought of Georgie who was waiting for us at home and remembered to feel grateful.

Chapter Thirty-Two

As I parked on the gravel in front of Gamekeeper's Cottage Molly said, 'Rob gave you this place? Seriously, no expense spared.'

The electric gate slid into place behind us. I said, 'Just goes to show how keen he was to get rid of me. And he does have a new baby on the way.'

'Of course. How's that going?'

Molly sounded nervous and artificially bright. I decided to follow her cue, and to try to carry on as if the disclosure she had just made really was behind us. She was Georgie's long-lost aunt, here for a flying visit. If we both behaved as if that was all this was, maybe we'd be able to get through it.

'Well… now Rob's got what he thought he wanted, he's not sure he wants it any more. Typical. Anyway, I'm sure he'll adore the baby, but right now he's being a bit hard on Chloe.'

'He was very smitten with Georgie when she arrived, wasn't he? From what I remember. It's all a bit hazy.'

'Yes, he was. I think of it as his one redeeming feature. Or the main one, anyway.'

Molly looked at me suspiciously. 'You know, the way you talk about him…'

'What?'

'Oh, nothing,' Molly said, and got out of the car. I followed her and unlocked the front door and went in with her behind me.

Georgie's denim jacket was hanging on the banister post, and there was a faint dusting of mud on the chequerboard hall floor and a lingering smell of burnt toast. From somewhere upstairs I heard a muffled giggle, then murmuring in low voices. I called out: 'Hello?'

There was silence, then the sound of movement upstairs. A door opened and Georgie called out: 'Hi, Mum.' The movement turned into several sets of footsteps, and Georgie came down the stairs followed by the twins.

Georgie said a shy hello to Molly, who said an equally shy hello in return.

'This is my aunt Molly,' Georgie said to the twins, then, to Molly, 'these are my friends, the twins from next door, Livy and Jo.'

'Nice to meet you,' Livy said to Molly.

'Sorry to hear about your stepfather,' Jo added.

'The cake came out pretty good,' Georgie said to me. 'Check it out – it's on the kitchen table.' She smiled at the twins. 'Eggs from Charlie II and Lola make the best cakes.'

'You should come and get some apples,' Livy said to Georgie. 'We've got more than we know what to do with.'

'Is it OK if I just pop round next door, Mum? I'll be quick,' Georgie said.

I glanced at Molly. She said, 'Apples are good. Especially stewed in a pie.'

'Sure, you can go,' I said. 'But you'll want to be back for the cake, right?'

'Yeah. Don't start without me! I'll only be like ten minutes or so.'

The girls went out and I shepherded Molly through to the kitchen, where the cake was sitting on a plate in the middle of the little round table with a large Tupperware box over the top of it. I lifted the box off to have a closer look. It looked as if Georgie had scored another baking success: the cake was a huge, fluffy-looking Victoria sponge, doused in icing sugar and stuck together with lashings of buttercream and jam.

I remembered the cake she'd made for me for my birthday back in the summer. It seemed like a million years ago. And now Molly was here. Without knowing it Georgie had made a cake for her other mother.

'That looks mighty fine,' Molly said as I put the box back over the cake.

I said, 'Are you OK? You look a little peaky.'

'I'm fine,' Molly said, though without conviction.

I offered to show her round the house, and she agreed and seemed to be relieved at the prospect of having something concrete to do.

She passed through the living room without comment. Upstairs, she peered in my bedroom and said, 'Rob really did a number on you, didn't you? It looks like something out of a nunnery. Apart from the massive mirrored wardrobe, that is.' Then she poked her head into the bathroom. 'You two are tidy,' she observed. 'I've got more clutter than that, and there's only one of me.'

'Georgie's not really into clutter.'

'She seems very sweet.' She said this tentatively, looking up at me as if she was unsure about how I'd respond – as if she didn't feel entitled to venture any opinions about Georgie, no matter how complimentary, and half-expected me to be angry and accuse her of overstepping the mark.

'She is,' I said. 'She's quite shy. Usually she's pretty quiet until she gets to know people. But you should hear her singing in the shower. She really lets rip. She has a good voice, actually.'

'I bet she does,' Molly said. 'You do, too. I mean, you were always musical.'

'Me? Not really.'

'Yeah, you were. You used to sing to me sometimes, if you were the one putting me to bed. Do you remember?'

We'd had a record of children's songs that she'd liked. She'd listened to it so much that in the end I'd got to know them.

'Yeah, I remember,' I said. 'You used to ask for a lot of encores. It was a great way of spinning out bedtime for as long as possible.'

She managed a smile. 'Rumbled,' she said, and we moved on.

Georgie's bedroom door was firmly closed. I said, 'This is Georgie's. But she usually only likes me to go in when she's given express permission.'

'I see. And you always ask, do you?'

'I always do.'

I could tell Molly was torn. Part of her was curious and wanted to go inside and soak it all in, if only for an instant, and at the same time she was afraid, and another part of her didn't think it was her place and was warning her to stay away.

All she said was, 'Well, we'd better respect her privacy.' She led the way back downstairs to the kitchen, where she settled at the table and stared at the cake under the box as we waited for the kettle to boil for tea.

I was sure that she had felt a connection to Georgie on the day of Mum's funeral. Some kind of physical recognition or familiarity. An instinct, or an impulse. But that wasn't a social connection. They'd never really met before. They were mother and daughter. And yet they were as good as strangers, about to face each other in a quiet kitchen across a chasm of lost time.

Was it possible to bridge such a separation, regardless of why it had happened to start with? The only way to strengthen the connection now was through words, and words were clumsy and confusing. Anything you said was a hostage to fortune, liable to be taken down and used against you later. And the same went for what you didn't say. And all that, the inadequate words and the loaded silences, might overwhelm whatever had been there to start with.

Then Molly looked up with exactly the same troubled but philosophical gaze that she'd first turned on me when she was a baby.

'Do you know what this house feels like to me? It's stuck,' she said. 'I mean, like the estate agents say, it's got loads of potential. I can tell you've done a bit to it, but still, it's like a person who needs a big shove in the right direction.'

The house. Yes, that would do. What a relief, to talk about the house. Something that could be fixed up and changed at will, and, if necessary, left behind.

'It was empty for a while before Rob got to work on it,' I told her. 'Tony, the twins' dad, told me that there was an old guy who lived here alone, who died here...'

'I don't think it's because of what happened before,' Molly said. 'I think it's because of us.'

She pressed her hand to her heart and stared down at the table. Her expression was so sad and so defeated I almost couldn't bear to look at her. Then she looked up and said, 'What it feels like here, it's like someone who's lost. Someone who knows they have to do something and has been putting it off. And I think that maybe part of that is that you've never been able to tell her about you and me, and what we decided to do after she was born. I know I once said I didn't think you ever needed to tell her. I know you always meant to do it, and you never did. But after everything that's happened, do you still want to?'

I couldn't answer. Couldn't move. The kettle clicked off and I didn't respond. I just stood there by the worktop and looked down at her and remembered the mix of bribe and threat that Rob had presented me with when he first brought me here. *Take this, or I'll tell.* And then, later on, *Take this, and take Georgie if you must. Isn't that enough for you? With things as they are, why would you want to tell her now?*

And someone said, 'Tell her what? Who are you talking about?'

It was Georgie. She was standing in the doorway with a cardboard box full of apples, looking down at the pair of us as if she'd caught us in the middle of a crime. My heart began to pound as if it was building up momentum to stretch to breaking point.

Molly froze. She looked as if she'd just been interrupted doing something deeply incriminating. I said, 'Hi, Georgie. We've just been admiring your cake. Why don't you put that box down somewhere and come and have some?'

Georgie slapped the box down on the kitchen worktop. 'Why are you being so weird? What's going on?'

And there was Rob, standing close to Georgie over by the door, scowling at me with the flinty disgust that he always showed for me when I didn't do exactly what he wanted. The Rob who haunted me, who lived in my head and maybe in my heart too, and probably always would.

I told you not to say anything unless we talked about it first. We're meant to presenting a united front. This isn't honesty. This is just recklessness and bad timing. And I don't think it's going to go very well, do you? What with one thing and another, you're clearly heading for disaster.

Georgie folded her arms and looked from me to Molly and back again. 'I want to know. Don't tell me it's nothing, because I know it isn't.'

She was half-smiling, as if this might yet turn out to be some kind of joke, but I knew from experience that it was a half-smile that could very quickly shift to distress.

'OK,' I heard myself saying. 'But you might want to sit down.'

Georgie settled at the table opposite Molly. She said, 'Mum, you're making me really nervous. What's happened?'

Molly was staring at the cake again and frowning a little, as if she was trying to carry out some complicated mental arithmetic. I sat down on one of the spare chairs I'd picked up so there were enough places to sit when Georgie had the twins round. Georgie was watching me and her sweet, perfectly familiar face was full of both trust and foreboding.

'The first thing I have to do is offer you an apology,' I said.

Deep breath. There was no breath deep enough for this. Molly was watching me closely, her mouth half-open as if she was tempted to intervene but either couldn't bring herself to speak or had decided against it. She seemed a million miles away. I couldn't tell if she was urging me on or was terrified that I was going to fail. Or both.

All I had to do was to tell Georgie the truth. Part of the truth. Not the whole truth...

'The truth is that in a way you have two mothers, and we're both right here in front of you,' I said. 'You have a biological or birth mother, and me. Molly is the mother who was pregnant with you and gave birth to you. Then she gave you to me and your dad to adopt. I saw you for the first time in hospital when you were a couple of hours old and Rob and I took you home soon after. Molly had been living with us for a little while before that but she didn't stay. She moved into another place close by. We formally adopted you a year and a half later and then Molly went abroad.'

Georgie was staring at me open-mouthed now, as if I'd just started going on at her in a foreign language and was expecting her to understand. I pressed on. My voice sounded thin and strained, like an actor's at a bad audition.

'You were very much wanted,' I told her. 'We were so happy to have you. You know I told you that I was in a car accident with my dad before you were born, and he died and I survived? The accident left me with some problems that meant it was going to be difficult for me to conceive, and when we found out Molly was pregnant and wanted us to have the baby it really was a dream come true. It was a miracle. The best thing that ever happened to me. I would tell you that was the best day of my life, the day we brought you home from hospital, if there hadn't been so many other best days as well. We love you. I hope you know that. Whatever might have gone wrong between your dad and me doesn't make any difference to that, and it never will.'

And then I stopped and waited to see how she would react.

She didn't burst into tears. She didn't reach out to embrace Molly, or me. She didn't storm out and run away. She didn't curse and condemn us all; Molly for giving her away, us for lying to her.

Instead I saw her take the shock deep into herself, as if it was a stone that was sinking slowly beneath the surface and out of sight.

She looked at me the way she had done once or twice when she was ill: bleak and pained, as if everything around her had shifted out of place and she had begun to lose faith that it would ever return to normal.

'If that happened... if she's my other mother... then do I have another dad? Or did Dad...' At this she peered at Molly with quick, flinching distaste, as if she was too embarrassed to look at her. 'Did he actually... you know?'

This was it, the hardest part of all. I opened my mouth to answer and couldn't speak. I couldn't bring myself to lie to her again. And I couldn't tell her about Lee...

'Rob was nothing to do with it. He isn't your biological father,' Molly interjected.

She sounded very calm and matter-of-fact and detached, and I was reminded again of how resolute and clear-cut she could be. And so often had been, where Georgie was concerned.

'I was going out with a boy called Jason who I met at the college I was going to for my A levels,' she went on. 'It wasn't serious. We were both just really young. Well, I was seventeen, and he was a year or two older.' She glanced at me. 'We'd just lost our dad, and I'd moved in with Mum and Lee. I was a bit all over the place. Which maybe isn't all that surprising.'

'So you're telling me this Jason is my dad.'

'Not really,' Molly said. 'He didn't have all that much of a part in it, to be honest. I mean, I barely knew him, and I have absolutely no idea where he is now.'

To be honest. Wasn't that always meant to be a cue that someone was hiding something? Like when politicians said *To be clear*, and meant the opposite.

But it didn't register with Georgie. She turned to me and she was suddenly distressed and angry and in that moment I despised myself almost as heartily as I despised Lee, but at the same time I knew the danger had passed and I could barely have been more relieved.

Georgie said, 'Were you ever going to tell me? Or were you just going to leave it until there was some kind of weird accident or someone let something slip and I found out?'

'I knew it was wrong not to tell you,' I said. 'I should have done. I had so many opportunities to do it, and I didn't take them. I can't excuse myself. The thing is… I wanted so much for it to be true. I suppose I wanted you to be all mine, right from the beginning, and for me to have been able to be your mum in that way too. I just couldn't bear to admit it.'

Suddenly I couldn't look at her. I put my face in my hands. I had never felt quite so exposed in front of my daughter – exposed as fallible, exposed not as a mother but as a person with weaknesses and shortcomings that meant I'd let her down.

All those years I'd been trying to live up to the role I'd taken on, to be kind but fair, to teach her right from wrong and to help her understand how to live in the world, as a good mother is supposed to do. And all the time I'd felt inadequate and fraudulent, as if I was only pretending. Like an imposter. I had been afraid that if I told her about Molly she would see me that way, too.

But maybe everyone who took on this particular role – whether they did it for days or years – felt that it was impossible to live up to. There was me, and there was what I had tried to be to her, and then there was everything I had been trying, sometimes misguidedly, to protect her from. Sometimes without even knowing what was there. I had always been aware of failing. But now she knew, and she was still here, and that gave me a glimmer of hope that in her eyes at least, I hadn't failed completely.

Someone moved towards me and I felt a hand on my shoulder. I looked up and saw Molly standing next to me.

'Your mother did her best,' she said to Georgie. 'She may not have done everything the way she ought to have done. But I don't think it was because she didn't love you. In her own way, she was trying to keep you safe. What she hasn't explained is that I always told her I didn't want to see you. She was worried that if you ever tried to reach out to me, I would reject you and you would be hurt. I mean, that was what I had said I would do. I warned her. I told her to leave me alone. I didn't want to be part of the family any more. I thought I could have a whole new life and not look back. It's only really since Mum died that I've felt differently about it.'

I forced myself to turn towards Georgie and saw that she was sitting up very straight, rigid and determined and unexpectedly fierce. She was staring at Molly with the kind of wounded outrage that means someone is very close to tears, but desperately doesn't want to cry or to show any kind of vulnerability at all.

'I guess you just never really wanted me,' Georgie said. Her voice was steely but with a slight tremor in it.

'Georgie, you mustn't think of it like that—' I began.

'Mum, no,' Georgie said. 'You have to stay out of this bit. It's nothing to do with you. I just want to know why Molly did what she did. Literally what happened, like in a history book. I don't need all of your feelings and emotions getting in the way. I just need the facts.'

The facts. Which were exactly what Molly and I had agreed I would never give her. Not in full, anyway. Not about Lee.

I realised then that the promise Molly and I made to each other would always keep us close, however far apart we were. It would tie us both to Georgie, too. But it didn't feel oppressive the way hiding the truth about Molly had been. It was a pact, as warm as a shared understanding. It might be wrong, it might not be. But it felt like the best we could do.

Molly took her hand off my shoulder but I could still feel her touch. It lingered the way any pivotal moment does in your relationship with someone you love. It was delicate and sure and I knew exactly what it meant, and that I would remember it any time I had doubts and questioned whether there might be a case for telling Georgie about Lee.

Remember what you promised. Leave this to me.

She was calling the shots, and I was going to keep quiet.

'I don't know if I can explain… I'm not sure if I can make it make sense to you,' she told Georgie. 'I'm not sure if it does make sense. My body made up my mind for me. I wanted to have you, but I didn't want to keep you. I couldn't do it and I knew I couldn't do it. I wanted Stella to have you. I knew she would do a good job of it. She'd been good to me when I was little and I always remembered that. And I have to tell you, it was a huge relief when she said yes.'

She walked away, over to the window at the front of the house. Her head was bowed and I thought for a minute that she might be crying, but she didn't make any sound.

Georgie said, 'Who knew?'

'Hardly anybody,' I said. 'Your dad, of course. Mum. Lee. But otherwise… We moved around a fair bit in the first few years, and we just didn't mention it. We let people assume. And they did. There is a physical resemblance, after all… People often comment on it.'

There was a small, intense silence. True silence. I couldn't make out Rob's voice at all. Not even so much as a small sardonic whisper. He had vanished.

Molly turned round and walked back towards us. She seemed to have composed herself. I didn't see any trace of tears on her face. She looked sad and triumphant at the same time, as if she'd been robbed and beaten but had made it to where she needed to get to anyway.

'Having looked through the old photo albums, Georgie, I have to say, what your mum told me is spot on. You do look like her when she was your age. Although clearly you're your own person, right?' She glanced at the cake on the table. 'Take your baking, for example. That is a magnificent sponge cake. Your mum's a pretty good cook, but she could never make a cake as good as that. Hers never rise. I don't know why not. They come out flat as pancakes. Or that's what used to happen, anyway. I think she rushes them.

She doesn't beat them for long enough. But I don't know, maybe she's improved with time.'

'I'm not that bad,' I protested.

Georgie looked from me to Molly and back again. Suddenly her face lightened. 'I couldn't possibly comment,' she said, and grinned at both of us.

It really was like watching the sun come out. I'd seen this happen before: after she'd been sad and worried about something, sooner or later I'd find the right words to say and it was like flicking a switch. The world fell back into place, and it was as much of a relief to me as it was to her. It had never been quite as much of a relief as it was then. But this time it wasn't me who'd managed to lift her back into feeling loved. It was Molly.

This was it, the moment that I had often thought of and hadn't dared to believe in. This was my chance to walk free. Georgie was going to be able to forgive me. She was going to forgive both of us.

It wasn't going to be forgotten. There would be more questions. But we were in with a chance. She was willing to believe that we had set out with good intentions. And we had. We had both wanted what any mother wants: for her to grow up happy and sure of herself and strong, and to be ready when the time came to step into her future and leave us behind.

'I do have one bone to pick with you, though,' Georgie said, and both of us stiffened.

She noticed, and frowned disbelievingly at us both. 'Relax! It's not a big thing. It's just that I think you're wrong about who I look like. Going by the old photos I've seen, the person I really look like is Gran.'

She got up and approached me, and I stood up too. 'I always used to think you were clever, but now I'm not so sure,' she told me. 'I don't know who I got my brains from, but maybe it's just as well it couldn't have been you. You were stupid to think I would reject you if I knew.'

And then she moved a little closer, which was her way of signalling that she was prepared to be embraced and might even welcome it.

I put my arms around her and drew her close. We held each other like that for a minute and then I became conscious of Molly standing to one side and looking as if she wanted to withdraw and leave us but couldn't quite tear herself away.

Both Georgie and I reacted in the same way and at the same time. We let go of each other and turned towards her. Now we were two points of a triangle and she was the third. I reached out for her and so did Georgie at the same time.

She began to cry. We drew her in close enough for the trembling of her body as she wept to pass through both of us, and we carried on holding her close until she was finally calm and still, and it was safe for each of us to let go.

Chapter Thirty-Three

It was overcast, and the light was just beginning to fade even though it was still early. It was that time of year and day that reminds you the nights are drawing in and there is plenty of darkness on the way. I concentrated on the road and we didn't talk again until I'd stopped in the drop-off spot at Barrowton station.

'Thank you,' Molly said, but made no move to get out of the car.

'You're welcome. Molly...'

'Yes?'

'I know you've got this job coming up, and you've made your plans and you're going abroad... but if you change your mind, and decide you want to stick around... you know, I'd be happy.'

But Molly shook her head.

'I'd like to come and see you again,' she said. 'But probably not until the spring. Things will have moved on by then. You'll have settled, all of you. Rob's baby will have arrived. And I'll try to slot into whatever kind of space you have for me. An aunt-shaped space. A special aunt, maybe. I think that's all it would be reasonable for me to hope for. I think, in the end, that's probably all I want.'

She looked away from me towards the station. A train was just pulling in at the platform nearest the car park – not the London train but the express service heading out west, to Bristol, near where we'd been living when Georgie was born.

'Georgie's a good girl, and she'll want to please you by showing she's OK. Go gently with her. Give her room to react,' she said. 'She's got a lot going on. She has to be allowed to kick back. But she trusts you. That's plain to see. She'll always come back to you eventually.'

She reached across and pecked me on the cheek.

'And remember, you don't have to tell your daughter everything,' she said.

She got out of the car and walked away towards the station entrance, and I saw that everything about her was subtly different to the way she had been when I picked her up. The Molly who had walked off the train earlier that afternoon had looked anxious and potentially erratic, dressed up in the kind of bold outfit that people sometimes use as a costume to disguise whatever it is that disappoints or disgusts them about themselves. But now the way she moved was light and free, as if she'd just enjoyed an unexpected success. She looked like a woman who knew her own mind and was going exactly where she wanted to go.

What we had just done – the things we had told each other, and what she had told Georgie – had changed her. I could feel it changing me too, like something in my blood and in the air, a transformation that would work its magic long into the future and in ways it was impossible to predict or foresee.

Molly turned back and beamed and waved at me, and then she disappeared through the sliding door and was gone.

Afterword

Ten years later

In a future I never could have imagined, I went to a riverside restaurant with Rob and didn't feel afraid.

It was the day of Georgie's graduation. And it had been quite a day – a whirl of queuing and waiting and watching, sitting in Brickley University's Great Hall with its high pale-blue painted ceiling, vehemently applauding after Georgie had gone up the steps to shake the Chancellor's hand and had made it safely back down again.

We had emerged from the Great Hall into bright sunshine to stand on the scorched brown grass of the lawn and gather around Georgie in a small family cluster. It had been slightly awkward – Rob in particular had been on edge – but at the same time we had all been united in our pride in her. We'd been surrounded by crowds of other people chatting and drinking and eating little bowls of strawberries, all of us enjoying the particular happiness that it's only possible to feel on a warm summer's day when everybody around you is celebrating too.

The graduates – mostly younger than Georgie, who'd had a couple of years out before starting her degree and then had taken five years to finish it – all had shining, hopeful faces. The young women had long hair and short dresses under their long dark robes and were wearing high heels, and the men were in new suits, and looked pleased with the novelty of being smart. There were very few babies around. Max stood out in his red summer hat and short-sleeved romper suit, his plump little legs kicking as he gurgled contentedly in Georgie's arms.

Georgie didn't usually baulk at including Max in situations where some people might not welcome him, but she'd decided against having us bring him to the Great Hall. Instead he'd spent the hour of the ceremony with Liam, his dad, round the corner in the university's film and TV block, where the graduation was being shown on a big screen. Apparently Max had slept through most of it, but he'd been wide awake by the time we saw him afterwards on the lawn. He'd still been cheerful was but beginning to become restless, and Georgie and Liam soon decided it was time to take him home.

Georgie had looked so happy... Relieved, too, as we all were, to have got through the family gathering without any real difficulties. Perhaps she'd seen it as a dry run for how things might play out if she and Liam ever decided to get married. She'd managed to navigate her way through the minefield of only being allowed two tickets for guests to go into the Great Hall, having been clear from the start that she wanted me and Rob to be there. In the end, on the day, she'd managed to get a spare ticket. Molly joined us and I'd sat in the middle between her and Rob. Luckily Liam had been quite happy to stay outside and mind the baby, as had always been the plan.

Max wasn't the only one of our little group who'd attracted the attention of the other people around us. As we all made our way to the exit Molly turned heads in her off-the-shoulder purple sundress, one of the most flamboyant outfits on campus. She had been in her element all day, basking in reflected glory, every inch the proud special aunt who was also Georgie's birth mother – though that was something Georgie only chose to tell people once she knew them well enough to trust them.

Molly in her current bold and unapologetically happy incarnation always irritated Rob. Earlier in the day he'd muttered something to me about how she was carrying on as if she owned the place, which I had chosen to ignore. But anyway, there was nothing he could do about it. I knew that the relationship between Molly and me, and the way it had changed and settled into a mixture of distance and closeness – the give and take of it – puzzled him. But there was nothing he could do about that either.

He'd taken it well, all things considered, that we had told Georgie Molly was her birth mother without consulting him first. The saving grace had been that Georgie had coped with it so well, so much better than I would have dared hope. Time and familiarity and the carrying on of day-to-day life had worn away the shock of the revelation, so now it was just part of the way things were, something we had all acknowledged and grown used to acknowledging. But what Rob still didn't know – and if Molly and I had anything to do with it, never would – was that, over and above everything else we had shared, Molly and I were united by what she'd told me about Lee, and our mutual resolve to keep that knowledge to ourselves.

After we'd left the campus Liam and Georgie and Max peeled off to catch the catch the shuttle bus back to the car park, but Rob wandered with Molly and me through the hot streets of the town centre towards the station.

We didn't talk much as we strolled. But Rob seemed to relax, perhaps because the occasion was nearly over. When we came to the river Molly kissed us both extravagantly goodbye and hurried off in a flurry of purple silk to pick up the Eurostar service that would take her back to her husband and their gîte in Provence. But Rob asked me if I was in a rush too, and slightly against my better judgement, I agreed to have a drink with him.

With his usual skill at finding the best place to sit, Rob picked out a table on the walkway right next to the river, which was as narrow and straight as a canal here and reflected a thin strip of blue sky between the bulky silhouettes of the modern buildings to either side. Across from us on the other side of the walkway, next to the glass frontage of the brasserie and shaded by its striped awning, a mum with a sleeping baby in a pram was eating a panini with one hand

and holding her book open with the other. At the table next to her a redhead was despondently scrolling through her phone. Closer to us, at the next table by the riverside, a man with slick black hair was tapping away at a laptop. He looked briefly up at us, as if searching for inspiration or perhaps distraction, and then went back to typing.

Rob ordered a large glass of wine and a dish of olives, and I asked for tea and a scone. When the waitress had delivered what we'd asked for I insisted on paying for both of us, and Rob let me. In the past few years he'd got divorced from Chloe and had signed over their house to her and his son, then had gone bankrupt. For all that, I could still make out the cocksure, strident Rob I'd known. He had stamina, that was for sure. Things might not have panned out the way he'd wanted lately, but he most definitely hadn't given up.

'You're being very abstemious,' he said.

'Yes, well, sometimes it pays to keep a clear head,' I said, carefully applying cream and jam to my scone.

He raised his eyebrows at me.

'Meaning?'

'I like to keep my wits about me. That's all.'

'You think I'm trying to flirt with you, don't you?'

'I wouldn't put it past you.'

He frowned. 'So you're not seeing anyone?'

I swallowed a mouthful of scone. 'That is none of your business.'

'Hmm.' He folded his arms and carefully looked me over. 'Well, you look all right on it, whatever it is you're up to.'

'Thank you.'

'You're still wearing your rings.'

'Well, I'm used to them. I happen to like them.' I flexed my left hand and examined the way the diamond still caught the light. 'You made a pretty good choice,' I said.

'Yes, and that's not the only good thing I chose for you,' Rob said, slightly bitterly. 'That place in Fox Hill must be worth a small fortune by now.'

I shrugged and finished my scone. 'I don't think of it that way. I just live in it.'

'Like hell you don't think about it.' He knocked back some of his wine. 'I'd propose a toast, but you're not drinking.'

'Well, you can still propose it.'

'I suppose.' He raised his glass. 'To our lovely daughter and grandson. It's good to see them doing so well, isn't it?'

I raised my cup. 'It is. And here's to our lovely daughter's boyfriend, too.'

Rob, who hadn't thought Liam was good enough for Georgie at first but had been through a slow process of learning to accept him, drank again and sighed. He said, 'Did Georgie ever say anything to you about Jason?'

My blood ran cold. I said, 'No. Did she mention it to you?'

'No.' He said this slightly reluctantly, as if he thought she should have done. 'I was just wondering if she'd ever thought of trying to track him down. Especially now she's got a child of her own. That does change things, you know. And it's much easier to find people now that everyone's just a few clicks away. Why shouldn't she look for Jason, if she wants to? She's entitled to know where she comes from the same as anyone else. And she's his child just as much as she is Molly's.'

'And ours,' I said smoothly, setting my cup down.

'I thought you might take a bit more interest.'

'Then you thought wrong,' I said. 'I'd leave well enough alone if I were you. She's happy. That's all I care about. And I think she feels like she's got a full complement of parents as it is. You're all the father she wants. Or needs.'

'I suppose you're right,' Rob said, looking mollified.

I checked my watch. 'Anyway, I should get going.'

'But we've barely had a chance to catch up,' Rob said, looking regretfully at his empty glass of wine. 'I'll walk you the rest of the way to the station.'

'No, don't bother, it's too hot to go out of your way,' I said. 'Your place is on the other side of town, isn't it?'

His face clouded over. 'It is,' he said.

He'd really thought he'd be able to persuade me. Looking at him sitting there – handsome still, but slightly dishevelled in the heat – I glimpsed the man who'd once thrown down a set of keys for me to pick up as I'd grovelled on a chequerboard floor. A man who was as impulsive as he was imperious, who could seek to rearrange other people's lives on a whim, whose love made you feel chosen and whose loathing made you feel cast out.

And yet the tie between us, which had once been so tight it had seemed as if I would never escape it, had grown thinner and weaker over the years until it was the lightest, finest thread, barely stronger than the fleeting connection I might feel to someone I didn't know at all.

I stood up and shouldered my bag. 'It's been nice to see you, Rob. Really.'

He said, 'What am I supposed to do? I'd have another drink, but it's not going to be much fun sitting here like a lemon on my own.'

His gaze settled for a moment on the lone redhead who was sitting near us, as if assessing her potential suitability, and then returned to me.

'Being alone isn't so bad,' I said, and leaned forward to kiss him lightly on the forehead. 'Take care of yourself, Rob,' I told him. 'I'll see you the next time. And thank you so much for my birthday surprise all those years ago. Who needs a husband when you can have a house? You're right, it is worth a fair bit now. But it's worth much more than that to me. I've been happy there. It really was the best gift you could have given me.'

Rob looked momentarily stunned. But then he raised his eyebrows, smiled and shrugged, and I saw another side of him that sometimes was willing to roll with the punches, and might try it on but didn't always expect to win. I knew how much he hated being thwarted. But he had perhaps begun to learn, through the brutal process of disappointment, to take it with good grace.

'Now I'm definitely going to need another drink,' he said. 'When did you get so sharp?'

It was my turn to shrug. 'I guess I had a good teacher,' I said.

Then I headed off along the walkway, and took care not to look back.

A Letter from Ali

Thank you for choosing to read *The Marriage Lie*. If you would like to keep up to date with all my latest releases, just sign up at the following link. Your email address will never be shared and you can unsubscribe at any time.

www.bookouture.com/ali-mercer

This is a lockdown novel from beginning to end, though all of it – even the conclusion, which fast-forwards into the future – is set some years before any of us had heard of Covid-19. Most of the key scenes were written towards the end of 2020, when we were living under a range of restrictions in the UK that just a year before would have seemed unimaginable. Perhaps inevitably, some of the mood of the times seeped in.

Being anxious, as Stella is from the outset, changes how you experience everything. For her, even the chest freezer in an apparently friendly neighbour's garage seems ominous. This is a book full of airless rooms, closed doors, barriers and claustrophobic spaces, with a narrator who is trapped by fear. But its open spaces don't always feel safe, either – at least, not to Stella, not while she is haunted by guilt over what she should have disclosed to Georgie and has not yet been able to bring herself to explain.

I'm drawn to stories about damage, survival and repercussions, and the forces that divide families and unite them. As I was writing this novel, different conflicts that reflected those themes went into the mix. I was interested in exploring the relationship between siblings who are treated differently by their mother, even to the extent that when she leaves, she seeks to take only one of them with her. I wanted to look at how this unequal treatment might cascade down the years and affect both children: the favourite's guilt, the vulnerability of the one who feels rejected.

As Molly and Stella's intertwined stories evolved, their relationship became even more complex, more ambiguous and more painful. I hope I did justice to its moments of generosity, courage, selflessness and love as well as to the sisters' experiences of loneliness, suffering and loss.

But what about Stella and Rob, and their break-up? I had in mind a scenario in which someone sets out to finish a relationship by taking their other half to the new place they've procured for them to live in, and leaving them there. That gave me my opening. This is a story with many kinds of gifts and many different types of gift-giving in it, and as Stella and Rob both discover, surprise birthday presents can have unexpected consequences for the giver as well as for the person on the receiving end.

Then there was Rob, one of the most insidious and intrusive characters I've ever put into a story. He's frequently infuriating, and yet I found him freeing (and fun) to write. He doesn't have much of a conscience, doesn't worry about what other people think, and wants what he wants when he wants it, being quite happy to leave anything else to other people to sort out. He isn't prone to feeling afraid – or, alternatively, perhaps he finds the experience of fear so very unpleasant that he's prepared to go to almost any lengths to control other people so he can try to avoid it.

What about Fox Hill, and the white house in the woods at the end of the lane? That came out of all the long country walks I went on with my son over the course of 2020. He is autistic and has a moderate learning disability, and both of us found home schooling a struggle. He quickly got bored of baking, but was still up for going out walking, although this was mostly conditional on me finding a new route each time, ideally one including a river or stream and a couple of bridges. We discovered various places near where we live in Oxfordshire that we'd never been to before, and our expeditions inspired my attempt to create the remote and dreamy atmosphere of Fox Hill. (If you'd like to see pictures of some of the scenery we explored, take a look at my Instagram feed – @alimercerwriter.)

School trips, crowded streets, celebratory meals in restaurants, visits to neighbours' houses, all kinds of formal and informal gatherings… As 2020 drew to a close and gave way to 2021, scenes such as these often seemed as distant from everyday existence as life on a spaceship. When I was preparing to write the end of this book I looked online at footage from graduation ceremonies that had taken place several years ago. Watching those gatherings felt like looking at something from another era, like horses and carts in town centres, or Edwardian swimmers emerging from bathing machines at the beach and splashing out to sea. That made it all the more of a pleasure to imagine.

I really hope that this book was as much of an escape for you to read as it was for me to write. I've always found both reading and writing to be a way to slip into other lives, to experience other times and places and to try see the world in new ways. Over recent months losing myself in other people's stories has felt more essential than ever, whether they're on the page or on the screen. It's such a joy to be hooked into another world and to be absorbed in it, to feel as close to it as if you were right there, to lose track of time and forget yourself and where you are.

And then there's the chance to share it afterwards and talk about it, whether that's online or face-to-face. Stories have given all of us a way to connect as well as a way to escape.

I hope you loved *The Marriage Lie* and if you did I would be very grateful if you could write a review. I'd love to hear what you think, and it makes such a difference helping new readers to discover one of my books for the first time.

Do get in touch – I'm often on Twitter and Instagram and you can also contact me through my Facebook author page. I love hearing from my readers.

Warm good wishes to you and yours for brighter days ahead,
Ali Mercer

 AliMercerwriter

@alisonlmercer

 alimercerwriter

alimercerwriter.com

Acknowledgements

A huge thank you to Cara Chimirri, my editor at Bookouture, for shepherding this book through the writing process to publication with so much sensitivity and insight. Thank you to the whole amazing, inspiring Bookouture team, including Kathryn Taussig, Kim Nash (all those Facebook Lives!), Noelle Holten (who does a brilliant job of managing my publicity), Sarah Hardy, Peta Nightingale and Alexandra Holmes. Your creativity, dedication and drive astounds me, and I'm very grateful to you all for knowing how to look after authors as well as their books. Thank you to Jon Appleton. And thanks to my fellow Bookouture authors – I'm looking forward to seeing you for real again one of these days!

Thank you to Judith Murdoch, my agent, for wise advice along the way, and to Rebecca Winfield, who looks after my foreign rights.

Thank you so much to everyone who has read, reviewed, rated, recommended and supported my books and spread the word, and to all the bloggers and book group members whose enthusiasm and love of reading keep us all turning the pages.

Thanks to my friends and ex-colleagues, local and less local, including Nanu and Luli Segal, Helen Rumbelow and Neel Mukherjee. George, I miss the tea-breaks. Here's to meeting up when we can. North Cornwall Book Festival – may you continue to thrive.

And thank you to my family. There are too many of you I haven't seen for too long, and I miss you and am thinking of you. Thanks to Mum for all the books you've given me down the years and for being my very first reader.

Finally, thank you to my husband and children, who made lockdown more fun and more interesting than I could ever have imagined. We were certainly never in any danger of running out of books. Re-integrating ourselves with society might be a bit of a stretch, but I expect we'll manage. I just hope someone in the household starts baking again soon.